To my parents, who encouraged me to be fearlessly
creative, and to the hundreds of people who
told me to shut up and write it down.

Predators are calling but the phone is off the hook...

CONTENTS

PART ONE

CHAPTER 1

The office was abuzz as the news of the new security proposals came in. Half of the team, six out of twelve, were reading through the paperwork broadcast into their Nadar Forge while the hard-working old journalist computers wrote the public interest pieces for tomorrow's edition. Gone were the days of trench coat wearing investigative reporter hungrily hunting leads on rain covered streets. Reporting is now the job of a few hundred computers mixed with synthetic minds hard-wired into the city mainframe with brand names like Media Type, Electric Feature, Cyborg Beat, and, his favorite oddly worded title, BeatWetPaper. Valentino thought that the Beat-Wet Paper publisher AI lost the record of the original title from a forgotten language, and it translated poorly. They need to work on a retitling to something more modern and less illicit.

Journalism is a dying art. In his city of over ten million, only one hundred journalists are still working; many of them write editorials, jamming out their emotions through the neural connection into the worldwide stream, as the machines can gather facts and write 500 words in less than one second. His paper served Area-Four of Borough-Eight, the robot in-crusted island of Manhattan, which was called Lenox Hill hundreds of years ago. He held on to the term paper even though no one has used paper in over 200 years.

Marrow 16, the name that he dreamed up for the primary AI drudging through the daily message traffic, was announcing the new security proposal with its dark English accented audio. He found the name of Marrow in an ancient journalism volume, somehow tucked behind a version of Sun

Zu and the tribulations of the first water wars. No one was sure why the machine had a British accent, but it did seem to offer a bit of sophistication to the drab office.

"19:48 hours, Zellum Security reform proposal number 1623," it droned, making Valentino think of dropping by the local pub.

"Is that the one about the robocops?" Valentino asked Cobb. While Robo was not the most accurate way to think of the new police staff proposal, most people thought of the new design as robotic or as a giant armed insect walking down the street on six tapered legs. It was not in production yet, but the plan was to use a biological-tech hybrid that is tough as a nano-brick and can heal itself by exposure to sunlight.

"Magistar6Ped was out earlier today. Number one thousand and six hundred, twenty-three is about city-wide constant Nadar Forge monitoring," Cobb said through his bushy beard.

Cobb was the editor, but in reality, he only functioned as an editor under the direction of the local news agency in Borough Eight. The news agencies coordinate releases with Public Advocate Jersey-York City Office. With the Marrows leading the publication and the minimal output of the human staff, Cobb edited very little. Most people in the office and the city overall stood around 6'2, but Cobb was non-edited, meaning that only natural processes determined his gene codes. At a puny 5'7, all the staff towered over him, which tended to increase his general spitefulness.

"Sheesh...insect cops," Valentino said, shuttering a bit. He was not a fan of anything with more than four limbs and only for cops with two legs.

"Escrito, run the proposals up to now through the crime stats computer, keyword cross-reference, and identified any crime categories that were not addressed or missed altogether," Cobb pointing Valentino to the file room. Dozens of various types of hardware dominated the room as if it was broken in half. He touched the center computer and thought, "cross-reference the Zellum security proposals against all crimes in Area 4. Divide results into the crime that were included - stats, stop, crimes that were not included – stats, stop, map out all crime by category over the last calendar year, each list if addressed by the new proposals."

A small light on the machine blinked green, and it started to whir.

He did not want this life. When he was young, he read through all the old journalism he could find, even attended a museum exhibit with original front pages. Those writers exposed corruption, environmental change and disaster, and organized crime. They cited scientists and experts to alert people to global problems. Reduced to telling a bunch of circuits to cross-reference administrative paperwork and covering Area 4 block parties, or the criminal activities of the Preserve the Building project, he was no longer a journalist.

Well, that was how he felt until three weeks ago when he got his first confidential informant.

While he was sleeping off a typical print journalism experience, eight double whiskey presses, his message receiving window on his ceiling began to blink a burnt orange. It seems that his stomach knew before his conscience minds as it lurched and rolled. His brain was spinning, and he finally noticed the orange through his eyelids. He opened his eyes and jumped out of bed. Well, he attempted to jump, because he went straight to the floor, holding his head, which was about to explode.

"Zellum is attacking the city. Please follow the instructions in the next message if you what to know more. To pique your interest, research the following: Zellum Security proposal 1623 will allow the government to monitor all citizens' Forges 24 hours a day. That will be released in three weeks along with over 2000 other troubling proposals. The result will be total government control over the population. Remember to follow the instructions in the next message. It will be delivered on your HUD tomorrow."

Painfully he rested his head on the edge of the bed, blinking fast. What? The sender was not listed, no personal code or computer address. His HUD captured the sender information, and he would try to find out more, but he knew that it would be fruitless.

"Store in Quato, and total delete from message bin," he thought, and his Nadar Forge logged the data. He trusted the source and would follow the instructions. He barely slept, which did not help his hangover, but his HUD was set to alert him of any messages regardless of the situation.

Halfway into the bargain price printed delicious roast beef sandwich, the message appeared midbite. He bit his tongue.

He threw his half-eaten lunch into his backpack and started for the 35 A 104 Level street transport platform. He often forgets that he is always one hundred and four Levels over the river and whatever is still solid ground. Rarely does he see the sun or moon. The one hundred and fourth Levels were commonly known as the "Cobbstoper," as the one hundred and fourth US president was well known for promises of glorious things in glorious speeches while only offering modest results. A place in between the grand and the mundane.

The heavy misters were puffing hot stream overhead, soaking the streets. Many kiosks had a neoprene various-colored tape hastily pulled over their goods. Once the mist floated down, the road was alive with color, remembering him of an old digital picture of Tibetan flags.

The messenger, whoever that was, gave him specific demands to follow. Rushing under the park trees, he slid into the sidewalk and stopped one thing that he would need. Today it was a simple white farmer's hat. Hats of all kinds protected the heads of any wandering citizens from whatever mysterious goop falling from above, sloughed off the slimy walls. In a world where a city was the size of a mountain with wonderous technology, that always made him smile.

"You picked the right time to cover your head," a man with the name tag reading Chow said. Valentino used to guess people's ethnicities as a party trick. Down here on Level one hundred and fourth "Cobbstoper," it still worked; further up in the Levels, all the people seem only to vary on skin tone; other than that, all were tall, strong, and high cheeked.

"Ya, thanks. Are they ever going to fix the mist timing?" Valentino asked. The weather function was supposed to create a "perfect" living environment, not too hot, dry, wet, or cold. Of course, every third week, the air pools over the park and begins to dry. Then the misters croak to life, dwrenching everything for third blocks. While the trees must love it, the end effect is a moist street for half a week.

"Méiyǒu, the dry air brings the mist, and the mist brings the dry air," Chow said with a shrug. Valentino nods ran his wrist under the payment scanner and mounted his bald head with the shining white hat.

Typically, everyone was so focused on scrunching over like a turtle to avoid the rain sliding down their necks, holding umbrellas, or a quickly printed Pancho over their heads; there were several pedestrians collusions. No one said a word. Comforted in the protective hat, he slid through the crowds and between the kiosks and stalls. Most of Level 104 was built with recycling materials, in some cases whole building. But within bricks and glass, colossal spiral towers rose to almost meet the Cobbstoper roof. Many of these helixes, each holding thousands of residents, shifted as the nano-walls realigned windows, changing colors, building new patios. A building across from his apartment would sightly move in angles, becoming a vast blue stripe of kale, seemingly to wave in the non-existent wind. His home is a 500 square foot flat in a brick building, which dates back to 2,200. Old as a Roman ruin, in his opinion.

Around the block, he lined up in a queue for the mag transport. Lunch was over, and many of the pods were out. He was waiting for a full ten minutes, reviewing various articles on the Zullem corp and the city security programming. For a city of 11 million, the security system was surprisingly simple. Each borough had a centralized reporting system, feeding into a city-wide dispatch. Officers, both mechanized and human, were dispatched to the location via roads or air. Reports of the new security proposals would vastly change the whole system, and they are up for a vote in a few weeks.

A man bumped him in the back, forcing him forward into a woman. "Sorry," he muttered, ignoring the elbow in his spine. What a jerk, he thought. The woman boarded her vehicle. No pods left, but he will be next. He scanned his wrist and waiting again. Using the code from the messenger, he brought a pod track. Val thought that the messenger knew that this code would erase any log of his travels. Valentino thought that the messenger was a programmer or security specialist judging by their knowledge of city security, well at least perceived knowledge, and the code's use.

A pod rolled up and parking near the queue, it's top flashing a light green - Ready for service. As he walked forward, he tipped his head up to see the street. Pods raced past colored a soft red, occupied, building shifted windowed changing exteriors; grand, swirling architecture housed self-designing residences in forms of a magic unicorn, all of it multicolored. He loved the city.

He typed in the code, and the pods opened. The code

would also enter his final destination, where he was unsure, but he was now an investigative journalist, a real Marrow, following a lead to wherever it would take him. He settled into the large gray captain's chair, allowing the spongy cushions to take his tubby weight, then punched the hand-sized button on the dashboard center. Silently the magnetic levitation cells in the street pulled the pods before, changing their pulse as the pods moving to different lanes. Slow exit lane at 20 miles per hour, speed increased to the middle land, over 45 miles per hour, and finally, the fast lane, which he had only used twice below, the final magic speed of 230 miles per hour. The familiar streets, blocks that he instinctively knew since birth, 35th street down to 158th street flashed by, the street sellers becoming divergent hues ribbons as he zipped to the closes rays of sunshine. Reflexively, he turned his head back to see the block recede until the sun caught his face, its warmth. The building-sized commercial advertisements, and dank alleys flooded by misters, now began the Jersey-York City's edge. The pods sped on a maglev track at a fantastic speed, only passed by a cargo hauler robotically piloted over the river. The acceleration forced his eyes into slits, and the afternoon rays reached through the tinted pod's screen.

At first, he looked down to reaffirm what he already knew. Rocketing over the track, the pod was three hundred feet above the river. Human structures soaring beyond the clouds caught his eye. Heading southwest, he viewed the metropolis built on a city until this physical glass and grey formation created on a grey and white framework seemed to be the entire world, with the ocean beyond.

The rivers and the bays meet before him. Clearwater sparkled, reflecting the afternoon sun to his eyes. The vast sea wall reaches at least five hundred meters, a green breathing curtain encasing the city, that looked like many cities organically growing from the earth. The first Thálassa póli sprouted from the bay, crowded but smaller versions of herself. People were about to mechanically pushed her out, passed the sea wall. Aquacities poli one had a population of 250,000 people, each one a citizen of only poli one. Crop fields around the central spire encircled them, all glowing a deep blue green. He read that her tower, well taller than his residence Level, and all her inhabitants would lower into the sea for her future journeys. The shaft grew from a floating circle of the fields and the central Area of aerial vehicles' transport.

He saw the construction Area stretching out into the bay, where cranes the size of Level 4 transported aquacity sections into or out of the sea. Due to the distance, this activity seemed to be the gods of mighty titans but was only vast machines chugging along. The track turned back toward another borough, and a forest of buildings impossibly tall blocked the sea, and Newark came into view. Through the soundproofed pod chasses, he imagined that he would hear a bustle of other pods racing along the track. The low grind of nano-walls and the humming maglev, buildings shifting to new positions, and the voices of all the citizens could seep into his imagination. All were blending into a huge den, but he only heard his breathing.

The track quickly brought him through Newark, and the last curve highlights the crop towers. Thousands of feet tall, these yellow-green shocked his sight after the repetitive eggshell and hard greys of the building entanglement. Three towers covered in a transparent organically woven sheath seemed to grow from the surrounding farmland. While much of the food was grown underground, these towers began with a simple idea, genetically formulate trees to create a natural production system. From a sprinkle of seeds to a 5,000-foot tower took only twelve years. Cosponsored by the Jersey-York City and an agricultural firm Castle Rewild, these will soon cluster around the few remaining population centers on Earth. He could see hundreds of rows upon rows of individual garden masts, all connected by yellow living water ducts. The track swung close enough that he sees barely make out a tiny human form among the greenery. Now he knew where the meeting was, outside of the city's tracking systems, in the fields.

"Approaching Hawthorne Algae Bloom. Final destination in 2 minutes, please buckle up," the pod's speaker announced. He has never been here before, this far from his borough. As the pods changed lanes, slowing, and the murky orange structure stood apart from the other fields.

The vehicle parked, "Thank you." Valentino cocked a finger to the machine, "Back at ya," and he stepped out into the half a mile wide shadow of the Hawthorne.

Crop fields spread around him, each managed with rolling thirty-foot-high robotic minders. As these vehicles passed over the wheat, barley, sorghum, beans, corns, and potatoes, human-sized mechanical arms softly pushed to an army of wire limbs where they were gently separating from the plants. The field was planted out to Newark's borough when people at the lower Level saw one benefit of their lower social-economic lives. These crops provided a myriad of colors to look on from the high Levels depending on the season. Palm yellows, bright greens, and white, only when the cotton was blooming, marked the ground between the towers, creating a sense of a reconnection with the wild, even if it was all manufactured. While the city loomed miles over the fields until noon, shadows peppered the growth Areas. Breed to be resistant to drought, temperature, and pests, all these fields needed was light. Every thousand yards, a group of yellow and orange flowers, called Noctem Helianthus or the nightsun flower, rose high above the crops. Being photosensitive, their brilliant

petals tracked the sun. They used a complex system of genetically designed reflective leaves and stacks spread the light
across the fields, creating an odd halo effect. It seems that a
host of angels was guarding these plants. Even at night, these
human-created flower banks emitted a low orange glow.

Valentino stepped away from the transport track on to
the powerwalk. Each step generated a tiny bit of power, coursing into the main city's power network. He loved that. Scores of
joggers prided themselves on how they were why Jersey-York
produced more energy than it used. Of course, he would never
start jogging; joggers were idiots, mostly when your jobs,
school, and apartment were no more than two miles apart.

He was told to find the part where the two nightsuns
were at a hundred feet from his shoulders at the center of
Hawthorne's shadow. The building was oblong and looked like
a colossal cartoon tongue licking up from the ground. The
entryway is a cylindrical education center, which tried to teach
the engaging the history of the project, but due to the looks of
the few tourists, failed every time. The structure stretched up,
widened to an upside-down teardrop at the top with no real
roof to stand on. All of it is burnt orange. It was essentially an
algae farm; water circled inside to provide nutrients for each
type of small aquatic plant, making the color shift was the red
moved into a cloud of yellowish green. Counting the nightsuns, he thinks that he found the correct stop. The shadow
seems along toward and behind.

"Ok, ok, I'm here," he muttered. As he was told, he stared
and the ugly structure, hoping that the tiny flora was having
a better time than him. While it was chilly in the shadow, he
adjusted his bright white hat as if he was sweating. Maybe in
his turn to find a real story, a proper investigating story, he was
in a rabbit hole of his own making. He decided to review some
details on his HUD. A quick scan of the current security system
versus the new proposals showed him little, only that the new
plan asked for more public monitoring. The crime was increas-

ing, and, as sections of the city were being moved, robotically by billions of tiny machines, for more buildings, Areas were becoming less secure. Everyone was talking about it. Even Cobb, who has no situational awareness, pointed out which parts of town were dangerous after the residents moved while the prominent city buttresses were exposed. The whole neighborhood was now empty. Criminals, even gangs, were taking up residence.

"Mr. Escrito?" a voice said from behind him. Valentino jumped a bit, and he deactivated his display, then he turned around. A heavenly muscled man stood only one foot from him. His skin was much darker, braided hair over his head and down his back covered by a vibrant green shirt sporting multi-hued parrots. Valentino began to step back.

"No, please, stay there and be calm," he reached out his hand, putting it on Valentino's shoulder. "People will see a couple, and they are uncomfortable public displays of affection." He stepped forward, inched toward Valentino. Now he was sweating.

"Ok," he calmed himself. "How you do what to do this? Do we talk about it? Exchange data? I have many questions."

"I'm called David Dario." Tenderly grabbing Valentino's hand. "I'm a private programmer, take odd jobs here and there. Hold my hand, and we will talk while acting like tourists." He turned and led the way toward the Hawthorne.

"I was contacted to write a short section of a program that would, along with the other sections, be embedded into the new Zellum security system. These sectional programs are common as companies do not want anyone to have all the information." He said as he pulled toward the building. Valentino started to notice the birds fleeting around; he has not seen birds for years. They are only into the other sections of the city. Amazing to see a natural thing surfing the air, beyond the constant hum of drones.

"Who set up the program, and what was it for?" Valentino asked. He activated the record in his Forge.

Saba stopped walking and eyed him suspiciously. "No recording, audio or otherwise."

Valentino shrugged and shut the system down. "Ok, but I need some type of notation system."

"I will tell the story and then, upload the data to your Forge. After that, it is up to you. Got it?"

This was not going as he expected. He expected a massive reveal of the city's secrets. "Weave your tale, then."

"Almost all the programs are written by other computers. That is easily tracked, cataloged, and monitored. I'm not sure what you know about this world." Saba looked away from the orange Hawthorne Bloom to the farms and then tinked his head up to see the sky. It was a beautiful day for winter, approaching fifty degrees. With his free hand, he rubbed his face. "I'm a criminal, a code hustler," he said.

"Typically, I write code that cannot be tracked or traced. Often, I do not know who hired me or the end goal of the program. I received a message on my personal account, which is weird because I never do business with anyone from that account, meaning they knew who I was. That is dangerous, and when I asked around, and several other programmers, some are friends, received the same message," Saba said.

"Were the messages all from the same location?" Valentino asked.

Saba went on without acknowledging the question, "we all decided to do it; the pay was great. Baker..." He let go of Valentino's hand and nubbed his eyes. "Sorry, no names," He said, looking up their bloodshot eyes. "A friend has a contact in various businesses, so he asked around and found out that Zullem is developing a new security program, and he is incredibly cunning. They thought that he was trying to hire on somewhere."

"Ok, to clear this up on my end, as you said, I'm not well versed in this topic. So, I have two questions. First, what does the program do? Second, why are you so nervous?"

Saba was shocked. "So, you do not know?"

"Tell me."

"Zullem is huge, one of the largest companies on Earth, well even on Luna and Mars. They build aquacities, space towers, international security systems, and manage farms the size of Australia. Power, weapons, and transplanetary travel."

Valentino did know this, but the question remained. Why is this program being equated to taking over the city? Playing dumb might be the best play, he thought.

"So," he said, opening his hands as if he were holding a small basket that Saba could fill with answers.

"Maybe, I came to the wrong person." He looked around; they were almost alone, only a few visitors by the Educational center out of earshot. Saba was getting frustrated, but he was here with a journalist, apparently a dumb journalist; he must tell the story. Then leave town.

"You're an idiot. Remember the people that also got that message."

"Yes, you just said that. Baker?"

"No names," Saba said, again putting his hand on Valentino's shoulder, gripping hard. "Out of nine, only three are still breathing. Two accidents, two muggings in low-mid town, one supposedly suicide, and one walked out on a pod track, smushed," Valentino swallowed, but tried not to show how uncomfortable the good investigative story, a real investigative story, was making him feel.

"Any contact with law enforcement?"

"No, they would have identified me quickly, and then, I would be dead too. I will leave town. As I said, I tell you the story, then I out. All the deaths and the program will be in the data. I already passed it to you, hack through your Forge. By the way, man, you ready need to update your security protocols."

Valentino looks at the palm; there was still a minor imprint where the information was passed via epidermis virus swab. No, the data will be written into his Forge for long-term storage.

"Great, thanks," Valentino jerked his hand to the side and removed Saba's powerful hand from his shoulder. "That better just be what you are saying." Anger creeping into his voice.

"Hey, man. I have one last thing to do, then I'm leaving town. There are plenty of places that need an illegal programmer. All the guys used their various ways of reaching out, some legal, some not, and we put all the superposition states together, each piece into one state so we could read. Of course, we used an old binary system, not connected to any city drive. The program is called Babel. The basic point is that Babel will allow whoever is in charge to see the neural nets to subconsciously influence people, erased peoples from any scan, and monitor all, are you listening, all activity in the city. Plus, no one knows about the illegally written program. It is invisible," Saba said, pulling away, moving toward a new group of tourists. "You have all the data. Thanks for meeting me; I hope you can let people know about this before those proposals are passed."

"Hey, wait a second. I need more from you and your contact information." Valentino's voice was getting louder. Saba stood ten feet away, still retreating, put his finger to this mouth. Quiet.

Valentino just stared at Saba as the tourist swarmed around him. Once the groups past Valentino, Saba was gone.

Great, now I have to review all this by myself, incredible, he thought sarcastically, just great.

"We found a trace in the croplands; he did not change his new eye scans fast enough," the hologram in the shape of a man in a business suit stated. "Remember what we spoke about, eye scans must be changed every half hour; if you do not know, then you last changed them, then change them imminently." As it always is, the man's face was in shadow, standing in a small office with no windows and optical electronics. Only a body clad in an expensive suit, shade over his face.

Drauger hated this part of the work. At the same time, money and freedom continue to maintain this arrangement.

"Get me a time and place. I will handle it. The other two hustlers will not be found. Luckily, as hustlers, no one knew that they knew each other. Even the Area 4 pigs would have spotted that string of deaths," Drauger said.

"Now that we have his identification, we know all we need. The target is Saba Dario, trained as a programmer but left the profession 42 years ago. Then, he disappeared, leaving only a few recorded sightings since then. I have the quantum working to untangle the rest of his life. Importantly, biometric and gait recog will track him. Work backward; we found his apartment, it is empty, so all he physically, on his person. The target must be deal with tonight. Also, he meets some in the fields. I will send you that information once I have it. Somehow, this person was a shield; probably Saba's doing. Saba is on a pod track to Brooklyn, likely the Manzana Orb. There is a sporting event tonight; he will be in attendance. You are sanctioned for two operators."

"At the arena or after?" Druager asked; he sat perfectly, still crossed-legged on the wooden floor. The holo was bright, casting on all the brick walls, showing the difference in their texture. The walls reflected the blue from the holo, with Druager seating as if in meditation, bathing in the dark.

"After, within the crowd, right after the anti-grav exit way. One should follow him down while the other wait on the exit platform. Make it violent, a spectacle," the man in shadow said.

"I will handle the hunting; you issue instructions. It will be done," he said with a low growl, a stern voice, but barely above a whisper.

The man in the shadow stood up, irritated. "You watch yourself. I control your payment, and your freedom, as a matter of fact. Should I look into reversing my previous decisions?"

Without moving a muscle or switching position, "No, all your instruction will be carrying out."

"Good, always a pleasure," the man in the shadow's hand seems to move toward Druager, and he hit the button to terminate the hologram.

'Spectacle,' Druager thought.

Druager leaped to his bare feet with the blue light gone and stood incredibly still as if he was in a trance. The meditation almost overcame him; he was preparing from a bloodletting. The target, Saba, will bleed out his hopes and fears into the world. He will be purified, cleansed. Within Draugers head danced fire and blades, each waiting for its chance to destroy. In the dark, he had found his true self many years ago; now he will help the target find itself free from itself in the violent blood-soaked beautiful...spectacle.

Saba enjoyed the game. He had never seen one before. Static Ball, brand name, worth billions. He found his seat and tilted the recliner up slightly, but most of his view was the static dome. While he was one of the 500,000 attendees, he still felt that the entire structure was designed for his personal best perspective. Almost a mile in length and width, the dome's video displays depicted the Static Riders as they whirled and twisted over the color-shifting ceiling down to the oval-shaped lower Level. Where he sat. Each person, quite a strong attendance this week – 300,000 on the base floor, could adjust their recliner, align with their favorite player, and modulate their screen for their pleasure.

Saba has no favorite riders or any knowledge of the game beyond what he just saw. Baker, a former friend, former because Saba had found him with an empty skull three hours ago, had the ticket on his Forge. Typically, Baker was a helpful guy and, Saba thought, help him arrange a stylish exit from Jersey-York, as some hazardous people wanted him. Two unfortunate things were pressing in his mind. First, the dangerous person was unknown to him, which could be the fat guy seated next to him. Instinctively, his eyes darted over the man, his face covered in an array of mustard and sheswan sauce; he would be a very unlikely assassin. The second unfortunate issue was that his exit pass in this horrible situation, apparently, committed suicide mere minutes before Saba enter Baker's apartment.

Having a borderline ambition with the world before rewilding, Baker has much of his apartment programmer to emulate buildings from 2,200, including a front door. This door, Saba had only seen wooden plates in museums, was largest, much taller than Saba, and had the color of dark cherry wood. The surface, still formed by millions of nanobots, was a deep red but looked nothing like even naturally grown cherry, not purple enough. The apartment door has ajar, and Saba poked his head through the opening, hoping to see Baker mounted in his computer space. Besides every other traditional aspect of the apartment, Baker used his nanowalls to build a customary computer lad on one corner. The wall bulged out into an ergonomic seat, sound-canceling headset, and as only Baker would use, with a keyboard. Each piece seemed to be sculpted from cast iron, while the chair felt like it was stuffed with down.

"Hard way to go," Saba said slowly.

The seat was dripping. Baker, a small, wiry man, was slumped in the chair, blood weeping from the red beard. A printed drill was between his legs, gore still clinging to the bit. Whoever the dangerous people are, they intended that this will be a suicide scene. It was not. While a quantum computer genius, Baker was friendly and a religious man, very uncommon in the code hustler community. Heartbeat was steady, but he knew that he needed to gather anything that could be useful. The apartment life scanned was probably deactivated, so the killer could step out unmolested. Likely this would reinforce the idea that Baker was an odd duck, as his neighbors saw him.

Baker's apartment was hued a deep gray and was immaculate, not a thing out of space. As a programmer, Saba knew the value of having a set place for everything, virtual or otherwise. Organization was vital to Baker's life; his data was just as tidy on his Forge, which read with an illegal scanned. Some said that Saba on one of the few people still on the spectrum; he doubted that, but he did have an emotional deattachment. Within fifteen minutes, Saba read through all the pertinent data and copied all the was worth having on Baker's Nadar Forge, banking codes, vital records, some illegal security bypass instructions, and, of course, tickets to this week's Static Ball.

Saba closed his friend's eyes and headed to the game, which was rather good.

Last round. Lions up by four on offense but down by two on defense. The Sharks, the away team from San Francisco, were trying to mount a comeback. Human piloted magnetic spheres, arranged in a team of eight, rolled down from the stadium's overhead port, each with a holographic mascot giving the spheres some electronic life. Running bright orange lions chased swimming great white sharks, and they whirled and rolled to various scoring ports. The pilots broadcast his perspective to hundreds of feet wide screens along the walls, while floating video drones darted around the space, filming all the action. As the collisions between the Static Balls were cast into people's heads, a large majority of the audience were twisting as the pilots crashing to a wall or dove into the blackness behind the ports. The electric cracks and smashes between colliding spheres created a din, amplified by speakers the size of buildings. Some excellent pilots would coordinate their paths and only crash with the intent of creating buzzing music. He found that irritating.

Saba was not sure if his brain could take any more of the sensory overload. He disengaged his HUD and shifted his chair into a sitting position.

He thought that he could maximize his situational awareness if he discretely left before the half-million overfed and sport drunk pardons clogged up the exits. The new "graviton stairs" were now in operation, and he wanted to try them before he boarded an outgoing aquacity.

He slid past the mustard-sheswan drooling man and walked to the exit ports. The seating Area was designed as an inversed thumbprint in the base of the stadium's electronic egg. Static balls roared past and overhead as he quickly followed the red-carpeted route through the seats. Finally, leaving the over-stimulated mind-numbing arena, he passed through the exit tunnel. He stood at the graviton stairs, looking down over two hundred floors wrapped in a swirling descending art exhibit. The world's history was depicted on the cylindrical tube walls peppered with windows to view the city. Saba knew that this was a new application of this type of technology; one step forward and he will be slowly floating down thousands of feet. Controlling his nerves and shaky knees, he stepped out.

He thought it would be like swimming, buoyant in water. He was wrong; other than the slight drip on his feet, as there was no ground to press on, he was still upright and slowly flouting down, inch by inch. His heartbeat increased in fright as he looks down to see no floor, just thousands of feet of emptiness, but as his arms when stretching into the air to stabilize himself, he knew that he was safe. The instruction mounted on the walls advised that one such look at the walls instead of straight down. He began flouting the rules and scanned the walls, each set hundreds of yards from him. The story of life passed as he fell. Luckily, no one else on the stairs, allowing his full concentration. While abstract, the painted walls were calming, that was the intention, and the tale of the beginning of life was soothing. Of course, the walls were only using the nano-bots' pigments to create the colors of a harsh volcanic landscape morphing into a green ocean, then into a single green leaf swirling around him. He thought that he was an antibody flowing in a multicolored organism. His ears were happy that the crashes and mini explosion of the match in the arena. There was no sound beyond his breathing.

Typically, his mind would be analyzing the minutiae structures behind the pigment changes in the nanobots and how the justly curved tubes within which he was floating could stand the pressure being at 15,000 feet. Still, all that drifted off, and he was indeed experiencing the exhibit with a compliant mind. Calming subliminal rays only crossed his mind once; then, he focused on the greenish-blue swirl of light resembling a leaf change into a small bush on a virtual beach. The nano-walls were tracking his focus, allowing it to alter the art's depiction to his center view as he fell, hundreds of yards now. Tiny black figures spread across the walls, each spinning like was dizzy letter then clustered around an abstract tree.

Life was moving inland. Green insect shells buzzed by and changed into butterfly wings.

Bones were forming; rigid white beams were enveloped by boiling raft of light greens and deeper earth tones. He was falling quickening, though he barely noticed. He found a window, and he leaned forward, and his descent slowed. Oddly, as his consciousness focused on the city beyond the printed transparent alloy, he drifted toward the window revealing its true size. His bedroom could have quickly passed through the window, but he was unsure if it grew larger as he approached. The stair was suspended within another transported tube, raising to a peak that could be seen miles into the ocean. He was moving through the exit of the Magnum Manzana, the big apple. Before the rewilding, this city was a drowning and diseased big apple; he did not know why. This towering reddish sphere mounted on a curved tube was supposed to remind all citizens of what we were and what we are now. Saba thought that was a sham, the whole function of this spectacular display was to generate funds, but the window did show a fantastic view of the city.

Living in a vertical city, it is best not to think of how many feet separate you from the ground. He had only seen dirt a few times in life and never ran his hands through it or touched plants. Area 12, Level 152 had no actual plants beyond genetically designed ones, no birds, and insects. Of course, a rolling "agricultural nature experience" drifted through his Area every few months, mainly for the few children. Most children were on higher Levels; he always thought as the incomes were up, so did the prospect of having children. He never went to the nature experience. He found his true city outside the window, glowing, shifting, outlined by the pod tracks' arteries, and topped by white or golden light crowning the heightened buildings.

Looking down to the city at night, he felt at home. He saw aquacities in the bay within the sea wall, like toys in a bathtub. The black rivers and bay cross-cut by shining tracks, each either outlining the great mass of the central borough or diving into the glass and metal heart between the slender tower within which hundreds of thousands of people could never live their other lives seeing real dirt. He knew that he would miss this place; maybe he will return.

Dinosaurs were forming on the walls, some as big as his apartment building, rising to eat from a tree. As the creature bite, the leave sprouted feathers and flew around the stair. He had almost forgotten that he was floating as he tripped forward to investigate the feathered things and reached out to catch himself. Hands found nothing to hold; his eyes saw the last few hundred feet, his heart skipped. The evolution of life spread through the last two million concerning geological time, fast. Dinosaur fells to mammals, mammals trapped throughout the virtual landscape. Humans were last, but as they spread, the earth was depicted in darker and darker colors. Fire and volcanoes showed the beginning of life, while humans' Anthropocene age illustrated that the darkness was creeping in, blanketing the world in black. Green was fading, and the blue was mellowing into a dull grey.

Saba looked away to the stair base; only two people speak and checking the HUDs; it seemed like their faces were dull. He scans back the extinction event; the walls were dark gray, drifting to black, only a few stories before his feet found the floor. A quick flash of red and yellow, like a fire, then total black. The last war, the almost complete death of the green. The black softened by gradients, and a single cartoon leaf sprouted above the landing station. Then, as the nanos observed the viewers' eyes and projected each color just for that viewer, the lone green blade shifted into a none abstract portrait of one beautiful leaf, with water droplets still clinging to it, flashed in intense verdant green. Then, the entire visual tube became a forest of leaves. The Rewilding, to transform the world.

His shoes touched down with a gigantic cavern of green

stretching upward.

Benny Batters and Jersey Joe milled about the stair's exit, a huge hall of transports filled with neon lights of the awaiting city, each looking at one exhibit or another. Joe loved the Liberty Stature, while Batters took never understand how short the buildings were. Pods were based at the left, while escalators and elevators were on the right. Between the two was that museum of the old NYC pre-sea wall. Interactive miniatures of the former city and its monuments, all small compared to the mega-cites of today. Both came together at the nanowall poster of the height comparisons. Liberty Stature versus the Spiral Tower, or the width of the aquacity against the central park, which was submerged long ago.

Both men were the physical opposite of each other. Batters was powerful; his muscles could be seen flexing and rippling under his shirt. Illegal animal reprogramming made it hard to find clothes that fit. While Batters was always the strength, Joe was extraordinarily adroit, seeming to float on air, never off balance. Nerve implants were responsible, and he loved it. Once, he chased a target, though he cannot remember her name, because she had sparkling green eyes. He wanted them and bounced wall to wall up to six floors as she tried to escape. The light failed from the eyes, which was a shame; he wanted to keep the eyes.

Their HUDs blinked. "Target approaching, check the stairs." The gravel voice of Drauger said. "Do you remember the plan?"

Both thought, "Yes." All their gear was woven into Batters jacket, using small pockets of a mesh of conductive materials. Drauger wanted no trace beside the body.

"Good, free the blood." Drauger thought back and disconnected; his connection light turned off.

"Ready to free some blood?" Joe asked Batters. Batters shrugged, his hands darting about his coat, finding all the correct pockets. Joe pulled off his gloves, showing the metallic polycarbonate knuckle implants.

Finding the two right pockets, Batters said, "Yes, I'm ready." Removing his new toys.

They read through the HUDs' instructions, staring off into the distance, sometimes murmuring instructions to each other. Then, they looked around and approached the target who has just touched down.

The odd pair was still off in HUD land, looking dull and oblivious, though one felt about his coat. The other was taking off his gloves. Truly an odd pair, mid-November, and it was a grand temperature of a balmy 66, no need to coat or gloves. Saba was wearing a light windbreaker, which changes color as it moves across his body.

Maybe they were from the lower Levels, always hot down there, he had heard once, and one must acclimatize. David turned, looking up at the Graviton stairs.

'Truly remarkable. He hopes that he will return to the city once, and use them again, maybe from one of the towers to the riverbank, as the promotions describe. From his angle, the paintings are dark, only allowing the viewers of life's story. He stepped toward the pods. He could still make the aqua-city departure time, and he checked his code hustler inboxes, hoping that his streams would not give him any more concerns; he has them off during the Static Ball tournament, flashing light would ruin the whole experience. Now there was one red light pulsing in his HUD on the outermost section of his left eye.

Check it, he thought. The alert light now flashed green,

and a short message passes before his eyes. He only felt that he read it for, in reality, the Nadar Forge feeds that information to the brain's memory and language centers, but Saba knew that and read as he walked.

"Stream reports that Saba Dario, subject 1, was detected at the twenty-second robotiller section of the crop zone. Stream reports that Subject 1 was not observed by any other scanning that will show subject one presence since that detection according to Stream's methods and sources. End message. Thank you for using Stream." It read.

Saba stopped, and he thought he could hear his heartbeat triple. His transport from the crop zone to seeing Baker's supposed suicide was half an hour, to the Static Ball was half an hour, while the game was three hours, then the stairs were fifteen minutes. Way too much time, they, whoever they were, could have tracked him and tracking him in reverse. As a code hustle, well, former code hustler, now he would be happy in any jobs, maybe driving a robotiller, he knew that he would have quickly built a program to track him in both times, even back to a child if the information was scanned correctly. A geometric representation of his face, the way he walked, even his slightly inturned right foot, would be following, and any signals would be logged. Soon, if the program were built on the property, they would know what he ate for breakfast on his first day of school. Of course, it is illegal to monitor children, but he doubted that would discourage "them."

His pace quickened.

Message to Escrito, Tracked, leave now, he thought, and mentally send the message. His next line of thought went to the pod, Aqua-city Launch Center, departure time.

His viewer read 12.42 minutes. Ok, good enough. Book pod dispatch. He was almost to the pod Area, a red line that serpentined the middle of the transport hall between exhibits of the old city, left at a 2,365 sea wall model, right at a six-foot intricate reproduction of the something called the central park. He might still have time.

He was almost jogging, then he stopped moving, and his eyes left the HUD and focused on the ceiling. Before conscious thought could help him evaluate what was happen, the air was forced from his lungs, and something was pulling on the left side of his face. Something fast and strong was forcing something inside his mouth with the speed of a snake. It tore his check back like a fishhook, opening his mouth wide, and the more air escaped with a wet rush. His feet left the floor.

He looked down to see a hand squeezing its partner over his chest, the muscles pulled like metal cables. The arms covered a coat, but Saba could feel how the unnaturally large muscles slid over each other like steely serpents fighting for a meal.

Bones and tendons were bending, and he heard popping from his back. He doubted that he could even breathe properly again if released.

"Enjoy for this sweet afters, mate," the man holding him whispered in his ear. Another hand popped a small sphere into his mouth and pushed it into his throat. While his body tried to fight with minimal seizures and jerks, the hand continued to force the object down, somehow knowing which tube led to the stomach. He swallowed it, and the hand withdrew without touching his teeth; it slipped out. The fishhook hand left his mouth, and Saba was launched like a doll toward the lift entrance. He hit the floor, knocking his head after the titles, ripping open his temple, and slipped ten feet just up to exit. On his back, bleeding from one spot outside and several insides, he laid broken. His insides snapped as his lungs were finally filled with air; each cracked rib crackled against itself. Blood pooled in the back of his throat, waiting to be shot out.

He still could not speak; only low muttering left his mouth. Rolling over, the blood began to flow from his mouth and melded with the small puddle from his head wound. Darkness was claiming him. The two-man walked over, carefully avoiding the spreading blood and the marks where his head bounced off the titles.

"Alright. This is it, man. Are you ready to become yourself?" Saba saw the smile of a crooked, teethed thin man speak to him. Saba could only spit blood.

"Enough," Batters said, clearly irritated. "This is a quick hold and blow, right? Get the remote, now."

Joe, still bending over the broken lump, waved his hand and Batters, indicating that yes, it was a simple "hold and blow" and yes, he would get the remote, but he wanted to look into the eyes of the fallen. Well, that wants the odd hand waving was meant to express, but it looked more like Joe was warding off a fly.

They pulled the remote out, a simple small black rectangular with a single gray button.

"Ok, ok, I got it. Step back," Joe said. "First, throw him into the stairs thing, alright, Benny."

Batters grabbed the bleeding lump and pulled him up to eye Level. Saba screamed as his boned fell in on themselves, spraying specks of blood on Batters shirt.

"Dammit!" Batters screamed back in Saba's face and lobbed him into the center of the exit way. "Remote the blow, Joe. Now, I have to change. Holymothar, disgusting…jeez."

Joe kept the laugh internal, and yelled to Saba, now twenty feet away, "We will show the world your glory, my man." Then, he hit the button. Batters turned to walk away; he never likes these parts. He was more about holding someone down with his strength than the hold and blow, and 1,000 pounds per square inch is messy.

Within the belly of Saba Dario, a tiny technological miracle was taking place. Like a little bird egg, a small ball created from printed metallic alloys responded to a radio signal. Each layer of the pellet was printed within a high-pressure system and once finished, contained enough hydrogen to destroy a section of asteroids with pinpoint accuracy. However, in this situation, accuracy is not a variable measure, and Joe wanted it to anything except a pinpoint. The radio signal affected the pellets layers, and each second, the layer folded out like crumpled paper.

"The hold and blow are coming," Joe yelled at Saba. Saba could only feel his bones were ripped free from each other, and his breathing was becoming difficult now. Jagged rib edges were grinding through his lungs. "The blow is almost here, and your glory will be flung against the walls. Hell, maybe up forty feet!" Joe was moving behind a transparent exhibit shield.

The last layer began to fold out. As he was going on to shock, he could not move his head, but Saba's eyes swung up to look at the blackness suspended above. The hydrogen burst out, and Saba was atomized into a red mist that was captured by the Graviton field. Joe bent over and laughed, then swung his hand over his mouth. His hand was moist, still covered in Saba saliva. "Gross," Joe said and turned, walking away, as he wiped his hand on his pants.

What was left of Saba floated, first in imperceptible minute blobs, then in tiny drops, and finally, as the game patrons began to defense into the scarlet cloud, became blood beads. The patrons started to scream when they saw each other become coated in red, all dripping while still suspended. Their faces dripping. The exit Area was covered by blood and visceral. No patron could find footing, each sliding in a surging red mess. So as the patrons above slowly enjoy the magical arts on the nano-walls or looked out over the city, they realized that something was wrong; they were themselves also covered in what remains of Saba Dario. The lightning of a coming storm lit clouds. The grandest attraction of the Magnum Manzana, the spinning sphere above the largest city, people dripped red and became part of a surging wet crowd screaming for an escape from the remains of a former code hustler.

The coming storms quicken Valentino's pace back to the pod terminal, leaving the cropland. Mechanical pollen gatherers buzzed past him, some diving under his hat. Through a fast glance, they looked like pictures of wasps that he had seen when a child, all bulbous abdomens with thin legs and wings as long as they were, but a closer look, which was impossible due to their speed, would reveal that they were more like flying squid. The idea of life, even artificial life, pleased Valentino, made him seem more in touch with the world. He had read about the small groups working their way across the national farms, which are the size of states. The unknown to him and most of the city-goers, a land of green and seasons.

The sky shed sprinkles, dapping his hat. Weather much be nice to wake up to, well...better than the fungus producing misters every winter morning, he thought. After Saba left, he studied the data he was given and made a long series of notes on his HUD. He must have looked incredibly odd, staring off into space and wandering out in the fields, cornstalks over his head.

Each problem started and ended with who ordered the mysterious program that Saba and his friend built. There is where Valentino will start. During his wandering, he crossed reference the data and the code hustlers involved into a simple matrix that he would run back at the office.

Only a hundred yards past the pod terminal was a small entrance to the city, looking like a circular hole gouged out from the gray and glass that towered above. He could smell meat cooking and sweetness in the air and passed the terminal. As he approached, he saw the remains of the plants fashioned into all matter of things. Cornhusk dolls hung from small shops just outside the city's entrance, thirty feet high, and pushed into the original girders and old steel until the hole thinned into a small street that only four men could walk abreast. Other shops, manned by weathered and cracked old women and men, sold woven baskets and even clothing. At the base of the city, Level one, everything was cramped, and, as intended, the initial designers planned to form into a solid mass to support the upper Level. Buttresses spread out hundreds of feet over his head, each holds thousands of tons of city, buildings, parks, and people. At this Level, the city was like a castle, brilliant above, but the dark sewer system was the only entrance.

The scent of meat pulled at his nose again. He stepped into the shadow Level one, found the meat vendor offering an unspecified meat concoction. He knew that it was not printed from a standard flavor box. Wild? He thought. He nodded at the ancient man tending the grill on a small cart. The cart was original, real wood, and painted with cartoon circus animals with human faces. Beautiful, creepy, but beautiful, Valentino through, a real throwback. Actual fire licked an open-air grill cooked meals for the regulars. The smell of burning plants drifted back and forth, blowing into Valentino's face.

"What is that?" Valentino asked, pointing to the meat on a wooden skewer. The man cocked a hand to his ear and smiled. His teeth were gray, and he had lively eyes.

"Skazhi yeshche raz...pozhaluysta," the man said through a face that folded in on itself. He blurred the words together, as he had said this phrase thousands of times.

Valentino's face must have shown that he was clueless, and the man bent toward him and said, "please say again," in heavily accented English.

"Ahh...the meat," he pointed, then put his hand to the mouth and mimicked eating it.

The man let out a huge laugh and yelled, "Krysa...soo

gooowd. You will like." With impressive quickness, the man grabbed a small roll, and the skewer dipped the meat wad in the roll, withdrew it, and handed it over. "Odin credit, just one."

Valentino examines the cart, found the credit scanned in the shape of a brilliantly painted tiger's mouth. He ran his wrist over it and nodded to the man. "Thank you, sir."

"Da, da. Enjoy the rats, very good," the man said and skewered another small piece of meat.

Valentino did not know what a rat was but enjoy his real meat and real bread sandwich as he walked to the pod terminal.

Rain pounded the pod as he glided into his borough, darkening the sky. The bay was lit only by the aquacities production, as they worked under all conditions, and the sea wall, constantly beaming light into the open sea. He assumed that it was for resupply vessels and sea cities lost in storms or without satellite contact. Rain was rare where he lived, though sometimes, the pull of gravity will push it down from the upper Levels; by then, the water was black and corroded.

At least the bonus is that the air is humidified, so the misters would reactive, he thought. Valentino hated the misters, but his home Level was above 15,000 feet and is isolated from the outer atmosphere, so some concessions must be made.

Some of the older folks, 300 years plus, still speak of before the atmosphere plain was fully effective, and some kids would always test the system. He is She would climb out to the furthest edge, looking down on the ever bit of the city below. Always trying to outdo their friends, stretch just a bit further, as if the child was elastic, then one slip, and the system fails. The city was covered in a microthin energic veil. If the microscopic network of layers were disconnected, even for an instant, and the pressure was slightly released like air rushing into a room, it would spell terror for anyone testing its limits. Little Jose or Helga falls thousands of feet into a park or birthday party sprawled out below. According to the old-timers, it took around a hundred hours to fix the shield properly. The designers even created a circular wind current to avoid large scale bird collisions. Sometimes, decades of work, with the citizens always on tiptoes, waiting.

Once in his borough's heart and approaching Area 4, Valentino's message stream began to blink in the corner of his vision. Various computers, including his favorite Marrow 16, continued to cross-reference and catalog any findings from the name and companies in Saba information, and that was a mountain of data. Within the system, programs on programs are burying inside the system, each link by one to a hundred names.

He was starting to get responses. Saba nocturnal code hustling adventures at Thálassa póli construction were mentioned in Brooklyn Area 6 police message traffic, which was then pickup by several local news agencies. None of it reach beyond simple city crime, and many Thalassa poli security analysts through it were industrial espionage, which Valentino thought was odd, as the aquacities plans are open. Only four cities have freely granted access to aquacity technology: Jersey-York, Dar es Salaam, Fuzhou, and Buenos Aires. Of course, it said nothing of the breach of the higher, more secure Zellum networks.

'I need help with this, never knew computer or the quantum systems, and aquacities are now used bio-computers,' Valentino thought. He makes a mental note to contact an old buddy who used to sell program interfaces.

His pod rolled up to his stop and exited. Peaking his head

out, the life of the city filled his lungs, and the wizz of the passed pods buzzed into his ears. As people turned from a food kiosk tucked into an alleyway, the smell of printed foods washing into his face. He paused for a second to look down 35 A, past the clutter of vendors, the shifting colors on the nanowalls, the cold light of neon signs, and crowds of people, trying to see the rain. He could still smell it swirling around him. The distance was too far; all of the stimuli became a red-hued gray mist. Shoulders fell, and he sighed but returned to the matter at hand.

He hopped on the first sideway, and it began to move him along toward the park slowly. He still had his hat to protect him from the dark goo that the misters had generated. The slime fell in droplets, spattering the large oaks. Of course, it had no smell. Tiny Hygieia droids spun on the grass, fervently addressing each drop, and all other litter, with rapid swings of incest-like arms. One skittered under his shoe but was fast enough to avoid being smashed. A woman dressed in a long overly tight white sheath dress dropped her synthetic milk box on the sidewalk as walk pulled her to her destination. On the same walk, he turned, watching the litter. The walk microscopic engine, currently pulling and pushing him through the park, engulfed the trash and would enter its molecular matrix, pulling out useful elements. The box simply melted away.

'Animal,' he thought of the woman, then a chart of animals formed on his HUD. "Crap, disregard," he said the air. The chart faded, and his HUD was no longer visible through his eyes. "Alerts only, left peripheral three-Level," he instructed the Nadar Forge buried under the skin behind his ear. The last tree passed, and he said, "watery hole."

The walk's engines slowed beneath his feet as he turned toward the Empire State. A lovely pre-rewilding themed antediluvian spot with real glass, and handcraft cocktails, none of that synthesized liquid. These drinks were not squeezed out from a drab pale-yellow box with "alcoholic fermentation substance; please add flavor and color to drink specifications" printed on the side. It was a wonderful, grand place where all the proper journalists had their specific booths, with all their proper journalism.

As a pre-rewilding operation, the door was mounted with hinges, opened by a knob, both of which were being blocked by two unfamiliar huge, tattooed fellows.

"Excuse me," Valentino said, reaching for the door. Both looked up with up, the sclera was dyed blue and morphed as their eyes moved and frowned in unison.

"Oi, have you heard?" one asked, cracking a crooked half-smile. The entire make of his face was amiss, dead eyes and bald eyebrows, and a crooked smile with a cocked head. The other equally ugly man looked up are the overhead protection plain several hundred feet above, separating that Level from this one.

'Boy, a face only a mother could love,' Valentino thought. "About what?"

The man reviewing the plain burst forth a guttural laugh, "See, dustbin dunt know his cobblers from his nervous tick." The other drunkenly shouted, "Cheese off, asrehole," right into Valentino's face, then asked again, "The ugly apple over the bay, the man exploded?"

"No, have not heard yet, but I will check up on it," Valentino said, hoping they would now allow him to pass.

"Ouu..." the man hiccupped and said, "yep, yep, look it up. Great story for you journalists!" He waved two fingers to his forehead and out as a parting gesture, locked arms with the other man, who was still staring at the Level ceiling, and strutted off. The door cricked as the weight of the men was removed, a sigh of relief Valentino thought.

The old leather doors swung out, and he yelled to the barman, "Hiyoudoing, Mikey?"

Mikey, always clad in some shirt printed with the image of a musician from a bygone era, nodded, "Usual, Val?"

"Yes, sir, thank you, gentleman. What were those two brutes talking about, something about an exploding woman and an apple?"

Faster than should be humanly possible, Mikey pours, swirls, and adds the zest, then serves up Val's drink. A perfect ancient old fashioned. "Yep, some guy swallowed an ERO asteroid detonation shell." As the glass slid to Val along the real wooden bar top, Mikey's hands came together then fly apart; he mimicked the noise of the wet pop.

"Gross," Val said. "Cheers to the whiskey tree of life, my pal." He took a large draw.

"Cheers back. Cobb is in the corner booth."

As Mikey turned to deal with another customer, Val found Cobb and took another drink.

If you did not know Cobb, one might mistake him for an albino goblin holding the darkest booth in the darkest corner. Short, balding, flabby, and lacking in all forms of creativity, he was the perfect essence of a modern editor to today's newspaper. Val slipped into the booth, "Cobb, I have a story for you."

Head down reviewing his HUD, Cobb all but ignored him, other than raising a small fat hand. Val surveyed the room, same people doing the same thing. Most journalists were working through their HUDs or technicians that had just fixed some faulty city mechanism. He had almost finished his drink and moved to get another when Cobb said, "What?"

"Story, story, I have a story for you," Val said and clapped his hands, thoroughly excited to share.

Cobb's face had not changed from his original resting gargoyle, and said, "Blood in the air, Escrito. Check your stream."

"Fine," His thoughts activated his stream. Several lights began to blink red through his view. He mentally began to click through them, and the blood drains from his face. He is barely able to verbalize a "wow," before he stood straight up. Arms went out to balance himself, as all his weight seemed to rest on his head.

"Val, real talk, youalright?" Cobb glumly asked, feigning interest. Val, still steading himself, began to walk away, his eye still on Cobb. "So?"

The floor melted together, and Val walked, each floor tile becoming one as the walk became a run. The stream message continued to play in his brain's visual centers, though his eye was pointed at his editor. Cobb never left his booth, but yelled, What about my story," and pounded the table, spilling his drink. "Val, get back here!"

Val was at the door now, starting to swing the door and step on the street. Mikey called, "Next time, buddy," with a tip of his head.

'Blood in the air,' Cobb said. Val knew what the grotesque men and Cobb were talking about: someone had exploded. A lump that was once a man exploded at the bottom of the fancy new Manzana staircase. That stair operation may be over, at least for a while. Until people forget about floating through red mist. It was the first use of graviton tech on Earth; the ownership built it with instructions imported from the asteroid miners. It meant to manipulate things with colossal mass. Here they have aimed a small stream from the base of the case, allowing visitors to float down within a gigantic art exhibit. He kept the volume off.

The base is dripping visceral and blood; hunks of the flesh are still floating in the exhibit. His stomach churned, and he tastes bile working its way up to the back of his throat.

Behind Val's eyes, a new feed back-traced the woman's movements.

Saba enjoyed her float down, looking at the art and through the window. A short video section was corrupted by static; then, she is a broken mass of unnaturally twisted limps. More static, some distortions from the cameras and scanners. The explosion was too fast for the cameras; she simply atomized. She was there in pain, unable to move, then, a red vapor took her place. All the stream feeds were replaying her last movement, floating to mist, from all angles. Val has thirty views on both eyes, stumbling through the street, others avoid him as he brushed off passersby.

He stopped inches from the pod tracks. He knew one thing but was not sure it was possible.

The distortions, these blobs, where the video was so degraded that the graphics were only binary pulses of black, gray, and white, were concealing a human form, which brought Saba's tale back to him. Programmers have been killed, Saba had vaporized, and if the news feeds could backtrace her, then he was in profound jeopardy. Something he has never been in his life. Here, in the city, humans are never in jeopardy. Pods stop for you; apartments detect your emotions through biometric scanners limited self-harm options, even the floors to swimming pools will rise to help a poor swimmer. Now, he was in for a real-life specter of death with a shotgun pointed at his situation. He was in the mouth of a shark, waiting for his to bite down.

'What a story,' he thought excitedly.

He looked around, hoping to notice any sinister glances or eyes peering out from a shadow. He found nothing, just standard foot traffic plodding along. Following the night meal, more people will emerge and crowd the places between the buildings. He took a sidewalk to his apartment, only blocks away, ready to write down, what he hopes will be, the opening chapters of his perilous adventure. Eyes were watching him.

"Ingress. Five minutes," a huge man with blue circling around the white part of his eyes said into his Forge. Another was waiting and are ready with its teeth.

Val was brainstorming on how to tell is his story as he walked home.

'With the explosion, or the mystery message?'

Storing the data is paramount, which he could do now from his Forge, but he wants a more secure location, as whoever is hunting programmers may be able to code hustler inside his private stream. So, he had another idea.

The Jongro Building was created from old parts of the city, some sections are still cinderblock, and the brink mingled together haphazardly. Since his budget was limited, his second story flat lacked the total nanowall, but most of the living room had large nano segments placed between a belt of bricks or a plank of old steel. His hand pressed against the atrium scanner, and the first floor opened into a lower floor mall. All things were bought and sold here. Over five thousand people live in this building, and many shops only here. He did an experiment, and he could live in his building without leaving for up to two years and twenty-seven days, and that limit was only set because he got drunk while writing a story, fell over, banging his head, and need a new Nadar Forge.

While jogging through the opening food court, his mind was running too fast for conversation, so he waved to Bora and her husband Jung, behind their BBQ shop planted in the center. Best printed BBQ meats he could find. Nodded to Adel, who was still making custom artistic scarves, and then to Jose, who was frying up the best spicy crickets. All called, "How you doing,

Val," in several different languages.

Rushing around the front desk, up the manual stairs, he loved the antiqueness of it, and through the hallway, he scanner to enter his two-room flat. As with much of his life, his rooms were cluttered with forgotten relics of the old world. Paper posters lined the walls, except for the nano segments, depicting scenes from a city that is now destroyed, music bands will color splashing across the paper or odd images of a cat doing pullups. Age-warped wooden or gaudy plastic furniture was covered by dirty clothes, which was itself woven from animal fur or from cotton that was planted six generations ago.

Notizie sprang and landed at his feet. She was forty years old and still as furry and cute was when he adopted her as a kitten. She began to yowl, looking up to his face. Of course, you want food, even though the feeder was set on an automatic timing. He tagged Saba's data and linked it with his personal stream data storage, a light in the corner of his eye blinks green.

Ok, next step, he thought. Mentally, he linked his Nadar Forge with Notizie Forge. He had it custom designed to store hundreds of times what a typical pet Forge would generally hold. Perfect for a guy for never trusted some stream cloud off in quantum-net land, instant storage. With a thought, his data was folded into a folder where no one would ever look. The cat just meowed at him, then, startled, ran to some unseen place.

"Good job, cat, move along. I have to work," he said, engaged his halo-board; in his mind, an electrically colored keyboard burst into view. He cracked his knuckles and began to type. His thoughts signaled to the walls that all items would be removed from the floors, excluding his bed. Everything else, the tables, chairs, even his hastily removed clothes that sat in piles in most corners were pulled into the nano matrix or pulled together and placed in an overhead bundle. The clothes seem to skitter across the floor as if they were drawn by ants, each shirt skating between his legs while he walked and typed.

Circling the living room, not that much living was ever done there, as he is continually wandering the streets, he walked cataloging all his memories of the meeting with Saba down to the color of her eyes to the hue of the nightsuns. There was much to organize and plot in a timeline. Over two hours passed, and he believed that he captured all he currently knew.

His feet took him to his bedroom, and he rested on the lumpy mattress, sinking into the pile of sheets. The virtual keyboard was still in his mind's eye; he overlooked the room itself. Rubbing his hands over his face, he knew it was time to rest, collect his thoughts. He set a reminder on his stream for him to comb over the newspaper files on a friendly officer and a good video specialist tomorrow.

Behind the sheets, something was gently pushing off the wall, inching its way toward him. It was waiting for him. Slight, though it was, its sinews have twisted a man's head inverse before, and all that aggressive caliber moved to an un-suspecting victim like a shark through water. It smiled in the darkness, showing an array of serrated teeth.

Val felt nothing, continuing to type, and muttering with each sentence. The blankets softly crinkled as they brushed past each other while the thing moved. Feet softly push into the sheets, finding purchase and, slowly, so slowly that the bed made no noise, advanced, its teeth bared. The gray sheets move as if they have gained life, their first steps, cautious maneuvers over a newly discovered terrain.

Concentrating, Val was oblivious, and he continues to type. Like a snake shedding its skin, a nude woman rose out of the sheets that fell silently off her into a mass of quiet syn-thetic cotton. Her heartbeat is slow, measured tones and body did not pop, soft breathing through her nose, utterly silent. Her body slides out behind Val's head, he muttered along, setting alerts, alarms, and reminders. Black hair flowed down her back, and her skin held a greenish gross. She inched her head toward his, listening to his mutterings. Her mouth was open, a jagged row of teeth on display.

"The death of a Code Hustler....No. Deaths linked to Industrial Corruption...Crap," He said, working on a headline. "It has to be...great to get the proper attention." His eye rolled up, staring at the ceiling, unknowingly baring his neck. "People need to know why it mattered."

Her lips were kissing distant away from his ear. She whispers, "My teeth would not care if it mattered once they lock into your neck." She parted her toothy smile, opening her serpentine maw into sets of serrated teeth, and bite him with all her power. His flesh parted like an open door from behind his ear to the mid throat. Quickly her jaw began chewing into his skin, then muscle. Her mouth filled with blood.

He screamed and flew backward onto the bed, blood spouting from the wound, spraying her in the face. Her muscles tightened as Val's scream turned into a raspy cough, red spilling from his mouth. His HUD was still engaged, still playing over the real world. All he could feel is the pain while rows of teeth sawed their way toward his spinal column and the copper flavored liquid running in his throat. Each tooth cut through muscles, tendon and finally scraped against bone. Her mouth was almost closed, chewing complete, half of Val's neck was gone, sheared off with hacks of teeth. His head hung to the side, over the bleeding void, like it was the natural form of a neck, folded over the red gap. The bite was so vicious that blood was still shooting her face as she withdrew. She spits out a mouthful of his neck to the floor. It made a wet thump on the nanofloor; the blood was immediately absorbed by the floor, as was the still pulsing hunk of meat. Their atoms were reformed into new building materials for the apartment.

'Recycling,' her thought. Blood had painted her from her

face down to her stomach, bits of Val clung between her teeth.

The assassin pushed the body off with her small feet, and it rolled onto the floor. A smile broke on her face, and she walked to the shower. Then, lights flickered, and the power went out. Darkness surrounded her; she froze in mid-step. Her HUD showed a total lack of electrical activity throughout the entire apartment building. Structural reinforcement, she knew, was happening in this Area. Structures moved from one support to another, temporary cutting power. In her home, the lower Levels, there was no more reenforcing. As with all other things in life, life there was always static.

Lights flickered, blinding her. Then a high-pitched voice announced, "Non-resident detected. The resident shows no live signal. Law enforcement and medical personal will arrive soon. Non-resident, please remain calm."

Rage filled her, blood flowing from her mouth as she screamed. 'I was guaranteed a clean kill,' she thought hatefully. She had plans for the skin and the bones.

She ran to the door and fled down the hallway, dripping blood from her naked form. Sliding into the stairway, she reached into her long hair, forming fists while still bounding down the steps. She pulled out, and her second skin broke, peeling away. Halfway down the second flight of stairs, she jumped forward, ripping the translucent skin out and down while pulling her legs up. The motion launched tiny flecks of gore free, spraying the walls. Airborne, she flew over the banister and struck the opposite wall with her head, the skin landing on the floor, still wet with blood. Her original skin was free and unblemished by any evidence of the attack.

"All residents, please remain in your apartments. Emergency services will arrive soon, and you will be contacted. Thank you," an overhead spoke stated with mechanical precision.

She jumped the next six steps and threw herself through

the doors into the entryway. The main door was lock according to the lit red light placed at its top and bolted clicked on the stairway door once it closed. Alone she stood in the entryway, looking out to the street. No one seems to notice a naked woman with no hair caged in an apartment building entryway; the passersby continue to walk. The overhead lights had timed out, dimming. It was well past seven, and only the streetlights were on now. She knew better than to try and force the door; nano-walls could resist an explosion. Her breath was rising, her heart pounding out of her chest. She screamed, rattling the glass in the main gate, shaking the painted Jongro Building logo in ancient type font.

Her legs found their way to the floor, a smooth dark gray marble cut, and she kneed down. She covered herself in a pretext of modesty and closed her eyes. Jersey-York Area 4 patrol officers cuffed her after she was found catatonic. Bits of flesh were slowing being plucked from her teeth by her tongue and swallowed; she avoided opening her mouth, only looked at them with her supernaturally large green eyes, that could enchant you like a circling python, an emerald depth of insanity.

CHAPTER 2

The again-walker called her Sharkteeth, but, long before, she was Marrazo Zuby. The pretend human beings, the soulless ones shifting around in skin suits, will never know what to call her, and never had a grasp of her essence. Staring past the transparent aluminum of her cell, she believed that she saw all. All the patrol police with their bright orange uniforms and heavy grey belts loaded with equipment, all the tactical operators festooned with black dull metallic suits, each ones' spine encased in an insect husk supporting false muscles crafted from nanofibers, and all the others, fettering around the station. She loved it, their imbecilic eyes making furtive glances at her, then darting away like scared fish. Only her eyes shown through the circular holes, peeking out from her confinement. She was uniformed in all white and felt pretty, even after the gene-soak. The cell with all its authority and conformity hides the real darkness in her. Twin viridescent orbs speared anyone looking back, transfixed them for a bit, then, only when she wanted, released them again. She called it her ocular magic trick. She learned it on the farm, a lifetime ago.

Mrs. Saxon thought that her eyes were controlling the room from her chair. Her questions continued through the finger-wide holes in the cells as if Zuby was a pet. She had spent the last hour rereading the same questions using different words to the bald young woman.

"Please state your full name and address, ma'am," Elizabeth Saxon asked again. Zuby caught the eye of a clerk, who almost tripped over a chair as Zuby smirked, still looking at him. Elizabeth turned her head and yelled back, "hold your focus,

Mieners!" at the clerk. Mieners pretended not to notice and re-shuffled the massive pile of paperwork he precariously held on his lap. The criminal element was busy this evening, and he was still rifling through the intake forms.

"Ok, ma'am. I will start again," Elizabeth said, brushing her raven hair from her eyes and tucking it behind an ear. The headache was starting again, and this reticent woman was not helping. While she ran through the questions again, the seventh time, knowing that the mute will not respond, she checked her handheld. It was dinnertime, and her husband will be waiting.

'Still nothing from Human Identification Services,' she thought.

The initial scan registered that the 5'5 and 110-pound bald woman was a 63-year-old Chinese man, whose most re-cent address was in Nanjing in the Jiangsu province. While Elizabeth was only the Area-4 prosecutor on duty, not a geo-political specialist, she does know that this willfully quiet thing before her is not Chinese, nor male, and is a killer.

'The journalist…what was his name again?' Elizabeth thought, as she was still reading the questions, 'Ah, Mr. Valen-tino Escrito.'

She brought up Mr. Escrito's autopsy report and read through it, preparing an oral agreement in her mind for the Large-scale Augmented Municipal Protection System (LAMPS) electrical review.

Emergency services found Mr. Escrito in his apartment following an emergency call issued by the apartment's AI sys-tem. According to the report, he was killed by a laceration to the neck, which severed the carotid artery with puncture wounds from serrated teeth.

'Serrated teeth?' Elizabeth thought imagining the scene.

"Teeth," the quiet one said, glaring at Elizabeth with

a hard-verdant gaze. "Teeth," she said again, quietly, barely opening her mouth.

Elizabeth's back shot up, and she held her breath. The woman had moved to the walls, and her eyes were still peering through the elfin windows.

'Maybe I mouthed the words,' Elizabeth thought as she pulled her chair away from the cell, grinding the thin faux-metal of the seat against faux-tile.

"What did you say?" Elizabeth asked, recorder in hand. The small thing just relaxed and leaned back.

'I have plans for the skin and the bones,' Zuby thought, 'A clean kill, and with an exact time, he must be told, and this will be corrected.' The lady in the suit droned on; she will not answer, will not play their games; no more playing since she left the farm.

She smiled, licking the rows of teeth. Her tongue traveled the ridges from the barbed peak then down into the serrated trough. Home, the Department of Agriculture Quad-state production system, where she began to become whole, a true human animal, even before he found her. A vast plane of corn extending on past the line of sight. Rows upon rows of corn columns minded by robotic guardians. Maintenance was her family's primary function, and everything had its function. Over 260,000 square miles, 1,000 people maintained agr-bots, and other machines, occasionally to spot-checked the crop. Five families were in her group, near the Des Moines ruins. Most of the ruins had been gathered and repurposed into mag roads, the ports in Lake Michigan, and shipped to the east for grandly built human housing like the Cleveland megacity. Some of it even was formed into the agr-bots and their creepy ten-legged bodies. She called them spiders once; the farm knew of bugs, while the city people had never seen anything smaller than a sparrow. But Dad corrected her, "They are closer to crabs, sweetheart," he said, "They do spindle around on those skinny things, but look at their mouths." He pointed to the opening between the first set of legs, a portal small enough where only she could fit writhed with hundreds of spiny insect-like arms. Dad would explain how each one worked, what it did, and how that brought all of us food. She just thought it was gross.

She was never able to work up the courage to touch them, always afraid that they would swallow her whole, and at ten years old, they seemed monstrous, ten feet taller than her housing complex. Sometimes she would low crawl like a sniper to get as close without risking death to watch their underbellies as they worked the fields. There she noticed the bits of brick and concrete embedded in their dully gray legs, remnants of the nano-triggers, when towns were recycled into agricultural insecta equipment and roads to grand cities that her Dad had spoken about in his tales of his life in the big city.

"Without answering, we cannot let you leave, ma'am," Elizabeth said, tapping her handheld. "You will stay here until I get some answers." She pulled her collar back exposing her long neck, and its felt like steam was venting. 'I should have been off hours ago. This person...is irritating,' she thought, mild anger flaring.

"Were you told to do this? Killing someone? Did you know him? Lover's quarrel? I can understand that it happens." She was varying off the department-generated questions, testing her investigative mind, hoping to get at least some reaction, whether a soft tear-full murmur or a twitching of an arm. "Did he hurt you? Attack you? Maybe biting was the only choice you had. He was much bigger than you, maybe stronger." Zuby stiffened, her head turning away. Elizabeth thought she found an opening. "It is ok; I get it. He hurt you, and you were defending yourself. Just talk to me. I can help."

'Ha, she can help. I was attacked long ago,' Zuby thought, "No, no one can ever help.'

She must help herself. She will attack back, draw blood, and love it.

The farm families lived and worked together. Their responsibility covered hundreds of thousands of acres, her father said when he was lecturing the boys. One big family making food for all the continent was his understanding of his life's goal and that of his family. And she was just a part of the family, a small cog. Soon after her birth, the family suffered its first casualty.

Her mother, a person the farm workers called Laura when her Dad was not around, left to follow a fisherman. He worked near San Francisco in aquafarming in the Sacramento bay. As a small girl, she had never seen anything larger than a pond. The idea of an ocean's immensity was lost to her, as was her mother's emptiness from seeing just endless cornfields from dawn to dusk. The drive to move forced Laura to run west until the land simply ended. Zuby guessed she did the same thing, hurtling eastward until the Atlantic made her pause.

'Fishing?' she thought while watching the bots, as she sweated under the sun, 'Trading one type of farming for another, trading one family for the next.' She understood that.

She hoped that Laura was just as scared of the aqua-bots as she was of the arg-bots, that she had night terrors, too. The walking fright plagued Marrazo, the relentless dread quaking her bones. The terrors fled her mind after the fire.

Her father strained to manage her two brothers and her sister, making her free to roam. Or that is what it seemed.

Having two of each gender was beneficial to her father, easy to form long-term relationship cemented firmly by marriage. People in the corn rarely leave the corn. Father and mother train their children in all the ways of the corn, and the children will take their parents' place when the time came. However, having no mother allowed the girls to have an extended childhood, running in the cornrows and swimming in the creeks while the complex tended to utility matters. Until other families' young men came calling.

She tongued her canines hard enough to draw blood. 'Not young men, only petty, clumsy boys with wanton attitudes.'

While the men and boys were in the fields, fixing this and that, the girls escaped to see the White Ghost, a quick hour hike south of Saylorville Lake, near the Raccoon River. What once was downtown was now just a grid of broken asphalt with scorch marks from burned away tar. Though she never understood 'downtown" because there was no Uptown, Skytown, or downtown, she knew that this was a place where people lived together before arg-bots. But here, there were trees.

"Downtown" was covered with trees, the names of which she did not know. Running under a canopy, climbing the branches, resting behind the leaves, the girls flew. They felt the magic under the leaves.

The Ghost was a huge white cracked sculpture of a cartoon girl with short hair buried to her waist. Her carved face with its pudgy mouth and eyes that stared into nothingness reminded Zuby of herself, and she pictured that this is the way her mouth looked.

The sculpture leans to the right as a massive oak sprang out from under its pedestal, cracking the stones. Weather and time had abused the huge, little girl, and plants of all kinds grew around her. Zuby leaned against her and thought about living in a big city, the ones with Skytown and Undertown. Places where towers filled the sky like the rows and rows of corn.

The boys jumped out, scaring the girls, all squealed as

they ran home, except Zuby; she was lost in her thoughts until a boy grabbed her while the others laughed.

Elizabeth's HUD blinked in her peripheral vision, Banda Aliquam calling. She stood up, straightened her suit, and made the quick walk to her office. Mentally she answered, "Lieutenant Allyqam, how may I help you?"

"Aliquam," he responded, clearing his throat.

"I'm sorry, can you repeat that," She asked, confused.

"My name is Aliquam, not Allyqum. Like, ALI-CU-AM." He is used to this. Mispronunciation of anything, either his name or an item from a Chinese restaurant, troubles him.

"Sorry, can I help you?" She tersely asked again. Her husband is still waiting for her, and this is taking too long. Knowing Miguel, he will have a private celebration over one of his projects.

"Hi, I'm the Emerging Criminal Enterprises lead detective over Areas 2-6, Level 75-125. Your subject is of particular interest to me, as I have prepared several workups and semi-cases on her and her group. The subject in your cell is Marrazo Zuby, a member of the Draugers. The Draugers is a gang in Under town, and they are very dangerous when they come skyward."

He coughed and cleared his throat again. "Have you checked her teeth yet?"

"Detective, no, we have not. By order of the Inquisitor's Office, we have several other items first. A mouth print will only be used if needed, and, in this case, I do not see the need," She responded, thinking, 'odd, her teeth, strange feature.'

"Ma'am, what was the weapon? I see that she is being held regarding association with a citizen's death." Over the line, she could hear other cops walking by while Banda silently shushed the other officers' hoots and hollers. Elizabeth knew why she heard quiet voices in the background. She knew why, as she always knew.

Like most of the planet's population, she was tall, thin, and strong, but her eyes and hair always caused a stir. Her tan oval face was topped with a mane of raven hair that wound down her back. It drew stares and comments on how it was always set perfectly, long curls that formed black ringlets. But her eyes were the stars of her countenance. Behind the gorgeous shimmer top, she surveyed the world through golden eyes that shifted colors as they darted across a scene. She hoped that the officers recognized her as a sensational lawyer and phenomenal prosecutor, but, in reality, she knew that they only remembered her because of those amber eyes. Luckily, her husband only commented about her genomes and the psychological effects of those beautiful AU lights, as he called them. Of course, he used the periodic table to describe them; AU or gold. Once, during a deposition, she inadvertently entranced the suspect; he stood there before the IA magistrate for ten minutes before realizing that he must respond to her questions.

Banda was still trying to get the patrol to be quiet when she responded, "Yes, a death. The victim was killed by a wound to the neck...Wait, her teeth...? She bit him; that was done by her teeth?" The dreadful scene was playing out in her head, the savage cutting marks of teeth as they ripped into the dead man's neck, and Zuby's nude body wearing a skinsuit.

'What was his name again? Valentino, yes, that was it.'

"Yes, ma'am, but I would not try to open her mouth; she might actually bite you. They were genetically altered, along with her whole mouth. I'm sending you pictures now. They were taken at a distance, but you will get the point." He tried not to laugh at the pun. "She is suspected in several other assaults and at least two murders."

"Banda, can I call you that?"

"Sure, can you upgrade her holding status? I need to debrief her today. Is that possible?" He was already walking to check out a Police Argus, mentally arranging his notes on his HUD, trying not to bump into the other clumsy officers that were going the same way, all wobbly with their patrol gear mag-mounted to backs and belts.

"Yes, I will hold her for you. But, please stay on the line, though. I need more information, Banda," she asked. She still wondered where this cop got his intelligence. "You referenced her teeth. Can you explain?"

"Mrs. Saxon, have you ever seen a picture of a shark's teeth? A shark is a big carnivorous fish."

"Of course, Detective, I know," she snidely retorted, though she only saw one image because her husband was researching for a military gen-device contract. "So, she has genetically enhanced teeth and mouth, as you said. But, could that kill someone?" Her stream pinged in her left ear; message received.

'Display images,' she thought.

Before her, a dozen photographs splayed out, each one a blood orchestra. All were vicious trauma to human parts and a few dead faces, hanging at odd angles. One was down to the femur, marked by pointed objects. Another had cut between the hand and the Radius and Ulna with a gruesome attitude.

"What, she did this with her face? How in the world?" she asked as she sat on the top of her desk, pushing over papers and pens.

"Yes, she is one of the crazier of the crazies, loony as a runover cat. The gang arranges for enhancements, and she chose teeth. My ichthyologist said they were patterned after the extinct Great White Shark but scaled down. Vicious thing."

'Ok,' she thought. 'A human weapon, female weapon, dissecting the issues, looking for an angle. Her mouth can be used for attack and defense. Now, is she the victim of battery, sexual assault? Who attacked her?'

"Banda, we have no physical evidence, beyond that, she was there when the victim died, no DNA, fingerprints, no witnesses, nothing. If these images show how she...kills, then bite marks might be a key; however, the IA inquisitor will not file it, and she has not said a word after long hours of questioning. SO, can you help me get her to talk?"

"One second, ma'am." Banda burst through the station's entryway, walking to the patrol yard. He ignored the portly officer who was checking out an Argus, which sat rumbling.

"Sir, that is my cruiser." Banda mentally commanded the vehicle to open the driver's side door, stepped in, and began adjusting the seat. "Sir, please wait," the officer's voice reached Banda as he hooked the Argus into his HUD stream. The fuselage tipped back as the metallic form came to life. It adjusted the nano skin from an inert blob into a slick dart of a cruiser. Tiny black veins sprouted from the concrete, lifting the Argus, as Banda tuned the controls from his stream, rolling it forward.

"SIR! That is checked out under my name! Hey, bring that back. SIR!!!" the officer screamed while he was running, pressing his head against the windshield. Banda waved goodbye with a small smile, and the Argus' magnetically controlled mesh straightened, and the spoon-shaped body hit cruising speed. After mentally inputting the police emergency code, which activated the mounted lights, Banda resumed the conversation.

"Ok, yes. According to a human intelligence source, she was raised in a corn production facility in Des Moines, Iowa, until she reached 14. A fire destroyed the facility, killing her parents...well, her father. Her mother already remarried.

Her siblings and ten other families died. From what I have gathered, she was the only survivor. I think that she started the fire, and she is crazy as a soup sandwich. That might have been the point that pushed her off the nutty cliff; not sure. I have tons of other information from a good reliable human source with a great reporting record."

"Great, can she recognize you?" Elizabeth asked.

"No, all the intel is from a corroborating individual. I have bio-vid-log images for my face confirmation, and, sad to say, but I will know by her teeth. Have your cell display a point of view of the corn farm and, maybe, sounds of the machinery with birdsongs. It disturbs her, shows her that she is not in control. The word in Undertown is that she tries to manipulate people with her eyes like there are magic or hypnotizing them. Flip that around."

"Got it," Elizabeth search through her HUD, found an excellent 3-D view space, and mentally told the cell IA to project it along with a randomly selected bird recording from the Area-4 Natural Museum F4 and add natural elements. She checked the subject's file for anything that might increase the subject's comfort and ease any traumatic feelings.

"Ok, anything else?" Elizabeth asked.

Lurking on the floor by the transparent walls, still trying to mesmerize the passing officers with her eyes, suddenly she saw only yellow, and she jumped back. The yellow began to sway like it was breathing until the picture came into view. She was in a drifting world of dull yellow as the sunbaked wind softly touched her body, bringing smells of a farm. The odor of rich black dirt, a brief hint of rain in the air, and clatter of stalks rustling reignited memories of her childhood. Thoughts of clumsy boys, a witless father, and flames flashed in her mind.

Her skin began to feel cold, the subdermal muscles tensed, raising where her delicate arms hairs would have been if she was not devoid of all hair.

In the distance, a bright glow of metal stabbed her in the eyes, and she saw many shiny limbs rip through the plants. The Crabs were culling their way toward her, each limb guided by hundreds of others harvesting the corn. The air was hot as if it was summer, disembodied voices carried in the warm bursts of air, though she never saw any human shape. One wall displayed a long rowhouse with ten doors. The squat structure was once hers. On the opposite wall, at the horizon, was the barn, a nano-printed hanger-like building to maintain the Crabs.

Breath began to quicken, and she felt paralyzed, tasting only the corn on the back of her tongue. They could not touch her again; they could not reach out to grasp her again with their fumbling hands. Jaw muscles ached, then she knew that her mouth was locked closed, and coolness on her cheeks told her that she was crying.

The sky was cloudless, just waving yellow and intense blue overhead. The sun was trying to bake her, but fear froze her blood. Blisters were forming on her head and neck; she could feel them swell but could not raise her hands to check the severity. The sun was giant, looking down at her with one big angry eye.

She started to shiver.

Banda sends the image to the farm rowhouse and the arson investigator report. "Ok, are you reviewing it?" he asked.

"Yes," she answered as she skimmed through the first few noted observations and locations.

'Yes, time, date, yes, yes, weather conditions, ok, ah-h…,'she stopped, focusing in on the essential details.

"The cause was a liquid accelerant that was drained into the air system, the first call was after 03:00 hours from a weather drone. Ruled as a homicide with 46 victims. Exits were blocked by Balarama devices. Banda, what is that, like a transport drum or a barrel?"

The metallic nuggets of the Argus were slowing and drifting off the mag-lev course. Minimal magnetic power now, the pebble-sized pearls of nano-created metal rolled in unison to the Area-4 Magistrate and Inquisitor's Office. "Ha, sorry, I did not know that you had never seen one. Well, it is an agricultural machine just on farms, horrifying to kids. Twenty feet tall and have ten limbs used for harvesting. Someone, likely Zuby, programmed them to sit in front of the doors. Heck, those things do not even burn."

"I'm going to continue my interview with this information, Banda."

"Fine, fine, but I want my time after you are done. I doubt that she will speak, but I need to try. My confidential individual said that she is semi-agoraphobic and fire seems to comfort her."

Elizabeth said, "I will hold as long as I can." She checked the subject's vitals through her stream, all were up, stress hormones, pulse, breathing. It is working. "The cornfield display is affecting her; cortisol Levels are very high."

"I have very little experience with her physically, be careful, as you have seen, she is really an animal," Banda said, the red images of ripped flesh flashing before his eyes.

"She is collared, and I will not enter the cell."

"Oh yeah, one thing before you go. The highest traces of the accelerant were found in the bedroom of two teenage boys. Probably revenge for something or something personal,"

Banda said.

A pool of sweat spread out from under her, her red eyes could see was a gray yellow that was all. The fantastic green was now soured by reddish white, each eye oozing tears. The laugh was back, echoing in her head and the pale phantom image of the sculpted cartoon face of the White Ghost rested to the bright sky. Lurid smiles, white teeth, probing eyes, and clumsy hands. And blood and endless fields of corn.

"Mrs. Zuby, I'm Elizabeth Saxon, chief of the Inquisitor Staff in Area-4." One of the walls flickered then faded. Elizabeth was neatly seated in a chair where she was before, looking refreshed and holding a neo-paper copy of the interview. "I need to talk to you about your past in the cornfield," Elizabeth said.

Zuby briefly scooted to the transparent wall and locked eyes with Elizabeth, flashing green against glowing gold. A low growl erupted from deep in her throat.

"I'm glad that I have your attention. Before we deal with what you and your mouth did today, let us revisit the night of the fire."

Zuby did not blink, the pain helping her avoid trying to rip through the transparent aluminum to wrench life from the suited lady.

The cloudless sky over an endless cornfield faded from another wall, and the images of the bloated burned bodies were shown. The cell monitored Zuby's eye track and dilation, gently adjusting the images' location, turning them on for maximum effect. The center of the wall showed the blacked husks of two teenagers, each with a skeletal grin. Zuby's eye widened, and a hint of a smile crossed her face.

"I see that you know these sweet young men?" the suited lady said with a smile and an arched eyebrow. Zuby's tongue again found its cut, pressing against her jagged teeth. "Were they friends in Del Moines?"

Zuby's lips pressed even tighter together, her mouth filling with blood. Slowly, her mouth opened, sending blood sloshing out to the floor. As her jaw lowered, her head tilted up to directly face Elizabeth and her red soaked saw-like serrated teeth spread over her face as if the fangs were creating the smile rather then her mind. The computer absorbed the liquid as the process of course for the test; however, all the tests rendered null results.

Her mouth hung open as a horror show.

Crimson dripped as Zuby said, "toy despoilers," then she glanced at the twin blackened bodies. Her hand rose with fingers licking the air. "Fire consumes," blood continually running down, spoiling her uniform. Elizabeth thought she looked like a lioness right after a kill, with a scarlet maw and energetic eyes.

Elizabeth looked down, away from Zuby's face, afraid that it might infect her. Muttering, she asked, "how did you know to program the machines?"

Zuby nodded and mimicked typing, closing her jagged orifice.

"What about your parents, siblings?" No response, just a red-covered face and green eyes.

"Why?" She said nothing. "What happened to you? Did the boys hurt you? I might be able to help." Elizabeth mentally notified the medical staff of a minor injury, and the subject will be escorted to the med-bay after questioning. Of course, this type of questioning may take a while.

Zuby's mouth stayed closed, blood bubbles formed at the edges of her lips.

"Ok, well, it was nice speaking with you. You will be booked on 47 murders and transferred to St. Thomas in the morning. At least you will see clear skies and open sea," Elizabeth bluffed, hoping that Zuby knew nothing of the legal process. The reaction in Zuby's eyes told her that she was right.

"I have heard that the trip is nice, transparent walls like an open-air cabin on the mag down there. Even a penal Thalassa poli, fresh wind, and an expansive view of the ocean. Of course, you will be permanently cut off from anyone that you know, but you should not have chewed on people's necks, you know..."

Elizabeth's mind instructed the cell's IA to follow her mental track. The computer raced through files faster than thought. New images were cast to the walls. Two boys, both in farming crew clothes, were displayed behind Zuby. The picture tilted slightly, and the bodies seem to move away from the background, their smiles shined presenting to the observer. Zuby hissed, scrambled back from the projected faces.

"You will regret this," Zuby said softly, still staring at the smiles, blood drizzling to the floor.

"Is that a threat? I hope you said your goodbyes. Communication is severely monitored and extremely limited. Do you have anyone special? I can get them a message."

Zuby saw the Again-walker's face, his black eyes and white skin, his knowledge echoed in her ears. Her hands became twin claws and her toes pressed against the floor. Jonas would want suit-lady's head and her heart. Zuby was ready to spring teeth bared, but a man joined the suited lady.

"Inquisitor Saxon," Banda said with a nod to Elizabeth. He walked to the cell, noticed Zuby's position, "This one was about to jump against the walls. Oh, that would have been fun, right, Marrazo Zuby? First, you would have been stuck as the nano-cells harden around you, then, the best part, you would have been shocked until you were unconscious. Fun stuff!" He cracked a smile.

"So, did killing your family and those rapist boys earn you a spot with the Draugers?" Banda asked.

Elizabeth immediately sent Banda a stream message, 'Really, rapist boys...you should have told me that.'

'Hell, you got her to speak; that is impressive,' was his response.

Zuby's glowing green eyes flicked from the smiles of the dead boys to the pictures of her family. "Them, you, no protection." She said, shaking her head vigorously.

Both Banda and Elizabeth HUD streams beeped, and each saw a green dot in their peripheral vision.

'Release orders, reschedule questioning, report biometrics to the Identify Department from the Primary Inquisitor's Office per city policy.'

Mieners was already preparing the proper virtual paperwork, and he alerted Elizabeth through his Nadar Forge, 'I'm on it, ma'am. Med staff is on the way down and I have rescheduled the questioning for Monday morning. She will receive all the instructions via a bio-chat message.'

Elizabeth shot up from her chair, and both Banda and she shouted, "WHAT!"

Elizabeth commanded the cell to return to the cornfield broadcast, and all outside audio to be blanked.

"Sorry," Mieners said, "per city policy. No evidence, no witnesses, no nothing. She can walk."

"No way, she needs to stay and talk to us, not only about this but other cases too," Banda demanded.

"No sir, direct order from above. The ID team is reviewing the residential monitoring data, and we can pick her up later if needed."

"Umm… Did you not notice that the ID team is called because she has no identifiers? How will we find her in a city of over 10 million? No scans, DNA, biometrics, nothing. She will be a ghost," Banda's face morphed into the human approximation of a bulldog and turned toward the clerk's face, fuming.

Meiners backed away, again losing his grip on piles of paper, which was physically separating him from the large detective. He summoned the courage to state, "Well, sir, that is a police problem, not my problem." Then, he pushed up the paper stack, quickly backed away as Banda leaned in. The detective was about to strike the little man, but Elizabeth grabbed his shoulder.

"Detective, we have enough to track her; I mean, she is covered in DNA. I will write up a request for a new ID metric set, and then she will be scanned wherever she is. Please contact your CI and gather any data regarding her residence, work, close associates. Or I can reach out to your Captain?"

Now Banda's bulldog attitude was directed to the Inquisitor.

"This is a load of nonsense!" Banda stormed down the hall rubbing his face, which had turned red from his rising blood pressure. "I will be back tomorrow. Such a waste of my time!"

Elizabeth smoothed her suit and mentally addressed the cell's AI. 'Inform the subject of the order and call officers to offer friendly guide the subject out of the building. Log all data for tomorrow's review.'

Verbally she said, "Cell, render transparent."

Zuby stood in the center of the small gray room naked; her bloody clothes were in a neatly folded pile tucked into one corner. Two officers opened the nano-door, each holding out an arm, pointing toward the exit. "Ma'am, please consult your bio-chat message for future instructions. You may leave, and thank you for your time," one officer said without looking at Zuby.

She sprang out of the cell on bare feet, walked to Elizabeth, and leaned within inches of her face. Elizabeth could smell the iron floating in Zuby's breath, and Zuby could catch a hint of Elizabeth's perfume. Her mouth spread into a grotesque smile showing a parade of fangs. Elizabeth did not move, their eyes connected, and neither seemed to breathe.

"Remember Inquisitor, fire consumes, and thank you for YOUR time," Zuby breathed. Everyone watched her leave the building, a nude woman being swallowed by the city.

Her heels were clicked against the pavement, annoying her, each toe awaiting freedom. As she brushed against the palm reader, a blue outline of the door appeared. She thought, "Open," and the wall began to dissolve. As the wall became a porthole, then an oval, she could smell dinner burning. He always enjoyed cooking. The bio-printed foods are much easier and infinitely cheaper, but he still loved to cut, slice, and pepper each course with what he called his flare.

"You are burning something, Manzana." She stepped inside, watched a slow curl of smoke linger over the kitchen, and the wall resealed. Their apartment was originally an eggshell blank canvas and could be preprogrammed into seven different formats. They agreed on the placement of the walls, but, as always, he changed the design every month or so. Today the kitchen, which is again extremely expensive, was on the right of the entryway. As part of the culinary experience, he changed the wall and furniture to various earth and forest colors. The love of the forests and deep tones came from his grandfather, she believed. For a man so involved in technology and always sequestered in his lab, playing with genes like a child with blocks; part of him has the gentle spirit of a gatherer.

Against the wall's deep evergreen, she could see a layer of smoke; alarm ran through her.

"Miguel!" Dropping her purse, she turned the electric stove off. A pan containing a blackened bio-printed salmon steak oozed out smoke, she dropped it into the sink, then ran water over the charred meal. The fire was not her concern as the apartment would dose anything above 350 degrees with foam, but he would never abandon his carefully crafted meal.

"Are you here?" she yelled as she walked quickly passed the table that stretched from the wall and noticed a faux candle next to the plates.

A lightning-quick scan into the living room showed nothing, and his lab door was closed, appropriately lit with his favorite dark green, indicating that it was locked.

"Walls transparent and air void!" she called. The fan clicked on over her head, and the smoked began to swirl up, vanishing into the ceiling. The forest tones remained.

"Walls transparent, Lola!" she told the ceiling. Lola was the current model moniker. No response or changes in the greens and browns, the darkness closed in.

She walked to the bedroom and found only a well-made bed and an empty closet. The bathroom was clear as well. The fan clicked off, and then, she could hear the slow grinding of the wall reshaping and low moans.

A low gravelly voice called, "He is with us," and she froze.

'Someone is in here with us,' she thought.

She commanded the AI to close the bedroom, but nothing happened, the voice was only several feet away. Her fingers typed her code on the paneling, the AI scanned the apartment for any bioForges as her back pressed against the wall. The response revealed that Miguel's Forge was in the living room, and he was on his knees. Her hands began to shake. The image displayed in her HUD showed a man painted in electric green, head on the floor, arms bound behind him. She keyed in the emergency contact number, some faulty software muted any response, just a blinking black dot in her sideview.

"Sweetheart, we know what you are doing," a high-pitched female voice spat. "It won't work. Come on out here. We took control over your house, your...walls. You know that your husband wants to see your face!" the voice screeched. She knew that voice and that she was being mocked.

'How did that voice escape?'

She covered the few steps into the living room, the longest steps of her life, each footfall echoing, as her dread rose. The forest faded into a grey plane, which morphed into rust. The wall colors changed with each step; as she entered the living room, the walls were lit by a roaring fire.

In the red and orange dance of light, she saw her husband bleeding and moaning on the floor. Two others stood at his back; the fire bright behind them. An exceptionally tall man kicked Miguel forward, and the short woman caught him by his neck, twisting him, so his head was at an odd angle versus the rest of his body.

Grabbing Miguel's hair, exposing his neck, the woman said, "You wonder what my love would think the next time he saw me," jerking her head to the man, who was still standing in front of the fire like a monolith.

"Well, Inquisitor. Now, you know. You can give him my message." The woman smiled, showing genetically altered serrated teeth.

The man stepped forward, and she could see his face of pure white covered with black tattoos. He raised a knife, which glittered in the orange light of the broadcasted fires, and locked Miguel's head in his hand. She screamed as the other woman began to laugh maniacally. Miguel was suspended by his head, trying to scream even though his mouth was stuffed with a cloth, and the man looked at her from one foot away.

"I do not climb this high up often, lady. We tend to stay in the darkness of this wretched city. I only come to say, don't threaten my people," he growled and plunged the knife into Miguel's chest, then dropping him in a bloodied heap. Air rushed to her lungs as her heart thumped against her ribs, but the air never left her body. The woman launched her arms out, one hand covered her mouth, and the other retched her head to the side. The serrated teeth sliced into her neck, finding an artery, shooting blood pulsing into the air. Miguel watched the fire dance in his wife's eyes while she bled out, the pulses spraying him in the face, slowly decreasing until the dance was over, and darkness claimed him.

CHAPTER 3

It was time to celebrate. He has finally completed the defense Nadar Forge and the gene match application. The data was being converted into the proper DNA fragments, each process being stored right behind his ear, in the best Nadar Forge on earth, in his opinion. While editing DNA within a human is illegal, and one could change one's genetic building blocks like fashion accessories, Miguel has added over one million blank genes inside himself. An alteration in the four normal base units of DNA allows him to code all the overwhelming data across the megacities and all the animals on earth down to each genetic code.

So, he was proud of himself. While his lab was the size of a walk-in closet, he was remarkably efficient with its shape. Each gene-editor was stacked upon each other, and the virtual display was jacked directly into the brain. Once as a child, he saw an orchestra, the conductor magically waving his powerful wand. Each flick issues a wind of complex notes. In his tiny lab, nestled within his small apartment, he felt like that as he moved his fingers and hands, and the machines covering his wall began to hum, each executing a different task. He touched the wall, thinking, "continue storage, rerun initial query, and then deactivate." Removing his lab coat, which was unnecessary, but he was a traditionalist, he locked the room and entered the kitchen, just feet away.

"Forest tones, all surfaces, entry 124, four-speed."

Slowly, the eggshell walls shifted into dark greens and browns. After spending all day looking through a virtual heads-up display, the color change always made him studied the floor; afraid that he might crush a fern or disturb a creature nestled in the undergrowth.

"Salmon steak, per specifications, and turn on the element," he said, removing the pan from a cabinet. As the electrical heat warmed the pan, he added some butter, that he had specially prepared with real garlic and herbs. It was worth it; the military contract was ready to fill.

He thought it was time to bring his flare when he heard the soft grind of the entry pathway.

"Sweetheart, I just started the food. Go and relax. It has been a tough week for both of us."

A breath brushed his ear, and someone growled, "yes, it was a tough week."

Then he blacked out.

His arms were numb, and he choked against the sock in his throat. He retched, but the sock blocked the way, and he could feel the bile building up, eating away under his tongue. A heavy boot pressed down on his shoulders, and he realized that he was on his knees.

A tinny voice screeched, "Quiet and still, or I will open you. Understand?"

The boot pressed harder, crushing the air from his lungs out through his nose. He tried to nod, as the boot pressed his organs against his bones.

He heard the nanowall grind again.

"You are burning something, Manzana," Elizabeth called.

He thought, 'we are just tubes.'

He knew that he would regret that thought later, but it

was so simple.

'Holes for food to enter and exit. Tubes, with append-ages. Limbs that would gather food, supplies, build shelter, play with a child, hug a parent, and love your partner...only appendages.'

As the blood splashed his face, the light in her eyes dimmed and then, vanished while he was partially blinded by the firelight. As the hues of fire, reddish-yellows, and oranges were cast across the room, it was hard to tell where the light faded, and the blood began.

Elizabeth was dead, her throat open, and he could see her windpipe like it was a window. All her blood flowed into his face, lying in a pool of red. Her eyes were halfway open, not focusing, just blank. The arteries and veins only oozed now. That face, which he saw every morning and night, was more beautiful than any other that he had ever seen, was now just a head of a tube with blooding appendages. His legs would not work, and he looked down, even though he knew what happened. A blade had entered his chest, plunged through his intestines, and lodged in his spine. He felt no pain.

The people, the monsters, had passed through the wall right after the shark woman ripped out Elizabeth's neck.

'Like ghosts. They want me to bleed to death while I stare at my wife's dead face.'

On the wall, just over his wife, they painted a symbol. A circle, no, a snake eating its own tail, an ouroboros. Inside the ring, an upside-down letter T marked the wall. The wall was still dripping, painted in her blood. Dark against the simulated fire, it was burned into his eyes, buried deep in his mind. He could either look at the drawing in her blood or her dead face. He chose the bloody snake devouring its tail.

'No. Not yet...'

Pressing his forehead against the floor, still virtually

burning away, he tried to pull himself toward her, but his head slipped in the blood. His stomach was warm and wet, and he knew that the white monster, with a tracing of black lines over its face, must have nicked an artery. His blue shirt was turning black as the death soaked into the fabric.

He thought, "HUD," the room went from fire and blood to a dark space with several glowing tabs across his vision. By movements of the eye, he triggered a call to emergency services. A face emerged from the blackness.

"Borough 8 Manhattan emergency services, Area-4. How can I assist you?" a virtual responder, a gray head with a simple artistic rendering of a human face, said. It blinked at an abnormally slow pace, but the system was already scanning the apartment.

He choked out, "help." The blood loss allowed him to see the veins in his eyes as his heart pumped harder, and the real world was breaking through the heads-up display program.

"HUD off," he said. He wanted to look at her, not his inner head program. He focused on her face, pretending that she was asleep or concentrating because her eyes were not fully open or closed.

'Just her, her face, that is all,' he thought; the light was escaping him. The bloody chasm in her neck seemed to stare at him, the hole of the windpipe as an eye.

He was fading. His face relaxed, and his eyes fell into the hole of the wound that was still oozing.

'No,' he thought, 'No. Sweetheart. I love...' He started to cough, not thinking anymore.

His eyes rolled back, head lolling at an unnatural angle.

"Tubes, we are just tubes," he thought.

His world faded from view, and the story of Ravin took shape behind his eyelids. He could hear his grandfather telling it over the winds when he was nestled in the tall grass, looking at the stars. The first two things, the Wildings.

He faded again, oozing blood; his heart had pumped it all out, his face resting in his wife's blood mixing with his own.

Then, he was gone in the sleep of the dead.

CHAPTER 4

Intercedent One:

New Jersey-New York Articulated Level Atlantic System, Two days after Halloween

2,112 AD

He arrived early, wanting to be the first one on the job, rain dancing off his poncho. Each drop ignited the cloth and started a chain reaction, powering the glowing yellow that surrounded him like a halo. Even with the illuminated cloak, he was almost hit twice by other crews hurrying to finish their work as they drove by on the small troop carriers. Through the storm, he jogged down to the dock to meet the team. Shift starts in 30 minutes, at noon, but the clouds have blocked the sun for three days, and the sky was a swirling grayish-black soup crisscrossed by lightning. He took a deep breath and opened the door.

They did not want to hear his given name nor his last name; they only wanted to call him Five, as he was the newest to the crew. He assumed that his new moniker likely was because many never returned after their first mission. It was a hard and dangerous job; a job where one returned home with bruised knuckles and a sore back. He took all the classes, training, and worked for several years at an Undertown water purification facility, which broke more than it purified. He knew he was ready.

"Sir, when do we head out there?" He asked the foreman as he was strapping on his equipment and webbing.

Extra flashlights - check, toolkit- check, radio – check,

and, most importantly, check the hoses to his embedded wet lung just behind his left collar bone.

He inserted the tubes into their slots and checked his wrist monitor, showing him a light-up display of his respiratory system. The single natural lungs were seen in green, and the wet lung was yellow. He tapped on the monitor, cleared his ears, and activated the electronic device. He heard a loud pop, poured some water in his mouth, washed it around, then sucked the liquid into the trachea suppressing a cough. He glanced at his monitor, he read clean, and the water was drained out through the tubes in his chest. "Wet lung clear, sir," he called to the foreman.

"Ah, got it, Five. We leave in two minutes," Mr. Fraser said, "Team, out in two minutes!" he yelled up to the tin ceiling, hurting Five's ears.

"Aye, sir," the four men yelled in unison. The men began to haul their gear to the ship. The trip to the wall would take a rough 30 minutes across the bay.

It was here, pushed by ninety-foot-tall waves and the wind of the gods.

Hot water off the coast of Guinea, locals reported that it was hot enough to make a cup of coffee, drifted off to the sea, then the winds started the spiral. Tiny droplets were sucked into the air creating a moist fog over the ocean; the trade winds captured the small squall, along with a dense choking industrial mist, like the Saharan dust blooms in black. Moving out along the equator and then up to the Caribbean, the storm formed into a monstrous swirling black force of nature.

One weather drone entered the storm at its outer edge; then, its signal was lost. Other drones flew outside of its reach, and all land measures returned null. It destroyed any measuring equipment was the conclusion. The western hemisphere division of the World Meteorological Organization viewed it as wise to avoid feeding the creature with any more aircraft.

It drew its breath over the Greater Antilles, collapsing the few remaining towns, and drained lower Florida's marshes before it attacked like a dragon spraying torrents of water and winds instead of fire. Satellite images show the land was crushed as if God has smashed a violent hand seeking to return the land to the sea.

The storm, now called Calisto, slowed and drifted back out to sea. Jacksonville locals reported that she festered for seven days before moving north again; gathering energy. The monster was rested, and hungry again. Overhead measures register over 250 miles per hour winds and short 275 gusts. She reached a new Level of storm, category 7, while she was renewing her power as she traveled past the Carolinas.

The cycle of storms drew her north along the Eastern seaboard. Like a good monster, she lurked out of frame, waiting for the best time to strike, gathering all its inhuman power.

The wall grew before Five's eyes as they bounced off the ocean, heading to their assigned repair section. Their craft's deep V cut through the waves as they were rocked by the airlock system. Unfortunately for Five, the crew, tangled in their gear, was packed so tightly that he felt like a sardine in one of the old metal cans. Their tin can skipped over waves towards a black wall. Raising over four hundred feet the New Jersey-New York Articulated Level Atlantic System, now call the Seawall or the Apple's Crust by the locals, was once one of the greatest engineering marvels. But over the last hundred years, time and lack of maintenance had reduced its effectiveness much like the Romans stealing marble of the Colosseum, making a modern ruin in the ocean.

Five looked at his monitor, and the repair section was minutes away on the right. The screen displayed red Areas that need repairs, and the best route was highlighted in a line over a map. His amphibian skin-covered fingers brought up the maintenance log. A crease formed on his brow. "Sir, when was the last repair to our section?" he asked, really wanting to know, so he could formulate a mental plan but still afraid to show any scrap of weakness to the crew.

Somehow, Mr. Fraser pulled his body out between the other crew members and leaned across Mr. Jackson's lap to gaze on Five's screen. Jackson was napping, even as the craft creaked and strained with each bounce.

"Yep, Kid. That reads right," Mr. Fraser said and squeezed back into position like an octopus. Five's crease deepened.

Crewperson Hendrick's log, last repair mission to JYALAS section C243, subsection C92 completed on time, and all crew returned to post, 17:43 hours, 2052 AD. Log out.

'Great,' Five thought, 'and Skytown waited until the worst storm on record for repairs.'

A foot thumped his knee. Crewmen O'Sullivan was staring at him and moving to his throat. Eager to impress the second in command, Five's mind was racing in circles, trying to figure out what the movement meant. Was one of his hoses misaligned, or his buoyancy compensator strapped in poorly? O'Sullivan kicked him again, in the shin, hard. Five's eyes squinted in on his face trying to maintain the look even as the craft jumped and rocked.

O'Sullivan's pinkie and thumb extended, and he placed his gesture to his helmet.

'Oh crap,' Five thought.

"Comms up, crewmen O'Sullivan connect," Five said and faked a smile to crewmen number Two. After an electronic pop and some crackles, Five heard a voice from the speaker.

"It's good, kid. No worries. Typically, I train up the rookie, but this storm is fast, and we just finished the Wall repair assessment," O'Sullivan said.

"Nice to meet you," was all that Five could manage.

A bright smile bloomed under O'Sullivan's red beard. "Yeah, yeah. It's great, right?" he said as he looked to the Wall and then to the black mess of a sky. "It is like hauling in a dead body to sick call and then yelling at the doctor when it stays dead! Skytown, idiots!" His smile grew wider.

Mr. Fraser said it was a simple repair, and they would return after the storm passed. A short was sparking its way toward subsection C92, possibly causing a lock failure. 'Fix the lock' was how he explained it, in and out. Two teams, one will find the short and disconnect it, the other will remove any obstructions to the lock, such as tons of metal that have not been repaired in 60 years, and drain any water that might have leaked into the main rooms.

'Quick, in and out,' he said.

While the boat docked under the sheets of covering, the sea was churning, and they could barely unload before being jerked back on aboard. Five and Forest, a gangly blond who has not uttered a word the whole mission, had to pull the equipment over, stow it in the Wall entryway before returning and hoisting the other members onto the flooded gantry way. They passed a set of double watertight doors as they fought toward the main entrance. Inside the main hall, Mr. Fraser saw that the Wall's internal organs were still running but overburdened. Low hisses as the batteries were overcharged, outside wind and rain smashing into electrical generation panels above the waves and in the sky. The powerful waves continued to pulse electricity by pounding the wave energy convertor that lined the entire Sea Wall. The computer was using all its tools to vent energy, sets of thousands of batteries lay glowing, and the lights were on a maximum, straining the crews' eyes. Flowing out from the entryway, Section C92 opened like a cavern to over 1,000 feet wide, 300 feet back to a grimy concrete wall. No need for decorations in the interior, or, maybe, any festoonments have eroded as every surface was coated in thick gray dust. Five could hear water rushing nearby, sounding like rain. He had never seen the inside before. The training photos did not capture its true essence of looking like a failed cement factory, gantry ways sprouting this way and then that way, a concrete maze. Some of the lights were throwing off visible crackles.

"Electrical short, my ass," Fraser said, "Ok, hop to it." He pointed to a walkway, then pulled up his shoulder bag, and motioned for O'Sullivan and Five to follow as he mounted some stairs.

"Comms check!" O'Sullivan yelled into his helmet.

"Aye, aye," the crew yelled in response.

Sanchez and Forest harnessed their gear and lumbered off toward the power supply without saying a word. The winds were tremendous, and the battery was likely bursting. Fraser, O'Sullivan, and Five wound through the maze of concrete passageways and hanging catwalks, looking for the command room C92.

"It should be around the corner," Fraser said as they walked into Passageway 973. The floor was metal mesh, and Five noticed cracks in the concrete ceiling. He felt water well up around his amphibian suit. Bubbles were spilling from below, and a small current was pushing against the back of his ankles.

"Sir, should I be concerned about the rising water?" he asked.

"Is your wet lung working?" Fraser said in a curt tone.

"Yes, sir." Five knew that he should not have asked.

"Did you test its operation?" Fraser asked.

"Yes, sir."

"Did you clear and check each part of your gear?" Fraser leaning forward, his face mask almost touching Five's.

"Yes, sir."

"Then shut up and follow the leader," Fraser muttered as he quickly turned away toward the command room.

The water was up to Five's waist in the so-called command room, which was more of an aquarium. Small fish darted between their legs stirring up the gray dust, dancing through a charcoal soup. Still brighter than noon, the reflections on the water and the oddly metallic clouds caused him to darken his visor. As they splashed into the C92, Five saw the gray clouds swirl around them, flowing down the hall.

"Sir, we might have a sea base Level toe breach," Five said, motioning to O'Sullivan.

"Jesus, kid," O'Sullivan planted his gear on a metal table in the corner. "First, call me Sully, second...What?"

Stepping back into the concrete tunnel, Five pointed to the dust clouds moving in the murk like an industrial accident. "I think that some of that stuff is seabed from the ocean side being pushed up from the storm surge. Chances are that there is a leak over us, and one below. Umm...making a water chimney."

"Chimney?" Both Fraser and Sully asked.

Five hoped that he was not stepping off a cliff or shoving his foot in his mouth. "Yes, sirs. Back in the day, a chimney was a vent over a fireplace in a house. It allowed smoke to move up and out without letting rain through. In this case, I think that since this gallery is not airtight, due to the leak above, the crack in the concrete, the storm is pushing water up, as smoke would have in a chimney. If the crack above was closed, resealing the air pressure, then the water would have no place to go, but…Section 92 is filling up with gunk and water. Water in from both sides. Might short-out everything and break the damaged lock."

Both crewmen's eyes were fixed on him. They could not tell that he was holding his breath.

Fraser tapped his comms, and said, "Team two, what is your status?" while still staring at Five.

"Sir, we are in position and have cleared part of the lock mechanism, but several modules are at the end of life. Also, a leak above us has filled the lower compartment near the seabed, so wet lung time in a bit, sir."

"Roger that, keep in contact," Fraser said. He moved closer as if he might need to read Five's lips. "Alrighty, smart guy, I agree with your unconventional risk assessment. In your oh-so-wise opinion, what is the greatest risk with the chimney thing?"

Five felt that he did step off the cliff and was in freefall. His eyes blurred for a second, then he remembered to breathe. Sully continued his assignment, flipping switches and changing fuses.

"Sir, Ummm…" Again, Fraser waded through the water closer, disturbing the gathering grey dust, and tapped Five's visor three times. His two prominent brows had netted themselves into one angry brow. Worry was in his eyes, and his knuckles were white behind his suit.

"No time, kid! Now!" he shouted.

"Section Failure as the water undermines the seabed, destroying the ground support. The lock will tip over once balance is compromised. Tons of pressure are pushing against us now. The section filled with water, the seabed, ripped up by the storm surge. Total and complete failure, sir," Five shouted back more out of surprise than being totally confident. He calmed himself, "Yes, sir. That is the worst."

Fraser turned away quickly, looked at his wrist monitors, then spoke with command and control, Seawall C2, onshore. "We have a structural failure in the gallery of C92. Unknown sections of the locks are damaged, and the gallery is filling with seawater from below and rainwater from above. Please advise?" Five could see his monitor view of the C92, blinking yellow, edging toward red. The lights overhead threw sparks, causing all eyes to shoot up.

C2 responded, "Copy that, Crew Chief. We are aware, and we advise that your crew should..." The other end's voice seemed to fall into a hole; they could only hear disembodied chunks of words, then radio static.

The sparking lights threw one last flash, then blinked out. Five heard a splash beside him. His suit ignited his visor display, a small cone of the room reappeared. Fraser was trudging toward a light that was flopping around in the gray soup. With one hand, Fraser pulled the three hundred pounds of Sully from the water and set him on his feet.

"Afraid of the dark, Sully. Making you look bad in the rookie's eyes," Fraser said through a smile.

Sully's head cocked back with wide eyes, "No worries, just slipped."

"Ok," Fraser put his hands behind his helmet, as the others looked on, "The storm likely took out the radio relay, and all this water finally shorted out this section. So, the only productive thing is to secure the locks, and the weight of the Wall should keep in place until it can be truly fixed after the storm."

"We close all the rooms with airtight doors, seal up some air in here, find and help team two, and get the hell off this storm breaker!"

The water-filled command room was closed and electronically marked as faulty, showing in large glowing red letters on Five's wrist monitor. The Gallery had few airtight rooms, just a vast concrete cavern, divided into lobes, like a human lung. Thin nano-layer sheets were placed at what Fraser called critical junctions, mounted in sections of cement. Each man was assigned an Area and began to pull the inset sheets across an elephantine space, creating a cellular structure within C92.

Five kept imagining pockets of alveoli being sealed away from incoming water.

The battery banks were clear; then the transmission room next to the gantry ways that led to the command. All sealed with layers of clear nano-mess that would, in theory, slowly drain the liquid out through a complex capillary action. Fraser explains that it acts like a tree, using water's strange ability to coalesce, pulling it up through the sheets, then draining it back into the ocean through roof vents.

Five asked many questions, but Fraser just shrugged and said, "They only told me enough information to showcase it for any tourists that walkthrough. You know how C2 loves their safety measures." He chuckled as he wrapped up a new set of sheets.

Gazing through the first cell wall, Five could see the water gathering along the lines of the sheets; he hoped the drain sheets would work quickly to seal the leak. As he squinted through one sheet, which began to fill with slowly flowing liquid dust, the floor flew out from under his feet, slamming his head into the concrete wall. Stars floated over his eyes between blinks, he was unsure which way was up.

"Piping failure," Fraser screamed into his mic, "The pressure of those waves is pushing water under the storm breaker! Levee failure!" Five still could not see straight, and he tasted blood running into his mouth. His training kicked in, and images from a training volume of a levee failure, an artist rendering of water, blue lines stretching under the structure, working to dislodge it filtered into his mind. "Five, come here," Fraser gestured like he wanted a hug, "Yep, you got rattled. Just sit there, focus on breathing," he mimicked each breath, "In through the nose, out through the mouth." He continued to speak to Five, but the words were garbled as another quake hit them. Sully tipped like a tree, rolling his shoulder on the way down, sending the drain sheets flying. The light flicked on again.

"Agghhh, CRAP!" Sully screamed, clutching his massive shoulder with an equally large hand. Five understood that. Somehow, he was on his feet again, trying to lift Sully's injured arm.

"Everyone...team 2, head to the evac ramp, now. I mean NOW," Fraser ordered, turning to them, "This breaker is tilting, and the seabed has shifted below. With that broken lock free from the other section, it will break loose, drown us with it. So, we move fast." Veins bulged from his neck, and his eyes seemed larger, picking out every detail. "So, move, move, move!" As he shuffled, he typed an emergency code into his wrist com, heard something discouraging on a private com-line from C2. He continued typing and then switched off the C2 line. They ran as quickly as their legs would carry them. Still, despite the urgency, their equipment forced them to slosh through murky seawater toward the other team until Fraser received a message on the open communication line.

"Sir," Sanchez said shakily, alarm crossed over Fraser's face. Sanchez was known for cracking jokes over the line, with no mention of 'sir.'

"Forest's waterlung malfunctioned…he is drowning…" Five heard sniffs and choked sobs on the open line like they were off in the distance. "I can't carry him…I'm calling Code Grey." The clunky uniformed armor clicked as Fraser's spine straightened. "Copy?" Sanchez said he was moving on the other side of the line.

"Code Grey received. Confirm?"

Through ragged breaths, Sanchez groaned, "Confirmed…Code Grey. Meet ya'll at the boat." The radio disconnected.

"Sorry to ask, sir," Five said, worrying that he was kicking a hornets' nest, "What is that code?" Sully gripped his arm, staring at him through a looking glass.

"Old hospital code we use. It means loss of utilities," he said, horror creeping into his eyes, "It means Forest will be left here as the Storm Breaker smashes into the seafloor." His face changed as if he forgot what he just said, "Now, we have to move." He let go and ran after Fraser. A crack rippled through the walls, shaking the floor under their feet; they stopped moving. The lights blinked off, then water began to jet out of any small, unsealed surface like a submarine implosion.

"HULL BREACH!" Sully yelled, his legs trudging mechanically, "KEEP CLIMBING!" The next few flights of stairs were water-free, but that would not last long. Five reviewed his wrist monitor, two stories by stairs, several turns, opened three sets of sealed doors, out through the loading dock, and the fresh air of a hurricane. He was thinking of how he will explain his first big day on the new assignment to his wife, not sure about using the phrase 'fresh air' as the largest and most powerful hurricane was barreling toward the city. Maybe just 'escape.' They hit the first set of doors, collided through anything in their way, dropped all equipment that could not immediately save a life.

"Boss," Five huffed, "Are these next rooms sealed from the inside?" he tried to look at Fraser, but there was not enough room in the hallway, and the visor blocked his peripheral vision, "I mean, should I be ready to engage the wet lung?"

'The second set of doors, water-free,' Five checked off in his mind.

Fraser angled his body so he could see Five, showing off his huge gap-toothed smile. "Almost there, son," he said as the last set of doors broke loose in a burst of high-pressure water, sending a steel gate careening through his helmet, then stapling him to the concrete walls. Five gripped the wall in a crouch, fingers interwoven with the metal mesh beneath the surging water. He froze for moments, just waiting to hear Fraser confirm that he was fine, just a scratch, now head for the door. Nothing came, only the sound of rushing water. He blinked several times, felt lightheaded, then understood that he was not breathing. Hands still mingling with the mesh, he turned looking for Fraser; he knew where Fraser was, at the wall, and will remain there forever. Sully floated facedown near Frazer's impaled body. Under his visor light, the water began to turn red. Five wanted to check on him, revive him, but he could not move and risk losing his grip. His fingers locked in the mesh held him from riding the icy waters down to another Level, a Level that would be home until fish ate him into a skeleton. He began to compartmentalize. Calculating life was the end goal of all his efforts since the first suckle to properly gearing up for today.

'So, THINK,' he told himself. 'The flow was weakening, meaning,' he thought, 'that the water pressure was equalizing. Now, the flood from above was consumed by the flood from below. Water has surrounded us through all the non-water-tight rooms.' He moved through the room full of dirty water, rushing like he was escaping a sinking ship.

After flipping a switch, his wet lung activated; he just waited for the first gulp of saltwater and then pulled himself forward to the loading dock and their small V-shaped ship. The cargo Area could be packed with carnival rides and concession stands, but Five only noticed the dim gap in the wall, where the storm was firing bullets falling from the sky, driven by hellish winds. The hallway descended behind him; the water was at his waist now, a slight current circulating in the cargo hold. Imaginary sea monster plagued these waters; he tried to keep it out of his head, but it was there, and he thought he saw yellow eyes staring at him from a blackened corner. With the haste of a man being hunted by monsters, he just trudged onto the pier.

The pier was three feet underwater, sometimes nine at a crest as the breaker began to tip. After being battered by waves as he ventured out into the storm, he mag-locked his boots to the main walkway. The rain came down like he was under a faucet while the waves tore up from the raging bay. As the troughs replaced water with air, he could get at least oriented; otherwise, the world was just seaspray. The ship could not sink, he remembered, and the air compression system will keep him safe. He could motor back to base regardless of any storm; only his mind needs help now. His wrist monitor told him that he was the crew chief. He was surprised at such a fast advancement, then remembered Frazer's head mounted on the wall and Sully's body floating away. With a touch, he reached out to C2, "I'm the only member left... Section C92 is disabled, water piping under structure leading to levee failure. The whole Section is being pulled back, breaking away from the rest of the JYALAS. Initiate emergency protocols," he said, fumbling with the ship's door and rechecking that his suit was still pressurized. His hand entered the correct code, the ship door cracked open, then the pier pulls away. He tipped forward, eyeing down into the black water, and his magnetically connect boots realigned his body. Another wave pushed the boat back to him; it crashed against the pier, smashing his outreached arm.

There was silence on the other side, then the simple word of, "What?"

"I'm the last surviving member of the repair work crew..." Five repeated, gripping his injured arm, "Boarding the ship, returning to base." Broken concrete slabs crashed together inside the main entry port, shooting water out like a blowhole. Five could not distinguish it from the other surges. As he steadied himself to jump aboard, he saw the lock at the edge of the massive seawall break open, water-spouting through the rips in the hull in grey fountains. Five's body was pushed back with each wave; they crested higher and higher until he realized that the pier was sinking into the bay. As the water receded for the final time, he deactivated the mag-lock. Through the spray, he saw another wave coming, the white breaking over his head less than a meter away.

He jumped to the ship as the wave struck, the water pushing the ship's open-door around him, capturing him like a ball in a mitt. His Dad would have loved it. Of course, his Dad would not have liked that Five's arm was broken along with three ribs. The boat's door sealed shut as it crashed into the pier's roof. The onboard AI automatically withdrew as the roof's metal planks scraped down the fuselage, then the dock was claimed by the bay. The metal groaned as it fell into the sea. The boat knew its way home and bounced over the windswept waves, cutting through the water. Five could not see where he was; the rain blocked all the city lights, only the momentum told him that he was moving. "Last crew member," he repeated again and again.

"Crewmember five, what is your name?" a voice said

over the radio.

"Last crew member...lastcrewmember..." Something in the sea moaned behind him.

"Confirm! Crewmember five, please confirmed your name on the live channel!" the voice insisted as if it was disturbed by something meaningful. The movements began to lull Five to sleep as images of his first mission played on the backs of his eyelids. Fraser was a strong man, a good leader; Sullivan had a brushy beard and liked to smile; Sanchez was sad at the end. "Confirm!" the voice yelled.

"C2 of New Jersey-New York Articulated Level Atlantic System, my identifying number is 546BV1..." Five mumbled, "I'm Campbell Saxon, confirming...returning to base." He disconnected the com-line, listened to Calisto rip through the storm breaker, and hoped his wife was on high ground.

PART TWO

CHAPTER 5

Jersey-York City, Borough: Peterson-Clifton

Maywood Island, Area-15, Level-12, year 2698

Miguel's little legs quickly carried his small frame up the stairs. Finishing the creation of the brand-new Bio-Bot toy set was of primary importance, but seeing Grandad's eyes light up is always the best part of a Tuesday. Besides, the toy's instruction stated it was made for 15+, and he was seven, so he figured that he had an extra day to build the neurological circuits and test the tiny muscles. He decided that its final form will be a mouse with a rhinoceros horn propelled by six beetle legs.

Grandad taught at the second-best college in the city, J-Y University, but in the best school, the Department of Physics. Miguel knew these rankings because Grandad told him, and, as far as Miguel knows, Grandad was never wrong by the purest definition of the word. The boy questioned his logic sometimes, though, such as the trivial idea of bedtime or the ancient traditions of dessert after a meal, when the caloric intake is the same whether one eats it before or after dinner. Sometimes Grandad would tell him the J-Y University, which peppered the city with smaller satellite stations, was the bests because all students could learn without any cost. Thus, surpassing all the other venerable institutes of learning. Grandad would lecture Miguel on many things, striding around in his study, speaking of regressive taxes, how the angle of 45 degrees inspires fear in humans, and how energy can be transported through an unseen web of space tunnels. Still, he always started by saying, "No man should escape our universe without knowing how little he knows, and a school will teach you the questions." He said that he stole that from a man, but that was ok because the man has been dead for over seven hundred years. Typically, his cousins would sit through these talks, only to raid the candy jar in the back of the study, but Miguel never ate the candy and stayed to hear his Grandad's wisdom or, sometimes, just the funny faces that he would make.

Miguel heard the wall buzzing, about to form an opening. His legs stalled, and he crouched down, imitating his best panther. The minuscule hole, the size of Miguel's pinky, grew in the wall, and soon the wall was gone, the portal opened. Grandad was there smiling, loaded with books, a valise over his shoulder, and briefcase in hand. Under the most immense eyebrow that Miguel had ever seen, Grandad's eyes sparkled, scanning the entryway, knowing to be on guard. Discarding all his load, he closed the wall and jumped to hide against the wall, spreading out, arms against it. From what Miguel knew through his extensive human movement studies for someone under ten, Grandad was spry for a ninety-year-old. However, the melding with the nano-wall was not a proper form of disguise; it might even make an object more noticeable. Grandad's face became a mask, emotionless, other than the brightness of his eyes. Slowly he hugged the wall, inching to the stairs. Miguel sunk to the step, even depressed his head to one side, one eye peeking out.

"Pops?" Miguel's dad yelled from the kitchen. "Are you home?"

Grandad's face was unmoved; he continued to creep to the spot of shadow between the main entryway and the kitchen opposite the stairs. Miguel could hear his dad's feet approaching from his right. Grandad slipped into the shadow on the left of the kitchen door; only the luster of his eyes showed his presence.

"Ok, Miguel, Grandad is home. Why don't you come

on up," he spoke down the stairs, not seeing his son. As he turned to call to his own dad, Miguel launched a mighty seven-year-old roar. Miguel's dad screamed, whirling to face the boy, then, Grandad's hand falls on Miguel's dad's shoulder accompanied by a resounding BOO. Miguel's dad screamed again and fell back into the kitchen, knocking pots over and scattering wooden spoons all over the tiled floor.

"JESUS," he cried. "Ustedes dos estan tratando de matarme!" Both Miguel and Grandad hit the floor, laughing.

"AhHH...no, no. We are NOT trying to kill you, just giving you a cardiac reboot!" Grandad chuckled and reached his large hand out to fist bump Miguel's tiny hand, who was still squealing on the floor, laughing in his dad's ears.

"Cardiac REBOOT...Dad," Miguel chortled, padding his dad's stomach, then continued laughing, rolling around on the colorful tiles.

"Yeah, yeah, ok," Dad said as he pulled himself off the floor. "Good one, like ninjas and shadow mixed together."

Grandad's finger shot out to Miguel, who was familiar enough to snap to attention. His smile disappeared beneath his white beard. "Three facts about ninjas, Miguel."

"Yes, Grandad, they were coveted warriors from Japan or Nippon, the land of the rising sun. They first trained in the ancient Iga province, and that Area produced professional ninjas. The first writings were in the...14th, no, 15th century," Miguel's voice became higher, suggesting that the last statement was a question. His eyes shifted to the left and up, a furrow formed on his forehead. "Yes, 15th Century!"

His eyes steadfastly refocused on his Grandad. The beard was broken by a huge smile of old yellow teeth, "Very good; I will teach you more later. Most of what people think is real is false, and sometimes false is real. So, what do we say?"

"I must know what I do not, and education will help me

find the real questions," Miguel said, his own interpretation of what Grandad had taught him; he did not like taking the ancient dead man's words without permission.

"Yes, I like it," Grandad picked Miguel up, slinging him to his shoulders.

"Ok, guys. Enjoy the night, but not too late," Miguel's dad returned to the kitchen, and Miguel could hear the pots clattering together and wooden spoons being dropped back into their container.

"To the backyard, my boy!" Grandad's extending a fist as if they were riding into battle, and they burst through the double doors. Miguel's house is on an island in the bay, and when the sun dips below the western horizon, as the twilight glimmer fades, the city brightens around them. The blazing multihued flickers of millions of bulbs make it seem to Miguel that he and his home are adrift in a sea of bioluminescent algae, all flowing on ocean currents. Miguel and his family occupied the Maywood island residence project's top-Level nestled under a newly created layer of new earth.

Often, Miguel thought that they were like dwarves living under their own hills. The rooftops of his block were all covered in grass with a filtration system leading to the fungus farms below, making it a wonderous place for Grandad's stories, curled up in the clean grass blades. They settled yards away from the house, and Grandad began to tickle Miguel's outstretched bare feet. Miguel wanting the stories to start, muffled his mouth with his hands.

"Ah, laughter. Miguel, did you know that all things started with a joke," Grandad's mane of wild white hair pressed the tall grass back, and he rested his head, "and the hidden things beneath the world we know laughed." Miguel nestled his small head on Grandad's large body.

"No one knows the joke, but their laughter struck a chord and started the first fire in the shapeless infinitesimal

void. The fire was a pinprick falling away into infinite blackness. The darkness was lit by the glow of a fire, a tiny glow."
Miguel looked to the stars.

Miguel's chest hurt as he laid in the darkness; chills
ripped through his skin like he was wrapped in an icy blanket.
Something other than himself moved his body; he could recognize it. He could not get his legs to move, not even a flick of
a toe. The air was vanishing from his lungs, and they began to
ache. The ice pooled inside of him, seeping in through his skin
and then into his bones. His hand moved. One finger against
another, his skin was sticky and wet.

"Full med-scan! BaladaFuse injection should stop the
hemo-loss and restore blood Levels, heart is stabilizing.
HealMed solution was injected five minutes ago," a woman
barked to others. He could hear them shuffling in the room.

"NURS lay him in one, two, three! Yes, that one. Damn it,
NURS, you rolled over my feet again. Saline," a man said, snapping his fingers, which hurt Miguel's ears.

He was being jostled, and he was starting to feel again.
Pain like flashing lightning danced through him, radiating
from his spine. Like a tiny angry creature, lightly squeezed
through his lids, people wearing white rushed around an ivory
room. Most of them had red marks on their hands and tunics.
He saw drops of blood drip to the floor, imagined that it was
he who fell, then exploding as he crashed. His heart thumped
wildly, pushing blood ever faster; it began to gurgle in his
mouth.

'ELIZABETH! Where was she?' He cannot hear her. He
wanted so much to feel her hand on his, her touch, feel her
warmth.

He began to seize.

❖ ❖ ❖

"Miguel, are you troubled?" Grandad asked when he noticed that Miguel was twirling his long hair. The darkness was fully formed around them. His eggshell suit was surely getting grass stains, and Granny will not like that.

"No, Grandad, but I have not heard this one before. So far, it sounds old, well, new for me but ancient on earth, I mean," Miguel said, fingers were no longer twirling. "Grandad, if you can, please tell me; I think I will enjoy it very much."

"Very well, young lad. This is an old, even ancient story from our ancestors. It is the story of the first four names. It is called The Wildlings, no worries, it is short, but does lay long in the mind."

Grandad cleared his throat and began again.

"The dark shifted and separated, like smoke rolls over black, charcoal versus night. The monochrome became marbled, gray, green, gold, blue, and then red. Gray spread out like blood in the water, shifting, moving according to some unknown plan created before man's minds were formed. Green, once generated, bloomed into thousands of shards, spreading into all places. Gold followed, flowing out, turning like the wind, settling along the edges. Blue explored as a mist, mixing yet staying separate between the other elements of nature; it rolled out as an immense wave. Red grew on the hues, sprouting red blades across the multiple colored world. Liquid orange rippling above, warming the swirl. Miguel, what do you think that uncommon language means?" he asked.

"Well, the colors suggest that they are elements of nature," Miguel said, staring at the city lights thousands of feet above, indistinguishable from the night's stars.

"Smart boy," the storyteller retorted.

"These had no form or structure, only hues floating

through space. Only two spots of blackness remained linked by an ephemeral flowing ribbon tying them together. These floating spots were not only black, but they also consumed color, pulling it in, coloring themselves, fueling their fires. The dark emptiness pooled around the first colors, like the universe's blackness between galaxies. They took form. The twin firelights began to move and gain structure. They grew limbs as they twisted and rotated around two swirling spots. The bodies comprised of nature's elements began to sprout arms, legs, wings, and fins. Their heads formed in all directions; eyes, mouths, noses grew and shrink, moving to find a place across their faces," Grandad said. "This was the beginning of the world, the rush of air from a joke, an eternal laugh."

Miguel asked, "What did the dots do? The world, well, the universe is much, much bigger." He spread his arms wide, showing the magnitude of what was just within his sights.

"Yes, much bigger," Grandad said, puzzled, "So vast that we are finding universes beyond our universe. The day is filled with hidden worlds. Well, these dots, as you acutely called them, maneuvered through the new space, finding ways to interact, like a baby crawling, then chewing its way through an undiscovered toy room. The dots, these newly evolved things, explored the flowing ribbons of color. They ran through the green, swam through the blue, sniffed the red, studied and felt the warmth from the orange, and scooped up the gold. The glow of the fluid colors began to solidify, forming a web of elemental architecture. They made the world through their minds and dreams. These are the first two creatures, the Grand Twins, the Wildlings." He paused to breathe in the stillness of the night air.

"The Wildlings forms were not one animal, as we see today; they were all the animals. The vast creation that was born from flame stretched out before them. As the ocean churned, they imagined swimming, so they swam. The blue and orange divided the space, one in the sky and one below, our land. The orange burned as it absorbed the day's heat, and wings sprouted so the Wildlings could fly. They swam and flew until the green caught their blooming eyes. Green became solid, in leaves and wood, covering the developing ground surrounded by the great ocean. The wood provided shade and cover. The Wildlings ran through it, then dreamed of the first grand tree that grew down until the oceans covered it. The dream became the base of the world; all things come from the first tree, the first thing to protect the twins."

The blood in his eyes spread out like branches, and he was looking through his own redness to a world of white, blue, and tan. The room was quiet, save the occasionally beeping and humming from the NURS-bot arranging things in the corner. Beige sheets were suspended from the ceiling, closing him in, and he could see his feet under a drab blue sheet.

Behind a hanging sheet, a voice snuck out, "No, no family, he and his wife were attacked. Yes, this violence is increasing, but only a little. The Bluemen said the attacks are only in a small part of the city, but people are afraid. No, no, homicide rates are barely above typical. So, who among you wants to speak with him? Another time would be best."

"Patient Miguel Saxon is conscious," the medical droid sing-song voice said through a speaker. "Hello, Miguel. The Doctor will be in soon; please be patient and remain at rest."

He began to fade, his vision of blood turning to scarlet, then purple. Black was taking him, and he thought of a ripped hole in a dripping neck. Then he was gone.

Grandad's face was inches from Miguel. He looked perplexed, "I thought I lost you then. Were you sleeping? Oh, you were miles away."

"Sorry, I just drifted off; I will pay double attention now," Miguel said, eagerly pulling himself up, then picking long blades of grass off his nightshirt. "Love you, Grandad!" He jumped forward into Grandad's waiting arms.

"Ah, my boy. Love you too, always," Grandad said with a blissful sigh. "Ok, the story, where were we…Ah, yes, the Wildlings and the Great Tree."

"The Great Tree was the foundation for all others; it was called Divony by later men. That is us, by the way."

"Really, is that written? Historically, I mean?" Miguel interrupted, wrinkling his nose. "In a scholarly work or a history book?"

"Great question, little wolf, but, no, only a legend, only in the mind of our ancestors. The Great Tree is called Divony, a term made up by men, for it has no true name, as it is the base of the world. The dreams of the twins forged Divony from the remains of the first fire. Even now, the dirt and sod were dim reflections of the Great Tree. All the colors merged, creating all things that we see, from the fires to the lights in the night sky. Before the Tree spread its arms, the Wildlings slept. They dreamt of the new world with their new senses. The seas rushed over the land, the earth rose into hills and mountains, and the plants overtook all they touched, rising to the golden orange glow of the Sun. The Wildlings dreamt what suited them, uncontrolled, free, and unspoiled. Dreams of green and blue; climbing, running, and swimming."

"Grandad, I like the prose, your telling of the story. It would be wonderful to travel in that environment. No waiting around for millions of years for evolution."

Grandad smiled at his grandson. Miguel was lightyears ahead of others his age but always aloof, distant. Now he and Miguel's father must focus on him before he really disconnects.

Although none of the little ones knew Grandad's actual name, except for Miguel. He knew his grandfather's birth name of Joseph. He was keen on details, always noticing unseen things. Like the boy, Joseph was what Miguel described as a polymath, showing expertise in many things, but always distracted by new thoughts, gears constantly grinding. He was consistently racing to focus his mind; only his wife could slow his thoughts to bring out his emotion and love.

'Miguel, please do not be like that. Hope all your thoughts bring loving wisdom and joy, not only the pleasure of gaining knowledge,' Grandad thought as he gazed at the little boy who was looking intently at blades of grass.

Over the years, he saw all his grandchildren playing joyfully together, excluding Miguel. He did not fit, somehow. However, he knew that Miguel was always first in any game, whether physical or otherwise. Of course, Miguel never mentioned his imagined wins.

Miguel shuffled and grabbed a blade of grass to tickle Grandad's nose. "Grandad, the Twins were traveling through the world?" Miguel said, silently questioning Grandad's memory.

Slightly irritated, Grandad continued, "The remaining darkness pooled under them, like water in a puddle. It hid from the light, the first fire in the sky. One of the Wildlings, now called Ravin by man, was hot from the first day, and the ethereal blanket of darkness began to swell, draining away from its sibling. The Wilds shivered, feeding the gloom as it grows from discomfort. Under Ravin's belly, it stirred and exploded out into the day, sucking in all light. Like water falls into an abyss, the dark expanded as the sun's rays were swallowed into the earth. Thus, the first night was formed. Of course, the fire did not wholly surrender, for the moon and the stars still radiated, holding the Fire's creative breadth. Ravin's sibling, now called Nebeth by man, gathered the remaining heat, filling it with joy.

Dreams became the Moon, while the dreams' whispers became starlight. Those night thoughts burst full force into reality as the Sun rose, all dreamt experiences formed by the flame's light. Nebeth warmed Ravin's back at night, and Ravin lovingly gazed into Nebeth's face when the Sun rose."

"The Twins continued to roam the land, flying high to touch the stars, swimming to the deepest, blackest parts of the sea, running over endless grasslands, and hopping through all forests. They only had each other for company, and as the years wore on, with no secrets held by the land, they became lonely. When the black took the sky, and the light held on with starlit fingers, they dreamed of others, others that can fly, swim, and run. Every morning for untold years, the dreamed others formed. The sun's first morning light shined on new creatures. Wolves nuzzled the Twins formless faces, while fish swam around their feet, and bluebirds spied from above. The new creatures transformed each land and sea until all land was full. Miguel, this is the good part, like in most genesis stories the earth is created and, then, comes family trouble, brothers fight, as do fathers and sons."

"I'm lucky that Dad has only one of me," Miguel said, still trying to poke Grandad's nose.

"Well, brothers and sisters are great to have; they form a team and can help you make your way down whichever path that you wish," Grandad responded. "Now listen. Each Twin saw this grand new earth differently. Nebeth, built from the first laugh and of eternal life, spread itself infinitely out into all great cats prides, vast dire wolfs packs and the largest schools of fish across the world. It tasted the life of all roving animals, as a man later called the creatures. Nebeth looked for Ravin, wanted to tell its sibling to come along, to feel and taste the world. Nebeth searched, sharing the creature's faces; it flew with a sharp beak or ran with keen ears and hunting fangs."

"But, the other sibling was different; its eyes were

clouded with fear. While Ravin looked at the crowded world and saw an unceasing terror. It shied away from the creatures; alone, it prowled the deep woods or caverns, always watching, ready to bolt. Gone were the free fields; gone were the deep rivers, as was the empty blue sky. The mixture of the Twins' dreams formed a monstrous plethora of claws, beaks, and teeth, each waiting to attack the twins. Ravin could see the hunger in their eyes while they twitched their talons."

"Each night for thousands of years, Nebeth shed its ethereal skin to be free with the animals, while Ravin dreamt of only its own protection. Nebeth spent less time at the campsite each night and more time with the animals. While each morning found Ravin larger, its muscles stronger and its countenance more ferocious. Each twin looked on the other and pitied them, hoping that each would see the right way to enjoy the world."

Grandad sat up, then tickled Miguel. "Now listen to the story of the brother and their LAST NIGHT!!!" he proclaimed, theatrically raising both his hands to the sky lit by billions of city lights.

"The last night of dreams came; Ravin woke and could not find Nebeth. Ravin spread itself instantly across the world, into each forest, pool, and sky, but Nebeth was gone. Only Nebeth's cozy white fur coat laid at the campsite, then the wind whirled, snatching it into the sky."

"The world had eaten all of Nebeth Ravin thought," Granddad yelled, trying to imitate an ancient god with a gruff voice, "Ravin searched where Nebeth loved to play, but it was not there, and Ravin roared, shaking the earth and rumbling the sea. Each tribe of animals ran in confusion, then fear turned them against each other as all the creatures' natural weapons were used for the first time. Antlers ran through other antlers, bared teeth plunged into skin, and claws snapped. Ravin saw the bloody carnage and, then, knew that these tribes killed Nebeth, his wonderful twin. Ravin, using all his mighty strength, attacked the tribes, and the tribes fought back. Now, the tribes did not know him; he had always fled from them because fear limited his life. They did not know that he was mad, ferocious, and immortal. Ravin tore into them, reddening the ground. These animals saw their own blood and feared for themselves and fled, except for one mighty white hind, who held up its mighty antlers against its foe."

"I mean you no harm; I only wish for you to let me pass,' it said, holding its head high and looking straight into Ravin's eyes. Ravin smiled; the years of dreaming protections had worked; he was the most powerful in the land. His terrible dreams formed a monstrous creature; scales and shells formed on his back, fangs and tusks protruded from his mouth, claws dangled dangerously from each hand and foot."

"He said, 'Your kind killed my sibling, Nebeth. Now all of you will pay the price back to the first fire,' Then, Ravin struck the buck, crushing its antlers and flinging it off a mountain. It fell back to the sea. The stag could not move, but it looked at Ravin, its eyes hoping that Ravin could see the right way to enjoy the world. Its face pleaded, holding great sadness."

"The stag looked up and said, 'Ravin, I am Nebeth, your sibling. Please be glad, and enjoy the sun, the sky, and grass. As the sea will always flow, so is the love I have in my heart for you, my one true twin. Farewell.' Nebeth died, and some of the good left the world.

Miguel's eyes opened. The room had changed, with nano-simulated floral wallpaper and a viewing window with counterfeit sunshine. The sun had not graced his eyes since his family died before he found Elizabeth. His thinking was like molding hardened concrete. His thoughts were running too quickly but not registering or turning any gears. Memories faded, everything was dust; once his mind tuning in thought, it became motes freely floating through the air. His limbs were numb; his tongue seemed too big for his mouth. Saliva had dried on his chin; he felt its crust.

'Where is she? Why am I here?' he thought, his panic rising.

"What…" he asked to the air. "What happened?" A hiss responded.

"Morning, Dr. Miguel Saxon. You had a medical emergency and are at the Jean-Martin Charcot Medical Tower in Area-10, Level-578. Medical staff will be with you shortly. Thank you, and please relax," a speaker mounted to the NURS medical bot declared. Its semi-human head looked to the door, a faded dingy yellow panel with a trans-aluminum sheet at eye Level. Miguel noticed the lack of a door handle.

The tinny voice jarred him, shocking his ears. He could feel the bones in his head ache as thoughts raced by but failed to grasp anything.

"What was I given?" he croaked. Both eyelids seemed to have free will and were closing independently. He reached for them, but he could not move his hands. Looking down through the blurry vision of one eye, he saw that he was restrained with a thick green biodegradable polymer, all bound to the polymer eggshell bed.

"Hey…!," he yelled, trying to arch his back, but his head was secured. "Help me," he demanded angrily.

NURS rolled to the bed, "Sir, please relax. All is well. The doctor is coming presently." Several metal limbs emerged from the robot's body, each coated in a soft rubber material, each one gently tapping buttons on his bed. "Please allow me to adjust your mode, sir."

"No! Get away from me," Miguel said, still struggling, but

the narcotics were taking effect. "Ssstttoppp," he yelled, punctuated with a spray of saliva. "Lizzz, wherareyou…." His eyes were rolling in their sockets, looking for her. He thought, she must be here, maybe behind him in the corner where he can not see due to the restraints.

'Yes, just over there, passed my peripheral vision by my ear. She could reach out and touch my head. Are you fine, sweetheart? It is ok, Manzana, she would say. She is right there, thinking of her parent's prayers, trying to help me. Liz, please help me. I want to see your beautiful eyes. She's fine, nothing to worry about,' he thought.

He fought to keep his eyes open, but the narcotics were winning, and the room was slipping away. As his pupils rolled up, he saw a symbol on the ceiling. A faint circle marked with a capital T in the middle began to darken. The white sound-absorbing ceiling tiles began to turn pink, then red. The ring became a blood serpent encircling a war hammer. Slowly to his eye, the symbol, an ouroboros, swelled with blood, soaking the tiles. They warped, and, as he lost consciousness, they broke, sending a waterfall of blood into his eyes.

Red, then black.

"What?" Miguel asked, quickly sitting up. "Ravin killed his brother because he was afraid? No way!"

"Yes, my boy. Fear is the great destroyer of life," Grandad answered. "Ravin fell back, misunderstanding. Its mind pushed the terror and sorrow into a new creation, built from all the anguish felt by a formless, faceless, and infinite wild. This thing was created in a split second from a half-formed thought for Ravin's protection, but it was malformed and wrong. Wrong for the sole remaining wild twin, morphing it into something new and dangerous. From deep below in the

Great Tree's heart, a creature grew, nourished by the despair, then it burst from the earth, sprinkling dirt clods on Ravin, who scurried away, fearing for its life. The thing poured out like a black liquid pooling around the fallen Nebeth. Now Chareth, as we call him, born out of sorrow and anger, was the first evil thing. Ravin created the first evil thing from his wish to have his brother back. Chareth has no heart, only self-perpetuating darkness. Its tendrils reached out, penetrated the deer, filling it with its fowl presence. Before its blackness was gone, it smiled at Ravin and said, 'Go sleep; only dreams can comfort you.' The deer, now dripping black, bounded away to spread its darkness to all living things. It was now the creator of all evil, then and now. Ravin's confusion created the first evil thing when it wished to have his sibling back."

Miguel turned to look at the Moon. "If Ravin helped create the universe, why can't he…reanimate Nebeth? It makes sense."

Granddad rustled Miguel's wild hair. "Well, while he is one of the first two creators, nothing can cheat death. Death is part of all creation because, without decay, there can be no new life. Chareth has no heart, only self-perpetuating darkness. Chareth's tendrils reached out and penetrated the deer, filling it with its fowl presence. Before the dark liquid was gone, it whispered to Ravin and said, 'Go sleep; only dreams can comfort you.' The deer, now dripping black, bounded away to spread its darkness over all living things, the creator of all evil."

"Grandad, this story is gloomy and dark. I LIKE IT!" Miguel announced as he jumped up. He was thinking of the mythical creatures and what will be 3-D printed first.

'Ravin, of course, with all his protections, like an amalgam of a gorilla, a turtle, and a Komodo dragon. A black deer is easy enough. But what will Nebeth be?' He wondered, 'Maybe he will build a magnetic chimera that could morph into any animal. Yes, that will be a good learning opportunity.' He told his Grandad his ideas, and Grandad agreed to help.

"But, first, we must finish the story. Now sit," Grandad gathered his storytelling voice. "With the deepest grumble, then a heartbroken wail, Ravin crawled its way into the deepest cave, tears streaming from its eyes. Its tears came like water but fell as black stones. Once in the cave surrounded by dark crystals, Ravin dug a hole that would house him for eternity; only its dreams will trouble it now. Thoughts of its claws smashing the white deer to the ground began to attack Ravin, threatening to rip apart its mind. As it closed its eyes for the last time, it thought, 'No, the world killed my sibling,' and dreamt of protection. Ravin laid covered in its sibling's blood and the remnants of Chareth's foulness, and he rolled in the dirt because all his dreams drove him mad. He is down there now, deciding if the world is safe enough to climb out of its cave. "

Miguel thought, 'I'm alive, hurting, but alive. Elizabeth is dead, her throat ripped out by an animal. Cold, she is cold to the touch, and her blood has been pumped to the floor. Only the gold remains in her eyes, a cruel joke, gold where his lover once was, just colored pigment. Maybe this is my dream, the dream of madness. Perhaps the world is a dream, and if I fight hard enough, I will wake. Like the ouroboros, endlessly swallowing its own tail. Dreaming for infinity. When I wake, there will be blood; my dreams will be for vengeance, a sculptured vengeance.' Blackness claimed him again as thoughts of black flowers came into his mind.

CHAPTER 6

Intercedent Two:

Emancipated Rita Blanca National Grasslands - Dallam County, Texas

Privately reclaimed cattle ranches collective – 2,153

The air was beautiful this morning, but he was sweating just past noon, and it was only May. Projected to hit a high of ninety-five plus in two weeks. His brother, handling another family ranch in Laredo, said it was almost one hundred yesterday. He will have to truck in more water to the herd. Clear, purified water, too, and keep them away from other ranchers' herds', always a must.

'Add that to the list: grain, water, built more paddocks, grain again, damn it is hot,' he thought, wiping the sweat from the back of his neck, 'More air conditioning in the old and new paddocks by June or they will all fry.'

"Ground is dry, too, Dad. It is crunchy under my boots," the boy said. He was right. At least, Kon seems up to snuff. He patted her neck. The girl named that fine animal; it was not until much later that he realized that Kon meant horse in Polish. Probably picked it up from Grandmother. She continued to speak that language even though her home nation was full of Russians and Germans now. From what he heard, those crumbling houses of Europe were not the best of friends, but they sure know how to carve up other countries. Grandfather said they were afraid of the growing Polish military power, blah, blah, blah, and their alliances. Well, their allies did not help them between two ferocious neighbors. Not many speakers left. He wished that he spoke some but was always too busy to learn it, and his dad always told him that speaking the American English was best. Be all American was what he was taught.

The hands were out on the ATVs, using up gas and the limited battery power, but he will, as always, ride Kon through the pastures, along the fences, and back home for lunch.

"I should have packed up my cold-weather gear in February," he cursed, unzipping his jacket, "Nothing more than a thin coat in May. At least the drought-resistant grain was handling the heat well, and the lack of rain."

His watch beeped, and he reaches for his phone. It was in his chest pocket, next to his pens. Several times he almost broke it trying to sign documents, mistaking it for a pen, pressing it down hard, trying to loosen a broken ballpoint. He hammered it on the table until the girl told him that it was his phone, then she giggled, thinking that Dad was hilarious, before skipping away. Pulling it from his pocket, he thumbed the access pad at the end, it folded open, and he heard the girl's sobs.

"Sophia, what happened?" he asked, turning Kon toward the house. Typically, Karen would handle this, whatever nine-year-old girl emergency, but Sophia was calling him today. "Where is your mother?" he said tersely.

"DAD, can you please come home? Charlette is visiting… her and her Mom. They're sad," she snuffled, "Mom is talking to Charlette's Mom. And her Mom is crying. Something happened to her Dad, something bad. So, please come home…Please." Her cries were of empathy, not genuine distress, but they could always break his heart. The boys wanted to be like him, an illusionary man's man, immune to pain, hunger, and thirst. And, he did not discourage that instinct. Like his brother said, fake it until you make it. That was his life, probably will be his son's life, too.

But Sophia was altogether different. Smart, with a keen

eye for details and a heart that felt for the whole world. Once the malady crept into his state, her tears for the culled cows could fill a river that would flow to the Gulf of Mexico. Tales from the tiny Emancipated Rita Blanca school reached her small ears, and she would bawl over the deaths of cattle across North and South America. One year ago, he would wake early to check the paddocks, inspect the bovine for any signs of infection, and ride out to scout for cow invaders that could spread the bacteria; he saw her rushing by each gate, through clouds of dust raised by the morning wind. After he recovered from a nightmare of a stealthy ghost of a trampled child, he questioned her, and she said that she was mentally blessing her cows. They were, really, her cows in her mind. Once bless by an eight-year-old, they could live a happy grass munching life until her Dad sold them off. She never knew what happened to them once they were shipped away. She thought that once they left the ranch, they were free to roam the prairie like her father was the warden of a livestock jail. He let her believe that. She has never seen anywhere more than ten miles from the ranch house. So, the tiny lie will protect her from the force bolts to her cows' heads, and he was happy to tell it.

"Will do, honey," he replied, tapping his watch to call in the drone, "Riding back now." Kon trotted down the low hill as the sun shimmered the flowing yellow grass. A few dead or dying trees dotted the soft rolling hills with over-chewed scraps of the prairie.

'I am lucky,' he thought, riding further north. It came to mind often, the day that he fought so hard to avoid. That day when the herd was shot down by soldiers, or he gave the final gift of the stun bolt before the bacteria spread throughout their system, peeling their skin and liquefying their organs. The last gift he could give them. At a short town meeting attended by the sons of the first reclaimed cattle ranchers, the USDA illustrated the reason for the culling, the life rending loss of hundreds of thousands of cattle.

A short film featuring a man dressed like him, wearing what they all wore, walked to the cow ready from milking. He set the stool down along with the pale. He knew the proper grip and stance as they all did. One of the first things they all learned. The utter was large, and the animal was in pain, waiting for relief, stomping its forefeet in anticipation. The sores were clear on its body, black slabs of crusted flesh, darkly oozing.

The man continued to pull; the crowd heard the milk splash into the pale. After several more squirts, the man found his rhythm. Familiar comfort washed over the cattlemen with the repeating sound of home. The man patted the cow, stood, and walked to the camera, holding the pale out. Under the camera, the pale revealed its contents, a deep red fluid sloshed within, shedding bursting bubbles. The view refocused to the man's face; he shook his head, then nodded. Turning his back on the camera, he dropped the pale under the cow's muzzle; then it began to drink its bloody milk, if there was any milk at all, not just the blood vessels disgorging themselves after each tug. Then the man put a stun bolt to the cow's head, and with a shock, he ended the poor thing's life. Beyond the gore, simply used to make their point, the film was intended to show that the cows will eat each other once the animal is infected, chomping at their kind like tufts of grass, spreading the malady.

He hoped that Sophia would never have to watch that; somehow, she would be spared. He saw Bob Curtis's pickup resting in the chalk driveway, driver door hanging open. Kon stopped at her custom hand-carved cedar horse hitch, though she never hobbles off, just chews on whatever is nearest. Casually, he sauntered up to the old house, noticing that several new wasp nests have set up shop and the second-floor windows moldings needed repainting. Sophia's window was open. Wasps fluttered around it, making him nervous.

"Whole thing needs repainting," he muttered.

Karen was hugging a sobbing Michelle, who was curled up on the porch swing while Sophia and Charlette lay on the rough-hewn boards by the main door. Karen left the door open, hoping that the coming heat will cool the house through the updraft from the open window upstairs. He grinned, thinking that somehow, she knew it will be a hot one today.

Slowly, he climbed the few steps to the porch, eying Karen as he leaned against a support post. Karen rested her face on Michelle, then touched her shoulder with a nod. Standing, she motioned for him to joined her. Leaning in, she whispered through a tear-clogged voice, "Bob killed himself...pretended that it was a farm accident. Crushed by a tractor," she shuttered, "But he lasted for two hours, before...he died." Tears welled up, filling her eyes as she pulled him close. "I told them that they can stay here for a couple of days in Alex's old room." She grabbed his weathered face, linking them eye to eye, "He did it for insurance money," the tears were rolling down her beautiful cheeks, "Their herd has the malady, and the debt was already crushing them. So, now, debt is paid and," she looked to Charlette, "They will have a little to start over." She gave him a gentle kiss on his cheek, then sat on the swing, hugging the widow. Michelle was in good hands. A few strides to Sophia, he bent down to the kids. Sophia was clear-eyed, always observant, and holding her friend's hand tightly as if any loosening, Charlette would float away and be lost to the winds forever.

"Do you guys want ice cream?" he asked, unsure of what to say to the little girls. He felt that he was breaking in on their moment, but Karen's chin was nudging them inside. Michelle was about to let the pain explode, and no one wanted the kids to see that.

"It is only eleven, Dad," Sophia pointed out admonishingly. Charlette was in shock. Later he found out that she was the one to find her father with his chest crushed in, mumbling through a bloody mouth. But, ice cream momentarily broke the shock, and she weakly nodded, mumbling a faint, "Ya."

"Eleven or not, let's get some," he offered a soft smile, rose, opened the screen door, and led them to the kitchen. The child's frame was weak; something was broken inside, he did not want to make her speak again. So, he ready two cream-colored bowls and planted a scoop of plain vanilla bean and one scoop of double chocolate fudge inside. Slipping them across the table, spoon in each, the girls were happy, but both still detached. He stepped into the hall.

The malady is here. Bloody cows chewing on bloody cows until the fields were red.

His herd was clean, surrounded by miles of fields, failing farmland, but still safe. Bob's land spilled into New Mexico and Oklahoma, a bit too distant for the contagion to spread. He hoped. Throughout Bob's holdings were three hundred head with hundreds of acres along with new equipment. That equipment, automatic gates, squadrons of drones, state-of-the-art moisture farmers, was the long game, a good bit until the payments roll on to each other. Creating a mountain of expense with little coming in, all ending with a caved-in ribs and your only daughter crying as she tries to understand your last blood garbled words.

'Cows will be gone, culled bolted out of existence. Lowering the overhead, and ranch hands went too. No need for them with no herd. They will wander about, looking for new postings. And the new federal protection insurance for cattle ranchers allotted by state agencies...New Mexico and Oklahoma, but not Texas. This is a chance to stretch,' he thought, running profit and loss figures in his head. Stepping through the back door, he found his phone, activated the call function connected to the pod in his ear.

"Hello, Hank. I need your advice as my business's attorney," he started his plan, "With some fancy big-city refinancing, could I buy up Robert Curtis's operation?" Hank asked some questions, but the rancher was already thinking of the proper payments to Michelle and Charlette, relocating them far away and expanding his ranch, a growing ranch. He will build a home of business opportunities, all protected by the feds.

"Oh, yes. He passed today...Oh, yes, it was a tragedy... Oh, sure. I agree. I can drive up to Boise City tomorrow to start signing the papers...Yes, we will take care of Michelle...Charlette, that's his daughter, sweet one too," he bent back to gaze down the hallway. Sophia was standing there looking at him suspiciously, eyes narrowed. His gaze shifted to view the fields, now his expanding fields. "Great, great. See you tomorrow. You know, you are the best Zellum Ranch lawyer I know...Of course, you are the only Zellum Ranch lawyer I know." He disconnected and reached for Sophia's hand with a bright smile, but she was gone.

CHAPTER 7

He brushed leaves off his shoulder and handed his railgun over to an assistant so it can be disassembled and cleaned. Helyettes gently removed the rail from his hands and began breaking it apart. The power source was aligned with solar cells ready for recharge, the armature was cleaned, and the rails were being detailed. For a man of such stoutness, Helyettes's huge brown hands moved with such swiftness showing his familiarity with weapons and the quick efficiency of his movements.

The sun was an inverted glowing bowl falling behind the forested hills. Each wave and ripple on the Susquehanna River briefly lit the forest as the trees captured the last lights of the sun before it dipped down for its daily rest.

'Glimmering water and black trees, real trees,' he thought.

A few dark-colored leaves decorated skeletal branches. Dark Northern Red Oaks, black cherry, and white blossomed hawthorn, all leaving dashes of color. He loved to be out here. The day was long, but the bear did not hear the shot coming, dying before it hit the ground.

The morning was grand for a city boy like himself with the maddeningly loud calls of cicadas chattering to their partners. He found the art of camouflage pleasing as he looked at the beautiful terrain, eying where he would place himself if he ever revisited this place. Hunter drones scanned for a full thirty minutes before his stream pinged him. Over three miles away, near a weathered strip of ancient railroad tracks, a behemoth wandered sniffing for fish. Even with the calculation performed electronically, it was a hard shot. The rail could hurl a round miles into the sky, but he had to curve the trajectory over the hill. Of course, his rifle was military-grade, and interfacing drones coordinated it perfectly. One tap of a button and the round was off at over 7,000 miles per hour. Half of the hairy colossus separated into a wet red mass, and all its fabulous fur was reduced to ash. The weapon was illegal for personal use, as was killing a bear, but seeing the fur light up and viscera spray the railroad track brought a long satisfied smile to his face.

Hunting was an art, excruciatingly planned craft of brutality. The animal or human, depending on his taste, should be respected and killed with precision. Once, he mounted an audio microphone on a bolt and fired it through a horse's chest. The bolt crashed through the bones with a crack. He could hear a gush of air, then fluid as the bolt passed into a lung. Just gurgles followed when it sliced through the entrails, finally, another snap of bone. Only sixteen and ignorant of horse anatomy, he used a holo superimposed with a 3-D equine image to trace the bolt's path, slowing down the audio files, fine-tuning it to hear each alveolus pop and the intestines shutter. He even heard half a heartbeat.

Zaldi was a great horse, regularly running on Jersey-York tracks generating money and prestige. Father very much disapproved of her death, but he got an accurate mental picture of how a knife feels while it plunges into a living creature. The experience was worth another month on Greenland. His hands were still cold from his handshake with Arctic survival. It was undeniably worth it.

Augustine stared at the sun until it retreated from his eyes.

"Augustine, come!" his father bellowed, anger sturring behind his eyes. Father was ready to play his part. He will name the bear after his father, Grizzly Excelsior.

"Yes, sir," he straightened, smoothing his clothes, and removed his targeting helmet. Walking to the circle, he took inventory of the guests. Half of the Jersey-York council sat, each sported tailormade hunting gear with Excelsior's gift in their hands: an ancient Winchester 1873 lever-action rifle. Only one had fired any weapon, and all the rifles will grace some type of display case. He hoped his father bought him one. The hill spread down from the campsite, a pebble-covered semicircle surrounded by meter tall granite blocks. His father stood with the fading twilight glimmer setting behind him as the darkness closed around the group, ready to address the members, thirteen in all. Earlier, Helyettes moved immense wooden posts to serve as seats. Father wanted the seating to fit with the rural aesthetic but not too comfortable. It was easier to hold their attention if they cannot truly admire the country sky. His siblings were sitting comfortably on the mansion porch, which pretended to be a large log cabin behind the seating Area.

"Thank you all for joining us today on a glorious hunt!" Excelsior beamed his wonderful smile raising his hands, and began clapping.

The smart council members propped their rifles against the side of their seats, but many tried to hold the gun while clapping clumsily. He heard his brother and two sisters clapping from the porch. Footsteps approached, and his brother passed him to lean on one of the granite slabs next to his father.

"Personally, I thoroughly enjoyed the parade today, and I will have all of your trophies mounted and ready for display," Excelsior bent down and lifted the body of the wolf he speared through with one massive arm. He chuckled loudly, rocking his muscled core, "I know that someone at my station should not mention it, but I will. It is wonderful and grand that the lords of the land can roam and exercise out in the wild. Where I think we should be able to. On this land, here," he stomped the dirt stirring up clouds of dust, "and, as lords should…And ladies, too, stalk the land's creatures! Look at my wolf! Amazing!" His perfect white teeth glimmered as he turned to the small crowd.

The others thought of what they hunted, tracked, and pursued. Beyond Augustine's grizzly prize, no one managed more than a Cervidae, only four dead hooves, much less than an apex predator. Richard, Augustine's younger brother, never even touched any of the weapons, though Augustine saw him sparring in the morning. As August was gearing up under the freshly risen sun, Richard was bouncing around Helyettes on the grass, who spun a thick bo staff toward his face. Then, Richard lunged with a high kick. Blood poured from Helyettes's mouth, indicating that Richard was winning.

'Odd fellow,' Augustine thought, he would easily take the machine designed to deal death than a quickly twisted ankle.

"Now, my servant will scan your Forges and terminate any bio-recall and transmission," he extended his hand to Hong Tai, who slipped from the growing shadows holding a small metal ball. He slightly bowed to council with his slim body dipping his head as he dabbed the sphere to each person's head. Tiny veins of red glowed on the sphere then turned green; after it touched the council members. The Forges were deactivated from recording and transmitting any of the following conversations. Tai walked to the center of the mini-amphitheater, bowed to the council, then to Excelsior. Once he stepped beyond the stone pillars, he disappeared, melting back into the murk.

"Thank you, Tai," Excelsior said, stepping forward, clearly in command. He stretched his solid chest, extending his head to the coming night, each muscle pulling at the camouflaged Treetech uniform seams; he commented, "So formal that guy," eyeing the shadows where Tai faded away, still smiling. The mansion's electronic lights were blocked by the granite slabs painting half of his face black, though his teeth still shined.

"All, I invited you to spend the weekend with us because we all have many things to gain if we work together," he interlaced his hefty fingers, "And I can offer you a unique opportunity." He walked to one section of the council and took one knee, inches from them. Augustine knew them as the most powerful council members, charged with sections crisscrossing over the whole city.

"While all have different ways to handle a problem, this is positive for each of us," Excelsior gestured to a pale diminutive woman with large eyes. To Augustine, she looked like a tiny mouse smothered in camouflage, holding her new rifle across her knobby knees. "Niva Lesnik," her neck stretched, and eyes narrowed, "you show loving care for the community and help the helpless. But, I bet, I bet, that you think that you could never work with Mr. Boto?"

John Boto snickered and nodded his head, leaning back his thin frame onto his pedestal. His skin was dark enough to blend in with the shadows. Niva continued to look at Excelsior with her fingers pressed together like they were part of an old architecture piece stemming from the old rifle.

Excelsior quickly pointed to Mr. Boto. "Of course, John here may think the same. I mean, how could the most famous genetically altered circus show do to help Niva's community? How could those strangely beautiful animals help the helpless? The ones in Undertown. The circus's motivation is only profit, while Niva's centers across Undertown are for generating empathy and care...right?"

Boto's face cracked into a massive show of teeth. "Ex, thas bitter koud, man!" Boto exclaimed, hands up in defense.

"We always help when asked; it is in my nature."

Excelsior's eyes flicked to Fernando Alemoa, a brilliant recombinant geneticist and ruthless businessman. "Fernando, can you help, maybe help them both? You know, with all those frozen genes and mixed bloodlines? Say, a recombinant solution?" His hands juggling the air as if he did not know the elements of Alemoa's work. He did know.

Augustine recognized his father's act and hated when he played dumb.

Fernando Alemoa did not move and casually stared at him under his Boonie hat, still drawn down tight. Illegal high explosive .50 caliber rounds were mounted in the elastic band around his forehead. He wore it like a crown.

"Of course, you can offer something, Fernando. And you too, Mr. Mani and Mr. Panhu. With my support, we can construct the largest communal wellness program between the geneticists," he pointed to Panhu and Alemoa. "And the circus owner," he nodded to Boto, "and the owner of the exquisite hall of the Manzana can allow us to use fantastic entertainment for a fundraising event."

Mr. Mani nodded back, clearly prebriefed by Ex.

"And, of course, Mrs. Lesnik, you would bring together the community that needs help, and you will have supporters. That is what I can do!" he announced, "For all of you. Now, my son will explain some further details where we can all help and can be, No, will be, extremely beneficial to all of us."

He stepped back and offered the graveled floor with a wave of his hand.

"Please welcome my number one and newly appointed vice-president, Richard Zullem," he smiled and left the dirt stage.

Richard stepped out from the shadow of the stone pillar with a polite smile. "Greetings, everyone. I'm glad that you could join us. I have some news about the planned security upgrades and details of launching the new Bluemen drones. First, please allow me to explain what you will be voting on soon…" Richard began to pace along the arch of the seated members, scanning across, meeting each one's eyes, forming a keen connection with each member. His father taught him that trick, the ability to have electricity flow from himself to the audience, whether prince or pauper. Heat rushed into Augustine's limbs and his mouth tasted of metal.

Augustine stood disgusted and walked to stand between his twin sisters, one typically drunk, the other monitoring her HUD muttering notes to herself. He tapped Mallory on the shoulder and mimicked gulping a drink. Her perfectly constructed face offered a woozy grin; she struggled to stand, then waved to Dad with the enthusiasm of a little girl. Both circled the porch to the French cedar doors. Cordelia was miles away, continuing her mental note-taking, and Richard's eyes caught Augustine, then returned to the council only showing a mild distaste that he quickly hid behind a business-like face.

The doors closed with a soft clatter, and Augustine exploded, "That son of a bitch! I helped write those plans and was the PA guy for father!" His knuckles were white, sweat rolled down his forehead. "Horrible, worthless, self-serving…" Mallory pinched him on the arm with a ferocious intensity, then she laughed. "Dammit," he cried. The high pitch cry from a fully grown man made her squeal as she attempted to pour him a drink; half of the whiskey spilled to the wooden table.

"Shut up, cry baby," she snorted as she poured hers; all the liquid landed safely in her tumbler. After a long pull, she asked him, "Why do you care? Richard version 2 will always and forever be the prince." After another long slurp, she said, "Just enjoy your station, young man." She pointed her finger in an amazingly accurate mom imitation and slipped into the couch, being buried by over-fluffed luxurious pillows.

"WHAT?" he bellowed, red coloring his face, "Why not? Richard is a Charlie mixed with a grumbletonian and a lout. Four times an idiot!" He punched the back of the couch, jarring Mallory as she sipped her drink. He finished his tumbler and poured another.

From beneath the mountain of pillows, Mallory said, "Hey, arse, now I need to change my dress, and I only brought seven!" Her hand shoved the tumbler out for the refill.

The night was cool; noises of insects chirping filled the chilly air as the council listened to Richard. In his mind, he knew that August was holding on to festering anger and pain. It was Richard to finalized the security plans and supervised the engineers. While he almost always agreed with his elder and dutifully followed his father's instructions, he did argue that Augustine should be involved. He hoped that his brother perceived that he was an intricate part of the new project. Father allowed him that success.

He had to sell the idea to the council for their votes, and each needed some pushing. The Jersey-York council was concerned by father's initial statements. Father might have used some less than reputable methods as was his way. Now, he had six Manhattan borough Area council members convinced to support the project. They all knew that Excelsior had eyes and ears out to Mars and back. At least, the hunting trip was a success; each member was lovingly gazing at either their kill or the ancient weapon, which was custom-made from surviving texts.

Now, the order.

While short and born from original genes, Mara Chort was ferocious if someone wasted her valuable time. She must be first. His stream activated, and her details spread before his eyes. Father trained him to speak publicly while mentally reviewing his HUD. As a child, he remembered that his first task was to practice martial arts and gymnastics while studying the company's expense reports. Within the first month, he cleared the med-cabinet out of all the hematoma reliever and painkillers. It hurt. Now, he could spar against two others while reading the news streams on his HUD.

He knew of Mrs. Chort, and her company, Myasofoods printed all meat variations from fish to buffalo. Locations throughout the city, always running at full capacity.

Formal is best in the beginning.

"Council members, I will address you individually to show that there is no malfeasance on my part with full honesty. As you know, each of you is essential to the upcoming vote, and I'm here to show you that the city and yourselves will be better for it. So please, allow me a few comments, first." A few grumbles, but all eyes were on him. He tapped his camo-suit, and it flashed to a light gray.

"Ok, Mrs. Chort and Mr. Leshy. Crime is rising. We all know that. The recent well-covered insecurity is affecting your businesses by delaying deliveries and your supplies. I'm sure that when you reviewed the proposal," he knew that she had not read one word, "you noticed that lev-lines would have increased security, as will the crop farms linked to the city. The new CHARM security portal units and the FAUN models will also drastically increase visibility and physical presence. Every criminal or...even a tempted minor will see law enforcement on the street at all times." Without changing her face or posture, she nodded. He assumed that was an approval.

Privately, before the hunt, just after his coffee morning solution, Bear Leshy told him that he would support the proposal "wholeheartedly" as he stared at the rising sun. His network of farms supplied half of the food to the Eastern seaboard, fresh Leshy LLC lettuce, and tomatoes on plates in all the three mega-cities.

'Check and next,' Richard thought as he reviewed the next candidate.

Joseph Mulunga was known as an esteemed lawyer and pillar of the community. Richard's HUD streamed Mulunga's details along with several issues far beneath the station of a community pillar. Nasty issues. Father must have gathered this data from every seedy back alley and motel. Always, Father covers every angle.

Mulunga lounged on the large stump motionless; he was starting to dissolve into the night. He was the only person to hunt in all black, from his folded Homburg hat to his faux leather boots. He enjoyed being a shadow.

"Mr. Mulunga. Joe, if you allow me to call you that, you have involvement with many of the guests here. And your constituency is employed by many companies that have been affected by the increased crime. We have all seen the news, the attacks, the stabbings," Richard passing to Joe, angling, so the light illuminated Joe's face. Only his eyes were visible. Richard saw the receive from recent gene editing for melanin enhancement.

'Odd. Most people opt for highlights of brilliant colors, a stripe of blue down the back, or red stripes on the forearms. Though, there is no doubt that the existence of a living shadow does affect courts and boardrooms in his benefit,' Richard mused.

Joe straightened his black uniform and clutched at his throat, likely trying a adjust a tie that he was not wearing.

"An alleged increase in crime. The Office of Inquisitor has not released the records. All we have seen is the news streams," Joe said, waving to the others, "As I see it, this perceived increase falls directing into your profit margin but may interfere with the citizens' rights, Mr. Zellum."

This is always the hard sell, the imagined rights of the anthropoid. He never understood how a person could believe that their view or vote could sway anything. Leaders make war, not the people. Companies make money, not the employees. Citizens pick another citizen, who will change things according to their newly found elected station regardless of the voters' intent. Real power should never be in the hands of one man: period, end of story. Of course, people believe in inalienable rights given to them by the state even as the state pulls rights out from under their feet. If these rights ever existed, then no flood would have destroyed the world while the other part burned to cinders. The population would not have dropped to two billion, and people would not die from the heat at the equator, or the arctic would be an icecap, not an open sea.

Richard's head dipped for a second, "Thank you, sir. That was my next point, and you hit it on the head." He placed his fingers together to resemble a steeple, dipping his fingertips forward for each point, almost like he was praying. "First, the CHARM system is interlocked to each borough synth-mind, which are directly connected to the Synthetic Amplified Neural-net, I call it SANN. If you approve, that network will correlate with the LAMPS, the Large-scale Augmented Municipal Protection System, and then to the SMPU. That last one means Security Mechanoid Protective Unit. Some of you know the current system well, and this is a major upgrade." Fingers still bobbing, he faced all the council.

"Not that I want to bore you with the complicated system or to drown you in acronyms, but the rights of the city and its citizens are the primary reason for the existence of the system. One of the ancients, a former leader of the United States, hundreds of years ago said that the great revolution in the history of man, past, present, and future, is the revolution of those determined to be free, and freedom is what we are offering. And freedom with protections at all Levels. Each synth-

125

mind is protected from the other synth-minds, with no cross data-bleeding. Anonymity is secure through the final quantum cycle."

"I love it!" Riverwell Kibuka yelled, wobbly raising his canteen, filled with a horribly tasting concoction that he offered to Richard before the hunt. Out of obligation, Richard drank it and swore that he would get Riverwell back someday. He could still feel the spices and tangerines burning his gullet. "Arms for Zellum corp and rights for all!" He took a long pull and stood.

"Richard," he slurred, "as we all know, Riverwell is part of the project. Kuzimu! I even designed some of the new weapons." He eyed the group, and he started walking to the main house. He turned his head back and said, "all nonlethal too!"

Mallory's snores disturbed Augustine as he was gazing into his empty glass. She pulled her blond hair away from her face; it rippled with tiger colors when she brushed it, black shifting to white, then orange. She rubbed her nose and arched a fluctuating eyebrow.

"So...what?" she asked.

A full breath escaped Augustine's lungs in a huff. Of course, she was not listening.

"Father will retire in a few years, and I should be chosen to lead. I earned it. I will be Excelsior 2, the shining one!" he announced to the almost empty room with only Mallory there to hear it.

"Ok, sounds good," she dug into her illegal suede purse, "I will support you all the way!" His eyes moved from the empty glass to her, looking astonished. "Until I don't."

"Dammit," he stood, rubbing his temples. "How much do

you make? You know, the profit margin?" Liquor sloshed when he refilled, and he was properly drunk now.

"Almost nothing, really just enough to pay the staff, doormen, couriers, lab techs," she responded, still snorting a black powder and rubbing the leftovers into her gums.

"Boy, I thought that I have troubles. Little profit for a highly dangerous trade. Lab techs? Really? Why not Fact-bot, or whatever those are called?" he said, refilling his glass.

"Tartersauce!" she laughed mockingly, "You would make a poor investment. All bots have memory and can be hacked. Last thing I need is for Dad to see my workshop. Egad, I'm the supplier for half the people at the company and most of the Skytown kids, unless they get a thrill from dealing with the Jeepers and Cracks. Everything is manual, as all good criminal work should be."

"Maybe, I should..." he hesitated, finishing another glass. "Drop by..."

"Nope, Rozzes would follow you, and I might get nicked, or, at least, have to move to another shop. Besides, I would give you some, anyway. It is not in your character. You stick to seducing secretary-bots and pretending that you crunch numbers." Her eyes were alight, muscles flexed, but her face was supernaturally calm. "What do you really want? I mean REALLY want?"

"Cutmen. I need help to accomplish my goals. Father always says build a proper team, and I need the Cutmen," Augustine said, looking out to the gathering of council members.

"That is a group that you should want to avoid," she suggested, "you have the life of one of the wealthiest men on the planet. Just enjoy, as I do. I say pas de soucis, et profitez de la balade! No worries, and enjoy." Somehow, he could see the excitement spread through her face while she barely moved a muscle. It was what lays behind her eyes, spinning fairies dancing through blackness. He had his problems, a mound of bodies could testify to that if their dead foul-smelling mouths could speak, but he saw that Mallory was becoming insane just like one of the phantom fairies hidden in her mind.

He pulled in a lungful of air and said, "I would say profitez de la tuerie. I'm heading back to my workshop in the city. I have many efforts to complete, some for business, some for my personal enjoyment...what you said, profitez de la balade."

"Well, please do something that I would not do," She snickered, "I will give your regards to Father and Richard. Adieu and ta ta!" She sunk back into the mountain of pillows.

He sent a mental stream to his Gatherer to find new subjects, then packed his bags.

CHAPTER 8

Red Sun issued the commands, and the Enswells responded.

Like one of the overpriced animal safari experiences, where an overfed and undereducated family stuffs themselves in a pod, body to body, so no one can breathe, waiting to see a gang of Bison or a North American Jaguar, the Enswell waited with either knife ready or a recording charged. In the cities, each building was clothed in a nanomaterial, which studied its owner's health and soundness of mind, down to the last breath or the placement of a table lamp. The streets were decked out with scanners reading peoples' gaits or the fusion of capillaries within one's eye, all creating the most surveilled place on the planet. Electronic eyes and ears everywhere. But without an interested party, like a jealous husband or angry wife or a business partner that was pulling some leverage to push you out, or a murderer seeking to remain anonymous, the piles of data were just spinning in a machine somewhere, just dots buried in a mountain of other dots.

The Cutmen's greatest strength was knowing people and what they wanted, sometimes frantically needed. If you had access to the Datamine, all the details of a sordid life, the audience with find you and pay you well. While the Cutmen was built on gorging out eyes and shining light into brain cavities, now they were made through pattern matrixes and information algorithms. And only occasionally brought out the knife and the bullet. Nothing moved in the city without him or his two brothers knowing.

Information is the keenest of blades.

Red Sun watched from the shadows and heard the code, "prelievo sangue" from the huge brown man. His HUD went up, and detailed orders were issued. Luckily only two operations, the capo won the other over. While he was told to allow the other group to be dealt with, he was distrustful. A trapeze artist is the only one that can grasp the rope, just as a killer is the only one to thrust the knife.

'Ru and Diego,' he thought.

'Dark Sun,' they both responded, the typical answer to a head Cutmen, the reverse of Cutman's title.

'Indicate identity,' Red Sun thought. Mentally, he shuffled through hundreds of prearranged identification images and flung one through the electric ether.

Diego was glad that he was seated when his sight was blasted by an image of a young woman wearing a white tunic over a sky-blue dress, her long blond hair weaving and hanging over her shoulder. Confusion gripped his mind until he saw what she was holding, a staff with a glowing skull mounted to its top.

"Tsarist Vasilisa, Dark Sun," he countered.

'Approved,' Red Sun responded, 'Received and report to duty.'

A craved bas relief spread before Ru's vision from a pinpoint in his HUD, carved thousands of years ago, and probably smashed to bits. He had to hold on to a railing in the Intercity transport car that bounced along the mag-track between boroughs. The wave of surprise hit him hard, and his body tensed gently, leaning on an unpleasant old woman. He almost freed the life from her, but he was still in training, so quickly brushing her with his ricin finger pads or injecting her with an air bubble from his modified writing pen would be frowned upon, possibly delaying his true Enswell membership. He worked too hard to get this far. The Undertown was far away, and he will never return to the stony shore next to the robo-net technical shops, sweating his life out while the machines sped on tirelessly. The drum on the gigantic wheel was maddening.

As she hissed at him, he stepped away. He lifted his body over the floor and hovered, hanging by one arm, thinking at supernatural speed.

The Cutmen intensely train the Enswell with imagery and use biological feedback surgery to dramatically enhance critical thinking and pattern recognition. Still, the reference images were flying past, and part of the training was that the HUD streaming was deactivated once the word was said: Indicate identity. He must have missed one of the refreshes.

'Report, Ru,' Red Sun thought, reasoning that the swab would fail because the idiot had not kept up with the recent refreshers. It happens. He felt it should not with a simple alert system in your HUD stream, then one would automatically log in to the Gauze-stream to download the latest codes.

'Idiot.'

Ru was trying to concentrate. The bas relief was carved into a terra cotta box, though only one side was visible. He knew it was Roman, and it was a funerary urn from the partially visible lid. A winged woman stood under an arch wearing a tunic from the waist down and a leather cross breast strap clasped between her bosom. She carried a torch.

'A guide to light your way...,' he thought, still suspended for the train car ceiling. It had wings. His mind filtered through hundreds of thousands of images stored deep. His augmented detailed oriented pattern recognition was flipping behind his brain.

'Roman....no, not Roman, Etruscan. Winged guide, guide of death,' each thought reorganized the images and brought them into the vision in static form. Mentally, they were aligned with his thought flow.

Etruscan death goddess, down to three images flashed under his eyes. The first two matched, draw with ink from a modern pen at a much later time, focusing excessively on the breasts and lascivious figure of the goddess. He dismissed them. The third came into focus.

'Match.'

"Vegoia, Etruscan death goddess," Ru said, trying to remain calm and realizing that he was holding his breath.

Red Sun retorted, "Received and report for duty. And Ru, set up your Gauze-stream refresh alarm, baichi! Red Sun sets."

The HUD went black and silent.

Mrs. Lesnik, Niva to friends of which she had few, had concerns. While the primary goal of the Zellum Corp is simply to gain knowledge, understand it, then profit from it, which was seen as positive, but something was hidden. She could not put her finger on it, but it was there, just the same. Like trying to spot a dust mote in your eye, once you catch it, it drifts off to be never caught. All you could do was to close the lid, temporarily blinding yourself, and wipe the eye, but the mote was still swimming once light was restored.

Not long ago, she worked with a young woman. Woman was an exaggeration because Violet, as she called herself, was only 85 pounds, stood 5 foot, and looked barely sixteen. Like many others that floated through the community center, tens of thousands, she came from Undertown. Undertown churned people like the nano-engineers did old buildings. Torn apart, stripped down to the most basic materials, then spit out new, but not like a new pair of shoes, more like a wet decomposed foot hacked from the original body. Fresh like a discarded tooth, smooth in some spots, and mostly worn and yellow.

Many people call it recycling. Odd pieces of ancient

bricks and ruined concrete dredged from the swollen ocean forcibly sculpted into the modern innovative waves of shifting buildings, supposedly part of the whole, but always different and easy to find. One could stick their finger into a building joint where Wall Street met Chinatown, then call others to see, the reused refuse of another society.

According to the Zullems and the higher families, the culture left class and stratification behind, like famine, and disease, off like a husk from a cicada. They were wrong; the husk was still hanging on the dead tree left in a dried-up river valley. Undertown had a way of lingering about anyone who was raised there, following them like smoke. Maybe it was living behind the behind, under millions, or the lack of sunlight. However, they have pills for vitamin D. Everyone was fed enough, exercised enough, and giving jobs plus some form of universal income. But something was always missing. That was that girl, Violet. She explained that she had no parents, just was dropped off from a mag-pod in her early teens at a lonely spot near the robo-maintenance shed without shoes. Her words made you feel for her, how the tiny breaks in the mag-track cut and drew blood from her feet, and the small cleaning nymphs robotically scampered around her legs. How old men leered at her young body as she slept with one eye open. Or the waves of sneering people that passed her small camp, before they traveled upward, to toil away so they can buy more trivial things. Maybe better shoes.

Lost and never having to provide for herself, she applied for her benefits and planned to live in a small row of bow-shaped buildings within sight of Long Island Sound. She sat in the mornings, on the gray preformed pebbles along the shore, in a new simple dress and printed sandals stitched with an image of a blue jay, something she had never seen. The pebbles, the Kisgep brand, turned black as they dissolved with time, then filtered down into the sea, stabilizing the great foundation of Jersey-York, manmade bedrock. The beach was constantly refreshing with gray and black pebbles, but they never burned her naked feet when she held her sandals. As she told her story, she smiled, but it was vacuous and full of pretext.

Niva liked her, how soft her eyes were, and offered her a job at the center. She could work part-time handing out meals and showing off her pretty, but not too pretty, face. Niva rescinded the offer once she learned that Violet put her thumbs through an older woman's eyes after stealing her shoes, a plain white pair, now dribbled with blood. As is often the case, the viciousness was unneeded because the woman had offered the shoes willingly, even with a smile. Niva imagined that the offer awakened a rage in Violet that spawned in Undertown's belly. The extreme anger could only be quelled by Violet's thumbs popping through the woman's braincase. Then, and only then, could Violet stop her anguished screams as blood sprinkled her face like soft rain. Something about the Zellum deal reminded her of Violet, the buried rage with hidden violence.

She will thank them and keep her decision to herself, but her mental pin will highlight the NO square when voting day comes.

Out of the hundreds of thousands of lessons that the Cutmen taught, catching out was the best way to move about the city without leaving any crumbs. Ru judged that it was easily the best, distantly followed by synthesizing tetrodotoxin with household chemicals, then a lightning-quick puncture of a femoral artery. The last two were up for debate, and circumstances typically decided for you. His Forge was preloaded with all the available codes and shortcuts; catching out was simple. He recounted the steps in his head.

Step one: Find a subject that roughly matches your description.

He noticed a man with a slender build and dark skin, matching thin English mustache. From a straight covert look, Ru's eye centered on the man's eyebrows, but that could be explained with a hunch, so he adjusted his posture.

'Ok, Check.'

Step two: Scan the subject and exchange the proper coding.

He lined up the needed codes in his HUD and slid into a line near the man. Mentally he toggled the receiving aperture mounted behind his hairline.

'Code hustling, Check.'

The right side of his vision blinded him with a green flash as he slipped into the physical queue; the codes and data exchange shuffled into the man's Nadar Forge like a curse. Luckily, the man, John, it turns out, was implanted with an aged Dadoswafer, when compared to his undated and spectacular Forge, it was an antique. At a moderate speed of a few nanoseconds, the stream cast through the local qua-com, rumored to be hidden in a pool table around a corner in a rough neighborhood. The Cutmen stationed them throughout the city, always hidden even from the senior Enswells. Once, he asked Bright Day the real purpose of the machines.

Bright Day responded in his heavily accented Italian, "the Cutman fears no man. We can blind him, take his ears out, but, the computer things; they see all." He flicked his hand to the left, then the right. "Now, these qua-coms lie to the very city, lie down to its bones. Placement cords over here, over there, over everywhere. Menzogna suprema. Now, the Cutmen blend into the street, between the cobbler stones. Hidden." Ru did not know what a cobbler stone was; he was sure that it was important and wanted to look it up but forgot.

Ru hoped that the fabled blending was true, as he, like a mental mechanic, virtually unscrewed and replaced sections of the man's code only a few inches from him. He could have outstretched an arm and poked John in the eye.

The peripheral dot turned green again. 'Code exchanged. Check.'

Finally, step three: Insert one's self in the line ahead of the code hustled.

He lurched forward, shuffling between large masses of people, all of whom were scrolling through their HUD or streaming meaningless information to other pointless people. From his perspective, these disgusting peoples' life goal is to waste the right to live by consuming useless things before the things join a pile of other useless things, then venturing out to buy more things.

'What a waste. Especially since the slovenly troglodytes can live for a long, long time, many of those things are recycled into new things that they will buy again.'

Ru was several yards ahead of John, 'a boring name, dating back thousands of years, he had unoriginal parents.'

The pod coach crept up, and the mag-unit depressed into the street, opening two sets of doors. The exit door frothed people in suits and skinny dresses, while the ingress door sucked in more people. The door frame scanner picked his identity as John Hammerblock, aged 27, com-assisted accountant, unmarried, 4,286 credits in Jersey-York City Bank, no warrants, and other socially ordinary constructs.

Once the electronic eye blinked green twice, he was clear to enter. When the real John tried to clear the door, his light shifted from green to orange to a blazing black, the alert black. Everyone hated the alert black; articles have been written of alert black psychosis. Ru imagined that John would step back alarmed and begin to yell, just long enough for JYC PD to send bots to accompany him out of the queue. His day would end poorly until the Identification Division clears the recognition mistake and then initiates a backtrace. Of course, the qua-coms would have scattered the input to the heavens, and Ru would be long gone.

The trip to Maplewood, Newark Borough was fast; just a few passengers boarding in-between. This was the high-end section of the Borough, closest to Skytown that Newark had to offer. Ru thought it odd that a community organizer could afford to live here. Unlike Manhattan, this Level was spacious, room to roam between lush gardens and under faux wooden overhangs from the luxury three-story apartments. One of the training Cutmen programs used architecture remembrances during the identifying process, flooding his mind with half re-called structures. Thousands of flashing memories of ancient buildings, like the abandoned sharkfins-shaped opera house to the forbidding city's monstrous tower shooting out of Asia, rolled through his mind. This building was reminiscent of an-cient Tudor England next to a strand of apartments the moved within a rectangular structure like a puzzle box. Each living box shifted to a new position each day. The thrill was to hunt down your apartment every evening, all your meaningless be-longings dropped somewhere in the building, like categorized shoeboxes. Ru could see how this is useful from a security per-spective, but not a living one.

'Humans are odd creatures,' he deduced, which is why he could live this life after flunking out of the Colonial Marines. Structure and training moved him, while the banality of shuffling to a place called work, then crawling back broken would kill him. He knew that.

The sunlight mirrors dimmed as he continued to walk away from the Area's outer sections; the organic lamps blinked on, casting a soft orange light over the counterfeit antique-ness. A few more corners and turns landed him in front of her building. The Area did not have towers between the Levels, only buildings up to five or six stories. The target's stood alone in its beauty and relentless posh.

"Wow," Ru marveled, "some community organizer, organizing straight into her pockets."

It occupied half a block, and the bowfront reached out with hanging gardens and massive bay windows. Cedar-colored nano-stone adorned the face, though he knew that each stone chuck weight less than a quarter-pound, and the windows were garlanded with black iron that curled around the edges, creating a story of fragility but held real strength. Her mansion, that is what he would call the collection of living technology, had four Levels with an actual door, no touchpad; however, his HUD lit up with all the passive sensors draping the building. His eyes darted over the building, but his feet continued to slowly walk by.

'Never stop in front of your target.'

Below the sizeable columned stoop, he saw a tiny door tucked lower than the main building; it was not surrounded by windows and concealed from the empty street.

'Breaking and entering never happened here, so one of two things will happen. One, no one will pay any mind, or two, everyone will pay attention.'

Judging by the lack of people on the streets and how this was a strict bedroom block, he betted on option two. He completed a circuit around two more blocks, weaving between Home-bot, nannies, and a few children. He had forgotten how annoying kids were, how their high-pitched cries squirmed into his nerves. He approached from a different street and engaged his gait modulator. Nerves signals were blocked along his spine, and his gait changed from a smooth pace of an athlete to a stuttering slog as he turned on to her street.

'Effect left leg and right forearm,' he instructed, and his body slightly shifted, 'Almost Quasimodo, more traumatic brain injury.' He slowed. 'Scan for qua-com,' he ordered his stream. 'Three miles away, fine, that will work.'

'Flashbang,' he told his HUD. Four orange bulbs lit in his peripheral vision.

He crossed to the center of the street, the HUD reconnected his nerves, and he launched himself to the small door under the stoop. From a slow lumber to a fifteen-foot jump, he landed like a cat then hacked the door's electrical lock. At low-Level security, the lock opened in a flash, allowing him to dance inside without making a sound.

Four green flashes blinked in his left eyes, and two orange in his right.

'Systems back up.'

Flashbang virtually blinded the entire block's sensors with an overload of information, like cutting a nerve on a sleeping man. Nothing but the flash.

'Location loop ten minutes, start,' he commanded. His HUD spread out before his internal point of view as he sat in the dark corridor. His left earlobe vibrated; he grabbed it and checked his embedded wrist display. One eye was lost in the HUD, while the other focused on his wrist. Just across the tendons, between the base of his palm and halfway down his forearm, an electrical image of the house showed him all the sensors. With a thought, he set them as dormant or playing the loop of the last few minutes. Zero life signed, and she was known to dislike robo help. His boss arranged for an eight-legged security FAUN to be waiting for him upstairs. He could hear it skittering around through the simulated wooden boards above.

He was clear; time to work.

The meeting was over, and Excelsior knew who was on his side, and truly his side was the only side. Hong Tai was monitoring Richard's group, but he thought he knew their votes too. Tai invaded the council members' internal systems and fed Ex their vitals down to their sweat's chemical readout and the respiratory intake as they looked at their new weapons. Some were hard to read, but he had Tai for that. Hong Tai, a man of many talents, was the best lie detector that Excelsior had ever met. Behind his almond eyes lurked a brain that could snift out a lie like a wolf tracks a herd from miles off. Ex expected that Tai gained the skill from a lifetime of perpetrating the most masterful lies ever told in this century. He could have sold you beachfront property in Miami even though that whole state had sunk like Atlantis.

'You have it all tied up?' Ex asked mentally, still scanning the groups of council mingling amongst each other.

'Yes, all agreed measures have been taken,' Tai answered.

He surveyed the group, noticing who was close to each other, what direction their ears and feet were pointing, watching for silent motivations and a sense of uncomfortableness. Feet pointed where people want to go, and many pointed to Richard. That could be good or bad. Finding non-verbal clues was the most critical aspect of his job, his life. His head ticked marginally as messages passed through his HUD, catching his attention; they were answered, then he responded to via an encrypted qua-com stream. His overtasked Nadar Forge continuously stored information and fed it into his DNA. In addition to the typical 23 chroms, he had 17 more, each packed with enough information to drown whole cities. He watched, took mental notes, cross-referenced them, made more notes, and stored them in his cells. While Richard was near peak intelligence and driven like a thrown knife, his advancement to polisci charmer seems too easy to plan. Tai started a new Marginalia folder to catalog anything that also seemed accidental or too uncanny.

HUD message received: Breach wagon, complete. Marked.

Tai nodded with approval and received was his only response.

Full night had reached them, and the fire sprouted from the posts on the sitting Area's outer edge. Ex's HUD sends his stimuli regarding the flame's brightness and the heat wafting away for the gas-fed fire, along with the mental attitudes of the party's guests. His sense of control was maximum, trying to control everything, even things that are uncontrollable. The minds, even the brilliant ones, were drifting, unfocused. The qua-com told him that these mixes of brain waves and other corporal signals were cast between arousal, affection, and empathy. Like Tai, he noticed that half of the party, meaning half of the assembled council people, were orbiting around Richard. Richard was still regaling them with a well-thought-out intermingling of hunter tales and, somehow, relating it all back to the business at hand. Still, he was so polished that it all seemed organic and flowed from one tale into a profit and loss allegory. His hands moving up and around during his telling, animated just enough to draw attention without overacting.

'I trained him well,' Ex thought, 'He will do fine, and he is only 87 with so much time to grow.'

Ex hummed a familiar thought around his head, 'Zellum InterSolar Corp, or Zellum Sol One, maybe Zellum Extraplanetary Corporation? Rich could lead them past the Main Astbelt out to Neptune's moon. Maybe interstellar.'

Ex smiled and stroked his chin, his fingers remembering where his beard use to hold residence. Ex thought about allowing facial hair production again, but he hated the need to call a roboclip for maintenance. The way those clips fly unnerved him, swooping through his manor like a small umbrella blown by its private storm. He bristled at the thought of this thing gently crashing down over his head. "Certainly not," he muttered.

'Lower flame output by 25 percent and illuminate the fire fonts with orange cascading to dark green, high granularity,' Ex commanded.

The cast iron forged into small skeletal trees lowered the flames, and the orange bloomed near the fire, then in long spiral lines shifted to light green, then to dark as there worked their way to the pebbled floor.

As the atmosphere changed, many eyes looked on the flames or high into the sky at the crescent Moon, set slightly off the horizon. Ex stepped between the stone slabs and back into the center of the outdoor theater.

"Everyone!" he hands folded out and up, like a show master, "I wish to invite you inside for refreshment and wonderful food. I have a great brand of whiskey that has waited hundreds of years for you to taste it and hundreds of wines from vineyards that were produced before the ocean claimed them back." Richard knew the game; his father would act drunk and gather information, testing the others' attention to detail.

Ex said with a slight gurgle, "I have tried several that are now expecting your attendance." He strode to Han Panhu and embraced him, high-fiving Mr. Mani on the way. Following a very long bow to seated Mrs. Lesnik, he offered her his arm. With a controlled tension, she reached out and grabbed him, then Ex's powerful arms lifted her to her feet. "Ma'am, may I escort you inside?" Ex asked. Just as she opened her mouth to reply, he said, "Yes, thank you, Mrs. Lesnik, may I call you Niva? It is a beautiful name, so lovely!" He paraded her through a break in the color-changing flames and into the house.

In the main parlor, several of Tai's men opened six bottles an hour ago so they could breathe. Each of Tai's servants had one shot from a decanter of light brown liquid, tasting horrible to them as they do not drink. They coughed as it flowed down their throats, but nothing could be spilled. Tai would not allow that, and his displeasure is extraordinarily painful. The harsh whiskey burned their throats, and one dropped the glass decanter. Matteo shot a foot out, kicking the glass. It bounced up as Bao slung his arm forward, gently pushing it toward the wall with a blazingly fast grace. The decanter rushed past his head; Luis jutted two fingers near the real wooden bar. He caught the bottle between the steel-hard fingers and shifted it in midair to the correct orientation. The 654-year-old decanter pulled from the waters of Islay, Scotland, gently landed, and slid to its original position. They all looked at each other, then nodded, leaving the room. One drop hit the floor, darkening the wood. That droplet-soaked into timber, increasing its value by tens of thousands. Before the tiny slick sunk into the wood, it shined like it was beaming with pride.

CHAPTER 9

Undertown was the same as Skytown; it had the same striations built into its social muscles. The main difference was that here, thousands of feet down, under the weight of the city's mountain, people do not care if you are noticed or not. Up there, thousands of feet closer to the sun and flowing air, so high that one walks on a needle head, everything is about being noticed. The Skybound want to be seen as intelligent, businesswise, or lavish by the other rich, or the best of all, overly extravagant. The Unders are only servants, never to live at a greater loftiness. Sometimes, they are prey for the Uptown slummers, but they did build this city. Not with hands and shovels; no, the nano triggers made everything, but with spirit and vigor. They brought life to the mechanical monster perched over the ocean.

Well, that is what Clarence Tyler told him and anyone else who would bend an ear. Alone, he barked with his carnival voice at Jonas, even though Jonas had heard it so many times that he would mock Clarence when his back was turned. Tyler called it Idolsophy, making the city the idol and the people its clergy. Once, Tyler's rule encompassed thousands, then hundreds, and finally dozens of simpletons that regarded Tyler as an idol. The idol was blown into visceral pieces in Atlanta along with hundreds of "clergy."

'The idol fell; it was about time,' Jonas thought.

Still, he did love Undertown, how people were closer to what they were naturally born to be. Animals. Fighting, screwing, and plotting like…natural beasts.

He slid back into the booth, sipping his coffee. He remembered real coffee, real as in it grew with help from the sun and the rain. This stuff, he looked to the dark fluid in the cup swirling around, had never seen anything natural, just lab powder. But, below Level two hundred, it was the best there is, and he sucked the last drop down.

The place was small, dirty, and tried to revive the diner décor, but the place seemed to have forgotten about the passage of time. Marcos Motor Diner was mentally operated by an IA and manned by staffbots, all scratched, bent, and looked like they won third place in the junkyard synthetic female approximation contest.

Tyler had been right about one thing before he detonated himself and spread like ashes over the last of the great southern cities. 'Well,' Jonas thought, 'I hit the button; he just so happened to be standing on the mass of perfectly crafted simulated high-explosive UN N-001-42.' Tyler stood on the pile of the deadliest munition east of the Mississippi as if they were shiny pebbles.

Tyler had mastered the one thing all leaders need to know. Building a team may seem simple, especially when half the world is having a seizure of rage, but no, it was the most challenging part of planning a rebellion. The team must be seen within the violent tangle of rioters and looters and drilled into tolerable order in an extremely short about of time. Tyler called it, First glance to divorce timeframe.

His passion was to generate a competent and driven team, the way an electrical generator sparks off electricity. One month into laying in infiltrators, Jonas watched, bewildered, as Tyler formed a crack squad in Tallahassee from two preachers, a fat mechanic, a gay English schoolteacher who hated religion, and four government workers based at the former US Air Force Base in Panama City. Tyler did what he was best at, gathering intelligence, building relationships, and recruiting the vulnerable, but also find the most qualified, then target them

The ink was still wet on the International Hegemon Charter, and the now UN-controlled US troops were ripping about the cities from Seattle to St. Augustine. Dropped from orbit, the rec-techs seared through the sky to fall along IH-10; personnel were under orders to crack all the dams in the Florida panhandle. While the little nanos attacked the cities with tiny swords and hammers, people moved to the preordained temporary camps in Jacksonville in the east and Pensacola in the west. The big green machine was to let the tiny destroyers eat all human structures from the state line to the Gulf. Removing all makes of humanity and returning the soggy lake basins to the Apalachicola Forest.

Tyler worked against the Rewilding and the Charter across the south and up to Montana. With Tyler and Jonas's help, the nine rebels devised a plan to incinerate the entire battalion and lead the Rec-tech nanos to the swamp. Of course, they failed, and the nine were reduced to three, and the three were reduced to a bloody zero. But the poorly trained and hastily build team caused three thousand men to slow a world government-ordered exfiltration of Florida's panhandle. He and Tyler had moved on, starting another rebellion, another crew, hundreds of miles away when the last member of the Florida Nine fell from the caverns that bullets carved in his body.

Tyler said, "A dead team means building a new live team." It was that simple with him, cause and effect.

He pulled up his gray coat as he leaned down to minimize any visibility from eyes on the street. He was a large man, and his massive shoulders are distinctive, like hills on flat land. Trying to not hug the tabletop, he signaled the staffbot with a wriggle of the empty coffee cup. The bot shuffled over, looked at him with its strangely erotic approximations of female eyes, then bent to fill his cup from a permanently attached pot as a man pushed in the door, and a cool breeze drifted in, disturbing the decades-old dust and the wild tufts of the bot's blond hair. Jonas knew that was his mark, the bagman. The man surveyed the diner, shuffled past the empty table and the staffbot, and slid into the booth opposite him. He looked different, wet otter dark brown hair and beard, with root beer eyes.

"Thank you for meeting me," he said, looking down to the table, seeing the ancient maps of the tablecloth. The ancient world was spelled out in roads and directions. Take the interstate to IH-95 to New Rochelle, then all the way through the beauty of some former state called Connecticut, keep going to exit 24A-B, finally Boston. All gone, hundreds of years ago, broken into the natural form of land and gravelly dust.

'What is an exit off a magnetic line?' the man thought.

Jonas only nodded, sipping the semi-coffee.

The man wanted some form of acknowledgment but reconsidered it after seeing Jonas's cold stare. Typically, he felt in full control, but he never had physically met Jonas, and the sight of a two hundred plus-year-old assassin and leader of rebellions took him aback.

He shrugged, "Ok, the arrangement will remain the same, but I have one issue that I need to speak to you about." His eyes returned to a mimic of reading the table maps. Jonas was surprised in the timidity of this man; he had thought him strong. The man did not cower; he simply wanted to take precautions against identification from passersby. Nor did he cower against the most dangerous thing in the room: Jonas. The dislike for the man was growing and morphing into disdain.

"Skytowner, what is the issue?" Jonas snapped in a low gravelly tone. He was unaccustomed to taking orders, and he knew that this would become an order by the time the man left the diner.

The man's short hair ruffled, bits of the natural blonde showed for a moment, then the chemically generated brown took over again. He popped in another pill for eumelanin pigment control. Jonas heard the pill crack against the man's perfectly white teeth, straight as a ruler.

'Unnatural,' Jonas thought, 'All this disguise. I could rip his identity from him with one hand.'

The man's glance shot up again but only held Jonas's steady look for two seconds before bouncing off and back to the table. "The female inquisitor," he said, it seemed as if he was shaking, "no more like that. I, well… we need to be like foxes at night. Do you understand?"

'Foxes at night, interesting phrasing,' Jonas mused.

"Foxes at night are quiet, yes, but even though they stalk like shadows in the darkness, they do not fear ripping the prey's flesh and breaking its bones once they sink their teeth into necks," Jonas said, hoping to test the man's rising fear.

The man's shoulder's hunched, his head dropped. A sharp intake of air sounded like a hiss. Through gritted teeth, he said, "Yes, violent quick action to procure nourishment… food," in case Jonas was an idiot, "but it was all planned. The hunting routes and type of creature, all of it. Nothing was rushed by emotion. It was clean and natural, you see. You need to follow the plan." His head rolled up, away from the map, away from fear, to meet Jonas's glare. They looked at each other for a minute, maybe longer.

'Hmm…the fear was a play. Hiding behind it, but I found you,' Jonas judged. He would be a great team member. Driven, intelligent, and apparently fearless when pushed.

"I told your go between that this is a joint venture, and I do not take orders," Jonas retorted, his muscles lifting his massive frame out of the nook in the booth. Even seated, Jonas was two feet taller than the man, but the man did not flinch. Nor did he try to extend his body or puff out his chest. He knew where his control laid and would not exacerbate the situation.

After decades of leading criminal industries, creating rebellions, large and small, and, due to unfortunate current circumstances, commanding Undertown with a gang of vastly dangerous killers, Jonas could spot inner strength, find the ability in a person to push so hard against an immovable object that you will shear off your muscles and break your own bones. That was his extraordinary ability to find those people, the ones whose souls were metal but were also dimwittedly stubborn.

This man was not only different in appearance due to the disguise but different in character. Not like a fox at night, more a spider.

The man stated evenly, "No more passion, until the end," he left his stare be the punctuation.

Jonas nodded and sipped his coffee. "I understand," he conceded. "You remember your word."

"I will, and you will get what was promised," the man said as he stood, pulling a hood over his head.

Their eyes locked again, and both nodded, then the man left the booth to slide through the diner door. Both understood the other, if either failed or compromised, they would attack like foxes, but Jonas knew that the winner would need more control. The winner would become more like the spider.

"Coffee," he yelled at the staffbot, leaning back into the booth, thinking. Not about his upcoming mission or the men he would lose. He stared into the black liquid circling in his cup and thought about the spider.

CHAPTER 10

He heard a conversation from behind his eyelids. Slowly, he moved his head, it was unsecured, and he wiggled it slightly. No HUD activity, and he could not open his eyes, but his limbs could move some, and he felt soft sheets. The effect of the memory suppressant seemed to be lessening.

'She was dead,' he thought. Ice grew in his blood, and his head slammed back, causing the bed to shake slightly. The snake eating its tail flashed before him; he could almost see it still written in her blood, dripping down the walls. He could not find the faces of the attackers, the black-eyed man, and the shark-toothed woman. Their appearances were lost, just words in his mind, gaging their shapes against the familiar space of his apartment.

Their apartment...now, just him, his apartment, single, alone. Lost.

Even the stab wound, though almost healed, seems a distant memory. The scar forming over the puncture itched, and his insides ached. He began to review the possible medical solutions that were injected into his body.

'Stabbed by a knife and impaled for treatment.'

Emotions were turning from cold to ice, forever frozen and unmoving. The chill was gnawing its way through him. Only two things were clear: a knife punched through his guts into his spine, and the beautiful Elizabeth with a wondrous smile was dead. Even blinded, he knew that he was in a hospital and heard the NURS wheels rolling through the hall. He needed to orient himself.

'Hospital.'

'First, BaladaFuse for blood loss, second Healmed to enhance healing.'

He listed off several liquid solutions that might be flowing into his veins, but Fulropamic was the most likely. The knife punctured so many holes that the NURS would fill him with something close to superglue until surgery. Fulropamic's main marketing program was for the military, he helped engineer the latest bio-produced batch.

'Plug up holes.'

Due to his size, weight, and blood loss, Pamethorudic was given to suppress memory, which will take a week or so to wear off. Gently he pushed one hand to the other, scraping across the sheets, and took his pulse, trying to use his medical knowledge and training. He barely managed, but he found a count.

'Forty-five beats per minute, typical respiration, too.'

His legs would not move. He focused on a twist of an ankle, but they were still. Fresh blood flowed over his face, and he could not move; he tasted it as it ran into his mouth.

'Rationalize. No blood. Calm. Ok, Hospital means treatment. Start with the toes.' Using all his energy, he curled the toes of both feet. The sensation was dull, but pain casually traveled up through his legs. His big toes popped.

'Ok, neural damage was mended. Neural bypass with accelerated growth, likely bio-silicone implant running up the spine. So, a roughly seven-inch knife puncture is mostly healed, blood pressure, pulse, and breathing are normal, weakness is typical, but memory is still affected.'

Some aching pinpricks shot through his back, angry nerves.

'Possibly additional surgery to clean up from the first.

Four days, I have been here for around four days.'

His heart sunk and then froze; she has been dead for four days. Her beautiful heart was being refrigerated to 39 degrees, or, much worse, she has been atomized into nothingness. His stomach lurched, but nothing came up, only pain.

The conversation continued, a little clearer now. The woman was young and assertive as if she had a position of authority. Whatever that authority was is currently failing from what the man had said. He sounded much older and held an irritated but professional voice, like a professor repeatedly explaining a simple stem cell to osteoblast regeneration matrixing to polycarbonate materialization.

The man said, "No," and the woman took a sharp intake of breath, then grunted.

Miguel could not hear most of the words, only the intent behind them. He assessed that the man was a doctor, who was lecturing her about Mr. Saxon, and she seemed familiar. Oddly, her tone and cadence reminded him of someone. He was troubled by this. It was like watching a virtual biblo but forgetting the title while you still remembered the whole plot. The mem-suppressor slowed his gears.

Her response grew more irritated and loud enough to sound as if she was speaking directly into his ear.

"Look, I'm telling you for one last time, I will wait here until he wakes up," she said loudly, not quite yelling but well above talking volume. A sharp crack sounded as she stomped her foot.

The man stepped back and said, "Now, Detective, he is resting, and I will personally stream you once he is conscious." Miguel imagined that the Doctor was holding his hands in front, palms open to stave off her growing anger. Miguel heard her sniffling, then heavy breaths. The woman's voice changed; it came out wet and almost manic. He heard a clatter and a hard thump. The mood changed. Her voice, now low and soft, was coming from his Level, she sat down, and the Doctor must be standing.

"No," she declared, "I'm here, and I will stay here. Got it, Doc." She cleared her throat. Though her voice carried sadness, she pulled it in, held it down, and put it in a pocket in her heart. The chair squeaked as she improved her posture in an unconscious effort to show the Doctor that she was planted to this spot until she chooses to move, and only when she decides.

His eyelids were starting to flicker, but his vision was still very dim. He saw flashing images of a hospital room as though he watched an antediluvian moving picture, one shot then another, humans moving like they were actors.

Through his gauzed vision, he saw a thin blond woman holding her head in her hands, sitting in the corner of the room. The Doctor, or someone with that kind of jurisdiction over the space, stood over her, with both hands planted firmly on his hips. It occurred to Miguel that he did not like this man; possibly, it was the attitude of power he attempted to use over the woman, who was obviously in pain. The man needed to correct her for an imagined slight. Miguel let out a heavy moan and shifted his head. He thought it was enough to break the tension, and he did not trust the unkind would be Doctor to notified her that he was awake. So, he took care of that.

The blinking eye movement was fading into rolling eyes, although his sight was becoming more crystal. His head lolled back, and he worked to focus his view.

Her head shot up, eyeing him. The Doctor mentally called a NURS and calmly walked to the edge of the bed.

"Mr. Saxon? Are you awake?" the man asked. Without waiting for a reply, he said, "I'm Doctor Yora, and I'm Area ten's Chief Attending at the Jean-Martin Charcot Medical Tower. You have been in an accident, and you have been here for several days." The fact that he was flipping through Miguel's chart on his HUD was plain, and his attitude was as if he was entering tax data.

"Miguel?" the woman asked, her voice smothered in pain like her heart was breaking from some bad news that she had not told him yet. Through his blurring vision, he saw that she was rubbing her eyes with a tissue, her head bowed. She was folded in half, shoulders bobbing as she worked to control each breath, just a mental flash from breaking down. Her hands cupped her face, and then she sobbed. The sound of her tears and the slight curl of her body in the ugly utilitarian chair was a lightning bolt, charging the room with mind-numbing anguish.

'She moved like Liz,' Miguel thought, and his eyes began to fill. He did not weep; he never had, the water just flowed down his cheeks, and his breathing stayed the same.

The last time he cried, he was with Liz, and he was reading off the stream mail. He was the primary contact for the Population Control Bureau because she said her HUD would break because she would check it so frequently. Immediately, he scanned it, and an eternally happy sense gripped him but hid that with his commonly dead face. Only she could find his emotions. He delayed the reading of the message just to torment her, raising the stress and her annoyance. He leaned on the bathroom doorframe and slowly read through the new notice in an overly long narration, stopping for several heartbeats between the title and opening line. It was one of his Sunday afternoon traditions, and he loved her so much for allowing him to put her through this type of harassment.

Liz squinted at him, a key indicator of her growing exasperation. "Hurry up," she urged, "If there is nothing worth my notice, then be off, husbando mine." She arched her neck, pointed her nose in the air, and looked away. Then, a giggle broke through the aristocratic pretense. "Come on!" Her nose wrinkled.

"Menter bill," he delayed for half a minute, "Thank you for your service in our wonderful printed food meal plan, total 45 UD credits." He exaggerated scrolling through the messages shifting in his vision by swinging his head as if he was watching a parade pass by, then announcing that he "Found another!" Luckily, she enjoyed a hot cup of molecular coffee and nestled on the bed wrapped in blankets.

He read all the senders in a second after activating his HUD, so his timing was perfect.

"Ok, Manzana. Last one," he turned into the bathroom, grabbed the dental mouthpiece, plopped it in his mouth. She only heard his mumbling beyond the loud hum of the mouthpiece cleaning his teeth.

"What?" She cupped her hand to her ear; now, the squinted was accompanied by a slight frown. He loved her and her micro-aggressions.

"PCB notice," he slurred as he pulled out the mouthpiece and flung toothpaste into the sink. She sat up, spilling her coffee, eyes alert. He continued to wash his mouth, swelling then spitting. She jumped out of bed, walked to him, wrapped only in a thin sheet.

He swilled and spit. She grabbed him from behind, and he turned.

"Hmmm...Hold on," he said, "What?" He pretended confusion. "Oh, they want you to go in for a physical examination. Wonder why?" He sneered, watching the idea reach full fruition in her face.

The most beautiful smile bloomed under her golden eyes, and she leaped onto him, wrapping her legs around him as if he were a tree. Personal connections, income, educational standards were all investigated, and all marks have been met. No illegal enterprises, and free from Undertown.

This was the P-EX's is the last step, and it really means

the license is granted.

Energy beamed from her, and he was soaking it up. The gold in her eyes seemed to glow, and he kissed her. Joyful tears ran down her face, and her power of passion entered him, and through that deep connection between the two, he began to cry with her. Maybe those were his tears, too.

Now, the connection was broken, violently rent by blooding shark teeth. Bitten in half, never to be sewn together.

He forced his head to look away from the woman, tears still streaming down his face, and stare at the wall.

"Miguel? This is Alcippe, your sister-in-law. I need to talk to you," she mumbled, trying to hold back sobs. The miasmic air held the words; Miguel only saw the ribbons of her blond hair jerking with each hard breath.

"No, ma'am," Dr. Yora cautioned angrily, holding up a hand to her as if his hand would bring silence. "No, Detective Anagnos. Now is not the time." He began to walk to her waving a finger.

The tears cleared from his vision, and Miguel thought the old man wearing a white coat was professorial uncaring to a battered woman. She stared at the man as bitter rage built. The chair popped and creaked as her muscles strained against it like she was about to spring into the doctor's face. Liz would have liked her.

Miguel had enough; his dry throat cracked, "Doctor Yora, Chief Attending of Area ten in Jean-Martin Charcot Medical Tower, leave." He thought he heard fractures in his windpipe. All movement was slowly coming back, but the pain sensors roared into his brain. The sutures pulled against his skin feeling like they would tear, leaving him an open blood bag, and every move burned.

"I'm sorry, sir? What?" Yora spun to face him. Miguel turned his head and stared at him, tears continually draining to the floor.

"Leave!" Miguel bellowed, pointing to the door with a shaky arm.

Yora crossed his arms, tapping one foot. "Sir, I will allow this visitor due to the circumstances, but first, I must inform you that you were in a medically induced coma, and you are at high risk…" The Doctor was pointing his finger at Miguel, now.

Miguel sighed, clawing back the urge to jump from the bed regardless of his limbs' uselessness.

"Yora, I'm aware," Miguel said through gritted teeth, "Initially, I was injected with BaladaFuse due to a massive hemorrhage. Healmed or something like it to improve healing. A version of Fulropamic to identified and stop internal bleeding, along with several surgeries. Neural bypass for partial paralysis and a dose of Pamethorudic to suppress my memory. All typical bio-measures are holding steady, and I have been here for around four days. Is that correct?"

The woman blinked, a small smile crossed her face.

The man was stunned. His pointing finger dropped as he stepped back. "Yes, that is correct," he said. "Now, Mr. Saxon, as I said, you were in an accident." Miguel looked at the ceiling, quickly losing strength. "After the accident, you were brought here. Sir, your wife…"

The Doctor did not see it coming; he went from a dictatorial authority to bruised face against a wall the second he said 'wife.' Alcippe held his wrist between his shoulder blades, her knees balanced against the back of his leg. She whispered, "You do not get to talk about her," she pulled the arm up until he winced. "Understand?"

His shoulder was inching closer to popping out of the socket; the pain made it hard for anything to draw his full attention.

"Understand?" she yelled, jerking up again.

"Yes, yes. I understand!" he cried. She pulled him from the wall and pushed him out the door. He turned to face her, but she closed the door in his face with a burst of air.

"Asshole," was her answer to the screaming from the hallway.

Miguel was looking at her questioningly, trying to place her face. The realization hit him like a blow to the stomach. The instant ninja act reminded him because once, years ago, he brought Liz home late, and as he made a halfhearted attempt to kiss Liz's cheek, her sister put him in an armbar. An attack from the darkness. If he thought about it too hard, his shoulder could remember the sharp pain. The woman was fast, caring, and Liz's sister. He tried to hold all the memories back, them laughing at a family gathering, a drunken Al purposefully bothering Liz with her work on a crossword puzzle, practicing some form of martial arts until they were both black and blue. And, of course, the sibling rivalry simmering just below the surface.

His connection to the world was being mended when he looked at Al's ice-blue eyes and her pain because he knew why she was here. Her true intent.

"Alcippe? What happened?" Miguel asked, his body sunk into the mattress, fully relaxed in the hospital bed. "Where is she?" Tears formed pools in his sockets, then they burst.

CHAPTER 11

His job was simple, deliver a message. While the primary goal was indeed simple, the application was much harder. Benny Batters rolled out of bed and pulled the drape away, revealing the Kansas River trailing off to the south. The F-printer dinged, he signaled by thinking 'breakfast,' a small garbage can-shaped bot served him as he looked out. It spit out a single morning meal, steak and eggs with a side dish of melon, and the eating implements. The salt mixture was not functioning correctly, and the fat was in gloppy blobs; he struggled to force it down, though it was better than MREs from the old jungle days.

"Water," Batters mumbled, holding out a degradable glass, the glass filled with clear water. Once Jersey Joe explained the process to him, something about baby crystals filtering the water from the air, but he forgot the details. It was all magic to him; he paid it no mind. Life was as simple as his job. Think it, and it happens. The microscopic machines that build his chair or give him food or transported him across the country were what they were, simple.

Having finished his meal and downed several glasses of water, he dropped the whole set into the recycler and watched it dissolve. The metal plate and translucent glass seemed to soften and melted together, becoming one gray slug, then draining back into the room's accommodations profile, ready for the next customer.

They still need to fix the salt mixture.

Rubbing his bald head while cleaning his teeth, he was

already bored.

He stretched his shirt over his body, and it almost popped the seams. Last night he popped another hypertrophy pill, and his muscles still ached. He retasked his customized bones and connective tissue cells to alter with the growing brawn, hoping that he did not push too hard and pulled a tendon from a bone.

His morning trip was fast and efficient, a quick pod ride, and a short walk to the farm's office.

His HUD called the foreman, and he sat in the shade from the dark red square building. It reminded him of a brick planted in a wheat field. Wheat spread for miles in every direction, each section marked by lines of trees creating thousands of yellow rectangle outlined in green. It will be a relatively cool day of 75 with moisture coming in from the east, from home. Manhattan was his home and will always be; concrete was ground into his bones. He will live there until the end of his days, and this is the farthest west he has ever been. In the service, he was deployed south to Amazonia and east to Parthia. Other soldiers had told him that the continent's center was boring, just farms and vast rewilding elements, hills of neverending forests and great plains where no one had stood in centuries. He could see why, it was just waving amber and a deep blue sky rising to the almost black zenith. Even the few sparse clouds seemed bored.

Foreman responded with a beep and a short message, "On the way."

'Maybe even simpler than I thought,' he wondered, 'Give the message and go home to the real Manhattan.'

The nation's home to the Agriculture University is in Manhattan, Kansas, which sported over 100,000 lost souls looking only to grow wheat, barley, Kamut, millet, and many others. All to be crushed and chemically dissected into some form of a printable paste. The view from his spot in the shade of gleaming waves passing through the fields of grain made him think of the overly salted steak and eggs. Not simple.

'Bad lives,' he thought. Of course, people need to eat, but MREs were fine with him. Easy and simple, just add water, and shove the chow down. Again simple.

At least he had a drink at the famous Auntie Maes on the tallest building in fake Manhattan. The bar was supposedly hundreds of years old, though it was relocated during the two thousand twenty-two drought and the following famine. Those ancients managed to save most of the original wood. All encased in translucent resin that is now illegal. The whiskey on a real wood bar in a transplanted college venue was good enough for him. He even managed not to get into a brawl despite some rowdy students casually brushing his arm.

The Blue Earth Tower view was nice, but nothing compared to the Manzana or the Spiral. The fields of wheat or whatever they were growing looked like fields, just fields. Nothing special to him. Of course, he was from Undertown, so the gritty concrete was beautiful to his eyes. Maybe with a little blood splatter for flavor.

Jonas told him to come and give the foreman a message, so he followed orders and was sweating next to the brick-like office. No one says no to Jonas, to his black eyes in his blank face. Batters was a killer, an excellent killer, even he had 592 confirmed kills, but Jonas was in a separate league. He stripped away humanity's false constructs down to the true animal that once roamed with primates and was seen by hungry tiger's eyes. He saw the real man, the man with a weapon, the man whose hands are blades. Batters thought that the earth vomited up Jonas, the late Drauger, the again-walker, to plague the planet. While Batters had seen Jonas laugh, eat, sleep, and even make love to Sharkteeth, he still doubted if Jonas was ever genuinely human. The man with black eyes tells you, you do it.

Simple.

No one was working today, maybe because it was Sunday, so it was just him and the foreman.

The solitude of the one-story office with a darkened window was beginning to make him itch like he was standing in the shadow of a rock floating in a sea of yellow. The easy breeze rushed the wheat into wavelike movement, and he could not understand how anything beyond the arg-bots could work out here. Ten dormant bots stood silently like a reef breaking the grain waves, but they were still watching.

Foreman was a few minutes away, time to start the message. The drones orbited overhead like a murder of crows and dispersed to the programmed coordinates. He began with the tree line around a thousand yards north. They buzzed the trees in a hatch pattern, dotting them with a white mist of hundreds of thousands of seeds. The next squadron of drones flitted over the trees, unleashing a brown haze. Even though the trees and the affected leaves were yards away, Batters could hear the hiss as the virus took root.

'Message sent,' Batters thought, rubbing his chin. The dust rose from across the tree line as the pod rolled up. The mag-ball settled, and the vehicle dropped, stirring clouds of dust. A huge man slowly climbed out of the opening portal, barely wide enough for his frame. Batters suppressed a smile as he heard the man cursing.

"What are you doing here?" the foreman exploded, trending through the dusty clouds as he plodded to Batters, not deterred by Batters' greater size. Typical farmer with a button-up shirt and denim, sunburned, and angry. "I told the last salesman to shove off, and I will tell you the same. We don't need nothing." His face was inches from Batters, and he was breathing hard enough to fill Batters' mouth with whatever he had for breakfast. A tinge of disgust washed over him, and he seriously consisted breaking the foreman's neck with a backhand.

Batters kept his face as it always was, bland and unmoveable, and said, "Not selling nothing." His hand shot out, catching the foreman just under the ribs, then launching him five feet backward with a powerful push. The foreman crumpled into the dust and tried to breathe but coughed until his face was blue. Batters dug his boot in the man's hamstring until he was sure that picnickers three counties away could hear him screaming.

"I have a message," Batters stated. 'Simple job,' he thought.

He activated his HUD and mentally thumbed a switch.

The tree line exploded. Flames raced up to meet the sky, and the superheated wheat became a lake of fire. The foreman struggled to lurch back from the heat. Batters liked the warmth, torching through his skin that was streaked by stretch marks of unhuman muscles. Most of his skin was scar tissue, cool to the touch. The man screeched as he wiggled through the dirt toward the pod. The pain coursing through his nerves confused his brain, breaking the Forge's neural connection; he swung his head furiously, trying to find his HUD in his field of vision. Batters thought that he looked like a happy dog with a dead chicken. Batters stream told him that it was now 140 degrees; his eyes began to ache as the moisture was sucked away.

'Wind is pushing the fire to another field. The air will cool,' he thought.

Batters yelled over the crackling and snapping of the fire, "No HUD service here for you." He lifted his massive head to the sky, where a dragonfly drone was loitering. "I took care of that."

"Why did you do that...TO THE TREES?" the foreman screamed, still trying to activate his HUD; his fingers were pressing his skull as if he would find a button. "Arg-bots will put it out, and Midsection PD will shock you to death!" he said as a laugh formed in his burned throat. Batters walked to him and hit a cognitive switch. A drone swarm rocketed over the fire, twisting through the thermal gusts. Hundreds of the insect-like fliers peppered the conflagration, killing the flame.

'Genetic genius,' Batters remembered, 'that is what Daxton called his source.'

One of his code hustlers bagged some guy who works on one of the Aquacities botany Levels. Daxton told him it was just a tweet to rapidly increase oil production and another tweet to create a non-flammable resin for the salvageable parts. Fire then goop, he said. He said it should smell like peppermint, and he was right. The hot breeze tickled his nose. One colossal hand pinched his nose to hold back a sneeze while the other gripped the man by the back of the neck.

"Ok, man. Drones have genetics in them. See, no more fire," he twisted the man's head to the dying blaze. "I have a message to give you, and that message must go to the owner." Batters slowly scanned through his stream, finding the text. "Ah, a man called Bear Leshy. Understood?" pulling the man close to his face, locking eyes.

"I met him once; I don't know the man," the foreman snapped, his arms gripping Batters forearm, trying to twist free. Batters tighten his grip, and the man's shoulders clamped against his neck, and his back arched. He started to scream again.

"Stop moving," Batters said, getting annoyed, "I need you to be alive. Bear is coming here tonight, to Manhattan, Kansas, to speak with you farmers. He will want to speak to you because of the fire and how the bots sat on their rusting butts."

"OK, OK, I WILL," the man panted, his muscles reaching exhaustion.

"1209 Hilltop Drive, Area 2, Level 23, daughter is Lilia,

son is Faris, wife is Banu," Batters said. "We know you and your family. Understand?" The man tried to nod between the crushing pressure of Batters fingers.

"GOT IT," he whispered. The man's substantial farmer's chest heaved as he started to blubber. Batters let go, the man falling to the dirt.

"You will tell him that Zellum will bring new security to the farms. You know, to prevent fire," Batters shrugged as if he knew this guy should already understand this, "and that a yes vote is best. Now, big man, do you understand the instructions?" Batters stood to his full height, towering over the man in the dirt.

"Yes, sir, I got it. New security firm bots...Zellum bots, right. They will prevent fires and vote yes...YES," he said through sobs, tears running like rivulets through the dirt strains on his dirty face.

"Ok, good big man. Also, tell him to check an account that will be sent to him via personal message."

The man only nodded, holding the back of his neck, thinking about the forming purple bruise.

"Clean this up, retill the land; the bot will deactivate once I leave. The Bluemen will only know what I tell you now, Lo entiendes? Ok, several big guys attacked you, the toughest farmer in town. Right? They forced you to turn off the bots. Beat you some, thinking that you are with their girl. Got it? Now give me your arm," Batters asked calmly. The man's eyes widened. "This fake fire and fake fight need to look real. Give one arm to me."

The crack reverberated down the man's spine and up Batters arms; he had to keep himself from laughing.

'Good, simple job.'

CHAPTER 12

'Second trip. Hate the hospital. It has been five days in here,' she thought, "Of course, he is driving the doctors mad, which is good.' She smirked and was sure that his regaining of consciousness was planned to shut up that so-called Chief Attending.

Lieutenant Banda Aliquam explained the circumstances, thus explaining her out of trouble for manhandling the Attending Charlie. How the patient was her brother-in-law, and the murder victim was her sister, how she had just come from a gruesome homicide scene, and the person of interest is unaccounted for, and she still has her sister's blood on her shoes. The Attending had two noise violations dismissed. But, Al will find him again later.

'What a jackass Charlie!'

Miguel answered all the detective's questions with alarming recall and accuracy, as his role was limited to being beaten up and stabbed in the spine, then watching the love of his life bleed out, the blood washing into his face. Tension had taken root in him, and its vines were tight around his heart. Even his short bursts of pain seemed to affect him less. He was a mystery to many, and the people that knew him, or thought that they did, would consider him unaffected and aloof, a genius psychopath. But Al knew the one thing that brightened him was when Elizabeth focused those incredible gold eyes on him, making him stir, and their laughter. His soul ventured out of his cave as he watched Liz laugh, forcing a smile. She was one of, if not the only, connection to the world outside of the intricacies within his mind while working in the lab.

Luckily, she was normal, her word for it, a normal worker.

She found a passion in her work, pursued it, and build a life beyond. Some people revolve only around work; she saw it at the station. Hundreds of Officers, especially Detectives, orbited around work, finding clues, intelligence leads, and returned to interviews until all other things were pushed aside. Friends, family, everything. Some only had the bottle left. Elizabeth spoke about it often, that push happened in both their workplaces, Homicide Block and Inquisitor's Office. Even the political top of the heap, Chief Inquisitor Matthew Griest, was guilty of it. You could see it working behind his eyes, a factory still churning away to produce another angle or calculate the next steps in some massive career advancement plan.

Miguel barely fit in this category. His secret engine that ran smoothly behind his face was well beyond the mind of anyone she had ever met. Her sister once described him as someone with a hunter's eye for detail and an intrinsic base of knowledge for the whole forest. Of course, Al had never seen a forest, but she was a hunter at the rail range. To her, he was a man with a boy's curiosity and a wise man's skills.

Now, the brilliance and unabated curiosity within Miguel had burnt out. She felt energy radiate off him when he spoke of the crime, pure rage, though, to people unfamiliar with his ways, he seemed calm, but beneath his stony face, there was a fire building. She hoped that she could persuade him to altered emotional center thought feedback, but she doubted it. Without the pain, his disconnection would be full, and then he might be a danger. Not to himself, but to others, to everyone.

Elizabeth told her about his projects. Adapting human brain tissue to reorganizing spatial awareness through synthetic printed primate neural pathways, then referencing UN worldwide structure data.

Al's response was, "What?"

Elizabeth sighed, smiling, and said, "He was bored and solved it in three hours. Since he has access, he was thinking about proposing a self-contained, self-generated Synthetic Amplified Neural-net unit with a passive connection to Earth SANNs. He has all the science ready, even working mini-units in his play space. You know, his lab."

"Ok, smart guy, sure, but why send a false brain to the moon? No way the Nations would sponsor it," Al sneered.

"Oh, first, since it would keep growing, like getting more complex, he wondered if it could offer any...life lessons, and, you will love this, if it wanted to harm us or take over, we could EPM it and nuke it," she snorted and rolled back lifting her wine glass, face beaming. She really loved that guy. Something in her, just like in him, flowered when they meet. Together and only together, they could feel the pulse of the world, even if that world was of their own making.

Alone, Miguel was a ship sailing without a Captain, with no direction, just bobbing along. While so immense and wild beyond her imagining, his mind was adrift, and Elizabeth was the only one that Al had ever seen to hold it, to grab that line and pull it to shore.

'So, that was him, brother-in-law.'

Tears started to form; she sniffed and cleared her throat. Parents were on the way, supposedly to confirm it was Liz's body. Dad and Mom were traveling from England as a pilgrimage to commemorate the death of the first and best born, the golden-eyed darling. They will be severely disappointed that Elizabeth will be a vapor job. She will forever be circling gas in a small bioplastic sphere mounted on intricately molded gold and metallic blue legs, ready to be placed on a coffee table or a mantle along with other dusty knickknacks. Elizabeth thought it was a good joke, as she and Miguel never believed in anything more than the good they could do in this world. The pious

Anagnos would be aghast, and the picture of Dad's face when he saw the sphere sitting on a mantle like a bird's egg, how red he would burn, oh, that removed the tears and created a small chuckle.

The NURS's tires screeched as it stopped in front of her. "Detective Anagnos, you may enter now," it chirped then sped off.

'Hope he is better,' she wondered as she approached the portal door.

His room was upgraded due to the case's notoriety, real Level 2000 status; touch portal, anti-gav bed, and an in-room skinwalker nurse, just meters from Skytown. At the edge of the city's rim, the window let in actual sunlight, with a grand view. She was still getting used to it; it was much brighter and a ting more yellow, while the internal lamps that shined in brightness now seemed too orange. Miguel told her, or maybe he just wanted to hear his voice after being stuck in a bed with only a bot to speak to, that millions of years of evolution created the human eye with its interpreting brain to crave Sol's brilliance. That is why the artificial lights are now so unsatisfying. The Skin-bot smoothly placed itself at the end of his bed and nodded, the voice box spitting out, "Hmmm...," and a soft, "Yes."

She touched the pat; the portal swelled, then she entered. Miguel was crouched on the window crook, wearing only his pants. The Skin was next to him, pretending to stare out the window.

She asked the robot, "Skin, what are you looking at?"

Its head turned to her, articulating, "Something of interest," then it swung back to where Miguel was staring.

She sank into a comfy deep chair and shook a bag of donuts. "Miguel, please join me in expanding our bellies. I skipped B-fast, and I need a sugar reload."

Moving his back up from the crunch marginally, he

169

asked, "Coffee?" and looked at the skinjob.

"Yes, sir," it chimed.

"Thanks, Miguel. Works been rough," Al said, realizing how stupid that was to say just after it left her mouth. "I meant, like…" gesturing to the room and the skinjob that was offering her a steaming hot cup of lab-grown coffee, "this is horrible, and I was…" Tears were building. She pinched her nose again and sniffled.

The sniffle woke what remained of his humanity. Still crouched like a predator reviewing the city below, a breath of society slid its way through his walled mind, and he felt something. Something passed the rage which surrounded the world. That sniffle reminded him of Liz, and his heart broke again. But he would run any memory of her no matter how wrenching it was; he would tear his heart to tiny fleshy bits if even a glint of that memory that was not totally stained with blackness, hate, and dripping blood.

He vaulted off the window space, sailing inches from the ceiling, and flipped to the floor next to Al. Startled, she lost her burning coffee into her lap as she almost fell to the fake cedar laminate.

"Holy Mother!" she shrieked, brushing her pants off. "Son of a bitch! Miguel, what are they giving you?"

Grabbing her arm to steady her, he looked her over, the sister image of Liz. Not Liz, but a blood connection, then he stepped back. "Sorry, I completed my review of the city. Well, from this angle, I mean," he said. "They have not given me anything past typical medical solutions; however, I have been stretching. Though, I think the neural bypass has fully healed to my spine, and my dexterity has vastly improved."

He thought that would answer her questions and then picked up her cup to refill it.

Al's fingers fluttered along her waistband, found it, then

pressed the button. The brown corduroy pants fluffed, extending each thread filament, and a sudden rush of air burst over her legs. She bounced around, pulling each leg to her chest until it was dry. Elizabeth would have made fun of her for dancing in a hospital room. She accepted the cup eyeing him for any more extravagant gymnastic displays, then settle back into the chair, which also air-dried itself. The hospital bed was wonderful, she wondered how the air suspension felt on skin, and the coffee was the best thing since the first breath this morning. He caught a donut that she slung his way.

"Thank you. I, too, skipped breakfast. Their food is not to my liking." He fingered the air in a circle; she assumed he meant the hospital, reminding her of his particular gastronomy tastes. Elizabeth raved about his meals, natural meals, which he touched, cooked, and seasoned by hand. Al thought it was strange; maybe an odd fetish. Perhaps she will ask him later.

"When do you get out?" she wondered through a mouthful of a faux-blueberry cake donut. Absolutely zero food matter plus no calories, perfect B-fast treat.

"Tomorrow morning, ten. I will be walking to the pod station, then home," he explained, then it hit him again. Home was not a place, not where you leave your things, but, really, a relationship built with others, with his wife. Now, he had only a small box where she bled to death. The glazed caught in his throat. "Perhaps, I will speak with Residential Services first," he stammered.

The gloom was taking her over too, but she willed it back. Not today, perhaps, later, when she was alone, but not now. The blackness lifted, and she could breathe again. "Want me to pick you up? You can see what an Argus is really like, anti-gav magball, lights, and sirens, the whole bit," she ventured, hoping and not hoping that he would bite.

"No, I think the walk will help." He looked to the window. "I need to be in the air, with other people."

"Ok, let me know if you change your mind," she demurred, "I'm off all afternoon, so I'm here," raising her hands to the room as if it was an amusement park. Guilt hung over her; she hoped that he would send her away or blame the police or maybe himself, but, no, he won't, not externally. All he wanted were answers, and Jean-Martin Charcot Medical Tower, in their grotesque wisdom, limited his stream searches, basically locking him in his own mind. As they called it, mental transition to a positive way of thought, some type of meditation, which was truly and utterly bullocks.

So, she knew the questions were coming, with answers that she could not share. Questions about law enforcement case sensitive information and multi-agency intelligence. Things that she should not speak about outside of a sensitive compartmented information facility with no scanners and heavily vetted personnel. Things that would cost her the job.

"You know what I want to know," he conceded. She raised an eyebrow, sneering as the tension built in her shoulders.

Having been trained in psychoanalytical interrogation techniques for decades, she knew that her mannerisms were natural for a woman who just lost her single sister and who is offering a helping hand to a distraught brother-in-law. But, she worked to tightly control each movement and breath. He gave her a quizzical look, peaking through the pretext to her private thoughts.

She had her nerve patches renewed last year; now, with the second olfactory nexus perched on the top of her throat, she could hear a suspect's heartbeat through her fingertips. She would be able to read a suspect, any suspect. Maybe she is more overtaxed than she thought. Sleep was hard to come by, and she had only clocked fourteen in the last ninety-six hours. The entire city had an average of thirty actual homicides and 4,000 virtual "deaths" per month, low considering the mass of people huddled together. Chief Inquisitor Griest, with his chewed bubblegum face, insisted on publicly flaunting those numbers. Those numbers, the quota, were for the Skytown bubs, who never saw Mid or Undertown. Their custom crafted shoes would burst into flame if they ever touched the lower Levels. These bubs were constantly swarmed with stern-faced armed bodyguards and rambunctious security artificial intelligence programs that run around on the virtual back-side, snipping, and clearing digital paths for the entourage. If Skytowners wandered the disheveled and begrimed parts of Undertown, the places where people IR tagged entire streets and public defecation would smear your boots, they would, if quick enough, find stinking dead bodies with the bioForges re-moved, then resold, before the city itself begins to digest the remain into its core. So, the thirty homs and 4,000 VDs was a figure, only a figure. In her head, the lingering Undertown kaleidoscope brought up one image: a snake eating its own tail airbrushed on a center column in a lower-Level neighbor-hood. The kind of neighborhood where families go to die from drink or synthetic narcotics made from melted-down robots, a neighborhood with a black smile.

"Yep, I know," she decided that it was best to start it off. "But I need something from you first. About the image that they put on your wall."

As he heard the question, he stopped, looked to the ceil-ing as his face changed to one of a man who just watched a mass murder. The ouroboros was forming in the white ceiling tiles, the red spreading out. He knew that it was only in his mind, like a song that continually replays hours after you last heard it: just an illusion, a brutal illusion conjured from his wife's blood.

"Ask," he blurted. Maybe he was reevaluating his thought process, or perhaps, after the hours of thinking, he missed something.

"Umm...Can you draw it?" her hand fishing out her handcom from a pocket inside her raspberry-colored faux leather jacket. She mentally told it to project a white canvass on the closest wall. "The picture will help me," she said dryly, dropping the donut.

He looked like a man who found his firstborn's limb body; sadness and shock pulling the strength away. Now, with the full acceptance of drawing the killer's message, he can embrace the coming agony with all hope gone. It seemed to drip from him, washing out all other emotions leaving him blank. She, his sister-in-law, had asked him to replicate the man's painting in blood, the monster's painting. The image was flicked and slathered to his wall as his wife's heart pumped it last. Chills ran down his arms, prickling his back. The media was her blood sounded in his ears. The warm red pool ran toward his face, threatening to drown him...with his beautiful wife's blood. Rage boiled in him for a moment, then subsided as if the flaming coal was flash frozen. An icy chill spread through his body, down from his focused eyes to his toes.

'Learn,' he thought, 'Learn.'

"Crimson, finger point," he told the machine, and he began to draw, still imagining he was coating the wall with her blood. In his mind, it was still dripping.

The crudely drawn snake circled, jutting forward its fangs, blood falling from a roughly drawn tail. Banda knew this symbol, the ouroboros. It had various meanings from Egypt to Rome, from representing a deity to the world's cyclical nature. In alchemy, it was used to describe the duality; the snake's head was black, while the tail was white, symbolizing all, no matter how different, remains one. It was linked with the philosopher's stone, a material that could turn base substances into riches and rejuvenate men to immortality.

Banda's forehead crinkled.

'Odd to use it at a murder,' logic told him, but the other token on the wall showed the scene's irony. A hammer depicted in fresh blood was within the circle of the snake. Banda was thankful for his Uni education; otherwise, he would only see an antique tool used to smash nails. The three-foot-wide hammer was drawn to summon the power of the Norse God of Thunder, so it can guard the community's well-being. It is a weapon of destruction and rebirth, tying people to the rule of law. Supposedly.

"Was this an act of defense or protection? And who is being protected?" he asked himself as he flipped through virtual files.

The apartment was sealed after the forensics team cleared out; a holo was taken, all the AI data was stored, and the body was taken to HQ. All cleaned up, nice and neat. Even the nano-walls and floors will have absorbed the last leavings of the dead so that it can be converted into a new carpet or the inner lining of a generated coffee cup. This is his last look at the actual defamation of the real carnage that was burned into Mr. Saxon's memory while he bled out with a knife stuck in his spine. The suspects took control over the entire apartment's AI, washing away any electronic recall with a virtual brush.

Even so, Banda knew the who and the why.

Zuby, a haggard semi-woman sporting shark teeth with spectacular green eyes, and Jonas, last name unknown, the leader of the Draugers, a man of massive charisma and muscles that could crush a pod's hull. Then the why was simple, plain old-fashioned revenge because Elizabeth insulted Zuby.

'Easy and simple. Probably not,' he thought with a deep huff of chemically scented air as a headache started rolling.

As a detective in the Emerging Criminal Enterprises unit, the typical motivations were time-tested and universal.

The main three were always money, sex, and revenge, and those are really prestige and power. The power of a gargantuan ill-tempered man, who finds it easier to crack a neck than to form a proper sentence, can feel safe and secure because behind it all, past the criminal record, the tough talk, and the blood-soaked murders, he is just a neglected child. His actions, whether judged as good or bad, were motivated by his need for self-aggrandizement.

In his judgment, this case was the same as all the others, punks trying to feel special.

One thing stuck out, troubling the detective. The who and why were checked off, but this is the highest Level, so a new why. Housing complexes just spitting distance from sea Level have gangs of all sorts, from just taggers to well-trained hitmen, but no groups venture to show their presence at this altitude. The evidence connected Zuby to two murders, both in Midtown. The petty gangs vanished like smoke above Level 200, seeking the perceived cover of the poorer masses.

And homicide involved the crime prince.

Other than the late assistant inquisitor, none have any known connection to the Draugers. At this Level, the gang only roamed police reports and intel briefings. Of course, the web of links to criminal activity could have reached the journalist, though his apartment showed that the closest he got to a breach of the law was spitting his gum on the street.

Roaming over the omission of facts from the case, he activated his HUD and mentally drafted a carefully worded message to all ECE units. Report any wrongdoing, illegal or not, amoral or not, where the symbol was seen. The stream coder virtually flipped open, and he created a net crawler to scour through any non-connected CCTV pipes and communal media. He crafted two duplicate versions; one searched the filthy section of net-life, out there with the quantum pervs and flaying hitchhikers, while the other was sent to LAMPS as a request for information with an official suspense date. He hoped the green receiving light should start blinking soon.

Anything with the self-cannibalized snake, along with a location and timetable, should be captured. He knew that the Undertown predators were rising, and he needed to understand why they thought they could enter his part of town. In a week or so, the new security protocols would increase police power, and people like Zuby should be feeling nervous. But high-Level killings are not the actions of a nervous suspect. There were the actions of someone who was emboldened, someone who is testing their wings. As his HUD closed, his vision refocused, and he found a spot of gore. It was black and brown, the color of a lousy sausage, leaching into the gray wall, waiting to be fully recycled.

"Heading out, sir," the last of the evidence team said. "Have a good day." Banda waved a hand at the air, not seeing the tech, only nodding.

"Sure...a good day," he muttered, then checked the collection process.

'AI current assigned occupant Saxon reactivated, Aliquam code Organic material and evidence collected, status cleared.'

"Good afternoon, Detective," the apartment's electronic mind chimed.

'Have a good day,' he thought; his mind kept repeating the phrase.

"AI, begin recycling and cleaning process," he said, walking to the portal, hanging his head low.

Black elements spread up from the floor, reaching up like ebony vines, searching for the dried brown blood. At contact, the blood began to liquefy; the black tendrils merged with the remaining dead platelets, plasma formed in a thin white veil over the surface. The entire gory painting, or what Drauger thought was an expression of art, faded into the wall filling up the hoppers for the next chair or dust mat. As Banda's overcoat incased his shoulders, he heard a low whine as the apartment's AI continued to clean by destroying, removing any mess left from the living and the dead.

CHAPTER 13

Deep behind the Jersey-York's mountains of nanotubes and neo metal and glass lay the Downtown Express. It laid buried under the towers that sprang taller than Everest, snaking from the continent's largest mega-city out to the others, carving underground burrows to keep the world moving forward. A vast web of vacuumed sealed tubes connected the cities with pods ready to ship off anyone permitted to travel past the two-hundred-kilometer line to the ever-expanding forests and plains. The land was clearly divided from human constructs to the acts of nature. The metallic black foothills grew over the land into the mountains of the last ten cities, but between these civilized anthills, the world bloomed from the Canadian snow-covered angelic forests to the Los Angeles desert out to Egdewatertown on the old lake. Downtown Express could transport a multi-city citizen from JYC to the inland sea of Sacramento Bay in two hours, time enough to catch some nice salmon and return for dinner. The massive aquafarm stretches across half of what once was called the state of California before the fires charred it, then the oceans took the rest. Along with these cities stands Seattle, the crowning jewel of the Pacific Triumvirate.

The Vihaan Basak Transit Line split from JYC to the flat mass of Kansas City, the agricultural colossus, or the industrial Cleveland with its sprawling recycling centers. One could roll into the arid San Antonio southern military compounds from the mainline, all cloaked in military camouflage for an extra fee. Second to JYC seaport in size is Jacksonville, dotted with hundreds of small islands and some of its history beneath the waves. A hub for the arg-settlements in the Southeast is Atlanta, which now reaches a height over Mount Mitchell, raising thousands of feet over the city that reduced to ashes in an ancient civil war. Shreveport is the Gulf of Mexico marine and farming hub and, to the nation's delight, retained Madres Gras after New Orlean surrendered to the dark waters of the Gulf.

Once, he thought about visiting these places that seemed so foreign, but Augustine had never been able to break through the JYC crust. He plodded through unexpecting passengers at the Downtown Vihaan Basak Transit lodge, occasionally raising eyes to find an attractive lady, but thoughts centered on finding a drink. The coaches, even privately booked, were covered in vacation decals of the wondrous and alluring ten cities, vomiting color everywhere. Smiles of partners holding hands silhouetted against the Sacramento Bay under the setting sun or treks along the old protective wall incircling Atlanta were plastered over the walls, floors, and ceilings.

He popped an Incitento pill, chewed it, then looked around. Hate filled his world as he wandered the station, the dank tunnels under the bright shining city stank of humanity and its filthiness. He felt inhuman under the orange lights that colored the larger hall. Overhead, modified vines gripped the ceiling shining brightly from strange glowing flowers.

'I'm scurrying through roots,' he thought, disgusted, 'Maybe I am a rat.'

He had seen those before. Small, dirty, and foul creatures lusting only for themselves, forgetting all others.

'Yes, a rat.'

Incitmento infused his body, arching electricity from nerve to nerve. His pupils dilated, and his skin flushed. The glowing vines spread above him and, with their wriggling light, ignited each crack in the ancient cement. Others scurried too, likely rats disguised as people, battering him to the hall's corner. As he looked at the bustling mob, he noticed that some faces were changing. Elongated noses and buck teeth were becoming more prominent, but he knew it was the drug.

'I'm stuck like a mad rat, though the diseased creatures never entered these grand halls even before the Great Dying,' he thought as he gazed up to the high expanse of ivory arches and stone-mimic buttresses. The main aorta of the line joined here, pumping the blood of the city. Cables of white nano-wire twisted above, continually rearranging and sprouting glowing filaments into the air. One Ph.D. architecture light studies student spent four years tracking the filaments' movements and found no discernible pattern; it was just another JYC mystery. The AI that timed the coaches and Basak Lines, coordinated the water devisor, and the food pastes directed the art at random. The lighting structure just...moved.

He wished he could move. The floors quartz tiles sparkled up to Augustine's eyes, blinding him. Not feeling his feet, Augustine had sauntered past the flurry of passengers to the center of the Basak hall, obsessed with the glowing structure as it spun. The narcotics madness floated around him like a cloud that might infect passersby. Like an organic flock, the lines of passengers avoided the damaged cell, plotting on, consumed with their HUDs, gripping someone's hand, holding a child; anything to avoid the crazy man. He collapsed into a bench and watched the rats with their dull looks and pointless fashion decisions. They carried on while his eyes darted over them. In his mind, his body melded into the seat, becoming one with the station. He was a god among the rats.

He streamed Mallory. She answered with a raspy voice as she was ending the three days of persistent intoxication. "Augustine of Hippo, what can I serve you for?" she said as if she was dreaming. Perhaps she was, her detachment from the material world was something a monk would strive for, and the amusement park in her mind was all she needed.

"I want to see your lab," he grunted.

"Fine, brother o mine. Two hours, Crown Heights, Level 547. I will send the direction once I'm on the way."

Augustine grunted and sniffed. The drug load was wearing off. "I need an education."

"Sure, sure. I hear ya, but first, redire ad gratiam," she murmured, then slurped a drink, thinking that she will need to arrange for a new liver in the next few months.

"Huh?" he asked. Maybe the Incitmento still pulsed in his blood.

"Latin, ass-hat. Return the favor," she jeered, "I will tell you when I want you to know. Just be there, you are taking my precious time. And it is indeed precious."

He heard the click, and the image faded from his vision, leaving two fat ladies bustling toward a leaving train, the amble bodies barely covered by the tourist garb. Each was huffing gulps of breath as sweat pouring down their faces onto the matching disgustingly mauve thin muumuu dresses.

'Rats,' he thought, 'all rats.'

CHAPTER 14

The symbol was complete. An ache ran through him as he imagined that the red was dripping, staining the wall. He chose red out of all the colors to represent his dead wife's blood, to truly show Al that this was extraordinarily painful. Something was lurking in his head past the genius and aloofness, something predatory with sharp claws and digging teeth. Alcippe had seen it before. A man lost his daughter to insanity after he found her locking in a virtual grease house, inversely hanging from a ceiling fan along with other young girls. The father attacked the suspect in court. His other children were there and had to watch as their grieving father was pulsed until he was a limp puddle on the floor. The suspect, a thin man with a wolfish face, smiled as the case was dismissed due to lack of witnesses. Of course, even the electronic AI-Mag commented that the lack of witnesses was that they were all now driven batty from the crime itself.

Years, maybe 34 years ago, Al responded to a terroristic threat call at a high-end apartment complex in the 900 Level, and all the occupants were aiming at the 1000 Level soon. The wealth and perceived influence clogged the windpipe of young officers. Typically, the AI Apt summons private security to escort the dispatched Blueman to the victim's residence away from any prying eyes. The victim met them at the portal shaking, and her white night shawl was drenched in blood. The suspect had flayed her dogs and nailed their pieces to the main bedroom's ceiling with hairpins. Al interviewed the suspect who held magically refined hate for the other because she stole her husband. The suspect seemed to expel blackness and loathing into the air like a tree shedding its leaves. Al had seen this at all Levels, from the mad screeching to the low burn of decades-long plans of vengeance.

Something else stirred in Miguel. She will find it, but she will answer his questions without helping to push him off the razor's edge of sanity. Her HUD captured the image on the nano-wall, which was drawn with such carefulness and exactitude, even the scarlet scales were seen in faint red wisps. She assumed that Miguel had memorized the ghastly symbol while watching life leave his wife's face.

"Ok, the gang," she spat, knowing this answer was coming, "They were once a powerful force donkey's years ago back during the reclamation troubles."

He nodded, face unreadable as he settled into the window seat. "Numbers, ideology, and the greatest threat to an individual and the city?" he queried.

'Maybe he is recording and cross-referencing,' she wondered.

"Is your HUD up?" she asked, concerned that a freedom of information request could have her name on it.

"No," he said, touching his temple with a finger, "only my human mind."

"Yeah, ok, then. The Draugers have about 300 members that I know of, and they are basically petty criminals in Under-town. They just put knuck to people for exploitation and theft."

"The threat? Mainly physical?" His calm and steady gaze made her uncomfortable, like a hawk reviewing his hunting ground.

She swallowed. "Yes, just the knuck. Kind of like the old Mafioso groups, each smaller clique paying up to the main boss. Down in the Under, smaller groups divide Levels and prey on the people; then, the Taxman collects payments or offerings up to the Drauger, like local leaders. Years ago, over one hundred, there were ten Draugers, now there is only one. He is called Jonas, no last name." The immensity of this conversation and factors of future actions concerned her as she saw Miguel's face change. He seemed focused. They were the enemy, the adversary, and they must fall.

'Banda could and should take me off the case. Well, in both cases, the throat ripped journalist, and the throat ripped inquisitor,' she thought, tears pooling in her eyes.

Her talented, wonderful, and amazing sister. Now, she could add another adjective, her dead sister.

She felt something warm on her cheek and brushed it away, then her shoulders cracked, folding in as sobs came. Miguel's mouth made an odd, clucking sound. It was unexpected. The void in his spirit was shoved so far down in his decentralized mental palace that it would never see the light again, forever dark. He stuffed it in an iron box wrapped with an ancient chain, so it would sink to where he stored memories of his Grandfather's face and his Grandfather's unfinished scientific work. Lost in his mind, a lock with no key.

He clucked again and realized that he must offer some type of comfort to get his answers from the Bluemen perspective.

"I know that this is hard," he blurted clumsily as he clasped her shoulder. Her shuttering slowed, and she looked up with red eyes, tears streaming down her face. He offered her a tissue.

"Urr....ok," she sniffled. "I got it." She brushed his hand off, stiffening. Miguel's face retained its mono-focus, and she saw no movement. 'Severely psychotically damaged,' she thought, and part of her heart cracked.

After a deep inhale and a forceful breath, she started, "Jonas is the current leader, and some say that he was part of the Rising Tide Rebellion in 2,568. After that many years, he has likely been restructured in some way or another. Illegal genes, of course, but animal and hardware, too. So, the bad guy with a bad body. From your description, he was the guy that stabbed you, and his mate is called Sharkteeth. Her real name is Marrazo Zuby; she has genetically altered teeth, hence the moniker. I'm surprised that he left you alive." Al felt the tears rising and inhaled deeply again. Miguel noticed that she flexed her fingers as her hands flitted around like they were in a dance competition. Stress relief, he suspected.

"Do you wish to pop your fingers or knuckles?" he asked, hoping that she could concentrate on relaying the facts after she felt more comfortable.

Surprised, she looked at her hands, which froze once Miguel mentioned them, as if embarrassed. Part of her wanted to look at him, but she could not. Afraid that he might see that she was broken and unrepairable, see the unfillable depths in her eyes with his singular focus, she kept her gaze away. His focus was troubling her again; it was too...predatory. She mentally logged on to her LAMPS system, making a mental note to ask the city-wide scanner for 24-hour coverage of Miguel. He was showing symptoms of becoming a danger to others and himself. His razor's edge was sharpening before her, and that blade could slice through concrete. She told herself that she was minimizing any threats by telling him these details. So, he does not wander around lower-Levels, offering a bleeding heart open to puncture.

'Help him so that I can see his point of view,' she thought.

An inner part of her, maybe the ancient amygdala, that could stir up rage, knew that she found the keenest blade for an unbalanced samurai. He would travel on a mission to kill, untrained but highly fixated down to a diamond's edge. Her rivets of pain will be healed into scars by his actions for good or ill.

She knew that he does not care about returning to everyday life or essentially living once the blood has started to flow. Without her, his wife and true connection to the world, who helped him see through all its distractions, he was blank, empty. Now, she was filling him up with all the details that she knew to fill the void, to aim him.

'No,' she thought, 'I'm just helping him to deal with her death. Yes, slightly easing his mind until he can slowly reenter the outside.' Insomnia was washing away her judgment, and she tried to fight it.

She cleared her throat. "He is paid from petty crime by underlings. I think that is what motivates him, not his human-animal tommyrot philosophy."

Miguel stepped to the side, drifting in front of Al's face. He looked straight into Al's eyes, his posture still perfect.

"Philosophy?"

"Oh yeah, you, the science guy, will like this. Ok, so this guy thinks humans were never supposed to build cities or any type of grand civilization. According to CI reports, he says we are all animals and should act like it," she quipped, mimicking clawed hands, "we are all just teeth and claws, the survival of the fittest, blah, blah." She made air quotes, "to return to nature, one must become a predator."

Miguel turned to the window, letting the sunlight warm his face. He thought of the story of the first two Wildlings, of the monstrous creature armed with sharp claws and ravaging teeth that slept at the core of the earth. The Ravin.

"Do all the members feel that way?" he questioned, rubbing his chin. 'Strategic advantage?'

"Most do, some don't. The group is a mixed bag. We have IDed twelve, all with different backgrounds, but most of the others come from Undertown. I can't give you their names; you know that, right?" She wanted to express all that she knew, unload it, and give it to another to remove the weight.

"I know," he affirmed, but his net crawler was bound to her Nadar Forge; it entered through the coffee. She was still sipping it, and the cup kept it hot. The nanos snuck through her stomach lining, simulating hemoglobin, raced to her brain into the elfin Forge implanted behind her ear. The nano cell-simuloid's protein coat accosted passing blood cells like a crude street worker, and the wolf whistle was the hijacking of DNA. Instead of protein production, the cells generate antiferromagnetic skyrmions, a swirling arrangement of atoms to store Miguel's data. Its task was simple: form a direct streamline into the LAMPS through an artificial police Individual Stream Coder (ISC), a backup Nadar Forge resting in his lab for all inventive purposes. Once she activated her HUD to reminder her to issue a track of him, she opened the door. Level 01, Area 01, Manhattan Borough, Neighborhood Officer Dennis Oswald Nut will now have unlimited access to the LAMPS entire system via light cast speed. He thought that the fictitious Officer D.O. Nut was mildly hilarious, though Al will likely break some of his bones once she finds out.

Suppressing a smile, he asked, "Can you tell me where they congregate? Maybe, and HQ Level?" Her base Level mental patterns created a map that he could follow through the system. This question was designed to stimulate her subconscious cognitive tasks as if she was hard lining into the LAMPS with the HUD. The question did the trick. Without answering, she unknowingly executed several processes and a decision tree matrix that would have brought her to the required question and storage to the reply. Unconsciously, she stored the question until it was needed. He made her leg kick out without knocking the knee with a rubber hammer, virtual monosynaptic reflex.

"During the Rising Tide, did he preach his...ideology?" Miguel asked, considering ways to mingle with the unwashed.

Shaking her head, "No, not that I'm aware of, but there is a video still-shot of him next to Clarence Tyler before the Atlanta riot. I'm not much in ancient history, but I think that was when Chosewood North American Penitentiary blew up. So, Jonas was a backroom dealer in the shadows."

Miguel had several more questions, if for nothing else, to see the law enforcement's attitude toward the gang or its members, but a metallic voice sounded in his ear.

'Visitor request, Mr. Saxon. Richard Zullem wishes to express his deepest condolences and wishes you the quickest medical recovery,' it chirped.

'Unexpected.'

"Mr. Zullem, the smart son, is in the building and wants to visit," Miguel told Al. Both of their eyes went wide. "This is unexpected."

Al shot up and gathered her things. "I'm out."

"What? Why? I thought you might want to meet the new leader of security?"

She wrinkled her nose, shaking her head so severely that her hair flew in all directions. "No, no way! I'm a Blueman, not my business," she groaned as she flashed her badge. "Like I said, I'm out. Can I drop by your place later?"

'Thoroughly unexpected,' Miguel thought. 'Visitor request accepted,' his thought reached out to the AI.

"I understand," Miguel demurred. She placed the coffee cup in the recycling sink and watched it dissolve when an electronically simulated knock barked from the embedded speakers.

"Dammit!" Al cursed, subconsciously back herself into a corner.

Miguel summoned his calmest smile and told the portal to open.

Richard Zellum walked through with a smile crafted for only those in bereavement, hand extended to Miguel. "Sorry to intrude, Mr. Saxon," He said in a soothing voice. Miguel gripped his hand. "I wanted to express my sorrow for your loss and tell you that Mrs. Saxon was a brilliant public servant." Miguel was stunned as the handshake morphed into a hug. Richard's grip was not too tight or too loose, and his last name's pronunciation was flawless.

"Thank you," Miguel stuttered, still recovering from the hug. Richard left one hand on Miguel's shoulder; he noticed the lack of typical hospital offerings, no flowers, no cards virtual or printed, and no other camped-out occupants: only Detective Alcippe Anagnos, the bereaved sister-in-law.

His free hand shot out from his suit to greet her. "Detective Anagnos," the smile brightened, "I'm, also, sorry for what you, both," his eyes shot between the two, "are going through. Hope that you two can find some comfort." His HUD was active over his left eyes, organizing stream messages and drafting his board meeting notes, scheduled for four-thirty.

Al returned his grip twice as hard, then pulled away, eyeing Miguel like he was a rattlesnake.

Miguel watched Richard's staff; a half dozen busy, intense people crowded the portal and hallway, each speaking to someone on the other end of a HUD display; fingers flying over virtual keyboards. Richard caught his gaze and responded with, "Sorry again. Excelsior tasked me with finding them jobs, but so far, they mainly interact with their counterparts in the business. Calling meeting to schedule meetings then talk about more meetings, you know." He mentally told them to wait down the hall with a sharp glance and a harsh gesture.

"No, I do not know," Miguel said, but he did know about the corporate way of wasting time, "but I understand. Thank you for your concern, Mr. Zellum." Miguel stepped out of his grasp and sat on the anti-gav bed. A flickering above Richard caught his attention; he disengaged from the conversation to stare at it.

"It is the new HummingCam," Al told him, her eyes following it, too. "It is a bio-reflective integrated camera system. Basically, a twelve-point fovea video records line-drived to the stream. Kinda rude and kinda violates several patient privacy laws."

"Oh, I'm so sorry," Richard said, embarrassment flushing his face, "I forgot that it was up there." He offered an open hand up, and a compact wafer smaller than his pinkie nail drifted down, settled in his palm, then rolled into a white sphere. "Dad, I mean Mr. Zellum, set up a reality stream show about chief executives at the company. My part is to act as a liaison for other chiefs, like robotics, weapons manufacturing and testing, and AI integration and development. But, since you are both here, can you please join me in a few evenings at a city function? Of course, as guests of honor. I will get back to you with the details. It will be a memorial dinner in honor of your wife," both his hands were on their shoulders, "and your sister."

"Her name was Elizabeth Marie Anagnos before I married her," Miguel said with his head hanging. His eyes gimbaled up, holding a fierce fire that could spark with the slightest breath. While Richard was likely unaware, Al saw this hidden threat and neutralized it, though she would rather vomit on Richard's face.

She pushed forward a resistant hand and said, "Yes, of course. Thank you for the honor." Miguel stared at Richard, hoping to melt a hole in Richard's suit that cost three years of Miguel's income.

"Great, great. Thank you, both," Richard said, drumming his fingers over their shoulders. "Ok, sounds wonderful," he caught himself and felt his stomach fall, "I'm sorry, not wonderful, but we want to properly give thanks and show what she has done for the city."

"Thank you," Miguel said, struggling to hold his rage in check. He knew that it was misplaced but could not suffocate it.

The bustle of his entourage prevented the portal from actually closing, and Richard the 5th, son of Excelsior, thanked them again and passed through into the hallway. The last thing that Miguel saw of him beyond his impressive smile was the launching of his HummingCam, which followed him down the hallway, taking videography of one of the most influential people on Earth regardless of any medical limitation, accountability, or privacy.

Miguel's jaw ached; he touched his chin, then realized that he was gritting so hard that furrows wrinkled his forehead and feral lines arched across his nose. He needed to remind himself to breathe again.

CHAPTER 15

As she walked in, Mrs. Lesnik dismissed the armed security FAUN from her atrium, its eight legs silently scissoring to the storage vault. While it was a gift from Ex, disgust was the only thing she felt for it.

'Typical human reaction to something with too many legs,' she thought, 'Hell, half the centers were full-on people who wanted to pull the machine's guts out.' It was after six, and the city sim-lights dimmed. Through the city shield, she could barely glance at the sun as it was wreathed in shimmering clouds on the western horizon. She dropped her bag on the archaic cherry wood table, one of the few items that were not formed from the nanosets, that and the Egyptian cotton sheets. Another gift from Ex was being dissolved in the bin; the rifle's polish of the wood and the shine of the gunmetal were almost totally gone.

'Horrid man,' she thought, 'Now, Richard, I can work with. He has potential. He can work with people, my people, the people of the ground.'

She fiddled through her desk until she found the trap door under the top drawer. She knew it was decadent to have drawers for folders of sym-paper, but why not. Her work was essential, and, sometimes, a handheld document felt better than an internal projection broadcast into the occipital lobe of the brain for only her mind to see. Out of the vast collection of things in her house, some fantastic or expensive, the desk was natural and real, much more than a place to hold papers or coffee cups. The finest artisans crafted the massive piece from the last surviving wooden paneling of the Green Drawing Room of Windsor Castle. Those molded boards once supported the bloated weight of the world's aristocracy and even King Marlborough before he suicidally invaded the Deutschland Empire in 2,351. It creaked as her small weight pressed into the wood, which was once the floorboards of the people who burn the forests and belched fossils into the air, made a microscopic giggle churn deep within her. The giggle became a gurgle. It popped up from her belly, almost escaped, then she gathered herself, and only the smallest leer crossed her plain face. She knelt, finding the compartment just small enough to hold her outstretched palm. The door popped open, and her hand entered, searching. It was there, she hummed to herself. The container was there. Pulling it out with relish, she quickly unscrewed the cap, opening the simple white bioplastic pill bottle.

Only two left,' she thought. One of the small purple doses found its way into her fingers, then into her mouth. Clear Logic Chaos diffused on her tongue, sending billions of mode-altering nanos and chemicals into her blood.

She thought she could hear her pupils dilate with a rush.

Energy swam from her heart through her limbs then back to her brain. Several brands offer something legal, providing the same rush, but none could show the joyous way of what a true drug could be, the illegality of a tested mind. In a city that changed the weather due to its enormity and casting miles of shadows, ran by a mass of AIs and populated by robotics, people live like termites in a vast hall, scratching out what life had to offer. All powering along from one take to the next. People always search for angles.

"Clear thinking has come, logic in thought, and chaos in application," was what sold her. At the center, she had seen every kind of intoxicating substance, from the ancient white powder to the newest Nadar Forge adapter, synthesizing the narcotics of choice from the chemicals drifting in the air. With the tech to destroy the world, also brought real recreation to all drugs, with no downside; one could snort a saltshaker of cocaine and be ready for work the next day. However, the availability of the chemicals physiologically affected those of weak mind and impure body. That is what she told the slugs that thought they were her betters, mainly to raise funds.

The addiction crisis of Undertown, the upper-crust's word, could be reduced to a simple deduction. The government of Jersey-York will support you and your family if you are cursed with a reproduction cert, in all circumstances. Uni income buys the citizens, food, shelters, and stream casts straight into your Forge. So, a family can be dry, fat, and happy with little personal investment. With an average lifespan reaching almost 300, the boredom slowly tracks you like an assassin, lurking in the shadows when you gear up your virtual Nova hand bolts, getting ready to battle an equally useless neighbor in the new cast: UN Dragoons: US Branch. Behind each simple repetition of endless days, it waits. City infrastructure allows the Settled, one residential movement among the buttresses once every ten years. The betters from Skytown called them the Settled, as they settled in the perceived dirt, like scornful parents commenting on mentally disabled children.

The citizen's plight: moving to a new neighborhood takes a decade, minimal employment is offered, low skill manufacturing when only a human hand can force two things together or stirring noodles, and, now, human life has slowed to a sloth's pace. Chemical suppliers fill the void and soothe the bitter taste of 28th-century life. Of course, the government will fit the bill. Many dejected persons with fragile hair, empty eyes, and taut skin are over one hundred years old, not due to age, but of the ever-present desire to chemically altered their own point of view, to be free of boredom. Unlike the poet Hobbs, her deduction is this; life is indeed solitary, easy, refined, and too, too long.

She came to this understanding after seeing an old man, close to three epochs, as he shuffled into a sea-Level center outside the city, escaping a one hundred and fifteen-degree day last August. Sweat soaked him like he just exited a swimming pool; his socks left wet patches on the floor as he stumbled along. He moved like an old man should, slow and tired, each step carefully considered. Approaching with an outstretched hand holding a globe of water, she saw that while his dingy shirt and ripped shorts were wet, his face was bone dry. His body had released all his water, cells were popped. She stopped and watched him, expecting him to die as under her eyes. His teeth cracked the water globe, sucking it dry, drier than his skin. Then he smiled with open, cracked teeth. His tongue was withered, a dead lizard in a desert. Like a tortoise, he meandered across the room to an equally old woman, who was freezing, covering herself with a large blanket, creating a barrier from the outside world. Their eyes locked, but neither face showed any recognition. He sat next to the bundled woman and tentatively extended a hand down by his side, brushing against her filthy blanket. In response, her hand shed the cloak like a snake and drop something in his waiting palm.

One blue tablet.

Niva was not sure how he gulped it down his barren throat, but he did, then stood. As he passed her on his way out, he smiled again, his eyes shined with life; his feet made wet plops until he reached the door. The portal opened, and she could still see him when he entered the street. Through the transparent nano slate, she saw him stand under the hellish sun, baring his face to the sky. The medics said that his heart stopped once he left the center; he was physically dead once his feet hit the scorching gravel outside. What she thought was an old man cursing the sun was, in reality, the last act of an already dead man. He stared into nothingness because he was already gone. His last act was to take the pill. He did it without a heartbeat and no blood flowing to that smile. Humans were not meant to live like termites in a mechanical crust nor cut three centuries into the life's belt, each more meaningless than the last.

That night she watched the old woman and sat next to her, trying desperately to ignore the stench of the unwashed. The hag never looked at her, just stared blankly off to what Niva imagined was a magical mystery land. Niva's hand crept down, offering a greedy palm. One pill filled it. That night changed her life, and the hidden layer of life unfolded before her. The woman whispered, "Bio-nihilism." Niva became a nihilist that night, or perhaps she always believed that the meaninglessness of her life was the actuality of its meaning.

She reached into the trap door again and took the last pill; two bursts of nano merged in her blood. Each set of chemical nanos brought the recipient a typical type of euphoric high but, while taken together, was something else, hence the illegality. Feeding off her Forge and its stream connections, the infinitesimal robots swirling in her blood formed a circuit to all the other stream-based devices, birthing the links a new life, unfolding just to her. Every movement of the nano-wall echoed with an agitation symphony blasting into her unheeded. More than reading and viewed elements on her stream, she was them down to her cells. As transports whizzed across the streets outside and she felt the tiny ferromagnet balls whirring together, churning beneath the passengers, speeding them along. She was with them, churning, pushing them. She spun forward, then back as small black balls. Even the security FAUN became her, and she it. She writhed on its legs and internal workings, losing herself and embracing the meaningless.

'Wall hum activate,' she thought, but she may have just willed it. The walls began to vibrate, pulsing to a pre-set tune. She was the house now, and she exhaled in wonder, waiting for the emotional triggers to assault her; the best part. Her eyes were open, but her vision blanked out for a moment. 'Maybe a heavy mag-lev passed disturbing the elect-field,' she thought. Once the lights returned, she expanded herself to the street with a deep breath.

The humming stopped, and she was back in her body; her nerves expected the rush of new sensations were now raw and painful. Concentrating closed off the pain, but her mental state withdrew into her fingers and toes, drawing back into her stomach. Her vision faded, narrowing to one black spot, and all hearing outside her brain stopped. No heartbeat, no hiss of breathing, and no humming.

"Hello," a voice said within her head. "Please be calm, or I return the pain." Chills worked into her spine, and she wanted to scream, but her voice closed off as if her vocal cords were removed. Losing all control over her body, she flopped over and struck her head on the desk, but she felt nothing.

The young voice with a slight Chinese accent told her that her body would be cared for by the FAUN, and if she feels that she is being moved, lifted from the floor, that would be some of FAUN's legs positioning her to prevent harm.

"Now, I will tell you a few things. These things are important, and you must remember them. Think of me as your home. Here, this place. Ok, now you direct a message to me," Ru said, thinking carefully about holding back his accent. Of course, his physical presence left hours ago. Still, Cutmen rules dictate that one must wholly minimize any personal identifying elements, whether cutting off a tattoo or removing an accent. One training Enswell bathed himself in steam to remove Yakuza tattoos that painted his body. He could have gone to a dermal printer, and the offending cells would have been vaporized, but each Enswell must remove all mark through his own means.

Those are the rules of the three.

After his skin blistered and fell to the ground in swollen, purple layers, he was reprinted. The dermal printer took three hours to apply his new skin, and it took twenty-four to cleanse the burnt flesh smell from the room. Ru always admired that Enswell.

Niva flashed at him, "Why?" then, "Take anything you want and leave," followed by a, "Please don't hurt me."

"Calm yourself. You will enter shock, and then I will be forced to turn you off. Please respond with either a yes or a no," his voice responded straight into her brain. Her heartbeat began to slow, maybe due to the voice's calming tone, but more likely, because of the soothing neural transmitters flooding her blood.

'It is like sleep,' she thought, considering the darkness around her, 'the real emptiness that I always wanted.'

Other than not being able to see herself, her hands and legs, it was as if she was flooded with blackness. She moved her jaw, hoping to hear her teeth clicking against each other, but the only thing she heard was the voice. Then, calmness took her.

"Ok, I'm here; you have me. Please tell me what I need to know," she told the man hiding in her head. Tears ran down her blank face, dripping to the FAUN's shiny legs. It moved her to her bed, gently nestling her body on the covers. Her head rested on a pillow, the tears pooled in her eyes. It was pro-grammed with sensors that mimic human nerves, so it had such control that it could play with a baby until the child laughed and giggled, while a quick jab with the same spiny limb could crush through a wall.

"Simple, Mrs. Lesnik. The security proposal will pass with your vote," Ru streamed to her, "You will vote for it, and, if not, these nanos will reform your internal circuits trapping you in here. In this…emptiness. Your drug use captured you, not me. If you could have refrained from the second pill, then you would be happily high, sitting by your desk and virtually riding your electronics."

She gritted what she imagined were her teeth, and pulled back into her command frame of mind, mentally shouting, "I can do what I want in MY House! You should not be here! Get out!" She thought that her body was shivering with anger as her mind was. Her personality, the intrinsic connection between body and mind, was fighting back, returning some body movement. Her body was vaguely jerking on the bed, though only the FAUN could notice. Her pulse had quickened again to the point of inefficiency. Her body's image was depicted on Ru's HUD, and sections were turning from orange to red, as in traffic lights, red means stop, a warning because shock might set in.

Ru interlock with her using the security drone began to weaken, his mental code hustle quickly reorganized the proper stabilization keys into her Forge, lacing his way back into her. Enswells were taught to code into a drug-fueled mind like picking a constantly changing lock; spring-loaded tumblers bouncing back every second, then finding the correct set of picks until it opens freely.

He must not have practiced enough; she was changing too rapidly.

"Please, Mrs. Lesnik. If you rachet, then you rachet. I just caught you, and you don't want to take it there," irritation was growing, and he struggled to shoo it away. He slipped back into local vernacular. Mental speak was always the hardest to keep clean, free of psychological interruption from one's own mind. In stressful situations, the ones with the most bitting teeth, emotions would buildup around the walls of one's self, only to spill over when least expected. In former education, a simple landman, the ones on the street, was taught to control it by using the easiest elementary orders, call a meal by number, call a particular pod off the track. Violence, both mental and physical, was his means of education. The extra load of bone-building nano-med osteoblasts floating around his fingers reminded him of his training.

His trick was to imagine that he was drowning. The urge to breathe only to be met by a cold liquid rush, then a sudden clamp on your windpipe as it slams shut, and all you can hear is your blood whirring past. He loaded that cycle in from a former business partner after the Cutmen were finished with him.

'Yes, that clears the head,' he thought, remembering the wet man slumped on the dock.

"Listen to this, Mrs. Lesnik," his calm returning, "Jersey-York City Council and all other JYC functions will support the new security proposals. You will do the same. Your second delightful pill has tricked your Human Augmented System by entering your skeleton. And there it will remain until I permit it to recycle out."

Her mind was all that she was now. She pulled it in like a bow and aimed it only on the voice that had skipped her occipital lobe, funneling into her frontal cortex.

A knife was pulled.

Once, she was threatened with a knife. She was young and stupid, hand-ups like she was in an ancient western from the flicks. She thought they were called flicks but was not sure. The kid was younger than her, but murder and hunger were in his eyes, calling her scream, possibly inviting her blood to the street. She focused, as she did then; a cry will not help and, in fact, will hurt. That SeaLevel punk kid's blade with its sharp death, opening the door to the vast emptiness, was easier than a second in her mental prison cell.

She told herself to speak to the voice just as she did to the kid holding the wobbly knife.

"Ok, I will vote for it. Yes, yes, I will. No problem from me," she sputtered, then collected herself, "How else can I help you? I mean, you have me here." She tightened her concentration, trying to hold away any panic.

Ru knew the trick, but it helped. "Mrs. Lesnik, I know that you will, that is assured. But I'm here more for who you are than what you serve. You are the great community organizer you were born to be, making them feel the way that I wish them to feel. Your community center, addicts, and all will start a campaign to increase security to the city, Level one to the Sky. I have embedded the instructions in a private message that only you can receive. It will be streamed after you wake."

"Ok, I can do that," she replied, thinking how this just got more complicated.

"No, you WILL do that. Now, since that was so easy for us both, here is the hard part. Once you wake, you will call the police to report several murders," he stated, his voice sounded as if he was reading from a prepared statement.

"What?" she puzzled, "No, no, no! No one can know about this." Her imagined arms raised in a virtual shrug. "I have nothing to say."

"Your system is being wiped for all the intoxicants and, in actuality, the FAUN will call for you, but you need to admit to three murders," he responded calmly.

"Again, no. I will NOT TAKE A FALL! How can I vote if I'm arrested?" she yelled, "I will find you, and you will suffer. You will be beaten to death! I know people, I can have it done. I'm the most powerful....." A blinking flash exploded in her head, her mental voice faded.

Once the mental attack wound to a close and she could think again, the voice said, "I'm only a cog in a giant wheel. Many others also serve the wheel, and some other cog will take my place when I'm gone. Do you understand? It is essential that you understand." The voice's cadence was the same, but there was a force in its hasty deliverance.

All the bravado, stress, and threats dampened her mental power; she replied with a simple, "Yes, I understand."

"While you may think that your situation will impede you in some ways, it will not. In fact, it will make you more successful, much more successful," the voice pressured, "Yes, you will be hailed as a hero and harbinger of justice."

She had no idea what he was talking about but wanted it over. "I see," she stammered, "I will alert the Blue. What then?"

The FAUN left her body and traveled to the atrium, rattling on its anti-ferro alloy legs. Its sensors checked the streets and passing traffic. No organics walked by, and the last Argus passed moments ago, marking shift change right on schedule. The time was right, and it always obeyed the time, the mechanical certainty of the automatic number flip from one to the next. It alerted the main portal; the house's AI formed a traditional double door with a mock deep red wooden surface decorated with a silver lion knocker, lined by two tall windows. Ru read of a military alert around the time Europeans settled this continent, some war about taking territory from a foreign owner, or some such, but the line stuck in his head. 'Two if by sea,' was the signal as all the other buildings on this block lacked windows lining the doors. Many only had a refined garden of ferns and hollies bordered by syth-maples. Around the corner, three wild-eyed men huddled. One noticed the change in the façade, then grunted at the others. The leadman, the one with the scars that were not printed over, took the hint and grunted back. They scanned the street, then approached. From their cheap clothing and jumpy manner, Ru knew that they were one or two rungs above petty thieves, closer to Undertown brigands.

Tentacles extended from a hatch under the FAUN's front frame, which magnetically creates a comforting human face out of tiny rolling balls. The polished appendages passed in front of the palm sensor, and the double doors flung open.

Blades sprung from two of the FAUN's insectile limbs as the other six legs skittered it into the corner just beyond the door frame. Two of the men rushed through the doors, stopping in the main living Area, with its mounted tapestries and many couches suggesting that the owner had a subconscious urge to be seen as sophisticated but appears as overly pretentious. As the third man's foot stepped on the atrium's tiles, his head was severed just below the jaw with auto-surgeon accuracy, the blade slicing between the connective tissue of Axis C2 and C3. Blood painted the walls and the FAUN metallic body red. The headless body began to fall with searching arms like it was looking for its removed skull. Before the dead man could complete the fall, one bladed arm caught it in the shoulder, punching into the bone, then the severed head was pierced, pinning the separate parts together again. The FAUN silently held them, preventing a wet thud of both head and body. The machine dropped the body minus head in the corner, then stalked on metal legs to the other men holding the skewered head forward like a talisman.

One man pulled a small flechette blower, ready to send a squadron of exploding darts at the FAUN's blood-spattered metal form. His mind blanked out, and he could not mentally command the weapon; it began to wave violently in his hand. His brother's bloodless face stared blankly back at him, still attached to the blade and blocking the robot as it moved the head around in a jagged pattern. Liquid in the FAUN's internal pneumatic cases were electronically superheated, and its girth expanded faster than the blink of an eye. The blade protruding from the forehead pushed aside the blower gun with a thud of bone on metal, and the dead brother's face slammed into the live brother's eye socket. The last thing that he saw was his brother's blood dripping into his eyes. While seen to be bulky, the FAUN swooped one extended arm under the other man's gaze into his sternum, then pushing its other legs up until the man was speared through. These executions took less than two seconds.

Another mechanical arm raised behind the speared man then broke off the blade with a harsh snap, and one body slid to the floor. The machine told the AI to engaged hyper recycling and covertly remove the last thirty minutes from memory. Spattered blood and assorted viscera melted away on the carpet and the walls, which were molecularly diluted into new materials. The FAUN, still cradling one speared body, returned to the bedroom to monitor the sleeping female organic. Her deep breathing was calm even as the FAUN picked her up and transported her to the living Area with limbs that were unsoiled by bloody remains. One limb reached for the blower, gripped it, and put it in the speared man's hand. AI will alert the police after the weapon is discharged, the FAUN instructed the apartment. The trigger clicked, and an explosion shook the mounted hanging draperies.

Ru thought that they had come to an arrangement.

"Excellent. Now, I will leave you. Please do your part, and all will be well. Management will be pleased, and management is always, I mean, always watching," he told her.

"Thank you for not hurting me. I will vote yes," she insisted, "It will pass." The darkness was changing, but she was not sure if it was the voice's doing. A distant whir echoed in her head, and the darkness was breaking as light leaked through her eyelids. She could not move, but she now had control over her breathing. She took two hard puffs, then snorted the air out through her nostrils in a long blast.

"When will I call the Blue? Where are the victims? Do I need to search for them? Are they outside or in the garden?" she questioned, thinking this was very disturbing and will deter her from some future drug use; it will work out fine. A simple YES vote, and then it was over; all done. She knew that this was Zellum's scheme, but that was fine too. Best not to poke the bear in the eye.

Ru thought for a moment about disclosing her actual circumstances. He decided against revealing anything. "Oh, you will see. Goodbye, and it was a pleasure to meet you," the voice departed. Ru stepped out of the pod-line, decided to walk to his favorite Xian burger spot; he deserved the treat.

Her vision was blurred, the distant whirring was closer now, muffling all sounds, but it was coming back. The first sight was the living room's ceiling flanked by German tapestries mounted on the curved oval walls. Her body was slow to reconnect; only her head was barely moving. She saw blobs with eye movements, then relieved that she was in the main living room. The colored lumps became couches, each rich in color crowned with pillows. Whiffs of something noxious filled her nose, something like melted plastic and burning oil. Due to extensive nerve plexuses in the toes and fingers, they recovered quickly, firing zings into the edges of her limbs then into the brain.

'Sticky and warm,' her mind gurgled. She wondered if she was lying in a pool of her own defecation. Her nose smelled something pungent, sweet, and tangy. Her head could move according to her volition, and it rolled to the right.

The FAUN slumped next to her with its metal abdomen blown inward, strange liquids pooling on the floor. Tiny shrapnel scars marked the metal plates and the wall behind. She pushed with her legs, but her shoes hardly scuffed the shiny tiles. Blood pulsed in her ears, and she noticed a thick salty, and metallic taste. Nerves were now working in overdrive as all the stimuli rushed into her. Her mouth was glued with some syrupy fluid, though she had enough control to spit it out onto the carpet. Before the rug began to digest the liquid, she saw it.

To offset the tiles and walls' colorlessness, she decorated

her space with many colorful items, from the wall hangings, couches, and animal printed carpets. The FAUN had laid her on an eight-foot by six-foot zebra print, pristine since no one had ever trod on it. Clean and slick, often admired by the few guests that she invited.

What flew from her mouth stained the bright white fur with bubbles of red. Her hands reached for her face, and a ten-inch blade fell from her dominant hand with a loud clang. Her face was wet with blood, not hers, but from the three bodies that were splayed around bent unnaturally. The living room was now an abattoir with her in the middle. The sight shocked her body into feeling, and all her muscles pulled in, each seeking to find the right footing to suck in the air. Her lungs felt that she drew in the whole room, and then she screamed. Even the nanos, each functioning just beneath the surface, vibrated from its force. Her blood began to solidify in her veins, and eye capillaries burst as her blood pressure spiked. She screamed until blood flew from her lips, then her nose peppering her crimson.

During an after-incident interview, the first officer said that he heard screams, reminding him of a posting at a horserace. A mechanical accident, when a metal cable was set free, severed a horse between its ribs. Its mouth screamed like a banshee while its severed back half continued to kick as if it was still running in the first place. He sawed off its head with a force bolt, not because the animal's life was over or because it was in horrible pain, only because he needed to end that noise before he stabbed himself in both ears. He could have had a vet tech patch it up with a quick print, so he was written up. That was not the most dreadful part. The worst part was that he could still hear it now.

She screamed like a horse that had been ripped apart, still trying to run in two separate pieces, the report read. The Blueman must have been an equestrian.

CHAPTER 16

Each move pushed him into defense, thinking about his last move, not the next one. Opponent pieces forced him into a fork. Crosshairs covered his king and blotted out the sun over his queen. He needed both pieces, and a little more thought could have saved them. A grave waited for the king or the queen: the leader, the head, or the fighter, the heart.

He made his move; bits of him broke away.

Hospitals weakened something inside him. The last time was after the fire. No family was there to welcome him then, just like now. After the medical discharge, the world shattered, and the pieces floated away, leaving him nothing and empty. He was ready to build a shield of protection and claw his way into the earth; maybe he already had carved his own cave of retreat. He did not need to imagine teeth bared or striking claws; he had seen them, knew the hurt. He was not scared of the world and its hard edges, not anymore. He will build a defense, a hard one, something of bone and enamel, something that bites back.

The release was truly that, a release from the building into the world. No counseling, no paperwork, no checkboxes, or forms, just a quick step out the door, and he was gone. He did not want to wait for Al, she had things to do, and he knew the way. A preprogrammed pod strummed up, and his HUD when active, a green light asked if he was, indeed, he. So, he entered and trolled past the other pods, all sealed in white, traveling eggs in the jagged mountainous city. Manhattan was still, regardless of Area or Level, a peoplescape, though the neon crowds and electric lights did not distract him. He was focused on the one thing that he was sure of, the only thing that was, in his eyes, real. That thing was absence, the loosening of any social bond followed by emptiness and freedom of the lost.

'Breathe,' he thought to himself, 'just breathe.'

All his nerves were fully healed; in fact, they gave him several rounds of muscle stimulants. Joints tested fine, better than fine, reflexes too. Before the change, this dreadful recovery, his routine consisted of waking with syth-coffee, breakfast with...her.

'Breathe, he told himself.

After breakfast, no, eating the morning meal, he told her goodbye.

He sucked in a lungful of air.

The pod took a sharp turn, and a drunken couple slipped into the roadway, all smiles and color. Without knowing why he pulled his head to his chest, doubling over, curling into a fetal position on the pod's white bucket seat. Once, he opened his eyes again, looking through his fingers. All the blood was pumped into his muscles as if a threat was lurking in the shadows. His finger bones throbbed either from his grip's pressure or the lack of blood as he pressed them hard into his face. He tried to string together a chemical process for a new contact, something about engineering and growing faux organic-electrical organs within leather gloves.

'Electric eel as handwear,' he told her. She looked at him with the beautiful knowing face of a woman that loves her husband because he is adorable and idiotic at the same time. He forced himself to loosen his forearms, his hands dropped in his lap like dead fish. The complex manipulation of the interlocking genetic code escaped him now; he could only think of the couple's smiles. Both faces lit up with life and joy, without a care in the world, until a pod smashed them into one red stain on the track. Even the clean mag-track would have the same effect as pitted gravel, tearing them apart wet globule by wet globule, streaking the black magnetically elements of the road into a lane of red viscera. One last look, and they were fine, drunkenly wobbling to somewhere, somewhere better.

"Ok, ok. Whoa...," he stuttered, closing his eyes, this time on purpose, and began to count. His heartbeat returned to normal, and his breathing stabilized. He could not think of her; her world was dead and gone. And he was left behind.

'Destination,' the pod announced as it exited the main traffic flow, slowing at the front of his building. Set in the middle of the block, his building stood, lower than its neighbors, that towered into prime real estate. Its street-facing garden rose to meet visitors, and the sidewalk lit in amber as his feet passed over it, a low flash with every step. The mechanic breeze slightly moved the hanging vines that were festooned by sun-colored flowers, and the thirty-foot-tall trees held their red bloom throughout the year. He knew that the entire scene was all artificially lit, genetically designed to appeal to renters that want to live beyond the city's enclosing walls but still wish for security on the human spaceship. After the greenery, the building was just another piece of architecture hidden under tricks of light and glass curves, only a series of boxes where people slept.

He quickly walked, almost ran, through the garden to the portal door. Vines jerked back before he could snap them. The glass ziggurat towered over him, and he needed to be inside, to be sheltered. With urgency, he thrust out his shaking and moist hand for the DNA entry code.

"Mr. Saxon! I'm so glad to see you," a nasal voice screeched to his right just behind a massive seedling that spilled out leaves that could cover a man. He heard her approaching footsteps, and he knew who she was, the representing officer of the Residential Bureau.

'Not now,' he thought as she swung around the corner

to face him. For such a large woman, she always seemed like she was only renting her body. Her hands were pulled in as if she feared falling off a rollercoaster, her shoulders so tightly scrunched together behind the pink blazer he had trouble seeing how she could breathe. She moved with jerks like a giant bird trapped in a purple pants suit.

"Oh, oh. I'm so sorry for what happened, and I feel for your loss," she blurted, walking quickly, head hastily swinging, surveying the garden for predators that prey on large birds. "But I do need to speak with you. Just for a bit. I'm sorry." An overly long finger jab punctuated each phrase.

Miguel did not move or look at her. He was a man frozen, and he was not sure if the contact with another human would help his flight into insanity or if he was afraid to open the portal and see what was behind the wall, to remove the last block and let the truth shine through.

"Due to the incident, I had the apartment cleared and made ready for you. The Bluemen left it days ago, and it was quite a mess. I handled it," she said, nodding, clearly very proud of herself, "The Residential Bureau called about relocating you to over there." Her long thin finger pointed to a small complex jutting from structural buttress hundreds of feet above, close to the interLevel transport way, that links the two Levels. From the lowest Level, down to the sea and black dirt, up to the Skytown, these interLevels chain the whole city together. Citizens can imagine a new higher Level, a new life maybe after decades of seemingly senseless work or a hundred years of saving the city com checks, but never back to where they were born. Like in an insect castle, these links were called "stairs" but were a series of escalators or pod chutes. He shuttered.

He did not need to move his head; he knew where she was pointing, "Why the stairs?" His face drained of color; his ears were burning. Sharp pain from just behind his earlobe jarred him until he realized that he was pinching it red. His fisted hand fell to hang at his side. She stopped walking, planting her overly long legs, bend her head forward as if she saw a delicious bug scrabbling across the concrete, waiting to gobble it up with a lightning-fast peck from a sharp beak. Her mouth slanted down, and he could read concern swiftly flutter under her features.

"No, no. I stopped that. You will stay here. They thought it was a…gift, because of the, well, the incident. But the place was consigned for only a single person. I thought that was uncouth, maybe in a few months," her pronunciation of "I" was too high, coordinated with a gnarled finger gesturing to the heavens shook him. Her "I," was just her, her motives and judgment. As if she was saving him from the floor of a building popping down from above, without knowing the true pain, not of the stab in the spine, being stapled to the floor, but of finding real emptiness.

'A city of cave dwellers. Stalactites,' he thought, 'we live in a human-made cave, and our structures are the minerals dripping down. We ooze construction.'

"Mr. Saxon, are you well?" she questioned with a snort.

Now he looked at her.

"Ma'am, bird lady in a suit, my apartment was broken into through some unknown means. Your company offers all renters a guarantee regarding security, yes?" he faced her, turning his head at an angle, like a dog deciding if it will pounce teeth bared or play with something fluffy. Her face reddened, wrinkles pinched it like a cold breeze. She tried to stand erect, but her legs and body seem to be printed from separate sets of instructions.

"Well…well. Of course. Of course, but the police said this was an extraordinary case, something new. So please don't concern yourself. Only I can open it; it is keyed to my print now. Well, you are aware of the incident," she offered a thin smile that he knew meant the opposite of the intended effect.

His voice grew louder. "Concern! Broken in to by thugs, bird lady! Control was taken from me; walls moved to THEIR will not mine. No alarm, NO ALARM!" he snapped, spitting each syllable into her face. "Bird lady, my wife was bitten to death, her neck chewed in half, while I was stabbed in the spine! Yes, I'm well aware of that, Bird lady!" His head was still on a slow circulation to the floor, and he was pulling his ear like he was trying to stop the rotation.

Bird lady's face retreated as if she was punched, and she let out a low mown. Like a general cavalry charging into battle, she brought forward her hand, and, like a perfect sword strike, she hit the portal pad. The apartment opened; a burst of cool air washed over him.

Her beaked face closes in on him, and she said with anger, "You are welcome, Mr. Saxon." Then she stocked off, fuming from such outrageous treatment. Antiseptic swirled in the air as he stepped in; he only made it as far as the kitchen bar before his feet locked, unmoving. The room changed; it was consumed with something dark, sealing into every surface and corner. The atmosphere carried the stink of iron, and his eyes blinked uncontrollably. He smelled something that his mind was not ready for under the metal tang, the stench of rot. Black blood coagulated in pools on the floor, stretching across the room. The self-eating snake dripped around the scarlet hammer. Both were still wet, marking the wall in a way that could never be entirely erased.

He knew that it was not there, the walls were clean, and the air was fresh. His mind was betraying him, making him want to penetrate the earth for the comfort of solitude. To retreat. The portal closed, sealing him into the tomb. He could feel the earth pulling his body into itself. Plants moved under the city, breaking away from hundreds of years of slow decay. Roots burst through the floor, rushing to gently grab him as dirt slid over his weary body until he rested in absolute black-ness.

CHAPTER 17

She had not toured her enterprise in weeks, but the sales have increased as the holidays approached. Something about spending time with extended family or narrow family, that is how she thought of it, thin like a blade, often inspired people to numb themselves. She could not be around her mother for more than a few minutes without a little bump up or one down. Besides, her mother was always floating somewhere in her mind, never really here or there. Often forgetting their names, so she saw no harm in it.

The legal intoxicants are the first to move. Customers snapping up synthetically designed alcohol under the pretext that it connected them to their roots. Linking them to somewhere else than JYC, or just the excuse to get drunk, then blame the intoxicant on not enjoying the time with a relative. Of course, in her frame of mind, the enjoyment started once the relatives left. Pills were the next to go. With a quick purchase, you could feel any way you pleased. In fact, a few pills could allow you to steal others' feelings, and those went fast. The standard euphoric and high-energy elements took lots of shelf space, along with the old fashion mellow sense of being high like an ancient beach bum. One brand was actually titled Beach Bum; of course, Mallory did not really know what that meant, but it sold, so it was fine with her.

At the Foil's Tip, the illegal ways sold too, sometimes too well. She liked the illegal one well, enjoyed the balance between total drudgery of modern life and the rapturous lows of the addict. This was a new shop nestled behind a syn-meat buffet called Carnealot Castle. A customer could squeeze past the line of bumkins waiting to fill their bellies with printed haunches and meat encased ribs into the corner of a recently recycled two building join. The tiny triangle of chemical ecstasy.

The hungry queue stood behind the meat craving customer, and the door was waiting for whatever the person wanted. A quick mind scan could identify the lack of experiences and mold a chemical substance to fill what the citizen wished and more. The art of flying was popular, as was slow-motion perception; some people's enjoyments were more exotic. At the grand opening, a party of thirty gathered to Nadar Forge into a slowmo-trip while watching an elegantly dressed man chemically simulate drowning. Every arch of his face and quiver of his limbs was absorbed ten times slower, and the crowds stood there, entranced for minutes after the man completed his trip. He ordered four more pills to use later. This establishment was owned by a Level-01 man, who would never see the façade or travel beyond Level-02. Receiving his identification codes, DNA scan, and banking records only cost a half-credit donation to his virtual hat. Bot-racks monitored the shore proper, while underneath the humans worked.

Carnealot Castle misted the line of hungries with a manufactured cloud of combined scents. Caramelized fat, the smell of heated pans, and blood greeted the customers, all to increase their appetite, but also required vats of an alchemist's array of biochemicals that were delivered to the opposite side of the building. For Mallory, the most enjoyable part of this enterprise was watching Level-1000 youths scrabble by to avoid being crushed by delivery bots as they worked to enter the Foil's Tip shop's dark side. Well-gened kids, but for all, she knew they could be on their 100th print from birth stock, parked privately owned pods blocks away, and looked around waiting for a police spotlight, which, if they were lit up, would be brushed under the metropolitan rug. The joy of selling was not the money; she had that in abundance, or for anything like affinity to the Undertown. No, it was simple, the sports of extreme people watching.

Buying was never a problem; adverse effects of drugs, even the old kind of narcotics, were quickly corrected by a new design; offending molecule out, a slick new molecule added. One could party until their brain melted and bones cracked, and the next day he would only have a slight headache with no lasting damage.

The problem, well, the police's problem, was morale, the esprit de corps of the city. The working class, which rumbled around the city all day and night, must continue to want to work to improve their lives. Basically, buy more things and Level up. Below Level-500, no one cares; they see the illusion of the entire system. Coms do the real work, the world is rebuilding itself after humans screwed it up, and people live in spaceships permanently mounted to the ground.

A vice-Captain's pillow talk taught her the only real things of life.

He looked down from her window, gazing at the city from fifteen thousand feet. He said, 'The city feeds you, clothes you, and shelters you for nothing with a gesture to the lights below. All you must do is keep breathing, right? So, why not be high if everything is free? That is why we fight so hard to maintain the illusion of a working city. If people accepted that they could be stupefyingly stoned all day, every day, well, the city would explode. The tinder would start looking for sparks.' Then he snapped his fingers, as he joined her in bed.

Selling certain things was illegal but not socially frowned upon, so no big deal in her mind.

Still, due to her station, she minimized her contacts. So, that is how it was in the last few weeks since she visited. She picked tonight because her idiot brother wanted to see a lab, and this lab and its location curtailed any information that he could use against her. She was always one step ahead of August. She climbed the stairs to the loading dock, watching for his stumbling gait to drift by. The meeting place, Two Saint Lightscraper, was two blocks away; she messaged him once she saw his horrible grandiose semi-velvet coat on the HUD casted closed circuit. He looked like a circus ringmaster.

She rubbed her temples as she though 'What an idiot.'

His walk quickened once he saw her, though, his brain was earnestly concentrating on maintaining balance.

As he came closer, she sidestepped him to place herself between him with the ugly and attention-grabbing coat and the street, hopefully cutting off any prying eyes. She send out her arms like a theater performer, imitating a hug. "Brother! What brings you to Level-547?"

His hug was always cursory; then, he regarded her with shifting eyes. "Cutmen, I said. I need Cutmen. But, first, show me the lab." He walked toward the Carnealot loading Area.

"Augustine, wrong way!" she snapped, striding off into the darkness. "Come with me," she said, snapping her fingers.

The graffiti-slathered building greeted them with its chem-printed and vacuum-sealed rooms, deep bass shook the walls. Beads were strung over the doors, making her think of ancient books that embraced the drug culture, though she was not sure if a drug culture ever existed at all. Everyone wore multi-colored Rastafarian neo-plastic clean suits complete with a helmet. People in the standard drug producers attire; red respirators, dark green goggles, and gold earmuffs, surrounded Augustine after the impressively muscled doorwoman secured the main door with heavy steel latches. Each cartoon character completed to their jobs regardless of the new visitors, whether that be feeding a machine a glowing powdered verdant substance or manually pulling a handle to press out pills in the shape of a unicorn. The corner mounted lights cast a low torchlike reddish glow, completing the dungeon atmosphere. Hundreds of beaded barriers clinked as she led Augustine through the maze of rooms. Incitmento still pulsed through his body, but its effects were lessening, but he was sure that she designed it as a labyrinth if he decided to lose track.

"Why are they wearing purifiers, and we are not?" he questioned, sliding through a threshold of beads. The overall effect was roiling his stomach, and the music shook his bones; it took concentrated thought to stop his hands from covering his ears.

She noticed his winces and messaged him through the stream, 'turn down your auditory cortex,' pointing to her head. He pulled up his HUD over his left eye, adjusted it; now, he could only feel the waves of sound rattle in his body. It felt like the walls themselves were speakers, vibrating in his ears. As always, her messages were coded so that he would hear her voice speaking straight into his brain.

He responded, 'Why masks?' pointing to the workers. Her eyebrow shot up, and she laughed.

Still brain to brain communication, 'We are the only ones who have active HUD with a stream feed, and the earmuffs and masks prevent them from talking or hearing too much. Everyone has their orders.'

'Fine, I dislike it, but fine. What do you need, so I can get what I want?' he said mentally. His face felt like sandpaper, the high was wearing off. He scanned the hallway for a drinking cabinet or even just an errant bottle. She pulled back the past column of beads, entered another dingy room smelling of stale smoke. Taking a seat on a hundred-year-old sofa, she offered August an equally old chair placed in the corner. Both have been spray-painted with cartoons, vividly colored smilesup and googly eyes looked up to him. He almost deferred, but her look was insistent, and he knew that was the only way he could leave this disgusting place with what he wanted.

'Ok, here we are,' the smile stayed on her geneticlly

crafted face, even brightened, 'Watch this, big brother.'

Augustine was surprised by her perfect posture as she clapped her hands, though he doubted anyone could hear it. Though his ears could not hear the clap, something did, the room blackened, and all sound disappeared. He could feel his chair change from an old greasy polyester entombed patting to something hard and prickly against his fingers. As he became accustomed to the darkness, veins of red highlighted the corners and drew jagged angles along the walls, like mechanical neon roots.

'Bioluminescence in a concrete box,' he thought.

"Look," she said with his mother's smile, "The noise was a subluminal instruction; of course, it was covered by the bass, and your routing the Forge straight to your little mind started the sequence. My clap was the trigger."

He let anger cover the confusion breeding in his face. "What? Wait, how can I hear you? Did you disable my HUD? Mallory, what game are you playing at?" he shook a fist, then stood. The ground stayed where it was, but his feet did not seem to fit; they wobbled as if adrift. Instinctively, he threw his arms out to steady himself.

"Sit down before you hurt yourself," she commanded with a tone that he had never heard before as her will took the mass of the room. An unfathomable growth pushed her out, filling the space between them. The electric lines continued from the walls, through the hard floor, and up the sofa's sides then tracing up her back. The crimson marks flowed into her eyes, which glowed like a stationary lighthouse beam.

'Oh God, it was like having mother stare at me...the insane intensity,' he reasoned, starting to sweat as sheer terror bolted him to the uncomfortable chair. His lids closed as tightly as his muscles could muster, hands groping the air in defense were met only by laughter.

"Wow, what a whiney baby you are," she snickered, "Open those blue peepers!"

While he did not want to open them because he would be forced to deal with his fear of his mother now that it was obvious, he did as she commanded. Back to her normal size, she was still sitting on the sofa, but that had changed. It was canary yellow with tuffs of feathers sprouting from its sides, forming a plumed throne. A new gown clothed her, rippling with an invisible breeze, whirling its colors, creating entrancing patterns of paslies. Her face had returned to typical scale, and her smile meant that she had just pulled a grand prank on her older brother. He thought he saw the Cheshire cat formed, then disappear in the gown's folds as her smile broadened. She never wore a dress, especially anything resembling an overwrought gown with pearls and lace.

"Am I in VR?" he grumbled, "It is not funny to scare me. I can become dangerous soon." A self-satisfied grin replaced his grimace as he sat forward. He meant to stand, but she stopped him with a hand.

She laughed again, pinching her features and pointing at his face. "Yes, VR, as I said, you helped me hack in, and, sure, dangerous, maybe, but we are in the presence of real danger here. Real, actual danger." She lifted a hand and snapped. The room disappeared into blackness, only cones of light hovering over them. Augustine heard crisp slaps on the concrete, someone's approaching footsteps. The thuds against the stone floor increased, as if the thing was running. He turned to face it, whatever it was, when a man whispered in his ear, and he almost fell out of his chair.

Through a thick Russian accent, the man said, "Hello, Augustine Zellum. Calm yourself. We are here to help each other." Augustine's head swirled, trying to find the speaker in the black, but nothing was visible beyond the limits of the illuminated cone, there the world ended.

"Oh," the man said, with a hint of happiness creeping into his rough voice, "I am right here."

August's head turned to the voice to see him. The man sat in a throne of pressed gold darkened with ages of patina draped in a thick charcoal fur cloak. His large head was covered by a rough helmet that seemed to be crafted from hammered metal. His cold ivory jaw and his eyes were the only skin that could be seen. He opened both his hands to the siblings and spoke in his miniature virtual universe. "I am Chern Yanoch, and I am here to help." The tiniest break on his mouth indicated a welcoming smile.

Augustine straightened his back to ask a pointed question, "Why are we here?" But, after all the decades with Father, he knew to keep it short. "Sir," he added for effect.

"Da," taking the title of 'sir,' meant that, at least, Augustine knew Chern should be respected. Chern continued, "Both of you want something. Augustine, I am your prize here. I'm with the Cutmen, and this is my place. I meet here to prevent any…unnecessary physical problems," he gestured to Mallory, "You are here because you need something from your brother, and you need an outside witness? Yes?"

Both nodded, and Mallory started with a series of requests. "Big brother, I need holding cells in every Thalassa Poli across the world. A cell that will be undisturbed by your people, only for my people. And, before you ask, yes, it is for drug distribution," She explained, stretching a tentative finger toward Chern; even her virtual self was nervous. "The Cutmen and I have a deal worldwide. Just need a secure place to launch it from…a place of privacy. I helped you in reaching the Cutmen, and this will all be kept in silence. Covert, if you like. Just between us."

From somewhere in the virtual world, she conjured bubblegum, blew it out of her mouth into the largest bubble that he had ever seen. Its pink body stretched up into the blackness, then she popped it. The bubble burst like a balloon, scattering pink pieces into the air, but each piece morphed into a new small balloon. Thousands of miniature globes floated away, disappearing as they left the light. August was not sure if this was only for aesthetics or was his sister's way of adding visual punctuation.

Chern's arm pointing in his direction got Augustine's attention. "Augustine, Yes, we have an agreement. I ensure that the various...customs," he groped for the word, "are paid and compliant. You have met me, and I have witnesses that she has properly asked you her question. Many items of discussion take too long and avoid getting to the real reasons for these types of meetings. Yes? So, this is the Cutmen way; a quick decision, and details later." He turned his helmet encased head to Mallory, spikes and forged wings cut through the air, then back to August. "What is your answer?" he asked. Somewhere in Augustine's mind, he reminded him of a kindly grandmother, like his own grandmother who left so many years ago. He considered his answer carefully, weighing the options on both sides. Now he knew that entering her spray-painted labyrinth and meeting this supposed king of the underworld had decided for him. His eyes flickered between their virtual avatars, reading nothing from their projected faces.

"Yes, I agree. I can do that," he was already organizing the proper paper-lightwork on his HUD as he responded. "Contact me tomorrow, and I will have it arranged." Mallory squealed and shifted her hips, mimicking the form of dance that only small children perform when offered a cookie.

"Chern...Sir, may I speak with you privately and outside of ...this," he flung his hand at the non-existence space.

"Of course, Augustine. My brothers will contact you shortly," he replied, then his face turned hard, "you must know that this arrangement is permanent, and only I can alter the details. When and if the deal is altered, you can express your concerns and judgments. After a future meeting the details will be confirmed, and you must conform. The Cutmen way. Do you understand?" The grandmother's tone was gone, and his warrior's clothing seemed to fit him as his chest pulsed into full strength. Fear crept back into Augustine's spine when he nodded.

Chern stood, revealing the chainmail and black leather padding under the furry cloak. He was the black night, ready for battle. "No, to complete the contract, you MUST say it! You must say da...yes, Augustine. That is the Cutmen way." Chern was less than a foot away from Augustine's sweaty face. August tasted the sweat as it ran down from his brow to his mouth and was amazed at the VR capabilities. The Cutmen's face was dead, no movement, or even wrinkles, just a blank plain of sculpted virtual ivory. Only the human eyes made the bone statue seem alive.

Augustine gulped and stammered a, "Yes."

The ivory clothed in metal withdrew, and a human smile broke across his face, ruining the statue illusion. "Good, very good. My brothers will see you soon. Mallory and brother Augustine, dobroy nochi, and be well." The dark warrior faded away in a flash, leaving Augustine back in the foul-smelling room with graffiti staining his ruby red coat, but Mallory looked thrilled.

CHAPTER 18

Dirt was under his nails, filling his mouth. An immense pressure held him down, and no matter how he pushed or shook, it would not move. Earth clogged his ears, he thought it was night, but his eyes were matted with mud. He kept moving, clawing until his nails splintered and bled. He pushed his legs up and down, hands grinding into the land, over and over again, though he was not sure his bloody limbs could find purchase as he churned his way through the earth. Maybe, he was a worm or a grub.

He did not know. Who was he, and where?

The last of his energy was spent, and soon he would inhale a lungful of soil. He wondered if this was the best way to end his time on the planet, the one that was hugging him so tightly that it was crushing all air from his body. There would be no burial, only peace after he stopped clawing through the loam. Just one last stretch of a gory hand and it would be done.

Fear enclosed him like a liquid blanket, seeping through the soil, into his pores.

His fear churned around him as his last breath softly pushed the dirt aside. His ribs were crushed, but the fear, like oxygen now, found its way in, filling his lungs. He shuttered and jerked; it flowed through him, changing his body and mind, down to the DNA. Earth was only tasting him before a much weightier meal. His fear will feed the land and the water will be blood.

'The dirt was...covetous,' he thought as his light faded.

The dirt was ripped through; his feet found footing. The

pain was gone; the weight of the planet was held back. His ribs popped as he flexed to inhale. He found his nails were claws, strong and sharp. Light filtered through the soil; the hole emitted a low white glow as he scratched with his new talons. The air held the smell of night mixed with blood, It found its way through the loam, drifted to him beneath the earth. He now knew he was clawing up to the ground, only a few feet away, energy building with each slash. Arching his body over, clawing down with new powerful limbs, dirt fell under his chest to be compacted by his feet, always pushing up. Pushing and clawing.

Up to home, up to her.

He surged from the ground like a geyser, continuing to claw at the air, then landed on his face. Reeling from the impact, his eyes closed, his claws covered his ears. He was a newborn on this planet. The smell was dark and cool; a gentle whir reverberated in the background. His strength gone, Miguel rolled to his back, eyes open. The Level ceiling extended a few hundred feet above him, jutting tangles for residential-slash-commercial stalactites. Lights flashed in all directions, from the twinkling lights of the Broadway transports to the orange streetlights all the way to Trinity Church Mausoleum before the massive structure blocked off Hudson Parkway.

'Christmas tree,' he thought, 'the city is like living inside a Christmas tree the size of Mount Everest.' His father always told Miguel that maintaining traditions was just as important as scientific advances when bringing families together. Traditions, like Christmas, pulling families, whole or in the past, into a wonderous living stew that can, once it is ready, satisfy everyone and leave the house smelling great.

That is what he said. Miguel did not like most of his family, not in so much as in active disliking them, but they constantly wished that the world was not what it is, and mere complaining words could fix it. Of course, they returned

Miguel's disdain, except for his father and granddad. His father would have told him that families are a tradition too.

He glanced at his legs and saw blood welling up from his knees. Then he noticed that he was nude, and his claws were gone. Only long piano-player fingers were left, weeping blood to the roof. The evening was sixty-five degrees according to his HUD, somewhere he disengaged it from the stream. Unsure if he was having a mental breakdown, he rose, looked around, halfway hoping that someone was up there with him, despite being naked, to tell him how he got there. Only an open portal winked back at him from the other side of the building.

The gap called to him, and he stepped to the edge. A step off would lead to a five-hundred-foot flight straight down, and the street would recycle him.

'Maybe I would end up as a new china cup,' he mused. Now, he was sure that he was in the clutches of a violent mental breakdown.

The building blocked most of the light as he stood in shadow, and the grand garden looked like a dark moat circumventing the structure. No one could see him here; the floor dropped into shadow. He was alone, mentally and physically. The nerves told him that he was crying before he knew that tears had formed. They fell on his hands, washing his wounds. For a moment, he thought that he might be crying blood.

Behind him, something was moving. No non-emergency drones traveled to this altitude, and the portal was still open, undisturbed. A soft sound of cloth rasping against itself traveled through the darkness directly beneath, then drifted to him. Unlike many adjacent apartment blocks, the roof surface was naturally rolling brindle ash, which made an aerial view look like a fractal Pollock painting. He jumped down from the edge into the inky black, took one step forward. It brushed to the left, then moved to the right. The person, or the thing, his heartbeat moved a little faster at that thought, was moving just beyond his sight, movement in the gloom, away from the city's light.

He stepped forward to the black; all his fear had bled to the ground. Any terror that once held his bones was crushed out when the blade splintered his spine.

A soft crunch of a depressed shoe and, then, a brush, like a sheet rustling, meet his step. His eyes adjusted, and he took another step further into the nebula. The darkness crushed and digested any entering light. He felt like he was walking into a fog that pulls power from candlelight, using it to strengthen itself. A black gateway to another misty world. Now he understood why Irish Stingy Jack held on to the turnip candle with both shaking hands; the intense pitch broke by a dreadful light to scare away the searching devil.

His face muscles began to hurt as he was opening his eyes so widely. Arms out, he began to walk forward. The sound of rustling cloth passed him on the left, and he heard the creak of a shoe. It was circling him, slowing, but circling. Swinging his head, he spun, trying to find something, anything to focus on. His legs folded over themselves, tripping him, his bleeding hands barely caught himself before smashing his face into the foggy floor somewhere below him. He cast no shadow, and now, he was on his bleeding knees being hunted by something on the roof of a five hundred story apartment block.

The scuffs, now emerging as slow steps, and the movement of cloth, was to his right again. Calming his heart, he looked to the only light that he could pull from the murk, the portal blue lantern. The blue glow from flagellates cycled through the whole apartment block, radiating everything from the elevator buttons to a night light mounted to the nano-walls to calm a frightened child. The microscopic creatures burn blue to soothe, to emit an astral blanket. That was his only source of light, his personal nightlight; the night air stung his eyes as he refused to close them.

The blue dimmed for a second, a silhouette shuffled along, rising and falling like a wave. It creaked as it went, then turned an angle to disappear into the blackness.

He sat, scraping the dried blood from his knees against the roof pebbles, and centered himself. That is what Grandad called it, a way to totally observe one's environment, taking it all layer by layer, then losing yourself if only for a moment. Sometimes his work required a split in the universe, a super-position. Miguel heard a crash in Grandad's office and was fearful as even he knew that all things must die. He was reassured as words that a young Miguel could not say echoed through the house. Slowly, toe by toe, he snuck through the doors of the study and found Grandad perched on his massive wooden desk with eyes closed. Miguel almost ran when Grandad breathed so deeply through his colossal old nose that he thought his eyes would crack open and catch Miguel in the act of breaking and entering. Grandad spoke, eyes still closed, "I'm splitting the universe because I just broke it." He jerked his head to the pile of papers and advanced mini-quantum networks lying to the side of the desk. "I'm centering myself. Come join me." He patted an empty scratched spot on the desk that had contained the pile moments before. Miguel joined him in exploring one's own mind, and he began to learn.

A thing stalked him while trapped in the illusory dark; he used what he was taught. His ears and fingertips were his eyes now. The air pressure was constant except for the air circulation system auto-time breezes. The city sounds broke through the blanket of the black, startling him as all the noise seemed blocked before. Without assistance from the neural Forge, his mind isolated the sounds. He silenced the nano's whirring from the streets below, the distance electric crackle of a broken light, and the rhythmic drum from an air vent. Each sound was collected from the city that swirled around him, analyzed, then discarded, leaving only the brushing and leather creaks. He closed off his skin, starting with his feet, removing all feeling, or more accurately, removing the sense that a mind has when it is feeling something, forming a mental tabla rasa.

The moving cloth caressed his shoulder, and two shoes creaked away. No, boots, two faux leather boots creaked and cracked as they were pulled along by something small. Traffic was gone, eliminated. The drone of the aerial vehicle stopped irrelevant input. The air blower's continuing low rumble failed to merit the mind's attention. All the extraneous stimuli faded, but the scratching brush of soft cloth remained. It moved over itself like lace, like a dress. He turned his head, angled his nose to the sky like an animal searching for a scent. The movement fluttered, and he inhaled deeply. Leather, the boots were crafted from natural leather. Small and soft footprints with the flourish of a bustling silk dress...the thing was a woman.

And blood, rot, and putrid chemicals. The woman still walked around him, slowly making a grand circle in the darkness, smelling of decay. Something that had left the Earth but, somehow, remained against the laws of the physical world.

Split the universe so that you can fix it. It was broken into a superposition.

Lace, the brushing of cloth was below his head, a light dress for a rotting woman. The black seemed to claw through his lids, and he did not want to see what was on the other side. He heard a scratch to his left. She was close. Apricot and vanilla wafted to him, then the tang of blood. It merged with his nerves, mixing with his cells, becoming part of him.

He began to imagine her; lace dress bustled at the waist, sheer with a rounded neckline, no sleeves, and the cuffed just above the boots, real leather boots. Then the dark broke through his eyelids, and blackness washed over him. The aroma of freshly pumped blood filled his nasal cavity, flooding into the back of his throat. He crumbled into a naked and scarlet pile. The dead pacing boots stopped creaking, and the rustle of the lace dress, a simple wedding dress, ended. The air was still.

It was her: his love and lighthouse. Her light was gone now, swallowed by the world's darkness that had crafted a cave in his mind. He freed himself from it with mania and bloody claws, but now, the muck was too thick.

"Shh, now, it is ok," a light hand touched the back of his neck, "It is almost over for me." A wet giggle echoed in the dusk. He shuttered as cold liquid dripped onto his face. He saw her now, sitting on the roof, in the dress, once magically white, now red with blood, a gaping wound still open and seeping. She looked at him as if he just told her a joke.

'A joke started the universe; the laugh lit the stars,' he told himself, and her smile was as right as the sun.

The light returned, but instead of shattering the surrounding darkness, it emanated from the roof itself. Red flecks peppered the gray floor, spreading out like a pattern. She sat in the middle of the scarlet display, white like a fresh flake of snow on a rusting metal plate dusted with dew. His knees began to ache again, and a fresh glance showed that his skin was slightly glowing. No, not his skin, but beneath it, the coating of Dying clots sparkled like sun-lit rubies. She sat only feet away, looking at him through dead clouded eyes, but she remained still. He pushed himself up, eyeing her suspiciously, but finally, he stood. He was in the hammer, and she sat where the snake was continually eating itself. Bits of gore fell from his hands onto the path he carved in his madness. With his liquid blood, he made the symbol real.

He was different now. His hands sported claws, his mouth hid lethal fangs, and his lighthouse with its extinguished flame of golden eyes lit the way. A dim circle of red light etched the roof as a canvas, drawn by the sacrifice of a bleeding living instrument. The ouroboros, the bloody life, death, and rebirth, was made from him; now it was him. His wonderous and beautiful wife, his dead wife, gnawed on by a beast, sat on one end, and he stood on the other.

Her bloodless face was beautiful; she opened a red smile.

He smiled back.

PART THREE

CHAPTER 19

It was so like her, Liz. Clean and organized, all cases in the correct folders, books properly logged on the shelf, but little touches showed the viewer or anyone who happened to walk in that she was whimsical and possibly irreverent. A clear and discernible juxtaposition. At the corner of her desk, sitting between a hand-labeled "in" piles of papers and three neatly placed legal pads with neat handwritten lines on each front, a black-framed photograph stood, barely maintaining stability between falling to the floor or just hanging on the edge. The fam, the first fam, before the religious schism that tore the family in half, elders versus the youngers, and before the youngers found a true calling in the city, this city, where the little sister will hunt her older sister's murderer.

'Decades and a lifetime ago. Well, one lifetime is over, now,' Alcippe thought, pushing around the pens and random office items on Liz's desk. She kept it so clear of her personal life; it was just a desk, a desk that any chief inquisitor could use, only business. Beyond the photo, the only thing that would allow her to pick it out of a lineup was the blue whale clown statue tucked amongst her black styluses. Al smirked, diverting the course of her most recent tears. She did not know that she was crying, and it was late, but that was what brought on the salty gush.

'I thought I would be dehydrated by now,' she thought, brushing them away with the back of her hand. She alerted her HUD stream to reminder her to increase electrolyte consumption. She knew that she would curse it and ignore it once the red light blinked over her right field of view. Or maybe have a beer instead.

'Stupid whale. Man, Miguel is an odd duck,' she thought as she picked up the statue. A simple, almost cartoonish rendering of a blue whale was painted yellow, red, and blue. It was small, roughly her thumb's size. It appeared to be dancing, flippers out and tail emulating a tap dancer. Tuffs of orange fluff were glued around the blowhole, and a huge red slash marked its mouth from one side of the head to the other. A painted purple bowtie was placed below its ridged lower lip. For some reason, Miguel found it funny and gave it to her sister, wearing a huge smile that only Liz could understand.

Maybe he thought it was funny because the animal's anthroporfication is a way that makes it human, but an altered form of a human, say a clown, is a sick parody of humor? Liz told her during that birthday party. The party had slim attendance, and for Liz, seeing the light in Miguel's face and his engagement with the dozen or so guests was her real gift.

'Odd duck. And he checked himself out of the hospital when I told him to wait.'

So, she buzzed over here to triple-check the files, as she had run every type of analysis possible in the pod on the way over. The only intelligence lead was to the murder of the journalist, as the wounds were the same. She shuttered as the images flashed before her mind's eye, the blood-spattered body of the journalist and her sister. Freshly gnawed gaping wounds were all greeted with surprised faces that morphed into two fixed faces of horror, one with miraculous golden eyes.

All crime sweeps were negative, and only Miguel's recall could place the subjects at the second scene. Sharkteeth and the huge man. Banda pulled both cases from her, as she was a bereaved family member, and it was likely that she would compromise the case. Chief Inquisitor Griest will serve as the inquiry director, meaning that all the bigwigs have noticed. That could be good or bad, depending on whose' toes have been tickled or trampled.

'At least Banda is still the lead detective,' she thought, hoping that he will keep her in the information loop that swirled around a high-profile investigation, whether imagined or real. While the casual homicide happens in Undertown every now and then, an attack, much less a murder, has not occurred to a mid-Level citizen in years and never to a court officer. Heads will roll, and she prayed that the system with all the AI magistrates and breathing judges would only drop the sword on the correct necks. The huge man and Sharkteeth have gone under, into the belly of the city, leaving little if anything to go on, and the scan problem destroyed any remote track.

So, she was just fiddling with her dead sister's stuff, trying to decide if she should visit Miguel at the crime scene, a place that was only days ago an abattoir soaked in Liz's blood, now sanitized, smelling of lemons.

'Argus location check for Lt. Banda,' she thought. A city map opened, covering half her field of vision with a green dot at PD HQ. 'When did his Argus check-in?'

The internal voice chimed back the time, fifteen minutes ago.

'Ok, let's waste some time,' she thought as she stuffed the paper files under her arm beneath her leather jacket, and some under her belt, then began plotting a covert way out of the office.

The Jongro Building bustled even at night, though night and day were now seen as social constructs. The overhanging Level cast a dimmed blue light over the street, giving her the feeling that the entire block was the subject of a noir painting except for the shining neon lights slung from the vendor stalls. She entered through the double doors on the eastside; the beautiful titillating smell of pork barbeque that wafted around the food court assaulted her nose. So many officers have crossed this path in the past few days that none of the typical prostitutes who proffer illegal dreams of children or necromancy, dealers of the few illicit drugs, and illegal body enhancement sellers even batted an eye. She took the freshly cleaned stairs to the Mr. Valentino Escrito's flat. Each step produced chills down her back, and she felt goose bumps form on her arms.

'Same as last time. Ok, time for Banda's trick.' Many detectives focus on one clue, one hint of something, something big, an item that could change the case or narrow it to a point, thus easing their work. Banda was the opposite, totally deductive. Collect the facts, then spit out what is in your head and see where it falls. Of course, this period only lasts for a moment or two; then the standard motives begin to apply themselves.

She knew that there was little to kill this guy for, no material motive, and it was likely that he was inexperienced in the ladies' department judging by the interior of his rooms.

She huffed, running her fingers through her sandy hair, trying to break up any lingering thoughts.

'Ok, forget motive for now.' The death was aggressive and brutal, but she saw the HUD cast of the Zuby interview.

'That lady was nuts, and that could explain it. Still, the choice of victim and the ability to disable the apartment's security change the whole game.'

The door clicked open, showing an empty space; the CS unit stripped everything. His collection of dusty ancient popular culture bric-a-brac was stuffed in boxes, stored under a shelf at PD HQ evidence collection, now covered in a new layer of dust. The place was clean as clean can be, wiped over, removing all marks of humans. Even his minuscule DNA traces has been gathered and liquefied into the building.

'Come over, Richie O'Bryan,' she thought, calling out her custom HUD command, and the room lit up orange dotted with lines of data. O'Bryan was one of the best Rugby players two centuries ago; her dad loved him. Sometimes, mother thought that it might be more than the true appreciation of sportsmanship. Even from the wobbly age of three, she could remember father wailing away, shouting, and somehow casting what he perceived as mental encouragement to the player as O'Bryan ran, juked, and smashed into others. Another reason that his name was a private joke to her was that he was a hooker, a term for a front row man waiting to mangle their rivals, all with the same thoughts of mangling. One of his many jobs was to pass the ball back to players behind him, and he did it with relish. The mighty leg of O'Bryan came fast and powerful, scraping to the bone of any opponent. Odd that the pious father enjoyed the brutal game with such delectation.

She liked it for another reason. Her time on the Vice squad was spent dressed as another kind of hooker, the kind with illegal geneware and catering to bizarre, unhuman exercises. As each cop, both men and women had to make up a name, a moniker, and a backstory to stick to when questioned by local hoods or Bratva thugs. She was O'Bryan, a failed athlete with an addiction to synth-glutamate. O'Bryan, the hooker.

'It was one of the few things from my father that I could still latch onto...a HUD call up,' she reasoned. The strange happiness of conducting busts on dark street corners faded and sadness took her. She breathed in hard, then her personal search resumed. Through the optical-cast, she stood in the center of the room, trying to clear her mind, cast off all other extemporaneous input.

'Black down. Play VR section, fifteen minutes before the arrival of emergency services with standard instructions,' she commanded the room. The false light faded, leaving her in the black; only her mind was present here. The wall began to form around her, and a softly glowing bar the length of her forearm drifted up from where her feet would be in reality. It rose like a ghost, grey and nebulous until her hand reached out to tap the fast forward button. Once touched, it emanated a lavish green.

'Ten seconds,' she thought, afraid that she might miss something, for the room was so still that even sped up time failed to show any changes. Her extended arm moved up from her waist, as did the projected passage of time. The portal began to glow blue, her arm dropped. She knew that Banda had done this several times and will probably dream about this room, but she, also knew that a tiny clue or half-formed thought might be hidden in this virtual world.

The report had summarized it correctly. He entered in a rush, clearing the flat so he could wander without tripping while he was arranging data on his HUD stream.

'Unfortunately, Nadar Forge data automatically deletes itself when the nerve center fails to detect a heartbeat. Of course, Banda said that was God doing so Bluemen can still have a job.'

She ran it over a dozen times; the victim came in, walked around a bit, stroked the cat, then went into the bedroom and his death. Changing the point of view allowed her to follow him through the apartment as if she were a camera screwed into his head, floating just above his receding hairline. The data stream in the flat and the overall building AI had a five-minute blackhole, likely when the murderer entered this place. He walked into his home, a place to relax, unsuspecting as shark teeth waited.

'Walking, wander, dead, over and over. Ok, shutdown play.' The room returned, and her anger rose as she ground her teeth.

"Holy God and son of a bitch," she screamed to the ceiling. She angrily grabbed her loose hair, pulling it back, and blew gusts of air through her nose until it began to sting. Her strength was failing her, and she knelt, mind starting to wander.

'Close to booze time,' she ruminated as that is where her mind goes most often. She will search for clues at the bottom of a shiny biodegradable glass filled with brown fluid. The extremely immaculate carpet looked comfortable, and she laid out in the murdered man's floor. She began mentally rummaging through the stream, lazily answering messages, and arranging for data transfers to an offsite storage PD facility for later review.

'Data transfer...hmmm. O'Bryan, play the interview with dead journalist's boss,' she thought.

A deep voice rumbled in her mind, 'Al, there were three separate interviews with Mr. Rannell Cobb. Which do you wish for me to play?'

She fine-tuned the HD streams vocals to suit her, deep and smooth with an edge, mentally forming a face for the voice box, that is a magical mix of a cynical Undertown street cop commingled with a SkyLevel poet sidelining as a part-time gigolo. Too bad it was just a voice broadcast in her brain.

'Section of the interview where he describes the last meeting with Valentino,' she told the voice.

'Roger that, ma'am,' it stated with even rolled tones.

"Make it 2-D replay with current background," she said, rubbing her aching temples. A fat face babbled about an employee meeting him in a bar. He seemed actually upset with red-rimmed eyes and a runny nose.

"I did not pay attention to him...," Cobb sniffed, "but, he said that he had a story or something. And he was excited about it, whatever it was."

'Pause,' she told the biocomputer in her head. Cobb's swollen, wet face hung over her; he was swiping at his nose with the back of his hand.

"Gross. The dead guy had a story that has not been reported through the news stream, something from the street."

She remembered from her first visit here, the archaic noir posters of a lone figure sharply cut under a harsh streetlamp, but half-hidden under the blackness of the city.

'Investigative journalism, if that still exists, might be able to hold off that blackness. He gathered something from the streets, something that was very important, at least to him. O'Bryan, were there any data transfers once he got back here?'

The voice responded with sexy gravel, "Yes, ma'am. One data transfer, 18 seconds after entering the residence."

Her heart jumped, and she blurted, "Play 10 seconds before the transfer, internal view only."

A screen snapped into existence, showing Valentino lovingly touching the white furball at his feet. The little creature seemed only to want his love and attention before it wandered off to push something over or claw a piece of furniture into ruin. A real predator was waiting just around the corner, only steps away.

"You were unfazed, you stupid little lion."

Her hands touch the imaginary screen, fingers pulling together, tightening the video. "Freeze frame. O'Bryan, what was the storage transferred? The bytes?" she barked, locked on the puffy cat's face. The Forge told her two petabytes. "Gotcha," she yelled at the cat's projection wired into the brain, brushed her hair out of her face as she sat up. Then, the search for the little lion began.

CHAPTER 20

Red light pierced his eyelids, and something sharp was poking into his back, threatening to break the skin. He was unsure whether he was awake, and the aching joints convinced him to stand. Edges of broken thin polymer shells spread across the floor, each glinting, reflecting the red light like firings in a winter's Viking camp. Open small vials were shattered, and whatever liquid that was once inside them had pooled beneath his sleeping body. His lab could comfortably allow for one standing person, and barely passed that test. He must have fallen unconscious here last night or...this morning. He mentally checked the Forge cloak feed from the city's satellite-connect.

'Nine in the morning, less than a week into dead wife life.'

Much of last night was gone as if his memories were part of a grocery list that he left in other pants. 'HUD replay from 0001 hours,' he asked. Letters formed in front of him, each flickering and solidifying, creating a short sentence. He had never seen this before; fear gripped him holding his spine until he read it aloud.

"Escape the cave," he said, dryly, his voice cracking.

It sounded familiar and foreign, like looking at someone you know well, but their disguise fools you. After he spoke the last syllable, the final magical silent e, his heart returned to normal, and his thoughts calmed.

'No rewind, only present,' he thought. 'Assess the present.'

He surveyed the lab under the red light, marveling at how everything he had worked on was gone or destroyed, broken, smashed, or missing. Years of work and decades of thought were splattered on the walls or had formed lagoons of ruined fluid under his feet. Oddly, he was not angry or frustrated at the loss. Thoughts of playing with a creature's DNA and Earth's menagerie's architecture seem in poor taste, so he dismissed it. Struggling, he cleaned a path through the debris with his feet, opening the frosted glass door to the living room, now an area where whatever this fluid was will dry, and left the lab; it's emergency red light still shining.

False sunlight glinted against the room, touching countertops and a chair tucked in a corner. A beam from the heavens, but the rest of the room was still dark, and the air seemed old and stale. Crossing over the threshold, the wall pulled on him like hooks buried deep in his skin. Of course, the nanos ripped apart the blood that was there, basically eating his wife's blood. Liz's blood. But he could still see it, it crudely painted the wall like a cave marking from 40,000 years ago, forever there, temporally immortal. After almost a week, it dripped down, staining the floor. His hand reached for the blood, pressing against the gray wall. He pulled his hand back and inspected it. Only pale skin with tiny cuts from the night before. He thought that his mind was now the madman in the rewilding, as Liz would have said. It just struck him that her smile will never bless this room again. The only shoes that clog the entryway will be his, laughter will die with her, and the world will be poorer for it.

Deep cold spread through him, quelling what once was a white-hot reaction. The rage was gone, and he needed to eat, his muscles were sore and aching for nourishment. Pushing past the soreness, he dressed and left, leaving the portal open. The place needed some clean air, something to brush off the depravity and restore balance or to remove it if it remained. The rooms needed fresh air to purge the dark.

◆ ◆ ◆

A corner vendor on Level 4 at 102nd and Lexington Ave sold him several printed meat empanadas and a synth-tea with extra caffeine, fueling him. His pace to the east river outlook quickened. He failed to avoid foot traffic, and he was stuck in a slow-moving mob walking against him toward Deca-Level Park. He almost lost all his tea as it spilled down his tunic and did lose a corner of his last empanada as its buttery-sprayed crust slipped from his hand, lost into the crowd. He thought of reversing course to the Dec-Level Park as he meandered passed, but only appreciating the hundred-foot-tall spiral of jungle build into Level 4. It cut through the city, a section of the old world, a forest sprouting from its massive vines. A place to reconnect.

'But, no.'

There were too many people there. The crowd surged on, faces of all colors and more languages than he could remember. He spoke five tongues at a rudimentary level and read seven like a fumbling elementary student. Picking up several words, he knew that many were talking about work, love, or food. He assumed that he could be dropped into any crowd everywhere on Earth, and the essential topics would remain the same.

He could let the crowd embrace him, but he knew that before long, he would resist, and someone would be hurt. Last week, the violent streak was always well hidden under high intelligence, customs, and his wife's thoughtful commentary, but now it was like a wave with peaks and troughs. He was riding emotions as if in a storm, and he did not know on just what island he would crash.

'Better with fewer people,' he thought, chewing the end of lunch, and gurgling the last of the tea. His tongue protested against the dredges of the synthetic in the syn-tea, then he spat to the street trying to rid his mouth of the remnants. His palm brushed a regrade pat, dropped the portable cup and the pastry paper, and he stopped to watch them shift into the black dust that reminded him of the clouds blowing over the East River. The city shielding was minimized at the outlook, allowing some of the River's true wind to kiss the tourists. Once there were two rivers, the Harlem and the East, they both expanded and rose as all watery bodies did before the rewilding, until they joined. As original as City authorities were, they decided to call it the East River since it was still in the east. For him, the view was one of the best in the city, a clear, unobstructed sense of material at peace. At five thousand feet, he could barely notice any waves. The river crashed over the submerged Randall's and Wards' Islands, spreading east out to the massive construction towers in College Point. Two miles of flat running water, the clearest view this side to Old Jersey City or south out to the Atlantic. The gray of the water met the industrial parks' gray miles away; all mirroring the sky, the heavens stretched everywhere. Today he was lost in an illusion.

He sat on a bench, rubbing his chin. 'Need to shave,' he noted, then noticed that the small cuts on his fingers and hands were sealing. Staring at empty space, which his mind would create when looking at the waves, calmed him, aligned his thoughts, focusing them like a knife's edge.

Grandad told him that with enough data, he could solve anything. So, he needed more data. Last night Al was wasting time, likely confused, and pulled from both cases. Now, he could not have access to the crime scene information. He planted a confusion cyber in her stream. Its job was to signal him based on her neural output from each JYC PD search. Most of her brain was only spinning, and her thoughts of an alcoholic beverage sent off several false positives. He mentally reviewed the cast and saw that she found two items of use: the journalist's cat and that the killer/killers can wholly control the artificial intelligence of the apartment block. At the hospital, a wave of displeasure washed over him when he back-slipped into her stream, but that passed quickly. The confusion cyber, he named it Clausewitz, scrambled the feeds to create a virtual fog so the proper stream response would ride through. Fundamentally, it gave Miguel time to react before she did.

Valentino carrying a large amount of data and stored it in the cat. He felt comfortable thinking of him by his first name; after all, the same serrated teeth that caused his death killed Miguel's wife. At Miguel's urging, Clausewitz entered an unguarded JYC animal shelter transfer system to direct the feline to the Pet Relocate Center two blocks away. He just needed a high view of the river. It was said that the city sheath was thin enough to slip through, and some poor souls have made an easy effort to fall all those Levels down, to be broken. Miguel thought they were fractured before they got here to view the magnificent river, the silver negative space between the cities' outstretched sections. They were broken on their walk here and in their successful attempt to wiggle through the shielding. But, once they fell five thousand feet straight to the always reforming nano-metal below, they were fixed and now complete. Without knowing, his hand reached to the shield, and only the feeling of rain droplets on his palm jarred him back. He quickly withdrew his hand, stuck the moist hand into his pocket under the tunic. He squeezed the drop from his hand as he gripped until his fingers turned white as he walked to the animal shelter.

CHAPTER 21

Augustine supplied all the necessary information to Mallory and through her to the Cutmen. While he was nervous, in fact, extraordinarily frightened that he had not left his floor in two days, he directed that a separate set of hardware adds to the Thalassa Poli number 47. His position and last name gave him override access throughout the entire "aqua city." He hated that term; it was a grand monument to his intelligence and pride. Well, not his intelligence, but his ability to gather the brightest minds and get them to create something new. The extra module, a simple semi-plastic encasement of nano-motherboard, was permanently mounted by the quacom receiver lines, just waiting if the need arises. A simple pale blue lozenge of insurance, but he was still scared.

He received the message minutes ago: regulations on request, twenty minutes, HUD disengaged, alone.

Once he read it and it faded from his internal screen, a map of Level 1023 took its place with a bright yellow dot marking his destination.

'Central Spiral Altocumulas lounge.'

"Get out of here!" he yelled over his shoulder, "Teza, Teza!" Shuffling and sniffling sounded from his bed; small feet scurried on the artificial wooden boards. 'Eliminate all DNA traces,' he thought. A low moan broke the sounds of women hurrying to the exits.

He stood; one woman out of five remained, still bleeding, lying motionless in his bed. Her naked mocha skin exacerbated the stark difference between his moon-pale derma and her body. The blood and other fluid had seeped into the sheets, leaving only the blood on her face and breasts. Apparently, he must have struck her too hard; a welt had formed on her temple.

Squatting over her bloody face, he bellowed, "GET OUT, WHORE!" No movement, only moans. Time was short, and he could not be delayed.

"You deserve this; I told you to take the medkit before we hit the sheets," he mumbled, walking to his behemothic hand-crafted teak desk. Once, Richard told him that the size of his desk reflected his insecurity; Augustine commanded his brother to leave with a curse. He swiped a letter opener, thumbing the tip.

'Poly-metal laser sharpened, yes, that would do.'

He pulled her along by yanking the sheets, she banged her fine legs on the wooden foot pillars, then he repeated his threat. "Time to go. Time, time, time to go," he breathed over her breasts, alcohol soured air rushed into her bloody nose. He stood back, knowing what was coming, only his hand touched her ankle, gripping hard enough to feel the bones shift beneath.

"Ok, fine, besides, this is the best part. The sharp-tip wake-up call," he said smiling, the glint of the blade flashed in his eyes. He pulled again, and her bare hips scraped against the lavishly carved footboard; the four pillars shook. Her eyes fluttered, and she moved against his pull with minimal strength. The tip pierced the skin under the balls of her left foot, digging in deep until the blade bounced off a metatarsal. Augustine thought the tip might have shocked her with electricity judging by how she shot up, jerked her leg back. The blade was shook loose, and the sheets were covered with a fount of blood.

'I must have hit a vein,' he thought as purple-red splattered across his face. His tongue ventured out, tasting it as it dripped down. She was just as spicy inside as outside. She grabbed her foot, screaming. He struck her in the throat, gagging her. Tears formed in her beautiful eyes; she asked him why, why would he do this.

Pulling her from the bed, she crashed against the floor; he said, "I'm on a schedule, dear."

The lounge was wonderful, clean, and perfectly ordered. He has not been here in over a decade, but nothing seemed to have changed. Even the staff was the same, or the manager recorded the original staff likenesses and printed them on the new waiters. Maybe the simulated accents might have shifted from one region to another. He will listen carefully.

The map guided him to a corner booth overlooking the city and, in the distance, out to the Atlantic. The horizon was over one hundred miles away, and the sea wall was below him, a greenish line stretching across the bay. The Manzana was to his left, and even in the sunlight, it still gleamed a ruby red. Masts fully extended to two thousand feet, the two Thalassa Poli sat stationary near the construction Areas in College Point, like smooth cacti sprouting from a verdant base. The central tower was the primary living and commercial space, which raised from the sea like a refined sea monster's neck over the waves. The tower is centered in a four miles wide circumference of aqua farming with traditional agriculture. Seawater ballast could be pumped in to stabilize the tower in a storm, while submarine craft launches would continue shipping. It was a transportable manmade island, the perfect grand city of the ocean.

'It was a good plan. Through a series of front companies, real estate brought up residences for the trade market. Agricultural space was provided, and the trade routes were approved. Submarine delivery. Good plan,' he thought, looking at the aqua cities beyond the sea wall, slowly traveling east, Mediterranean bound.

"Good afternoon, sir. I'm Doreian, and I'm here to serve you. We have several specials. Would you like to hear them?" asked a man in a flawlessly fitted white suit. Augustine recognized the smiling face, but the minimal Eastern European accent confirmed that the owners required the staff to wear the original waiters' faces printed over their own. He wondered if they had a printer in the kitchen, vaporizing skin cells then instantaneously replacing them with a person who quit over ten years ago or if it was an outside job.

Augustine lifted his mouth into a seemingly sincere smile, something he often did to pass within typical human entanglement, "Thank you, Doreian. I will have the most expensive whiskey, neat. I have a friend joining me soon. So," he pointed to his eyes, "keep an eye out."

The waiter HUD transmitted the order wordlessly, "Thank you, sir. Also, sir, your friend is here and waiting for you."

Dorian point with an open hand to the rest of the restaurant. Augustine looked up in irritation when he saw that the entire staff and the patrons stopped moving and faced him. Other than the sizzle drifting in from the kitchen, the room fell quiet, and forty-two eyes locked on Augustine. Sweat formed under his shirt, and the nape of his neck felt cold like he was in a winter shower. When he thought about it later, in those short moments of clear consciousness between whatever intoxicant he was taking, he felt that the room consisted of the whole of Jersey York City. White, German or Irish, mixed with Japanese, and Chinese, together with Nigerian, and Ethiopian, all continents and creeds.

What frightened him was the hollow black eyes and lack of facial expression. They were receiver synths, good ones, too. These were not produced on Earth; these were off-world. Military used sleeper cells, programed with enough to function, and, then, when needed, tactical killer mode is activated, and entire cities burn to the ground. He brought, played with, and killed an exotic one, once.

'Excellent use of my funds,' he thought.

"Sir, I'm instructed to receive your request, then, soon, you will be contacted regarding details. If there is an issue with the request, I will notify you immediately," Doreian said, still wearing the false smile with false white teeth. Anger overcame his fear, but Augustine knew that a cross word could have him literally ripped to pieces by these things, which sat unmoving, some frozen in midchew.

'Straight to it then,' he knew with some mental resistance, blowing out a lungful of air.

"I want you, the Cutmen, to kill Richard Zullem within one month," he exclaimed, finally happy to say it aloud. He stared at Doreian, waiting for the response, trying to measure the traffic within the synthetic mind. Dorian's smile drooped slightly and then returned brighter than before.

"Sir, unfortunately, that request has been denied; however, we believe that a compromise can be reached that we can both be happy with. Would you like to hear the suggestion?" he asked, as the only other ambulator waiter approached to deliver the whiskey.

"Sure," Augustine said, "Shoot," then he drained his glass.

CHAPTER 22

Typically, Miguel avoids two things throughout his life, groups of people and animals. He did love animals due to their essential place in nature, which was always outside the city away from him. The same could not be said for people, especially the vacuous, loud, and whiny set of brutes in the Pet Relocate Center's lobby. He knew the call number for the cat, Notizie, and had prearranged the adoption. They were thrilled to offer a pet to the recently bereaved. He has always avoided news-streams, except for placement-biblio with the feeling of being physically and mentally immersed in a wonderfully crafted scene. But, now, he logged in to see the broadcasts. He wanted to know what, it seems, everyone else knew.

His story and his loss.

As he stepped through the sliding glass doors covered with images of possible pets, from a pygmy panda to a winged mouse, he could hear the nearby staff speaking about him and Liz, the fallen inquisitor, a lost white knight. From the way people looked at him with pity and sadness in their faces, he played the part of the bereaved well, so he put his head down. Something in the back of his mind was alerted, barely about to maintain the balance on the razor's edge. The idea of buying a hooded shirt occurred to him as he saw eyes tracking his progress.

'Eyes up,' he thought, trying to maintain any semblance of normality. The building was more of a pet emporium; extinct animals and somatic gene alteration breeds to the left and basic pets to the right. He passed playful giraffes running about with polycarbon enforced bones in one clear holding cell only large enough for two toddlers next to an enclosed strip for racing mini-bears. A careless worker had inadvertently left open a case of winged mice, that were swirling down to steal pet treats from conical containers or trying to borrow into a woman's extravagantly blonde high bun. A man walking a dog that shifted into rainbow color strode by, and the animal sniffed a lazy orange elephant reaching his knee. His feet flew faster as his gaze shifted from the underfoot tiles to the struts of the ceiling, then back down to the floor. Only another fifty feet to the checkout desk.

It was a madness of color.

His Forge signaled his arrival, and a woman with a red tattoo that bled into her eyes greeted him. "Sir, thank you for coming in. I'm sure that the cat will love you and your home!" she chirped. Behind her, two other staff members, each wearing a matching blue vest and an equal number of piercings scattered throughout their body, looked at him. They reviewed the cat's file and, in his opinion, likely commenting on how a man who just lost his wife could be here adopting the cat of a man who was killed in the same vicious manner. His head hung low to the point where his shoulder muscles began to hurt.

He murmured, "Yes, the cat, please." He quickly transferred his information to the Animal Center, then Clausewitz scattered his data until he pulled the DNA transfer from the animal, which was now irrelevant. Though, it was what someone would call 'cute,' with a white mane and intelligent eyes.

The woman with the redeye tattoo squealed and said, "Oh, this is great! May I get an optical scan image with you?" Without waiting for approval, she waved to her coworker, who must be her friend due to his affinity for metal rods in his skin and tattoos. He approached with a smile of black teeth marked with a green zigzag and stared intently at Miguel. The teeth decoration was the style in this part of town, as he had seen others on the street with similar dyeing, in all colors. Some of the street vendors offered composite enamel bonding complete with a dentist chair attached to the street cart.

"Got it!" he said, giving an overly demonstrative thumbs up, then walked into the back. She stopped all movement, holding her head with both hands as if that could help her concentrate on the incoming image directly beamed into her brain.

Her face lit up. "Thanks, Z," she called out. Having collected herself, she began scanning through the thousands of folders to fill out the proper adoption questionnaire. Fusing Miguel's information and the form was quick, and she looked at him again, extending a gray sphere. "Wonderful, all is ready. Please sign, and I will go get your new pet!" The redeye tattoo lady beamed with the joy of connecting an animal its new owner.

'Her brain could probably only process one thought at a time, but she seemed nice, unlikely that she would want to be modified with shark teeth,' Miguel thought as he grabbed the sphere. Then, he wondered if he would judge all people by that metric. The dull gray sphere glowed blue as it scanned in his fingerprints and DNA to serve as a signature. "Ok, I will be right back," she said as the ball faded to gray again.

After a fast about-face, she disappeared behind a yellow wall covered in images of happy humans with happy animals. The shuffling of people continued, and Miguel raised his head, feeling more camouflaged in the sea of changing faces. Only the eyes of a woman glared at him, but he did not know why. Her head stuck out from a woolen sweater like a turtle, and her furry garb was various discordant colors. Miguel thought maybe she was secretly a spider, spinning her own clothing to camouflage herself with the humans, assessing her prey. Petting a gene-altered iguana with locks of hair that changed to every hue of the rainbow, her predatory eyes stared him down.

The lizard's silken hair shifted from multiple colors to deep scarlet along its body and black down to its tail.

'Probably to indicate its mood,' Miguel thought, noting that its eyes, onyx holes in an alien moon, mimicked the woman, and he was not sure which set of eyes was more disturbing.

He could tell how old she was, but her stare was ancient, and her skin seemed thin. She began to walk to him, maybe to spin a web around him. The hair of the lizard swayed in exact motion with the strands of the sweater. The animal's mane shifted from red and black to a deep blue as she stopped in front of Miguel, who had forgotten his purpose in the pet store, all the other people bustling nearby. Her finger disappeared into the hair of her cold-blooded friend, creating an optical illusion where her technicolor sweater becomes the many-colored mane of fur sporting a long tail.

Her voice cracked when she opened her mouth as if she had not spoken for a long time. "Sir," she said, like she was asking a question. The lizard held tightly to her arm and pulled its head into the warmth of the sweater, snuggling, trying to sooth her, as her eyes began to fill with tears. "Sir, I'm so sorry," she sighed, "I'm sorry for your loss." Miguel gulped, stepped back, and looked behind the counter for a distraction. She pulled her hand out of the lizard's blue hair and lightly touched his shoulder. "They got my son, too. Only days ago. His was…," tears rolled down her cheeks, landing on the lizard, who was now a vibrant green, she swallowed and continued, "killed in the same horrible way. You made it, though. The police can't help anymore; we have to tell them enough is enough." Her touch was now a grab, and she shook him as her anger rose. "Enough is enough. My boy is gone," a dam burst inside her, tears fell in cascades, "Your wife is gone, but at least she tried to help. She was on Valentino's case. She was…helping."

"I'm sorry, ma'am, but I can't," Miguel whispered, grabbing her hand trying to loosen her grip. She was a strong woman and pulled him in close. His body was held in lock by his terror and pain; he could not look away from the torture in her eyes, the soul-eating anguish encasing her. There was no wailing or sobs; she did not have enough energy, only the tears and the strength of her reaching out to a man that had suffered a similar fate, another broken soul. Miguel thought that his emotion should have built up so much pressure that they would explode into psychosis, a weeping madness. But, they did not. His face did not falter; all the emotion has been drained, pooling in an unknown place.

"Ma'am," he said evenly, "I want you t…"

She released him, stopping his thought. "My name is Sophie. Please forgive me. I should be babbling on," she sniffled, wiping her nose; her eyes darted around like she had forgotten where she was, searching for something familiar, a landmark.

Without thinking, Miguel shot his arm out, grabbing her hand, and squeezed. "I'm sorry, Sophie. The people, the ones who…killed your son and my wife, will be hurt. They will not be allowed to continue," he rasped into her ear, then turned away, avoiding her gaze.

She stiffened. "Continue to do what?" she asked, pulling her hand free and returning it to petting the lizard, who ruffled its fur.

"I'm back with a new friend," yelled the young woman with red eyes holding up the white cat, who looked as displeased as Miguel. She set the cat on the counter and engaged her HUD. The counter rippled as four thin elements sprouted up over the cat. The four wires joined into a solid metallic ball that began to spin, launching elements the thickness of a human hair down to merge with the countertop. A screen was woven around the perturbed feline until it determined that the living wires' movement was not a threat and laid down for a needed nap. "Ok, carrier ready, and you are off," red-eyed said to the cat, "Thank you, sir." She made a tiny bow, then ventured back around the corner, vanishing into the back of the Center.

Grabbing the carrier, which made a loud click as it detached from the counter, Miguel turned to leave. Still crying, Sophia blocked his way. "I do not understand. You said not to continue. Continue what?" she stammered with tear-stained cheeks. She looked as though the sweater was slowly eating her and the lizard was her only contact with the world, the one thing that could save her if she held it long enough.

"I'm sorry, Sophia. I am. For your son," he said like a man speaking to a child. Something in Miguel changed; something clicked from emotions to hardness, sandstone to diamond.

Miguel's head rose from between his shoulders, reaching full height. He sidestepped her, face emotionless, seeking to lose himself in the vast store, invisible among the aisles.

He turned his head so she could hear his voice as he strode away.

"Yes, Sophie, I did say continue," he said just before he vanished into the throngs of shoppers, "they, I mean all of them, will not be allowed to continue to breathe, not be allowed to continue to live." Then, he disappeared.

O'Bryan took longer than expected to electronically coordinate with the JYC animal shelter transfer system to find the proper cat, she thought, hovering somewhere between a brisk walk and slow jog toward the Pet Relocate Center.

'The message stream is...,' he beamed into her brain, "as you would say garbled."

"Report the issue to the Communication Department. I want a trace back to the source, bounce through all the local AIs and synth brains if needed," she told him out loud, drawing stares.

As an officer, she cared little for odd looks; she only noticed the strange teeth decorations. Vibrant colors with lines around the enamel, or, in a few, she passed, words. Things like BEEF, or Internal OS. People will always play with their genetic structure, whether for ornament or polycarbon bones, with transmittable broadcast recall.

'Hell, I never even dry my hair,' she thought if she would ever what non-job-related enhancements. It was a decidedly NO.

'I reported it; the Pet Relocation Center has informed me that the cat is no longer in their custody,' he transmitted. Her walk slowed like a windup machine to a mid-step.

"What?" she barked through gritted teeth.

"It was allocated to a man fifteen minutes ago. The scramble com-line just reported it to me,' O'Bryan thought to her, just as chipper as before with the electronic sexy voice pattern.

She calculated who might have found the cat's worth and picked it up. The maths added up to Lieutenant Banda. Still, in mid-step, she began drafting a message that cautiously inquired about the Escrito murder case's recent details without total relieving her true feelings, which were starting to claw their way up the back of her throat. Banda, great guy that he is, would not tell her anything, and she might earn a well-deserved counseling letter in her file. A group of young men concerned with joint listening to an internal vox tune bumped into her, knocking her forward.

"Hey, watch it, Charlies!" she exclaimed, losing her train of thought. Of course, they thumped into her, because she was mentally composing a stream message while still standing in the middle of the walk path, but she still thought they were a bunch of stupid Charlies. Simultaneously, each of their three auditory centers was jointly trained on one song; in effect, both committing the same social faux pas did not form in her mind. They were simply jerks.

"O'Bryan, who adopted the cat?" she asked, still eyeing the backs of the youths' heads.

"Al, adoption is no longer the proper term for sharing a residence with a living creature. Some examples are sharing a life, or living a..."

"SHUT UP," she yelled, causing a man walking toward her to jump away and stumble. She pointed an empty palm at him, she thought to align any fears, but he turned, changing his entire route to avoid being within arm's reach. "Who, O'Bryan?"

"Of course, Al. It was Miguel Teague Saxon, your former brother-in-law."

Former. Former brother-in-law that made it final, didn't it. An electronic voice connected to all the information in the world said it. This thing knew the answer to the two trains crossing at such and such speed, to the height of a tower by its shadow, the whole of Pi, it knew all of it. So, she was dead, and those excellent gold eyes have now faded, forever.

Tear were held back by a dam, and the case was still there, still unsolved.

"Dammit, Miguel!" she screamed, walking to the pod queue.

CHAPTER 23

He could still feel the sense of refreshment from seeing the beautiful city rising above the Atlantic, the shining jewels on the tiara of the Eastern Seaboard. The black lines of his elegant personal pod sank back into Manhattan; it was like being reborn. He stretched his muscles, feeling his jacket tighten and the shirt underneath complain due to overstress. Jonas sent him a video link once he reentered the towers.

'Already on a call,' he thought, 'it was nice to be needed.'

Massive blocks of concrete and buttressing blocked out the Sun as he slid through the city's sheath, only to be replaced by bright fluorescence of vendors' stalls and the neon dancing on the nano-wall. Against the pod's AI warning, he touched the pod hull, opening a small window. The air hit his rough face, much clearer than the outside filth, and the populace's ramble returned the feeling of home to his bones. The preprogrammed pod swung around the last corner in Area 7, Level 437, and Batters saw why Jonas was in such a hurry.

Chaos was brewing.

What was first a potluck of protestors of all types gathered in the historic Governor's Mansion Park was now a churning sea of human mass and anger. Different knots of people formed, screamed, and broke off until the sixty or so yards were too packed. The once private cohorts formed into a cohesive horde as wide as the park and over a hundred yards back to the pod track. From his time as a crowd dispersal demoman, he figured that over 70,000 poor sods were out here, all complaining about one thing or another.

He knew what Jonas asked of him. Demo dispersal, and a click, then a boom. It was so, so beautiful.

The giant amoeba of human mass roved near the outside gate of the historic Governor's Mansion. Thousands milled about raising signs or shouting on hand-held loudspeakers like waves of a hurricane that he watched from inside the city shield, crashing, rising to a crest, and crashing again, chipping away the old concrete and rock. The yelling was more like unintelligible screeching now.

The vendors were smart enough to push their carts across the street, giving the human mass a paved square all to themselves. The crowd was ringed by a pulsating wave of projected multihued lights, seeming to form a bioluminescent cell wall. The wall closed in angry vibrating vacuoles of agitated citizens near the bright nucleus of the ancient Governor's Mansion, the only building older than the rebuilt city. He stepped out of the pod, found a dark corner, and waiting for the others as thousands of people marched by.

"Save the building! Enough trees, save the building, enough trees!" a bearded man yelled to the sky as Batters walked by. "Enough trees!" Similar calls shot up from the crowd in all the languages spoken in JYC. However, his advanced pattern recognition inbuilt Forge enhancements had to translate the din into an ascertainable word because he could barely hear his breathing. Even the pavement seemed to shake.

Clusters of tribes formed along the edges of the mansion park and around the late governor's statue. Ten feet of New York Governor Edward Stella stood in golden bronze with one leg up on a small pedestal posing like an explorer. His molded hand shaded his eye from an imagined sun while the other was waving to a nonexistent friend. Batters would never understand it. Out of all the buildings of great renown in the 2,200, they picked this one to preserve. After the water riots, when the original brick structure was burnt to cinders, the state commissioned a five wing, five-story white stone monstrosity. While the outside was fabricated white granite, the internal was an odd composition of every architecture style since the BCs, containing any effect that bordered on a structural vomit.

'Maybe some trees might look nice there,' he thought, 'and a great place to burn down a stupid protest.' He pressed against the bag strapped to his thigh, the chemical elements inside sloshed. He hummed, 'Yes, it knows it is time. They're ready to go.'

From the semi-blackness of a Neo-Berlin style deli over-hang, he saw the totality of restless and desperate bodies struggling to reach the wrought iron fence, then beyond to the moving equipment directly next to the ugly building. Huldu-folks had already shifted their thin, sharp six legs into a phal-anx of interlocking organic metal arms. The robots' seething strength of nanos was pushing bar-like extensions down from the planted limbs, which Batters thought looked more like tree roots. The nanos were simply a barricade, and each overzeal-ous protester that somehow managed to get a handhold to climb over was swiftly swept back into the oncoming flood with lightening quick metal lashes.

Unaware of any local politics, he did not know why these people were upset or why they cared, though he did notice that the city buttressing structural system had changed since he was here last. He assumed that a field of greenery would sup-plant the five-story building of the last governor of New York; all the signs and yelling could no more stop it than a child on a pod track.

The mansion's grandeur was blocked in on three sides by various sizes of massive moving equipment, which was not so much essential for moving, but only for managing the tight turns of the tons of obsolete wood, plaster, and piping. Un-fortunately for the city's reforesting project, the only exit was through the amateurish protesters, who have nothing else to do all day. Entire neighborhoods have been resettled by careful reallocation of nano framework, all while laboriously maintaining a city's critical balance that reaches beyond the clouds.

'Sure, I will hand paint a sign that will stop an AI sponsored reshuffling of hundreds of thousands of citizens. Sure,' he thought, 'The nano-megalopolis could flatten us, all of us, in a moment, like turning off a light switch, and then continue to build masterless construction projects all its own.'

Referencing back to his time in the service, he imagined crosshairs on the loudest, and with a cling of a finger, it would all dissolve into streaks of running humanity. He understood that people feel powerless and afraid, but he thought, 'Hell, speeches, banners, and mobs! Good luck.'

"You gonna get us some sandwiches, Benny?" yelled Joe, striding up, carelessly through a wave of disjointed militants. He slipped between them catlike and gestured to the deli. "Oh, they are closed, man," he said, hoping for a full stomach before they began to cause so much trouble.

The sea of rebels was focusing on the bronze statue of the dead governor; someone was climbing it to speak to the ears nearby. The din was mounting, and Batters stepped into a street inlet for cleaning droids, hoping to cut off the sounds. The droids were jerking between the protesters' legs, mopping up the disobedient civil dregs.

"How's it goin, Joe? What's the news?" Batters was still looking at the churning mass. Joe cocked his head and pointed across the paved park.

"Fine, fine. You see um?" his hand mimicked a handgun aimed straight at Zuby and Jonas, each carrying a large, heavy backpack, seemingly made of unmoving stone amongst the fluid crowds of protesters. They held up signs that match the others, but neither screamed nor moved in chorus with the angry mob, statues of dead among the riot. Zuby was in a new skinsuit sporting long platinum hair, the synthetic skin shined under the dim light.

"Yeah," Batters shouted over the noise, adjusting the bag taped to his leg, "Ok, let's start."

All their HUDs linked, green lights blinked twice, then a countdown appeared in electronic red numbers. Jonas sent their bioForges an audio message, 'I spoke to the man, and we are covered for a short period, but not long. Newcams will be all over this place soon, and the program would affect JYC scanner systems, not newscam or especially international cams. So, command starts at OP word Blowback, duration 2:30 minutes, i.e., one hundred and fifty seconds. Roger?' Even for someone used to command and having absolute respect paid to him, Jonas was starting the sweat.

Batters and Joe responded with exaggerated head nods that could be seen a hundred of yards across the park. They looked as if they were bowing to each other, an extremely polite deadly pair.

"Warren and his cronies are out there too, and they will be audio-linked in. They know us, but we do not know them, so I wired in an ID modifier through each of your HUDs. If trouble comes between you and some punks, HUD clicks the orange button; the Ouroboros will appear on Warren's guys. If the trouble does not have the Druager symbol, then you beat it down. You four will shine yellow. You guys ready?" Jonas said.

Batters and Joe each raised a single flat hand in the air, a sick salute to a long-dead god, then Jonas returned the raised fist and faded into the crowd. Zuby ran in the opposite direction. Both dropped a short tube from their backpacks. It looked like a mat black monkey was clinging to their backs as they shifted between mobs of people, the tube swinging with each step.

'Roger, Blowback,' Jonas mentally spoke to their HUDs as they dashed further into the crowd, igniters ready to be flashed.

The ocean of angry faces was not prayed for, but it was welcome. 'This was the second call from Red Sun in a few days, a very positive sign to promotion from Enswell to Cutman,' Ru thought as he adjusted the magnetar flashback to the correct setting.

"Ru, you circle in from the back. Leo, straight down the middle to the statue. The target just began his speech, and he is surrounded by manifestanti," Diego commanded from the front seat, "Each of you, grab the occultamento." He gestured to the dull white ball placed between them. Ru picked it up; it barely filled his hand and squeezed. His HUD blanked out, causing a feeling of revulsion in his stomach. Typical for his age range, his HUD, with all the extra senses that it pumped into his head, was implanted when he was six. Back when he still believed that animals could talk, and the urban fairies were flying just beyond sight. The organic nerve-imbedded Forge, the size of a freckle on a man's hand, flooded a brain with so many stimuli that he could scarcely continue to exist without it. He doubted he could maintain basic physical functioning lacking the input.

Within his field of view, only the impulses along his optic nerve streamed information to his brain, nothing else. Then, with a brilliant flash, only seen by his mind alone, the system rebooted, and a new black dot hung at the center of his vision.

"Do you, have it? The dot?" Diego asked, plucking the ball from Ru's hand, looking at him quizzically.

"Aye, sir. Black between the eyes," Ru answered as he shook his head, his heart returning to its typical pattern. Diego tossed the ball to Leo. No signs of discomfort gripped his face as he snatched it from the air.

"Ok, now that this is taken care of, tell me the plan as Red Sun told you," Diego growled, attending to his weapon, a water gun. Opening the catch, he poured a viscous fluid, then shook it until he could see bubbles forming through the transparent biodegradable polymer.

Ru started. "Walk to the protest line, drop the hornflash, then approach the statue, so the target canna seen me. Have the hornflash trigger ready and wait for your call." He rooted around in his mind for any extra and pertinent details; coming up dry, he nodded.

Diego nodded back, "Good. Leo?"

"I approach the target on the statue with my...," Leo looked at the same model of water gun that Diego was holding, then shrugged, "weapon hidden, then wait for you. If interrupted, or molested, avoid contact and meet you back here." He eyed the cab space with a face showing that he knew his instructions but was not bright enough to think beyond them.

Ru had separate directions. Red Sun told him that if he were interfered with, he would thrust the molded printed knife that was strapped to his forearm into a low strike to the femoral artery just beneath the pelvis. Any interloper would recoil stunned, then find their legs running red. He had seen it happen once. His friend Boa, an idiot Charly, but still a friend, returned from a failed mission in Nakhon Sawan. The Thai prince had escaped and launched a formal protest to the Southeast Asian Conference. This was unacceptable, and, of course, Boa knew that. As opposed to following the proper Enswell training, the amurresufeiru, the traditional separation of the arm below the socket, Boa spoke back, accused the Cutmen of wanting him to fail. The entire incident was their fault.

Their fault, them, the Cutmen. That, too, was unacceptable.

Hundreds of years of Cutmen history narrowed its eyes through the faces at the table. Red Sun and Black Night both sat cross-legged behind a low black table; each face sat unmoved beyond a quick glance at the Iga blade. All the eyes of the consiglio lifted from the blood strained floor mats up to the blade, which was over two thousand years old, but could still split an iron bar as if it were tissue paper. The punishment was enhanced to the last level, the final punishment. Through rapid breaths, Boa began to apologize, but he knew that it was too late. He took a different tactic that had been tried and failed countless times before, frontal attack. Ru knew Boa; he was a friend, and Boa thought that he could likely take at least one along with him to the grave, or worst, the whole reprint with neural augmentation.

He covered the few steps in less than a second, the unsheathed blade was held high over his head. His muscles have been programmed to assume the kiriotoshi stance after years of training, and he fell into the pose without thinking. Ru did not see it, but, somehow, Red Sun was inches behind Boa, staring over his crouched form. Quiet as a shadow, Red Sun bent forward and whispered into Boa's ear, then tears ran down Boa's face.

Both of Boa's arms straightened, still holding the gleaming sword aloft as he turns to face his teacher. All watched as the two looked at each other. We all knew what would happen next, and no one moved. The dark of the meeting loft obscured any details beyond the sword. The light licked it, sending fragments across the room, catching the dust motes. It fell, swung hard with excellent technical form letting gravity do most of the work.

Red Sun was gone, now sitting back at the table. Boa looked down as if he were kicked in the abdomen, air rushed out of his open mouth with a spray of spittle. He dropped the sword, the clang startled Ru as it bounced off the mats. A red wet patch spread across Boa's white linin pants, while he gasped for air like he was choking. The meeting of floorboards creating channels for the dripping blood, all of it flowing toward Ru in crimson rivulets, though he knew better than to move from his spot. A light grew and flared on the table as Red Sun lit a soft white candle.

'A real wax candle,' Ru marveled, disregarding the channels of blood.

"The punishment has, now, been advanced," Red Sun said, extending his hand. He held a small knife by the handle, barely large enough to fit in his small hands. The candlelight glinted off the short but thick blade. The edge was glowing white as he gently placed the sheath over it. "He will live, after the reprinting, and he will have time to reconsider his actions this day."

Years later, Boa told him what Red Sun whispered that night. "He said, 'You should have a better teacher," Boa explained breathlessly pointing to his thigh were the tip entered, cut, and deposited health-knitting nanos. That same knife was in his hands now, and he was ready to use it with quick, deadly efficiency.

The three Enswells, future Cutmen, walked into the tumultuous human sea, ready to complete their mission.

CHAPTER 24

'Wow, that was easy,' he thought. The symbiosis lab was rendering the data, which was, apparently, a lot, reams, and reams of data. Though not as much was code and compiled DNA, he concluded after the machine formed it into readable documents, over 12,345 pages and a quantum attachment.

'Beagle, isolate the last gene-drive,' he told his HUD stream.

The invisible text hanging in front of his eyes dropped to 8,394 pages. 'Scan and sort into three sections: similar content, similar patterns, and temporally. Create an index for each section.'

'At first, I feared that the data or the cat, maybe a PHISH, allowed someone or thing access to his drives. However, he ran everything through his qua-com that was UN DOD approved, assuming that anything that could batter through that heavily guarded wall would have had him killed while he was still carrying the feline.'

The first 8,394 pages faded into transparence, then slid up to the corner of his vision, and three bright white sets appear. The content read like scribbles of a madman, arrows pointing to other pages, and circles surrounding branches of paragraphs. He clasped his hands together then slowly spread them; each movement mimicked by the biological computer resting in his skull. The pages separated in three dimensions forming an electric hedge around him. Arrows ran from one page to another like an aerial firefight. Tracing them with his eyes was beginning to give him a headache, along with the increased pain from his bones and joints.

'Did I drink something, inject something?' He may have wandered the night, sampling all the intoxicants throughout the boroughs. He rubbed his face furiously, then inhaled to calm his mind.

'Circles: blue, arrows: red.'

He followed the arrows as they darted from one page to another.

> Official procurement virtual work. Preventative techniques spun to the Large-scale Augmented Municipal Protection System (LAMPs) programs, such as concealment neural-net and masking proper practices and tactics.

Another arrow began with a circle around text describing Nadar Forge integration to the primary JYC LAMPS system, then shot thirty-nine pages into the document, which noted that the synthetic amplified neural-net could connect to all nanos within the city shield. Splaying his hands out, he stepped of the virtual cloud of sheets. At a distance, even the small one created by stepping back a few feet, the arrows and circles, red and blue colored respectfully, the cloud was not purple. A sporadic mess of loosely connected possible thoughts and believes, each referring to other loose connections that may not exist.

'Isolate common phrases and word linked by arrows in set one, and isolate common phrases and word linked by circles in set two. Start with the ten most common, disregard common English sentence grammatics,' he told Beagle. With the protection of his lab, his Forge brought up two sets of text dropping columns.

> LAMPS, security, proposal, extra-structural nano-technology, neural-net, crime, Zullem Corporation, synthetic mind, and quantum processor amalgam-

ation, concealment neural-net, and masking proper practices and tactics.

Zullem proposes increasing inner-city defense, a synergy of the mind and physical technology, nano up and out, expansion, and growing police prepense and influence. The city is the citizen, and the citizen is the city. We are building this to fill this expanding need, protect the citizen, and the new programming.

'New programming and some type of defense,' he surmised, he knew that from the news broadcasts. He streamed while walking with the cat, who would not stop its constant meowing. Two news items dominated. The Zullem security proposal and the increase in crime, of which Elizabeth's death featured prominently. The timing was odd.

'What is the first date of the documents?'

'February 13th, 2,786,' Beagle responded tersely.

'Research JYC media, highlight increases in crime, particularly in Levels above 1,000.'

'Open sources report "increase in crime" or a similar phrasing begins on July 9th to present. The most recent article discussed the murder of an inquisitor at the address...'

"STOP!" Miguel yelled, then, regaining his composure, said, "Query response was satisfactory. Hold current file drop, insert into a folder titled First glance." His blood was running hot, focus was fuzzy. "Is there any programming in the file?"

Acknowledging that its owner had spoken out loud, it followed suit. "Yes, sir. The quantum attachment contains coding; however, that is a minimalized file, which is password protected. A qua-run could possibly break it given time."

"How large is the file?" Miguel asked, sitting down, energy ebbing from his system. He was mentally exhausted. Each heartbeat drained him further.

"Including quantum source, logical, instructions, and synthetic neural coding, it is composed of approximately over four million lines, with additional instructions to offline systems," Beagle retorted in a randomly selected extinct Boston accent. Beagle was permitted to find an ancient Earth accent once a week aimlessly. The machine calculated that Miguel thought that it keeps him on his toes.

'Great, I know just the guy,' Miguel thought. "Load it onto my Forge and feed the cat," he said, running to the door.

He drafted a short stream message to an old friend, then fired it off. The cat was tracing his path toward the portal. The fear of an animal escape crept into him, though he typically was not an animal person. Lining his legs up at the portal to prevent the cat from escaping, he opened the portal while still watching the creature. The soft groan of the nano shifting for opening heightened his awareness of all the creature's mannerisms, and he braced for its movement.

"Hey," he heard as the portal ground open. Turning, he saw Al, then a blur. The blur focused into a tight jabbing fist, and only blackness after that.

He intended to circle the mob along the outer edge, tracing his way along the barrier concealing the moving equipment, which sat as a vast motionless mass just beyond the dull burnt orange metal planks. The mob was growing like a living creature. What was once several large groups of hundreds of people germinated into thousands, all falling into one bustling mass spilling out over the pod track and merging with a neighboring set of raging persons. Unfortunately for Jonas, the pulling and pushing, like blades of tall grass in the windswept field, could not control his movement. He was pulled off the barrier, spun, and pushed to the pullulating nest of spikes from the Huldufolk net. Barely retaining their humanoid form, the very city's grey law enforcement extensions were now linked, thousands of them, creating a metal forest of sharp boroughs and branches, each arching over the protesters.

'Impressive,' Jonas thought, 'no one can climb that without a puncture in a limb, but the countdown is still running. All, remember, this is for maximum shock. Just as the man said.' Virtual 'aye ayes,' were relayed back. He thought it will be quite a show.

He allowed the human amoeba to cast him aimlessly as he opened the tube hanging from his backpack. White liquid gushed out, splattering the pavement stones just below knee Level. The mass did not know; they sloshed and sprayed it amongst their shoes and boots, stepping on each other until his wake was covered inflammable fluid. After thirty seconds of hard-won jostling, he was almost on course, being pummeled between the line of outraged bodies on the Huldu-folks' blockade and the statue. The crowd's flow was changing slightly, ebbing toward the middle of the square, around the statue. He thought that he saw a man there, speaking to the passing crowd, like Tyler once did, as the lights of battery torches flashed, then he was pushed to the side.

'Perhaps they knew no one could penetrate the barbed-wire phalanx of the Huldufolk police barricade,' he wondered, or something was grabbing their attention. Time was short, and the human barbeque will not serve as many as he would have liked, but it will have to do. The idea of the flames sprouting up from the legs of the crowd quickened his heart. Light shined in Jonas's eyes, and a grin spread like a fissure breaking the ground on his large face.

Quickly, he adjusted the webbing and slung the backpack lower, the tube now spraying the passersby feet. His massive back muscle ached because of his walking crouch to avoid someone noticing his commanding height.

'The plan has changed. Zuby, I'm yards from the statue

and will circle your way, then drop the backpack heading to the street at 8th and 5th. Copy?' he ordered.

'He is speaking to me, straight into my brain; it was like God licking my cortex,' she moaned inwardly. 'Yes, copy. I see your indicator and the others too. I will draw over your trail, then follow. Copy,' she responded through the Nadar Forge coms line.

'Understood. Batters and Joe, are you done?'

"Almost, just finishing the circle now," Joe verbally answered. Jonas could barely hear him over the crowd's roar and the smashing of rather unfortunate bodies against Batters bulk; he is causing micro-fractures as he hulked by. He glazed over the heads of thousands to the street; two glowing yellow dots were flickering as people passed them. They were working from opposite ends toward the middle of the square.

'You guys, go to 6th, then meet us at The Cellar,' he cut off the line, pushed his way past the statue, then turned toward the street. The human cattle circled too tightly around the bronze late governor, so he cut a broader turn, still emptying the backpack. Then his ears were crushed in by overpressure, and the chants became screaming. People like stones pelted his back as they ran from the main protest line; signs and banners floated on top of the sea of faces like jetsam. The lights were set low to simulate an early winter's evening, but he could see the blood-splattered over the confused faces rushing toward him.

As he dropped the backpack, his HUD reached out, 'Draugers, drop packs, break off from encirclement, evac. I repeat, EVAC,' he commanded. While it was not actual volume when speaking mind to mind, he hoped that his full force of will would have the same impact.

His senses were dulled by the stinking glut of humans, even by the city itself, but he knew the energy would change due to the shedding of blood and anguished cries. A spark was struck, and the electricity ran over his nerves readying his muscles. He bent into an exaggerated cat-like angle, and a flame roared over his head, pointing to the platform of the statue.

A man's face was lit by the burst of fire. He was yelling at the human sea. No, no, powerfully speaking to them, explaining. The man only blocked his face from the fire with his hands, then continued to speak. His face was in the shadow of the statue's great arm, but his clothing, neatly fit and looking luxurious, showed his appreciation of power. The din drowned out the voice, but Jonas could see the faces light up and the anger fade when the people saw him. Shouts of "Yes," and "Yeah, preach it, brother," sounded around him. A child was awkwardly climbing the platform, which was just a few feet wide, to be closer to whoever this man was, to bask in his glory. Then another, followed by a third.

'Too many people,' Jonas knew, 'Violence on one side, the push for freedom on the other, then a speaker in-between.'

Even under the shadow, this man was like Tyler, the great rabble-rouser, the driver of the rebellion. Someone in the crowd pointed a torch up, highlighting the speaker, the divine provocateur, and the sound of his voice finally reached Jonas's ears.

"Citizens, citizens! I know you think that I'm rich and know nothing of what you feel, but I DO! I AM WITH YOU! Gather round, come, come. I can help to fix this! Together, we can fix these!" he yelled, continuing his speech. The torch's flash repainted the man's face in light, displaying him for the crowd to see. "I'm Richard Zellum, and I AM WITH YOU!"

'New opportunity.'

'Zuby and Joe meet me here; everyone else gathers at the street opposite. That includes you, Warran and your guys. Batters, find out what happened in the east of the square, then report,' he thought. From his point of view, the orange light flickered, times almost up. 'Blowback time is almost up, so separate yourselves from the packs.

A Charlie covered in a thick coat rushed by Jonas carrying a pistol of some kind, aiming it toward Zellum. Jonas knew the smell, a deep Earth mining organic fluid that erupts into flame once oxygen filters through the first layer of the waxy substance. 'Bad stuff. I remember it from under Moscow, deep under. Russkies were a tough bunch, even when they were on fire.'

The Charlie, whoever he was, kept astonishing aim in the jostling crowd; even someone with Jonas's bulk could barely find sound footing. He was holding fire until the crowd put him right on target, the perfect deadly sway before the practiced trigger pull. Jonas covered the yards in quickstep, feet bouncing between rioters like a dance; he dodged a large mass of limbs or spun from one side to another. Then he was within reach of the armed man. Upon closer examination, the gun was bioplastic with a resealing plug over the barrel. It was small, green, and could only have enough fluid for one more shot. Jonas relaxed, allowing the crowd to rock his colossal frame with the man. The man waited for the time to strike; Jonas waited for the moment just before the finger released the fire. Both their heads went right, looking past the statue to the vast array of apartment blocks filling the city plaza with artificial light, then slowly left, inch by inch toward Richard Zellum. The finger was unhurriedly tensing, inches then, and fire would hurl toward the collection of bodies.

Close enough now, Jonas's hand struck like a snake, jabbing his giant finger behind the trigger, then wrenched the weapon back. The man's supernaturally white face spiraled as his arm was pulled back, freeing his own hand from Jonas's crushing grip. His eyes grew, or more accurately, the skin around his eyes drew back, empowering the powerful muscles to push toward the oversized eyeballs to focus on Jonas. Assassin's eyes, Jonas could tell, but not with the gene-alteration.

The coat flew up along the man's arm, masking his face in deep shadow, and he retreated, crouching into the blackness under the crowd's knees, as if he were being trampled. Then, he was gone. HUD systems could not find him in the 360-degree scan, nor could it plot his escape by tracking the possible disruption in close by protesters.

A hand grabbed his shoulder from behind, and Jonas jumped to the side, almost cracking his fist into whoever made that a gamble. But his hand was hanging in the air just over Zuby's head, and she was looking up to him with glowing green eyes. Her new skin suited her well, her smile taut over her beautiful teeth. Joe was behind her waiting for instructions.

The team was ready.

He walked past the general protesters quickly, automatically, paying them no mind. Rolling on his shoulder under a group, then sliding under their outstretched arms, but he continued his forward progress, making the mob think that he was a jester place out of his time. Ru, clad in a dark robe and red boots, crept along the eastern barricade fondling the horn flashes in his pocket. The human sea ebbed like a withdrawing tide, and passersby scarcely touched him. The trouble would be at the police nanowall. He turned his head to the side to register any details, just long enough for the HUD to hold the image. 'Show still image over the right eye,' he commanded his Forge. As he reached out to caress the wall on his right, he viewed the image.

The outer edge of the visual representation was occupied by curious pedestrians gathered in small groups. The mass of heads recorded the protest through their eyes, feeding the vid-log to their Forges, clusters of anxious citizens framed the image. Further in the image was the sportsmen of the mess; furious, drunken members ferociously shouting to the sky. They were all the violent ones, the ones enraged at the city, the system, or most likely themselves. The collection of outrage pulled the most violent together into a churning, hungry chaos of red blood without leadership. In the background of Ru's mind, the enhanced subconscious tactics filed through thousands of images feeding to his semiconscious pattern recognition system, all searching for a match. Regardless of light, angle, or color, the neurological system could distinguish all manner of things beyond Ru's conscious mind within a fraction of a second. Often, it annoyed him. He could interact with the world through a dream-state, without conscious thought, because his body knew what was coming before his mind did.

'Got you.' His eyes targeted Leo, while the man was casually walking to the center of the largest group, hand in his pocket, finger already on the trigger. Ru stepped past the youths, each showing the validity of their point of view with the loudness of their voices. He will always think of these people, city people, as youths, so little has passed through their small minds. He merged with another group of rebellious youngsters heading toward the main crowd between the statue and the thick cluster of bodies on the Huldufolks. While he thought that the Huldufolks look like a child's drawing of stickmen, their ability to shift into any other shape and their incredible strength made them something to wonder, something to always respect. His adopted group intermingled with another, the constant bursting of bubbles and forming of new ones. In his view, they were all in a hurried to drift from one place of disgust to another. His feet switched directions as the new members joined, he included himself in the new angry bundle of curse yelling city dwellers. A shower was early awaiting.

The air was one of the main things that told him the social class of whatever bunch he had encroached upon. The atmosphere in the Cutmen's pod was sterile, lacking any scent, cleaned until nothing remained of the last ride, while this brainless wandering company was all Undertown, and likely its dregs. They massed at the edge of the largest part of the mob, raising arms and voices to protest. The Unders yelled in all their languages and dialects of the city's faults under the pain of a razor wire just inches from their eyes, but they all slipped from his mind because of the stench of the bodies and their breath. He could only handle so much. He knew the stink and was subliminally forced to push those thoughts of his past away.

'This place was good enough.'

Covering his face with his coat, he opened his pocket's inner lining and dropped one of the horn flashes. It fell inside his pocket, bouncing off the flagstones, losing itself under the feet of the mob, the one that formed to tell the city their demands and hold the elite accountable, or because they had nothing better to do and were bored. The hornflask would not have cared either way, torn flesh is just torn flesh, just as blood was blood.

'Mark me, first one is set. Heading to the Blueman line behind the statue,' he told his Forge, relaying the commands to Diego.

'Roger got it, position marked. Leo, I'm sending you the mark,' Diego responded, sounding bored.

'Wonder how long it had been since Diego got to play. Several decades?' Ru thought, 'Now, he is only a predator caged in a castle, sending knights out, but his arm will never hold the weight of a sword again.' As opposed to waiting for nature to take him, in Ru's opinion, the only valid goal of a Cutmen career is the Slavnaya smert by blade or bullet. He did not want to make a solid long final breath spewing a bit of blood.

Approaching the Blueman line through a concentrating crowd of people, he stooped and dropped the other hornflash. He spun it like a top. It spiraled out and came to a stop behind the more recent group, who were trying to climb the elaborate forks of the Huldufolks' arms, now spreading needle-like into the air. A more hands reached for a solid hold, the more the metal arms forked, rose, and became finer barbs aching over the protesters. Each armed with a diamond point. The gray stones of the hornflash were batted around like miniature footballs; then it vanished in the nebulous mixture of shoes and boots.

'Mark two. Second flash dropped,' he thought.

On Diego's HUD, the square was marked by two blinking red dots. 'Enhance,' he told his machine, focusing on the metal icon of the fallen governor. He pinched the air, then extended the imaginary manipulation until his HUD was filled with Richard's face.

'Intel confirmed. Target is on the statue. Ru drop the last, then walk west before crossing back to me. Leo, avoid the flashes, and get into position.'

'Roger,' they both responded. Another flash dropped from his pocket as he pushed through the horde. He heard it clattered, then lost it as the bodies past him.

'Mark three,' Ru thought, quickening his pace. He saw the target as he shouldered through groups of people that were barely of age. Mentally, he organized the first, second, and tertiary triggers waiting for the order. An instantaneous rumination on any of the number display in his left eye would activate the primer.

'Leo, are you in position?' Diego asked without any urgency.

'Diego is probably cleaning his nails,' Ru thought, ruefully.

'Yes,' Leo responded, 'the crowd is agitated, moving, but I can get a few shots off.'

'Ok. Ru, trigger the first, then get moving.'

The electric yellow number faded, replaced with a red slash. Ru was running as fast as he could, bumping and crashing into anyone ahead. He did not want to be part of what was coming.

The first hornflash was still inadvertently being kicked about two hundred feet behind him, casually floating over the flagstones, before crashing, then launching again by a hapless boot. It rattled across the ground, and the smooth oval surface rended away as dozens of sharp protrusions emerged. The metallic core held them, the angled metal slugs, for the next phase of ignition. The signal came in an instant.

Forty solid metal barbed horns erupted out in several straight magnetically traced lines, ripping through and puncturing bodies sixty feet off in the crowd. A circle of death shot out as the barbs ran through veins, lungs, and hearts; any viscera between it and the end of its magnetic arch. A man clad in a protester's black coat and designer stomping boots was splattered with his friend's blood as the horn ripped through his skull, leaving a gory half-face, air rushing in red bubbles where a mouth once was. The metal glint caught the protester's eyes, he closed them tight, but he knew what was coming. Tears formed and leaked through, cutting their way through the coat of blood. Finally releasing his breath, he opened his eyes to see the barb motionless in the air while his section of the group was screaming for mercy or help from someone, anyone. Seemingly held up by the air itself, blood dripped from the barb to the flagstones and onto his friend's mangled face. He jumped away, skidding to the floor in the viscera, still staring at the red piece of metal. It began to rotate parallel to the stones, turning slowly, then quicker, building up its gory borrowing power. A magnetic arch pulled it, along with all the other murderous barbs, into a spiral drawing back to the flash, ready for another throw.

Jenny always wanted to be part of a movement but never found the time. Her stream alerted her if a boycott or march was happening in her tiny neighborhood. Rarely, did her feet cross the street anywhere more than four blocks away. Tonight was the night, and she relished the change to do something beyond her ineffective office role of moving bits from one place to another. Her joy was not diminished by the marathon effort to persuade Li to forget the VR spacedragon battle or whatever it was, to join her. Their hands met as they jogged to the square, they both smiled, and she knew that he was happy, and she will pay him back tonight in the bedroom.

She read protests or civil disobedience were a real value to the community, but this one was like a toddler waking from a nightmare. While it started slowly with group singing and shouting chants, it swiftly began a full tantrum of flying glass and attacks on the Bluemen. Luckily no actual humans with badges had arrived yet. She heard sirens wailing behind her. Wanting to see, she turned to face Li, then wiggled in Li's arms. Finally, she stepped on his feet, bouncing up to see over his shoulder.

Li encircled Jenny with his arms, hoping to protect her from the angry dangerous crowd of sharp knees and elbows. He was worried about their safety, but he thought his arms could control the bodies bouncing off, safeguarding her. She turned to look at him; he wished that she saw how he was a brave protester, venturing against the city. A firebrand, but, no, she was trying to pinpoint that sound. The mush of bodies muffled all the sounds beyond arm's length, like wearing a pillow strapped to your head. He cocked his neck to upturn his ear. That sound, the wailing that clawed its way into your skull, was not a siren. It was a chorus of screaming. As he realized this, his heart and Jenny's heart merged, just a bit. The jagged hunk of metal shredded its way into his back, pulling bloody bits of his heart, then exited into her chest. Both fell dead without feeling any pain, knowing only shock, then a comfy blankness. They sprawled among the other dead forming a carpet of growing red. The returning barbs spiraled back to the core, creating waves of blood and bodies and a fiery melody of the ones not yet dead.

'Ru, trigger flash two,' Diego thought, and Ru mentally activated the small stone, then pressed on.

"Sir, we need to go. Any security that this had is deteriorating quickly, and if I pull my guys up here, then the pod will be exposed," Helyettes yelled over the crowd; the cries and chants were now just one noise pitching up and down, vibrating in his core. Braced up his heavily muscled arms to the lower base of the statue, he looked up to the employer's son, hoping that the concern could not be seen in his face. He had trained this lad, worked with him until all weapons were his friends, and his fist could now join them as the deadliest.

'Richard, the boy...,' Helyettes thought, 'He will always be a boy to me, but would have passed all the tests that my people would give, and be awarded the final scars along his spine. Those scars would blossom into sun sending out thirteen rays of scarred tissue in thick white marks where the knife cut between the shoulder blades. Even if he is not from my blood, I will always be proud of him. But this is too dangerous. I know this type of work.'

He eyed the surging groups of people through growing anxiety. The marks of a horns flash were clean; he was sure that there was more than one. The cores held energy for three bursts, but after seeing the yards of dead human carpet, that was enough. The northern part of the square already born the marks as a zombie circle was trying to rise from the bloody floor. That is what he was taught so long ago, the hornflash leaves a "zombie circle," even in the field manual. It starts with the first strike, then the runners come, spurting blood, too filled with fear to scream. Then, the ones with loyalty to the fallen pull broken bodies and amputated limbs of friends or family somewhere, anywhere but the zombie circle. He has seen it before. Bellies were open, ripped clothing struggled to hold in torn guts, creating a child's finger paint masterpiece still wet with blood. He saw the stragglers from his elevated position, and the reason why it was called a zombie circle, wandering souls, lost eyes scanning for loved ones, some holding severed limbs. The zombie circle ends with screams dying into whimpers, hands grasping for some imaginary item that hung between life and the forever sleep. The hands never find what they were seeking. Richard did not see it yet, and that delay is how one becomes a victim.

"We need to leave! NOW!" Helyettes rumbled at him, his voice close to shouting. Richard's attention was on the faces in the crowd, and those faces looked up in adoration to an elite champion, overlooking the shrieks from the other side of the square. He lost all vision in one eye as a flare blasted toward Richard. The fire shot up from the crowd; heat lingered on his face. Dropping down, he surveyed the people close by; all their heads jerked down like turtles retreating into their shells. Just beyond, a huge pale man with black tattoos running up from his back over his bald head was staring at someone in a cloak. That man raised something to the air, and the flare burst into the sky.

The angle was off by degrees he knew, doing the math in his head, but others crouched and shielded their faces. Richard pressed the children on the platform against the molded statue, blocking them from the fiery burst. Helyettes feet turned, and he shot forward, demolishing the wall of human bodies between him and the cloaked man. While he was an exceptionally large man, a massive moose when compared to many in the crowd, his battering way required him to push through like a glacier sheering off boulders. In the crush, he lost the cloaked man between the heads being pushed aside. The pale man was something else entirely. He was a tree made of moonlight; he was the landmark. After smashing through dozens, the crowd parted, possibly fearing his enraged bulk. The sound impacted him, bubbling up beyond human tolerance. This was an experience without any concept of time, just his raging shoulders and the mass of things that may be human or not. Helyettes, the bullet.

He broke past the last line, his head emerging through confused mass like a rock during a tide. All the others wanted to be home and safe, not part of this enterprise of fire and madness, they backed away from him quickly regardless of the spouting fire. Grabbing the men's shoulders and thrusting them apart, he saw the pale giant grappling for the weapon, a neo-plastic gun, then, the other man disappeared into the crowd.

Both of their ears pitched up, listening to the growing wails that broke out high above the din. The second horn flash was activated. The pale man pointed to Richard, then with the other hand toward the pod. Helyettes nodded in acknowledgment then turned back to Richard, who was still guarding the children pressing them against the statue, which was now the center of the exodus. People were stampeding over each other, rabbiting to the street, jammed chest to chest, pushing east and to the barricades along the side.

'Zuby, ignite once I pass the statue,' Jonas ordered into the ether. He scanned the crowd, caught the glowing forms of his crew outside the maelstrom. 'Need to move quickly if I want to avoid becoming a matchstick,' he mused.

'Got it,' she thought back, smiling internally.

Jonas pushed the rambling mass aside with violent thuds, running with Helyettes to Richard, who finally climbed down and was handing the bairns to their parents, or, any adults that might shuttle them to safety. They scurried off, losing themselves in the crowd that was hemorrhaging like a deep bruise, releasing the blood of the human wound through the vessels of streets. The buzz of newscast drones circled overhead. The legend tells that the squadron was so thick that one could jump from one side of the square to the other without their shoes touching the crowded floor. This was no longer a protest the relocation of the Governor's Mansion; terrorism and gang riot dominated the stream, meaning human Bluemen will arrive soon. Once they arrived, the stakes go up and the price of shredding drops.

Helyettes rammed his way through, grabbed Richard's delicate coat, lifting him from the ground, and enfolded him in the thick cables of muscles. Launching over the bodyguard and the master, Jonas rolled through the dispersing mass like a bull. As they turned around the corner of the statue's platform, disappearing from Zuby's view, the orange light of Jonas HUD icon faded; she hit her mark.

Ru's knife was out, ready to execute several expert strikes on the concentration of human parts pressing him against the barricade when he saw the blue light. The sharp electric blue danced between the feet and darted up legs before expiring below the waist, then it found life again, jumping to another leg. People failed to notice the fire as it bounced from one to another, flashing to life, stomped out by hammering feet, then spreading below, dancing over shoes. The living blue flame played beneath their feet.

Losing his breath under the growing pressure, he struggled to mount his feet on the flexible barrier. With extraordinary effort, he squeezed his body over the riot of hands and desperate faces, all fighting to push back against the more tremendous pressure of those thrusting forward, motivated by the grandest rationale. Fear. Sliding over bodies, he righted himself, sheathed the knife in a flash, then dropped into a momentary empty space. Having worked with accelerants before, he knew that the flame would not bloom under the charging feet. As the crown thins, air will rush in, and the fire will do its only job, to consume. The entire panicked mass will run, spreading the fire like a disease, transferring from cloth to cloth and hands to head. His brain thought of burning butter-flies landing on dry hay.

Separating from the flammable clutch was best, he cogi-tated his escape. He triggered the third hornflash, hoping one side of the human amoeba will direct east, splitting the weight of the hurtling chain of strangling feet. Over the crush, he could not hear any change in the volume. The square roared like a wrestling match between thousands of people. He had his knife, Ren Sun's knife, but slashing would only cover him in blood and delay his flight.

'Ok, up and over.'

A flurry of lightening kicks to groins and stomachs offered lower shoulders and necks to haul himself up. Lean-ing over, he grasped the barriers' top edge and took advantage of the tightly packed bodies hopping from shoulders to heads, then back to another shoulder. Though not built to full fru-ition yet, the blue fire was growing beneath the crowd, blue flame licking the air between them and arching out to empty flagstones.

Others followed his example; scores of bloody and crushed people clambered up the barrier, which began to wob-ble. Soon, hundreds of people balanced on top of the fence, while thousands more pressed it from the base. His timing must be perfect. He paused at another rise of the barrier, legs constantly shifting on the trampled, then was forced up by the deluge of incoming bloody people. The border buckled, falling over the swarm, and he threw himself, rolling down a rock-fall of human boulders on to empty stones, then broke into a sprint. The fire bloomed up his boots, licking a fiery tongue towards him, then was snuffed out with each jerk of his legs. Two unnaturally large men were pulling away from the crowd, running into the stampede, their power drove them through. One was holding a smaller man over the bulk of his massive shoulder. They were moving like a train, efficiently rushing through the few subjects still entangled in the Huldufolks line of twisted arms.

'Blockers,' Ru thought and jumped over a fresh group of protest escapees like a deer. His HUD lit over the smaller man, wreathing a red circle around his head. 'Target located,' the HUD text read as Ru slid under a tangle of human limbs collapsing over his path. "Diego, target located," Ru screamed, "Please advise!"

"Where is Leo?" Ru heard Diego's boredom because he was stuck in the pod, though now it was in the thick of running former protesters.

"Don't know. He missed his shot. Target is conscious and unharmed," Ru yelled, shouldering through groups of people, whose eyes showed that they were only concerned with flight and not much of anything else. The overwhelming instinct of animal fear gripped them, the wild-eyed gazelle look right before the lion's teeth sank into their neck, then the snap of bone. Confusing claimed the square, the quaking minds were frightened of everything from the water to the air. In what was a genuinely human exercise, the crowd was now filled with boundless dread, a quivering subconscious alert of something that might be consumed by feral teeth and rending claws.

"Follow to assess the target's condition, then return to Ringo Headquarters. I'm leaving. Out," Diego barked, disconnecting from the Nadar Forge network.

'Great,' Ru thought as he ran breathless, skirting between frighten mobs and blue fire flashes. At full sprint, he removed his jacket, threw it over a man's face as the blue lingered a bit too long, threatening to climb up to soak his shirt. Then, he scanned the crowd to track the target. The massive men carrying the smaller target cut across the now open square to the Huldufolks line; then the police bots parted, revealing a pod. Still running, carrying a man or not, they fled into the one corner that was free of blue fire and frightened protesters. An expensive pod, more luxurious than the Cutmen's fleet, was set near the construction equipment. The huge dark man gently placed the smaller man on the pebbles of the construction site like he did not want to wake a sleeping infant. The target was not short or tall, after closer inspection from what Ru's training had taught him, was quite able to supply massive muscular strength from his lean limbs. The well-muscled men were protecting him as if he was a rare jewel. Ru drew his blade, slid toward the remaining barricade fencing and crouched.

'Assessing,' Ru mentally told his system. The blade was not for the target, though if he were forced, he would use it on him. The keen blade was for the massive men, he knew that regardless of his combat training, he would be crushed. He heard yelling between the darker man and the target as he was bouncing off the large man's shoulder like a man falling off an elephant. Now, he knew his name, his position in society. Richard Zellum, philanthropist, video stream darling, and trillionaire, in so much as the castled society has trillionaires. And, most importantly, the most critical linchpin against his father's aggressive and manipulative policies.

"Thank you," the dark man hesitantly yelled to the evener taller pale man while pushing Richard into the portal of the pod. Compared to each other, these two specimens looked like a mocha coffee next to a glass of milk, though the pale one had black tattoos tracing up from his shirt, charting darkness over his skull. Ru gasped when he saw the man's eyes, ebony points against the moon's surface.

Richard swung around, resisting his bodyguard's mighty strength to stare at the other man, apparently a well-timed savior. They said nothing to each other, only locked eyes. Slowly the target reached forward with an open hand; the other man of moonlight enclosed Richard's hand in this monster grip, then Richard and the bodyguard entered the pod, and the portal closed, leaving a black surface like a river stone. As the grind of the pod magnetic propulsion steers them through the great towers of the construction equipment, the man walked into the darkness beyond the lights of the square and vanished. 'Transfer the pale man prints, gait, size, and physical markings to Diego,' he told his Forge; he wanted to know that man.

Squadrons of newsdrones orbited from above, catching the scene as it grew from scores to thousands bursting from the square of the late Edward Stella and the Governor's Mansion. The groups merged into a mass of humanity that did what all large groups of people do, they bled, burnt, and screamed, hemorrhaging outward like a bruise from a gut-punch, filling the streets with agony.

The butcher's bill counted over one thousand eight hundred dead, another eight thousand six hundred fifty-two injured. The field of play was chaos, and Ru, Jonas, Zuby, Batters, Leo, Diego, and Joe played their parts well. Blueman circle the square but were ordered to hold back. Nothing in the city could burn beyond flesh; even the clothing of the victims ignited only to dissipate into the air leaving the smell of charred chemicals. The buildings and apartment blocks were vast constructions of what has left of the nano-triggers fire on Earth so long ago, build from elements from the ground and sea. The minds of the city will not let it burn.

Only the people burn, and they erupted like a forest fire.

Fragmentation barbs was the beginning of the transfer of fuel, trees falling from an ax or collapsing from years of rot, piling up, until, under the sheer weight, crashing forth and breaking through the surrounding timber, sending branches and sprigs falling to the ground. The fear of the wooden crumple brought the running feet of the fuel, the fleeing of melancholy and mad. The nightmare pushed the kindling into the waiting flames, which were circulating in blue sparks rustling underfoot.

Soon, the wind of the crowd's own movement carrying blue sparkling embers into the old wood and the saplings: the people. These embers ran until their hearts exploded, spreading the blaze, which traced after them like a fire roaring over a dry hill, consuming everything. Heat shrouded the embers, wrapping them in a torrid embrace, freeing their clothes to the air, leaving only a black smoking remains, like charcoal. Like leaves, once touched by an ember, the flame sprouted to create tiny fires that grew and grew until the whole scene was burning. Blue flames streaked across the flagstones, then fire claws ripped over a person, chemical burns down to the bone. The host spilled into the street, but thousands still remained, and blue-lit bodies darted from within. The screams that started from general alarm swelled and reached a higher tone until the Dying's last wails became a physical force shaking the officer's very bones across the street. The local qua-mind activated the flagstones; walls burst from the pavement, trapping tens of thousands in the square. The liquid accelerant was quelled as the road engulfed the escapees, draping them in a gray foam.

Somewhere, likely in Skytown, an order was given, and the walls grew higher, entrapping the remainder. Due to maintaining the structural integrity of the city buttress, the fire dousing foam was not used, even as the officers saw skin bubble and melt from the few that attempted to climb the nano-wall with burning fingers. The sight of flaming bodies being ripped apart by other roaring roasting bodies was lost on them. They could only hear it. The cries became one sound, a thunderous roar, then heightened into a stone shattering maddening shriek as all the voice reached the maximum level of pain. The officers stood to block street onlookers, and the sound drilled into their minds. They bit into their lips, drawing blood to prevent the tears from forming as they waved away all the other citizens.

Newscams and mosquito sized drones recorded it all. Dropping low to swirl like actual insects, they scanned bio-Forges of the entire crowd, accounting for the total butcher's bill, creating a catalog of the dead even before the last of the blue flame turned the final piece of flesh to a cinder. Provocateurs leered that the protesters got what they wanted, the mansion will remain, the statue will be replaced with a monument for the fallen. AI news commentators' artificial voices trembled through speakers blaming this person or that policy, fingers pointed in all directions. They beamed directly into peoples' skulls that the tragedy was an act of terrorism, discounting the real motivations of the crowd. Through it all, one fact remained true: the city wins, as always.

Emergency services will benefit from the tragedy. It will be used as a teaching opportunity, and experts worldwide will be called in for comment. The young, well-liked Richard Zellum, his bodyguard, and an unknown figure will receive ac-colades and honors for protecting little ones, though the news will not report that all the children are cinders, burned black, now ground to ash along with their parents. Security forces will search for the unknown hero, but Richard tells the com-missioner to let the man rest and be free of scrutiny.

Finally, the fear of the citizenry, while it was not proved true, it was real and must be dealt with.

The entire stream field is alive with docudramas con-cerning the nano-triggers' troubles and how entire popula-tions reacted with broken brick violence to their neighbors: explosions and blood. Even more ancient archives were raided. The constant soul bleaching broadcasts of archaic attacks by both state versus non-state actors, or non-state against the state, the blood, and bloated bodies, bombarded the city, even the world. So-called talking head experts verbally combat with genuine vitriol as screens played videos of planes crashing into buildings, smoke billowing into the sky following an explosion in a tube train packed by innocents. The citizens become martyrs, while the city continues, bustling with industry.

The sounds of the street changed as new calls were heard from the angry public. A breach of public trust had occurred. The city must unite. Luckily, the Zellum Corp provided a new enhanced public safety and security policy before the council. 'Yes, that will save us' and 'Thank God that someone can provide peace…safety,' could be heard at busy corners.

They will; someone will; we must just wait for the freely given solution. Smiles glittered in boardrooms, and stocks quickly rebounded from a sharp dip.

Yes, a savior was found, the economy guided into positive territory, and JYC will soon have the tools to address the growing increase in violence and crime.

Electric municipal calendars clicked to another day. The council moved up the security proposal vote by one week from the unforgettable day: the attack on the Governor's Square. One week, then the vote, then security protecting the streets. The whole city will be shielded from within and without.

The people are just…waiting.

PART FOUR

CHAPTER 25

Intercedent Three:

> Washington District of Colombia, 2,134 AD
> Eisenhower Executive Office Building – 10:00 AM
> Presidential Press Conference covered by staff reporter George Sipriz of VideoDex

He thought he was selected because of the three billion subscription members of the VideoDex hub. They want to reach out to younger voters, pull them in, and lock down their ballots for the next election. Basic politics.

'Simple,' he thought, have a video blogger write up a quick piece about whatever political business that the Press Secretary babbles on about, then, at least, the viewers will know the President's name. 'Name recognition is the name of the game, heard that somewhere.'

'President Charles Horace Roberts comments about, say, the hydrogen explosion on the South American branch of the World Rail or, maybe, the new Chinese asteroid cluster out in the belt, or the methane bubbling out of the ice-free Arctic. Whatever, the viewers will glance at it before jacking into the newest Cinegame into the VR system. Maybe even drawing in more subscribers.'

The idea made him chuckle. The rugged yet attractive face of the prez, half-accountant, half-cowboy-movie star, was broadcast to in-vid displays, virtual newspapers, radio casts, and billboards in-games where the player is immersed in a novelized land, fighting whomever. Say, an intelligent intergalactic jellyfish, infected by a virtual virus allowing it to stalk you in your dreams. All the background telephonic and motion video played the prez. Digital billboards showed his face, buildings made of code depicted that presidential look and words spray-painted across the virtual bricks were his. He was everywhere.

'Brilliant,' George Sipriz thought as he looked to the real journalists who were streaming into the small briefing room, fighting for the best position among the rows of seats. It was odd that the briefing was held in the Eisenhower Executive Office Building. He did not know much about the building other than it was old, few hundred years old, and held a long dead prez's secret offices. He almost got lost in its hundreds of rooms. Luckily, he got there early.

The Press Secretary should come out soon to start the formalities, so George activated his watch, a screen was cast across his forearm. Holding up the left arm, he read through the news reflected off his skin. After cycling through the games news, which was lackluster between new releases, he scanned the world news. US political and international actions bored him. Hell, he was only here because a buddy offered up his name for the occasion. But, he thought it was best to brush up on one of the general topics of discussion.

The world offered up the typical stories of famine, disease, and war, both virtual and physical. Resource struggles dominated, some with only fists flying, but most with artillery. The clicking of pens and shuffling of folders broke his concentration, and he realized that the Secretary would soon mount the stage. All hands touched their watches or wrist bands, activating records or implanted eye cameras. Two security men in suits that were too tight over their tactical vests closed the wooden doors on the rear wall, then each posted up in the back corners. Two others approached the deep blue curtain that was separating the briefing room from a door beyond. The men scanned the crowd as they gripped the gilded ribbon, separating one half of the curtain from the other.

'It is like a boss battle in the old games,' George hummed thinking of the old favorite classics, crafted long before the code would adapt to the player. He thought he was ready for this type of reporting, but subconsciously shrugged his shoulders. Years of covering college frat parties and student elections were his journalist preceding battles, all bringing him to this. In his imagined boss level cave, with the dangerous boss waiting within, George sharping his tools of war, loading the specific high-powered weapon that was only be gained after its owner was defeated. Then, he pulled out his pen, his sword, while his imagination, its sheath, was placed on the mighty shield of his work, his notebook. The other journalist, the real journalists, looked undisturbed, some reading the newscasts on their arms, others making old fashioned notes on paper. The plain brown podium sat on a small stage, just inches above the green carpet, was readying itself for a new occupant. The microphone quickly emerged, rising like the head of a coiled snake from the slanted top, and the connection lights on the electronic communication module blinked until all were solid green.

His watch vibrated with an International Cinegame VR stream alert: Eastern Europe downloads interruption – millions of viewers down.

'Weird, Moscow games stats were out?' George surmised, flipping through other data streams looking for an answer. 'No, no, the system is still up.' Flipping over his forearm, he watched as Russia, Poland, and Belarus transits nodes blinked off, marked by a flashing red on the map of Europe. He typed into the general system to analyze any trends. 'Slight dip at sunrise, well, dawn in D.C. Then, a steady drop around an hour ago.' Another alert buzzed his wrist. South American regional nodes report less traffic centered in Venezuela and Brazil.

'Oh, man, this is the real story, hundreds of millions of angry gamers! Some of these people have not seen the sun in years! Energy drinks will be flying through windows!'

He drafted a quick check to IT, which he carbon-copied to his editor, but he failed to notice the room's collective attention shift to a television mounted to the left wall. Pens clicked, paper rustled as the reporters dropped them to the floor. A giant woman, clearly a German Amazon, stirred the entire row of seats when she turned to focus on the screen. His fingers mistyped, possibly the emergence of idle gamers' thumb disease, when he was jolted. Turning to find the disturbance on the screen, he saw an edge of the city along a jungle; small huts peppered the land, surrounded by the massive trees just beyond the corrugated steel roofs.

The branches of the trees were moving like a herd of elephants were rumbling through the underbrush. Shrubs and saplings at the end of the tree line snapped, and huge insect legs broke through, sending clouds of floral debris into the air like green smoke. The visual was captioned, and the picture was grainy as if shot from a great distance. Some technician pulled back the field to show a larger neighborhood near a large city's highway arteries. Scores of the mechanical Tulums six-legged shapes emerge from the thick trees in a tactical formation, twenty in a straight line with five on each side, creating a triangle.

'Rapid Action Battle formation,' George guessed, huffing out a long breath. Three years ago, George was luckily picked from the squadron of VideoDex games reporters to cover a Department of Defense and Boei Armor Bastion System joint exercise. The goal was, of course, recruitment into the DOD; everyone knew it. George himself almost signed up. His spine was ready for the neural implant and tactile finger nerve modifications. The armor perfectly matched the guests so it was like slipping into a warm bath with a bottle of whiskey. Five other well-versed gamers mounted an attack against a series of tunnels by using the Tulums, a military monster with six metal legs and missiles aplenty. At the final count, the digital mis-

THE CASTLE OF ELECTRIC BONES

sion was accomplished, and the very mountain was reduced to photorealistic virtual rubble.

He knew that these small tanks were neurally cast to soldiers in a forward operating base somewhere nearby, possibly a Naval ship just off the coast. Overwatch was provided by a nest of AI drones circling high above, monitoring the metal beasts as well as all the biologic creatures from the smallest beetle to a dozing baby.

Skittering out from the canopy, all the automatons folded in their six legs, allowing the tracks under the chassis to hit the ground, then scrambled through the narrow streets. The picture blanked for a moment, then returned from a separate viewpoint. At traffic speed, the dump truck-sized attack vehicles zipped about the poor unguarded neighborhood. The formation diverged into groups of three, each craft piloted by a nerve link to an unseen soldier. The huge mechanisms bristled with weapons fired on already crumbling rusty buildings, so common in the tropics. The destruction dust and debris added to the desert sands that continued to blow in between the palms. Falling into blockades, which cut off access from the major roads close by, the Tulums raced toward the highways that crisscrossed the beginning of the real urban area. The drones net switched to another view; a murky river wound across a deep green forest dotted with the chaos of growing suburbs. Orange roof tiles and palms marked the small collection of homes outlined with roads of dark mud, where the jungle once ruled. Following the river, more hamlets appeared clustered near a major bridge, cars already forming a logjam.

Trios of Tulums rammed through people like charging boars as they, whoever they were, ran from their destroyed, burning homes, then the heavy high-power artillery was deployed. Tulums sped under the elevated highway, while some set up a cordon separating the road from the village. The surviving residents were too bloody and busy searching for loved ones to mount an effective counterattack, mainly throwing bottles and poorly made bricks.

Light from the rockets flashed against the houses, and the bridge disappeared into the black water, now claimed by the river. Even at this height, the Tulums could be seen rocking with each explosion as houses were blown away, their entire frames pushed to the ground and tossed as a tornado struck them. The video had no audio, but George could still hear the blast's rumble and the sound of crumbling concrete. The madness lasted only a minute, but all the reporters grasped their ears, tugging at an earlobe to activate their phones, desperately trying to breakthrough back to home office, all hoping for a scoop.

The curtain was pulled back, and all the reporters were quiet as President Charles Horace Roberts stepped out, resplendent in a perfectly tailored gray suit with a red tie. His smile shown like a lantern in boundless fog as he nodded to reporters that he personally knew. The room filled with a clatter as bottoms hit the assigned seats, and pens clicked again, ready for notes. No one said anything; even George adjusted himself subconsciously, seeking to be as elegant as the speaker of the nation. Four others panned out behind Roberts, each with a somber expression, their eyes never fully meeting the pack of reporters, only glaring at the back of the President's skull. A woman in full military garb blocked the door behind the curtain, looking unsure of herself.

George had seen their faces before, people of importance. Political people.

The silence was broken by a barrage of questions, which Roberts cut off with a decisive wave of a hand. "Everybody, everybody!" his voice thundered across the room, "No questions yet, not yet." His smile shined.

Silence returned, and Roberts nodded to a technician at the back of the room. The television screen clicked into action. Roberts turned to look at the political people over his shoulder;

they nodded. He returned the gesture brightening his smile. Facing the crowd in the small room, he said, "Thank you, thank you. I wish to send you my genuine gratitude to all four parties and their leaders for joining me here tonight." He dipped to his right, then left, indicating the uncomfortable people behind him.

"I have seen the state of what once was a beautiful America," he continued, "Now, I see this wonderful nation is suffering, and its proud citizens bare the cross of allowing others to control the drive of prosperity. Previous administrations, from all parties, allowed the United States to be hampered and willfully dissuaded from its proper and righteous path. They and other intrusive global actions have treated the United States as a child. Now, we will free ourselves and stand up for what is right!"

He paused, clearly used to cheers and applause. Finding that lacking, he looked at the podium, considering. Anger rose in him, turning his throat a pale scarlet, then the red ran to his face.

With a fiery tone, he said, "Tonight, I will tell the American people that all the sacrifices and concessions that you have made over the last decade will now be relieved." He smashed his fist into the podium, then lifted both hands and jerked that fist in the air as punctuation for each point.

"The burden of tariffs and illicit political will of the United States opponents will now be challenged on a global scale with our partners. Today, right now, representatives from nations worldwide have rallied to our cause; they will join us to restore equity in this land and in many others. A Joint national security action to protect the Earth's petroleum reserves, refinement, and exploration, has been launched by a worldwide alliance led by me, the USA." Calm fluttered over his face, he stepped back, face slightly twitching.

"Many other leaders will speak to their citizens, and describe what we are doing today, the great lengths that have been taken, and the battles that will be fought. We, the world leaders of the free, are all together." His closed hand rose over his head, held like a firebrand.

"Some people, you know, the Washington people," he smiled, and nodded like it was an inside joke, "told me to avoid this action, to talk and talk. But I will not do that. Instead, I will fulfill the promise that I made at the beginning of my third term. I have created a place where Americans, ALL Americans, can feel free, a place where all of us, each one, is safe. Energy is a human right and a right earned by American sacrifice of blood and treasure over hundreds of years. I, we, have fulfilled that promise, America will lead the world yet again."

He stopped speaking, leaning over the podium, staring directly at the reporters' faces, hoping to connect with the living humans on the other side of the implanted camera. His twitch lessened. Changing from a Hollywood star to a grandfather, he crinkled his eyes and lowered his voice. "Long ago, some may think it lost in the mists of history, but, no, it was just in the past, a man stood up to a foreign king, and his people stood with him. He stood up to intolerance, injustice, and tyranny."

Pulling back, he Leveled his voice somewhere between a war cry and a reasonable call to arms.

"We will rise up today, fight back all the oppressors, and take what is ours!" Roberts nodded to the technician. A few clicks later, and both walls were lit with projected scenes of war. The audience was against the backs of their seats as if repelled; not a note was taken. Only a few hard-bitten veterans still had their mouths closed.

Roberts's stern face turned to the woman in the uniform. "General," he said, stepping away. She dipped her head in acknowledgment and stepped to the podium.

"I'm General Janet McKenzie, and I am now serving as

the acting Chief of Staff of the United States Army." Over his shoulder, George heard fragments of two reporters hushed conversation. "Holy mother, she is not even the deputy chief of staff!" said a man rapidly reviewing something on his forearm while still looking at his cellular phone on the same arm.

"Where is Lodlow or Freeman? No news has been reported about their dismissal or reassignment. Call that Pentagon guy, you know," said a much rounder man as he elbowed the first man in the ribs. The color drained from both of their faces.

"Earlier, you have seen the first releasable footage in the final step of the securing of a strategic port. Our brave warfighters have fully taken that area and will continue until the entire petroleum infrastructure in a joint operation with multiple other nations," she finished. Her face showed no emotion, only stating facts and plans.

A bombardment of hands rose each seeking an answer for a question that was begging to be asked. Looking around the crowd, she was unsure and unsteady, she turned to the President. Resuming, she continued, "In foreign lands, we have brokered a worldwide force that will capture and secure oil and gas fields, processing facilities, and refineries in all active areas of responsibility. A council of one hundred thirty-seven nations has lent support, either through providing strategic-level transport and supply or by offering troops. Military updates will be provided via the White House Press Office." She concluded, and returned to her spot, eyes cast down.

Arms raised like extending for a brotherly hug, Roberts regained his spotlight.

"The first video that had you was so enraptured was Laguna de Pajaritos in Veracruz, Mexico. That is a key petroleum receiving port, and, up from the wonderful Central American forces, and down from the grand and brave US troops, Mexico Petroleos Mexicanos will be forced to liberate its vast resources," Roberts explained. "China and Europe are working in a joint operation to guarantee the safety of Russian supplies. While Turkey, along with Egypt and Pakistan, are managing the Middle East resources," he said, then touched his ear. "Wonderful news!" he clapped. "Russia has, just now, volunteered to join the global oil reform. A raising tide floats all ships. Indeed, it does! Colombia and Argentina have secured Venezuela and Brazil. All these areas are now free to all...In a global effort," he announced, smiling, ticking the points off on his finger like a checklist during spring cleaning.

Alerts continued to buzz on George's wrist. Outages spread across the planet, and the war games were now real.

Roberts droned on and on. The newly minted Army Chief of Staff haltingly answered questions, and the four political party leaders remain quiet in the background like shunned children.

Years later, while researching for his book, *The Raiding of Earth's Black Castle*, George interviewed all the people involved, excluding the one that was serving out the rest of his presidency in the secured cell at the psychiatry ward in Walter Reed. He often thought of the juxtaposition of the entire endeavor. The world at war, which lasted eleven years, seven months, and fifteen-days, burned more oil than the previous fifty years. Exacerbating the global trouble, the destruction of facilities and disruption in electrical supplies drastically reduced any carbon capture, thus raising the carbon Levels in the air and sea. The Earth itself began to choke. The essence, the last oil war was a bloody way to burn over half of the world's reserves and destroy almost all the offshore rigs while staging photo ops with smiling politicians. George thought it was the same as all others.

The Army Chief of Staff was forced into the position as her two predecessors resigned, one by gunpoint. Her eyes still widened as she spoke about it. As always, the party leaders were blackmailed by other politicians or business cartels. After the honeymoon period faded, each lost their position, only to be followed by backers of the mad project, which, each in turn, was replaced. The revolving door of Washington.

George wrote a chapter on how Charles' war became popularize with propaganda. The national news channels were threatened by the possible removal their broadcast licenses. Some refused the pressure and continued honest reporting, only to be followed by dubious tax scandals and arrests of key personnel. Then, they folded. The others, the ones that now did the government's bidding, claimed the homes of the precious black fluid had banded together to subjugate the rest of the world. Posters of the with classical racist tropes lined the streets and the airwaves. Adults recalling their childhood villains: an Arab riding a camel with refineries on its humps and a young Latin man charming pretty Anglo-Saxon women while drinking an oil cocktail.

In large cities down to small towns, youths marched, calling themselves "Charlies," parading in their agreement to Roberts' ideas and his "securing" of earth's resources. George, too, was caught up in the global error, joining the US services late in the war as the tide turned against them. While the war was a disaster, he was proud of his service as a Tulum pilot in the later years and as a host of several other Air Federation bomb-droppers. Like many of the soldiers, he never left the States, only reported for duty at the local NeuralGear Center where his game skills quickly outpaced the older veterans. Nevertheless, his pride did not allow him to stain the wall of his solar-powered home with any military metals' shadow-boxes.

Though, sometimes, as the sunset beams its last ray up and over the horizon, he could still smell the noxious odor of burning oil as the winds churned it up, stretching all the way from the Middle East or Venezuela down to his house in Cathedral Heights in the third ward. His book was a hit, and now people call idiots "Charlie," thanks to his carefully planned words, but he still could not sleep. He coughed up the dark air, knowing that the workings of the world never really change.

❖ ❖ ❖

Like a bear in its cave, the pain was not dangerous; only when it ventures out to feed its hunger does the immense threat become obvious. His pain was chewing through his bones. Someone was yelling at him, but he still slept, not knowing which world was real. Until the nibbles on his femurs and biting within joints brought him straight out of his dreamless sleep. 'Evaluate,' his mind told him.

'The floor is at my back, so I fell over. Face, no, chin hurts, achingly sore,' his mind began taking a catalog. The tang of blood flitted over his tongue, but all his teeth were in proper place. 'Might have injured my cheek when I was hit. Cannot move my wrists; they are tied together with…metal. I'm still in the apartment, that is good or bad considering.'

He kept his eyes shut, so he did not alert whoever was there, and he was sure that someone was watching him squirm on his own floor. 'In here, where she died, choking on her own blood. I will see it again, the blood still wet and dripping.' Anger broke through his calm, but he was able to control it. The corners of his eyes crinkled, he used all his strength to prevent them from opening, though light still bled through the lids. Something soft and furry lightly brushed his face leaving small hairs in his nose. He coughed.

"Good, you're up," a female intruder said, then kicked him softly in the ribs. "Get him again," she chided, dropping the fuzzy thing on his face. The warmth of a small animal blocked all the light; he was glad until the wakefulness allowed him to understand that he could not breathe. Groaning, he rolled to one side; the creature slid off to patted paws.

'Ready to open,' he thought, 'Yes, I'm ready.'

Lounging in one of his chairs, Al stared down at him, her eyes were trying to drill through his skull. The cat stared at him too, large human liquid brown eyes to smaller green silted cat's eyes. Inhaling deeply, he blew at its face, and, only mildly perturbed, it slowly walked away.

Al pushed her boot before kicking him again, this time squarely in the shin. "OK," she screamed, "Wake up, you jerk!"

It felt as if the bones were shedding sharp, brittle pieces into his skin. 'Block pain receptors,' he told the Forge. After a few seconds, the pain lessened, and he choked out, "Hello, Detective Alcippe Angelica Anagnos." The room was still red, though the blood was smeared along the wall like a madman's vision of art. Pools were forming on the floor, slowly rolling toward him.

She screamed and jumped from the chair, bent over, and screamed into his face, flinging spit. Rage coursed through her, filling her face with heat, just waiting to explode violently. He dismissed the seriousness of her visit, calling her by her full name, a thing that he knows she hated, almost offered her the will to smash his head to bits. But, he had other concerns.

The flow of his wife's blood was creeping toward him in ripples, a pulsing red arrow, and he tried to stand, but the manacles linking his hands made that problematic, and he flopped over. "Ouch," he moaned, more from the grinding pain than the fall, but Al broke out laughing.

"Good," she sputtered between laughs, "Serves you right."

'Disengage the cuff,' she thought. Thin flat wire bound to a simple black ball released, dropping his arms. The wire crawled into the sphere, then it rolled to Al's feet before levitating to her outstretched hand.

"Al, what did I do?" he asked; she could hear the real question in his voice.

Terror and agony descended, grasping her, holding her down, and she sank back into the chair. "The cat, you idiot!"

As tears formed in her eyes, she rolled her head back, holding them back, then staring at the blank light gray ceiling.

"Oh, I see," Miguel said, "But I thought you were off the case." With an unapologetic gaze, he looked at her, understanding her emotions, though emotions were not in his bag of tricks. While his own were scattered and muddled, other feelings and their reasons were as clear as the human genome. Complicated, but clearly discernable giving study and he studied all his life.

The cat's small paw prints left scarlet smudges tracing around his head. He held his breath, willing the world to return to normal, though he knew in his soul or the biochemical approximation of one, that this was it. Blood will follow him like his footprints.

Sniffling, rubbing her nose, Al said, "Yeah, yeah. Whatever. Why did you take the cat? What is your point, Miguel?" accusatorially gesturing at him with a finger still wet from a tear. Her mind was reeling from assaults from all angles, and he was a convenient target.

His question as to her status as an active investigator was unanswered. Thus, he conceded to answer. "Escrito dropped data into the cat. I assume that due to the time of his death, this data is likely connected. So, I removed the cat from the horrible shelter, which I will file an official grievance about later." He marked the term shelter with exasperated air quotes.

Rolling her eyes as far as humanly possible, she asked with a half scream, "What about the Bluemen! What you did was against the law...knowing what you know," still waving her finger, "Many laws, in fact. I should book you now and have you up before a LEX AI in the morning after a wonderful night in a cell."

"If you wish," he said, holding out his arms. He knew the game and was a master. Grandad told him that if the Uni offered a Doctor of Philosophy in manipulating emotions, he was born with it. Knowing that he was perceived as somewhat thick in the mind while still seen as brilliant, he decided to go with the simple play first.

"I'm sorry that I disrupted police practice, but I want to share something with you after I fully understood it." Feigning ignorance is a key tactic, as was offering something of value.

Now standing, she grasped her spherecuff, its thin wires that will constrict if forced apart began to loosen. She drew them like a weapon muttering to herself, not hearing Miguel. His facial structure melted into a look of pure sincerity, tears welling just within his eyelids. Holding his offered wrists together, he rubbed his face with a forearm pretending to wipe away a tear. She sniffed, faltered a moment; that was his last chance.

"I want to show you the data because you were taken off the case," he pointed to the cat, that was swirling bloody paw prints around Al's boots. The prints morphed into the gang's symbol, the self-eating snake, making him shake his head; trying to shake away the coming insanity.

Blinking out of her emotional pain, she hissed, "What." He got her, now the layout.

Quick to fully capture her attention, he blasted all the details, "A large amount of data, a tremendous amount, was acid loaded into the cat's Forge, all encrypted. I cannot break it, but I know someone who can. I have an appointment with him later." He extended his wrists again. "I know that you are doing the fullest to complete your duty, but I was going to ask you if you will join me."

Jamming her fingers into her eyes, she dropped the spherecuff and slapped one wrist with tremendous force leaving fingermark red welts. Something about the marks focused his mind, the light stamp of her hand slightly damaging his minuscule blood capillaries like four rope lashes. They appeared as his flesh swelled, blood ran free through in the microscopic rents in the vessels, then reversed, leaving Miguel's typical dusty skin tone red.

He pulled his tunic sleeves over both wrists with a flourish and pointed to his Forge with a small smile.

"All the data is here," he tapped this skull behind his ear, "Can you help me stiff through this and see what we find?"

The cat darted between them, flinging its tail casting blood to AL's face. She did not feel it because it was not real, but it still dripped a long thin red line to her lips. A red bead hung there, resting just above her mouth. Her sister's blood, the last thing that would ever come from her, the final message, the pooling circles of her liquid self being pumped by a failing heart.

Miguel looked away, then started to the door. He had her on his side again, though he was not proud of how he snared her, it was real, and what mattered most.

"Come on, catch the ship, the appointment is soon, and I'm starving," he said, pushing the cat away as it tried to stroke its bloody fur over his feet. "I do not like cats, you know!" he blurted as if Al was part of the staff.

"Then you should not have stolen it, huh," she retorted, brandishing another finger, but this one was upturned. Stepping over cherry pools, he hopscotched to the portal while she watched him.

'Record all interactions from this point and use off frame scanners. Store in personal drive only.'

"Of course, ma'am," O'Bryan replied in a smooth accent.

As Miguel reached for the portal pad, a shadow emerged, a dark man wearing a dark hat stormed the door. Miguel startled, and jumped back as the portal grind opened like a disrupted small mammal ready with its teeth and claws. The dark man entered the apartment before the portal was fully open almost like it was design just for him.

"Where is that CAT?!" he barked, scanning the room until he caught Al against the wall, who was spreading herself against it in a ninja pose as if she could disappear. "What the hell?" he yelled, panning for Miguel's shocked face to Al, "are you doing here?"

"Banda," Al cautioned, "Please, let me explain..." her hands were out extended in two stop signs.

"Detective, I'm your Lt, and at this moment, because you are pulling a supreme Charly, you will call me that," he snapped, "and you have, while you are a victim of a horrible crime, misallocated police property." Stepping forward into Miguel's face, nose to nose.

"Technically, the cat was up for adoption due to Blue-man malfeasance," Miguel responded dryly, now heading to the door clearly not letting Banda's presence dissuade him from his meeting.

Banda sidestepped to block him, bringing up a hard hand to Miguel's face. "Yes, true, that is why I did not call up a Huldufolks to enter your place," Banda growled, spreading his arms to block the portal, then angrily touching Miguel's shoulder, ready to set up an armbar. Al intercepted Banda by pulling Miguel to the side, her hands out in surrender.

"Sir Lieutenant! Yes, he has the cat. And, yes, he was trying some of his own detective work, poorly trying at that. So, I ran a scan, found out, and came over to retrieve the animal to properly placed it in our custody. The cat just ran back there," she pointed to the lone hallway leading to the bedroom. Banda eyed them, looking for any misdirection. Seeing only a small enraged, possibly psychotic man, and his former trainee with blood-shot eyes still holding back tears, he instructed Miguel in a calm but assertive voice, a real cop voice, to bring him the creature.

Stepping in from the entry, Banda saw the apartment was immaculate other than the open door to the lab, where broken clear neoplastic littered the floor. The room was entirely gray with no wall projections or nano-bas reliefs. Clean and dead. The man with a developing bruise on his face was barely mentally functioning, and his relationship with his sister-in-law was under threat. A quick mental data check revealed that Mr. Saxon returned less than forty-five minutes ago, and Al fifteen minutes after.

"Lieutenant Aliquam," Miguel stated, "This animal has some bit of data, and I was going to return said data, then speak with Al so that she could inform the proper authorities. Mr. Escrito loaded it to an enhanced pet-Forge the night of his…exsanguination. So, I was about to talk Al through the small bits of the information."

"Thank you, sir. That is gracious of you. But slightly beyond standard JYC police procedures. I will discuss it at the station once I return with the animal. Sir, please, get me the cat, and none of this will be added to the official review. Understand?" Banda said, tired of the assumption of the air of eruditeness, but Miguel could hear the growl in Banda's voice.

'Arrange for mandatory counseling for the victim at the current residence,' the Lieutenant noted on his stream, and added Al to the recipients.

"Fine, fine, I will get it," Miguel blurted with flailing hands, slumping his body as if remaining in the apartment was draining all his energy. The world was often predictable when Miguel organized all its particulars. He liked it that way. Though Elizabeth would deliberately disrupt his carefully laid out patterns and, much to his chagrin, he would walk along unfamiliar paths holding her hand as they both smiled. The bedroom had been lonely for over a week, unused, basking in darkness; only weak semi-sun lights cast from the transom to the restroom. Miguel had not entered it because it was, as all the home was, a reminder of what he lost.

Of course, the cat can see in the dark, and it has no respect beyond its own private, selfish needs. The cat was nestled against the bed, pawing furiously at the blanket that spilled over the side. Mentally, he closed the door, cutting off its escape route, and slowly approached the cause of all this disturbance. This was a waste of his time.

While the pain was ebbing, his muscles weakened; he tightened his focus to prevent the telltale signs of exhaustion. Gratefully, the animal was white as pure snow, gleaming in the dark room. Shakily he reached out for the animal; it was so consumed by the blanket it failed to notice; clawless paws patting the mattress behind the fallen blanket, over and over. Rolling over the cat fur as if he were about to start a thorough petting, he grabbed it, pulled it to his chest. The blood was gone, just a white cat relaxing in his arms, aimlessly staring around the room as most cats do.

The mattress was average, typical, what a bed should be, a mattress in a dead woman's house. The nano-intel wires adjusted the linens to order with a plain flat surface, increased by the weight of a human form. He was afraid that the tossed and tussled blankets would resemble a person asleep, a slumber that never is broken. Pulling the cat closer, feeling its heat, Miguel turned and almost commanded the door to open when he saw the dark shape huddled in the shadow by the portal.

Within the pocket of deep darkness, a human form was curled, a black mass hemmed in by shadow. Crushed bones formed points on the small black mass like a skeleton made of ink, just protruding from the shadow from the semi-sun wall casts. The darkness pooled in the corner, pulling each shadow and lack of light to it like liquid. Barely discernible, the body glinted as if covered in a raven fluid like oil, but something sinister and angry. He knew it was her. Her head was covered by gnarled rotting arms positioned up at unnatural angles.

"I like cats, Miguel," it hissed, staying motionless, only its eyes, her golden eyes, shifted between the dead arms. "I never told you that." Her... its breathing was anti-breathing, pushing air out without any intake. The words came in bursts of ragged air streaming out from her, the shadow holding her pulled on all the other shadows, a hungry pool of black.

Her arms ground like a nano-portal as they fell like dead leaves freeing her face. Her grey skin was speckled with black spots and was falling away from her bones like an overlarge dress on a starved child, revealing what was hidden, opening the negative space of horror. The only source of light was her eyes; the sclera beamed as a sunrise. Her dress was threadbare black, now, and in tatters, pieces attached to the liquid shadow by an ethereal glue.

The endless breath said, "It is ok, Miguel." Her head turned as if looking for an answer; Miguel heard bones crack. "I'm here to set the path. I am the footprint showing you the track out of the cave, my dear. Thousands of years old painted handprints all pointed to the glorious ways back," she whispered as an unnatural smile fissured over her grey skin, revealing slimy black teeth.

"We need to talk about our future," she reached out a gnarled hand withered with death, "Come, walk with me." He reached back.

"I know, I know," Al told Banda, squelching her head, then arching it back over her shoulders. "I almost killed him, too." She spilled everything, well, almost everything. She held on to the faintest vestiges of hope, the elemental ideas that she could be of help to her...dead sister, and through that, to Miguel.

Banda seated himself, evaluating her position, the trace of her words, word choice, and other indicators of stress. HUD found the typical Levels of the bereaved, along with measures of confusion.

'Glad that I pulled her from the case,' he thought. 'Load all case information gathered from Detective Alcippe Angelica Anagnos in a confidential informant intelligence nexus file under my name disseminated by only my permission,' he instructed his HUD.

"Ok, I will take custody of the cat and say that he," he flicked a hand to the bedroom, "was seeking to join with a pet that was related to the case. Simple confusion from a lost soul. While you came over to help him, then saw the cat, etc. Got it?" He fingered his thin mustache, thoughts lingering.

As Al's back slammed into the wall, she thought, 'Miguel, I hope you know what you are doing.' Her belt poked her in the side, and Banda believed that her grimace was meant for the brother-in-law.

"Al, it is ok. I have been ruminated, and I think this might work. I will assign you with simple, NONessential tasks," he said harshly, but not too harshly, "just so that you are not officially on the case but just assisting in other matters. Then, you must help that Charlie, giving him some measure of control, for his fragile psyche?" Banda said, slapping his hands together. "Problem solved."

'THANK GOD,' the thought exploded in her mind, 'thank god, thank god, thank god!!!'

"Sure, that will work," she calmly asserted, using all her training to avoid any significant tells that Banda will catch, he always sees one, even from well-trained Bluemen. Breath in check, her focus was blurring, but appeared as if she was in deep thought staring into space, peaceful movements with economy of motion. 'That should work...Refocus when speaking. Think bereaved..."

"Yes, sir. I agreed, and he does need something to do. Hell, he didn't even sleep here last night, just out there wandering," she said with a shrug.

Banda rubbed his chin, calculating all the known facts and some of his most valid opinions, setting each chess piece in its final place, then trying to remember the game backward. "Al, as your superior officer, I command you to accompany the victim to his next few appointments, for his safety," Banda told her, extenuating this statement with air quotes.

Confusion flowed under her like an iced-over river, but her face seemed unphased. Lips that she thought should be shaking and bitten through said, "Yes, sir. I will take care of him." Sweat was spreading down her back and under her long hair; but her hands never shook, her voice was always steady. "It will help me, too."

The bedroom portal open with the accompanying grind, and the cat ran to Banda's feet. "He is ready, Lt," Miguel grinned as he stepped out of the shadow, strangely calm.

"Great," Banda scooped it up, fumbling for the carry fob in his pockets, "Not sure how you could see in there." He nodded to the dark bedroom.

"Oh, Liz, loves the dark, it seems to...swim in her," Miguel gushed, casting back a glance to the blackness.

Al questioned as she knew her sister would become a glowing star if it were possible, but kept her mouth shut, not wanting to spoil the mood. Banda found the thin metal oval, placed it over the squirming animal's head by a few inches. Somehow, the tiny metallic parts moved out from the oval like a mindful liquid and spread around the creature until the cat was within a perforated carrier shaped like a football.

Banda nodded his apperception and said gruffly, "Sir, I have assigned Detective Alcippe Angelica Anagnos to escort you to your next few meetings. Will that be agreeable to you?"

Al and Miguel exchanged quick glances before Miguel answered, "Yes, yes, that will be fine."

"Wonderful. See you later, Al," Banda mused as he turned, withdrawing from the room without a look back.

Al shot Miguel a stare. "What about the darkness?" she prodded. Miguel said nothing and started for the portal.

"I'm starving! Come on, walk with me," he yelled back.

CHAPTER 26

His voice broke through the smoke as his head arched back into the only light in the room. He was the only one making any noise; all the other faces were made of stone. Sweat dripped from his body, pounding against the padded floor, creating a rhythm that answered the strikes against his back. A leather goad slashed across, ripping skin, which was simultaneously reprinted with enhanced pain receptors. Each slash more agonizing than the last. His wrists burned as the nano-multi wire was pulled tight on the stone pillar to hold his back bared to the seated members.

"You have failed," Red Sun stated, barely loud enough for the others to hear. "But, not unexpected," with a loaded voice, meant to ring in the others' ears.

Red Sun turned his face to the assembled Cutmen and their Enswells. Even trainees Monsels crowded the dark hall covering their young faces from the smog of incense.

Red Sun tensed for a moment, then released the red strained false leather and blood spray. Then, the thin metal arms blazed around Leo's back, replacing the torn cells. The memory loads have been transferred to Red Sun immediately after the failed attack. Ru calmed himself enough to recount what he saw without any jitter of nerves. The mention of the tattooed man drew questioned from all the Leading Three and some of the Seax and Protegers as well. He answered the best he could. No scan identified the man, the gait, tattoo pattern, and skeletal structure. Nothing sparked any database hits, nor anything was found the nets or even a worldwide nerves cull.

Nothing, the man was a ghost.

Ru knew that it was not just nothing. The faces of the Three and some of the underlings seated to the left and right showed that, while searching through the vast web of electronic data revealed nothing, that nothingness of the huge man meant value, something to hold firm. The knives, Seax, and the shields, Protegers, shifted and conversed lowly in the benches was not uncommon, but the slight movement of the Threes' eyes to each other's faces indicated something...different. The Three were godlike, stoic, and the most experienced. The eyes brief exchanges, lightning-quick flashes, scared Ru. Whatever and whomever the tattooed man was, he is dangerous.

"Failure is a part of life," Red Sun declared to the hall, slashing Leo's back again, flinging droplets of blood across the young Monsels seated on the stone floor, closest to the marble pillar at the center of the hall. The Three, masters of all, held the back wall in simple wooden chairs made from the Cutmen's home territories' trees. In a smoothly carved block of olive wood shaped just enough to provide a seat, Bright Day relaxed, hands closed over his muscular body. In answer to Bright Day's simple seat, Black Night's armored form laid back in an intricate carved throne made of twisted branches of a Russian Mulberry wound between each other, circling to the stone and back up forming the base of impossible complexity. As his name suggested, Black Night has a face made of brickwork, rarely breaking into any emotion, giving only action and stern judgment. Empty sat Red Sun's chair, a Japanese maple construct of odd angles and rough chunks.

Ru knew what type of tree he will choose when he joins the Three. Each new member will replace their fallen brother's tree with his own; in his case, if he ever survives long enough and preforms with grand efficiency, a birch straight back chair with real fur overlay will claim his spot. His spot will only be his place when he is ready, lifetimes from now.

Facing Leo's sweating face, the rips across the man's flanks stirred Ru's muscles, sending them rippling with each strike. Blood dripped from Ru's face ruining his traditional white formation tunic, but he did not sweat or tremble, though he knew that his turn was next.

Failure was and always will be addressed like a cancer, cut out at the root.

Red Sun intoned, "Leo's failure was due to cowardice, not due to circumstance."

His lightning hand broke open a rupture along Leo's right shoulder blade, sending a splash of blood to the stones. The printing arm followed the lash with artistic fluid movements, circling up to avoid the leather strap, then darting back down to reprint over the split flesh.

"Ahh, the man, the tattooed man inspired fear in Leo. Fear is not a purely corrosive element in a Cutmen's mind. No, it allows for us, the Cutmen," he spread his arms to the right and left, encircling them all, sprinkling blood on one Monsel's face. The fair hair teen was instructed correctly and remained still, letting the trickle run down from his forehead, between his eyes, and then resting on his mouth. His face was motionless as the liquid warmth crept into his skin.

"Fear hides nothing from us, it clears the mind of all things...," Red Sun said, closing his eyes, "inconsequential. It frees us as long as we know our purpose." He whipped the lash up Leo's side, which broke open, showing a rip in the yellow fat that oozed just above the ribs. Leo grunted, letting only blood flow from him. He knew the rules.

Red Sun turned, bent to ask his bloodied student, "Were you afraid of the tattooed man, Enswell Leo?" The whip tapped lightly on Red Sun's hand, waiting for a reply.

Holding his pain in, building in his scarlet face, Leo could barely breathe, much less speak, but he found the strength to force up one word before biting into the woodblock in his mouth.

"Si," he breathed, holding tears back. The grind of the printer continued.

"Cutmen Matteo, please ask the Three for judgment of this failure and cowardice," Red Sun demanded. A short, burly man shot up from the lines of full ranked Cutmen, closest to the Threes' stage.

"Yes, sir," Matteo acknowledged with vigor, turned to the Threes' elevated platform. "Comandante in carica, Shihai shirei-kan, and Pravyashchiy komandir, I ask for your judgment. The Enswell was flogged for the failure of his mission, and his blood runs on the floor."

Each member in the hall stomped their left foot. "Blood runs the floor," they chanted.

Black Night responded, "Da," while Bright Day said, "Si."

Red Sun walked to Matteo, bowed, and asserted, "Hai."

Matteo returned the bow, strode to the amurresufeiru mounted to the stone wall, lit by the only concrete beam of light. The naked sword caught the beam, reflected it to Matteo's eyes as he bowed to it, and he remembered the generations of Cutmen that passed before him.

"The final judgment will be of the continued membership of Leonardo of Sondrio on the charge allowing his fear to prevent his true duty as a Cutmen trainee. The Three of the Cutmen, please, announce your judgment," Matteo spoke loud enough for the members throughout the entire hall to hear. Three times heals thumps the stones. Straining against the binds, Leo looked to the platform of the Three.

In order of negative seniority, the leading Cutmen announced their verdict.

Closing his eyes, peering into an internal set of universal

rules, the thin muscled Bright Day shook his head, making his grey beard quiver. Opening his eyes to face Leo, he said, "Son, son. This is a day to learn," he raised his arm to the entire company, "for all of us to learn."

He stood, bowed to Leo. "Ragazzo, ti ho deluso. Ma, a sua volta, hai fallito gli uomini del taglio," he vowed. Leo's face crumpled, he fell and the bands binding his waist jerked him up, leaving him hanging with bend knees.

Bright Day, the ruling member that invited a young boy who lived with the Unsettled in the former Italia region to join the Cutmen years ago, pulled a dagger from his belt, showing it to the crowd.

"This is the answer and my judgment. I choose the final cut," he murmured, his voice falling.

His blade slashed against his forearm, gorging a wound from the waist to elbow. Blood ran down, dripping to the floor before the healing nano in his blood sealed his skin. He looked to Black Night, who nodded, sheathed his dagger, then sat in the carved block from the trees of his homeland. Rising from his throne, Black Night pulled his ax from his belt and simply said, "Final cut," before replacing the bladed weapon in his black fur belt.

"I will explain to the Monsels, the new one," Red Sun addressed the rows of trainee lining the stone square around the pillar. "You may only see the blood and pain inflicted from a simple failure in a difficult mission, even a mission that was only predicated on another enterprise." He paced a few steps to stand next to the defeated Leo, who was still bleeding, pools forming on the ancient stones. Red Sun kicked off his teat sandals, touched Leo on an unbattered shoulder, and stepped into a pool of Leo's blood.

"I'm standing in what was once him, this ketsueki beneath me," he said, lifting a toe, drawing a line from one pool to another. "These pools are the Cutmen. We exist outside the whole but are the truth of the essence of…" he bent, crouching to the floor, listening to bubbles pop on Leo's ruined face, "The body. Yes, good. We unite the body of humanity. The leading Three formed hundreds of years ago by forming a common interest. That took bravery, focus, dynamism, and duality." Leo saw the ruling in the master's face, the tight muscles in his neck like steel cables slackened, but he maintained the gaze into Red Sun's electric eyes.

"To be promoted from Monsel to Enswell, then the final dedication of your life, to Cutmen required all four of those qualities. But all those are compromised by fear, uncontrolled fear. It robs us of purpose, like a frightened animal. No fear, because we are a true element of the essence." Turning to Ru, Red Sun slashed Ru across the face hard enough to loosen two molars. Ru did not move; he willed his blood to flow, spilling to his tunic, soaking him.

"See," Red Sun gestured to Ru, "no fear. Leo, I'm not here to tell you my judgment. For your brethren, the Cutmen kenshusei, the Monsels, what is your judgment? What is your sentence?"

Slowly, Leo's bare feet found pressure on the stones, lifting him to tower over Red Sun. From somewhere deep, he fashioned the courage to find his purpose. He bowed, knees wobbling, to the master, then to the audience. Holding his bow, lifting his bound wrists, he yelled, "Final cut," then, the bands separated, folding into the pillar.

"Final cut," Red Sun affirmed, eying the trembling bloody man before him.

Red Sun bowed to Leo, motioned him to the glinting amurresufeiru near the platform of the Three. Weakly, Leo made a few steps, then cringed, hands falling to his knees. The pools of blood followed him with each step, and Matteo reached him with a supporting arm. Red Sun watched from the square as a silent magistrate. Even though he turned his head to watch Leo, increased the red stream from his ruined cheek, Ru was in awe of Leo's final strength.

Lifting the ancient sword from its stone mount, Matteo proffered the blade to Leo, whose eyes lit with the possibility of holding the sacred item, a sword that claimed so many lives. He held it gently like a baby, afraid to use too much pressure.

"Final cut," he whispered, tears forming, and blood drippling down his lips.

Ru hardly heard him. Leo steadied himself by spreading his bloody feet and extending the sword away from his body at chest Level. The blood loss pulled power from him, but he held the blade out with the stability of a master swordman. Shifting his grip, he turned the cutting edge up to the ceiling. "THE CUTMEN CONTINUE THE FIGHT!" he screamed as he twirled the blade over his head then returned it to the same position. He was ready, focusing his mind.

The light beam shattered as the metal flew through the air in a final stroke as Leo spun the sword with incredible speed and power in a clean line to his neck. The blade struck just below his jawline, driving clean through the sinew and bone. His hands still held the handle after his head fell to the stones. Red Sun clasped his standing body, so Matteo pulled the sword back, cleaned its blade with a flick, and returned it to its stone mount.

Pushing the headless body to the center of the stone square, Red Sun echoed, "The Cutmen continue the fight!" All heals pounded the floor.

"Now for you, Ru. What is your judgment?" Matteo called, pointing to Ru, who was still wet from Leo's blood. Ru found his strength and faced it without fear.

CHAPTER 27

The pain returned, now branching out from his bones to his skin. He made little attention to the ride across the East River and into the Meadow. Exiting the mountain of Manhattan was like birth, a blinding glare into the sun, before the quick death of entering Queens. Just a few short moments basking in the sun shining through the transparent pod hull, then thrusting into a dark hole. The pod track made a hard turn; the road shimmered, everything glowing in neon light. The track tube was large, pods zipped by, dozens of other flyers descending into the darkness of the Queen's ridge.

'The whole city is tubes, tubes up to the middle atmosphere, or tubes across the water. Just tubes. We live our lives in simple connections of nanotubes. Ants' tunnels spread across a dead tree trunk, all scurrying to avoid the heat of the sun,' Miguel thought. Their pod shot through parts of Brooklyn, then turned northeast. The track dipped low into the Meadows' AI hub. The Meadows were once a wetland; hundreds of years ago, it threatened to sink away as the water rose from the ground. Buildings have fallen or shifted as wet fingers pulled them down, streets cracked as their foundations simply melted away. Rec-tech nano-triggers burrowed to the bedrock guided by an unknowable artificial intelligence algorithm, rebuilding the site from squatters' paradise of broken, abandoned homes to the qua-com and synthetic brain capital of the western hemisphere.

The center of the pod's dashboard lit green as it took the last turn swinging them past REMeter headquarters, a collection of red-veined brain-shaped constructs linked to a tower that reached the Level ceiling like a hat clustered coat stand in a low-ceilinged room.

"Did to call ahead... to him? You know, to arrange this meeting?" Al asked, absently staring off, checking her internal stream. Only targeted ads, from the content of faux leather goods and to skin adhering holsters, the targeting team must think that she is an archaic cowboy.

"It is arranged," Miguel said dryly, looking at the floor. The tracking tube opened to display the bustling center of commercial AI development. Entire Levels were devoted to one firm. A whole city of trademarks, the section yelled at any passing traveler that this one, this tech, is the best. Whether it is the new stream linked computer or REMeter Dream Join, or virtual, augmented instructional tech, it the best, maybe the best that will ever be. While Miguel vastly appreciated the electronic mind's enhancing power for DNA coding and mind-numbing calculus of impossible sums, the easily discernable exploitation of the citizens was too much for him. He was happy in his lab and had little time for prancing around in a lion's dream or a virtual block party with Nippon friends. His conscious mind was his place.

He shot the parking instructions to the pod, and the dashboard light changed to orange. The building greeted them with the flourish of a coral reef. The structure mimicked an imagined ocean, battalions of magnetically bound bots climbed up the sides, dangling thousands of feet up, or drifted through a channel of buildings, reminiscent of glowing crabs. Chromatic heli-drones swam in the air between the different department of the vast array of his friend's business. Pixelated walls showed a fluctuating color across all the organic build-ings. Al gasped, wearing a huge smile of awe, but Miguel's head began to throb.

'Helmet always love the sea,' Miguel thought as the pod zipped into a skeletal chink in the bright yellow massive section jutting off from a Colosseum-sized pink disk. The flashes of color lit Al's eyes as she was enraptured by the oddly decadent yet natural form of Helmet's firm. Black Stump Engentronics was built to improve the interplanetary artificial intelligence networks by using dream patterns from Helmet's brain.

"Wow," Al said, lost in her wonder. The enteral structure was dimly lit, and the continually wandering drones dulled themselves into the cloudy blue spaces, then flashed with electronic red blasts.

"The master's inner sanctum," Miguel leered, "It is a bit too much. My lab is better…was better." Irritated by his ire, Al shot him the finger, but he was unfazed or did not notice, but she knew him well enough to know that he sees everything. The track seemed to end between house-size yellow buds that rippled with manufactured coral growth, but, as they approached, the buds morphed into lips, yawning for their entry. While not sexual in nature to Miguel's eye, the intense yellow seemed to mirror the manipulated air waves action in perfect balance.

"Ugh…Gross," Al muttered. She was checking the Forge's stream connection and the function of all the internal police vids in her personal profile. Miguel chuckled. "What," she said distracted, though she knew the origin of the laugh. "It was like a cartoon just swallowed us. A little…deviant," she said, waiting to see the man who designed this, trying to keep a sense of humor about the artificial intelligence that rendered cartoon lips ingulfing visitors at the enormous commercial space the size of ten city blocks. Miguel remained quiet.

They sped along a tunnel decorated with bioluminescent stripes, twisting in a random pattern. The randomness amazed Miguel with its beauty and the emptiness. Maybe it was only random to a human, not to a qua-com calculating in 32 dimensions. Or perhaps the human eye cannot clearly see the recurrence due to the inability to see beyond its simple spectrum. Once, he thought about ordering the Forge to interpret visible light as IR but discounted the results as disappointing.

'Let the mystery remain,' he thought. The lights brightened, the typical JYC structure was revealed in straight lines and grey walls. Though Helmet constructed the illusionary coral to fade slowly, the flat grey showed diminishing gaps of flourishing semi-coral, and bursts of embedded color broke the traditional wall, all the way to Helmet's office at the end of the tunnel. As they stepped out, Miguel turned and appraised the pathway. The bioluminescent streaks thinned out to form glowing grout between the amber tiles, while the vibrant displays of the nano-coral shifted to the ceiling of the hallway, creating a slight marbling texture. He stored a note to ask Helmet if it was the computer or if Helmet played a hand.

Under their feet, the grout dimmed around the room, except for the line that leads to the sliding glass door, which opened, calling them inside. Aquariums lined the walls with reengineered fish from across the earth's oceans, all lit in a sharp blue. A gleaming yellow circle marked the end of the pathway edged around the last door. Irked by all the pageantry, Miguel half jogged down the hundred feet and slung the door open.

It had been ten years since they last met, pairing ended with a drunken hug that Miguel almost did not accept. The Canal Bar was full of Helmet's employees, celebrating a large capital investment deal and jolting income from the initial public offering. Typically, Miguel was seated in a corner barely visible under the neon's glow promoting the newest spirit. The scene replayed in both of their minds.

'I think it was Yoruba Fiji Rum,' Helmet thought as he turned his chair, a neat construction of bamboo perched on a nano-mount.

Hel, as Miguel called him, had to use the Forge DNA read to find him as he was squirreled away, trying to avoid attention. As a key member of the programing team, Hel offered congratulations and thanks to Miguel. He had to guide the development team by mapping the interconnections between the Nadar Forge systems in the larger synth-minds into a more protected organization modeled on coral reefs' growth. After Hel found Miguel in the crowd, he slowly coaxed him from the corner, Miguel launched into an incredibly dull lecture on the evolution of a reef and how insulating each synth-mind based on the root branch could help security as a coral pod grows together as a collective just interlaced with coral inherent protection systems. Rubbing his face, Helmet struggled to remember which jokes got him out of that mess.

He crossed the room to greet his friend, one of the few that regardless of temporal distance, always brings his heart joy. Somehow, both were wired that way; a strange connection beyond their invariably calculating minds. In a straight, determined pace, Miguel walked through the office, failing to notice the floor to ceiling windows that open to a vast aquarium or the models of future construction in the Pacific, just straight to the waiting handshake.

"Miguel! Come here!" Helmet yowled with his thin German accent, grabbing the friend in a powerful bearhug, pulling Miguel's gaunt face through Helmet's ginger beard. Not really willing to sidestep this display of affection, Miguel accepted it and hung in Helmet's brawny arms, with his own dangling at his sides.

"I'm so sorry, my man," Helmet said, dropping Miguel, then gripped him by his shoulder, squeezing hard. Miguel, unblinking, stared only at the floor. While Helmet was ever a laid-back bachelor, the look on Miguel's face broke him. This was not the typical emotional repression or any instability; it was a broken heart so lost that Miguel could fall into madness. Feeling tears welling, Helmet picked up Miguel again, holding him even harder. While Miguel was thin, almost skeletal, he must have been working out or using the electric muscle stimulators. Miguel's body was a tense ball of muscle with rock hard shoulders. Surprised, Helmet thought that he was squeezing a stone pillar as he set Miguel's feet on the floor again.

"Hey," Al said quietly, seeing the emotion between the men, "I'm Al," reaching her hand across to Helmet. He grasped her hand with both hands and pulled her in for his typical bearhug. She noticed that his bread smelt of an unknown plant, maybe lavender, it soothed her anxious mind.

After placing her on her feet, he said, "Yes, ma'am. Nice to meet you, and I express my sincerest apologies for your loss," he bowed, still gripped her hand, but he was gentle. Deep regret etched into the lines of his face. Since this happened, the attacks, the blood, the rending of her only sister, she sought to bind her face in a model of mental fortitude, but it was cracking, her tears melted it away, and fell, splattering their joined hands.

"Oh! I'm...I'm sorry," she murmured, yanking her hand away as she stepped back. Her tears washed over her face, tracing lines down to her mouth.

"No need, darling," he said gently, ignoring the tiny wet spots. With a lightning-fast pluck, he offered her a handkerchief, the color of the calm sky. Shaking her head, working to gain back her composure, she dabbed lightly, then handed it back with a small bow.

"I have code in the Forge, and I need it to be discreetly translated," Miguel chimed in, walking passed the elegant marble desk and the wonderfully accurate sculptures of sea life.

'Always straight to business,' Helmet thought as he instructed the AI to disconnect the link to external systems and to raise the console. All the room décor magically floated to the corners as if it had minds of their own, and the center of the room dipped to one foot versus where they were standing.

In the depressed section, the carpet parted, a bright red pillar emerged from the floor, complete with a keyboard and grouping of monitors.

"Physical viewing?" Al said amazed, stepping to the monitors, touching the immaculate screens. "Speakers, too."

"Yes, Hel is traditional. He uses what birth gave him," Miguel declared, "Should I load it into you or the console?"

Hel hoped that this was a meeting of friends in a time of need, not a search for intelligence leads, but he knew Miguel and how his mind works. Reach out to me was how Miguel found a personal connection; hopefully, one that can be his north star.

"Ok, ok, touch the green button, and transfer it to Weber-white-papers-documents-452 under Black Stump folder stream store," Hel answered, stepping down to join them, then typed the proper instruction to his personal qua-com. "Alright, I have it. All scanners have been disabled, and, once you walked in, your Forges' communications dropped off the grid. So, we should be alone."

As he quickly reviewed the data and mega held within, his heartbeat elevated, and his chest tightened.

"Oh, junge, Oh junge! What the hell is this?" he gasped, his German returning, "Ok, well, I'm glad that we are virtually disconnected." His hands flew across the keys, sounding like a chorus.

"Why? What is the deal here?" Al questioned, her police instinct returning. Blood rushed away from her face as she realized that Miguel was, in fact, not losing his mind, and she internally debated if she should alert Banda. This is a violation of police protocol, breaking the chain of evidence, and could jeopardize the case.

'Well, if there is a case. So far, with facts available, it is unconnected.'

Hel looked to Miguel, who sat on the stairs of the depression, facing the carpet. "What is this, Miguel?"

Lost somewhere else, somewhere dark, Miguel spoke robotically, "All I know, is that is some of the new security measures up for Council vote. From the little that I gathered, multiple code hustlers were contracted to generate sections, that when put together, allows the code to take over the city's systems and route everything through a Zellum controlled synth-mind. But, it is, once in the larger system, undetectable. That is all I have."

"Alright...uh," Hel said, "I'm separating it by apparent function and creator using code tags. Whoa, that is a lot of data. I can't see it all, but one section needs another, then another to properly work, spread across the city's qua-coms. Like...uunn...chromosomal gene function...right? Ok, this will take time, even for my personal qua-com and my amazing skills." He cracked his knuckles over his head, stretching his coding muscles.

Exhausted and only driven by this one mission, Miguel laid on the floor, nestled in the rich yellow carpet. "Codes that behave like genes...great," he said defeated, then closed his eyes. Through his lids, he saw the light was becoming brighter; he ground his hands and feet into the rocky soil. The tunnel ended.

What is in the outside world? What is behind the pain? Will there be a sky?

"Wake up, Miguel!" Al yelled, kicking him in the knee, "Get up here...Hmm, well down here." She gestured to the console depression. As Miguel struggled to stand, he heard Helmet's babble on about the symbiotic relationship between qua-coms and synth-minds, how to operate effectively, to have a real artificial intelligence they must work together like the cells of a brain. Al nodded, but Miguel suspected that she neither understood nor wanted to understand.

"Interesting" and "Wow," were her common responses.

"I'm up," he said, joining the others. "What is it?" he rubbed his temples. A dream echoed in the mind, something about digging, looking for light from a place locked still by the weight of the Earth's stones.

"When the Council adds this to the system, they will be giving away the whole city! Maybe everywhere…," Helmet blurted, likely just to himself, as the others' ears were less than one foot away. "Again, I'm not sure yet, but this will work its way into each element of all JYC components. How did they not see this?"

"Yes, bad stuff," Miguel said, still dwelling on the cave and the endless effort to escape. Al punched him in the arm. Her hand jolted bone by bone, leaving her hand throbbing.

"Damn! What are you wearing, Miguel? Is that a sub-sonic penetration protection shirt, those weird liquid crystals?" Al said surprised, holding out her aching hand, eying him suspiciously.

"No, just me," he said, turning to the screen, "Hel, what is the plan?"

"Well, sorry to delay things, but I will call you once this is decoded and its make some kind of sense," Hel answered, grasping Miguel's shoulder. "Should be a day or two. Sorry again. Want to get some lunch? Wait, what time is it? Whatever, we live in a robotic cave, so I can decide I want lunch whenever," he opened his hands, displaying an imaginary smorgasbord, "How about it?"

"Absolutely," Al accepted, "Sounds lovely!"

In unison, Miguel said, "Yes, I do need to eat."

Laughing, Helmet grabbed them both, lifted them with one arm each, and walked to his private dining room. "Alright, let's eat!" he bellowed.

The predator is Miguel was hungry.

CHAPTER 28

This was highly unusable, and he knew it. This place was huge, an entire apartment block wrapped in these nano-walls. The air pressure hissed as it gushed through the vents, and the sea rose out before him. The window, though it was essentially a transparent nano-shell of reinforced crystal technology, gave him a view of the shimmering Atlantic. He was high above the city lights; the building's shadow was a dark stain on the shore. A sense of vertigo passed through him, and he stepped back because he did not want to tarnish the transparent pane. The height of the Spire muted even the dying day sunset. Only a break in the silver clouds allowed him to see the sea, which seemed to be a flat blue blanket thrown over a plain.

'So, this it Skytown,' Ru thought as Red Sun tapped him on the shoulder. Hiding his fear, he turned, bowed, and asked, "Red Sun, how can I help?"

A small smile crossed Red Sun's lips; he returned the bow with a brief nod, answering, "I will introduce and, then, you answer his questions. He is a powerful client, but only a client, so be truthful. Understand?"

"Yes, sir," Ru said, adjusting his black robe and red ceremonial belts that were tied behind his back. No weapons were allowed past Level 2,000, but he had his hands, which were good enough.

As the door opened, he heard the wood squeal, a real wooden door hung on natural wooden panels. The floor below his sandals was a dark maple, and the walls were lined with deep shelves holding more books that Ru knew existed. They were all real. Not that he had ever read one, an actual physical object containing the printed word. Beyond the city shield and the floor to ceiling window, which was large enough to pilot a boat through, the whole room was real. Actual, from the iron table alongside the leather couches in the center to the man, now, sitting in a timber high-backed chair behind the espresso maple desk. Beyond the genuine timber, the walls were festooned with bas reliefs of dragons circling a massive tree, spreading across the room from above the desk back to the wall behind him. Eight flying lizards in all, they flung fire from their wings, set in all hues that wood could hold, but the tree and all its leaves were held stable in wood, unburning and true. Ru thought it was carved by sweating workmen during the great wars before people became settled and safe. Too safe, Ru knew from his time in Undertown. Society's nerves were now too long, the pain from the ant's sting in the tail could not be felt in the head. It was all an illusion.

'I'm in the city's head now; standing in front of one of its kings,' he ruminated on his path forward. Red Sun and Ru were pacing to the desk, and the man glowered down from his perch. Concentrating on the simple walk forward, matching Red Sun's stride, Ru almost smashed into several priceless artifacts, but he avoided them, making it appear like he was dancing with the furniture.

Red Sun stopped, and Ru halted abruptly.

"Excelsior, this is Ru, and he is the witness. He was one of the Enswells at the Stella riot. May he speak?" Red Sun asked, then slightly dipped his shaved head. His face was emotionless and still. The man, Excelsior, was plainly angry, blood boiling into his scarlet head. Ru saw the crimson through his neatly parted black hair. Ex did not move, but Ru thought he heard the seams in Ex's business coat creak as he tensed.

"Yes, Hong Tai. Speak!" he ordered, then closed his mouth so hard that his teeth snapped. Rage rested in his muscles, barely calm enough to remain seated. Soon it would explode and destroy everything near.

Unsure of his part, Ru looked to Red Sun or Hong Tai. He had never heard that name before, but the Cutmen have many monikers.

"SPEAK!" Ex yelled, his knuckles grew white, while his eyes turned a touch crimson. Red Sun noticed that Ru started, though no one else could have seen it. To Ex, Ru was as still as a post. Then, Ru lifted his head and relayed the details.

"A team of two, including myself, entered the park while the protest was forming. Each of us had one assigned goal. I circled the mob and planted hornflashs as instructed, while my partner targeted the mark, who was on the statue plat-form. The explosives ignited, disturbing the crowds; however, the goal was to humiliate the man on the stature. It was not achieved, and the mission failed," he said in an even tone, hid-ing the fear that welled inside.

"Yes, I know that," Ex said, whipping his hand as if to throw away the foreknown information, "Why did it fail, En-swell?" Ex leaned back, linking his thick fingers at his chin.

"My partner fired the torch several times. Close to the man, hoping to intimidate him into fleeing. However, the man sheltered several children that were climbing up to see him. So, in essence, he was seen as a hero," Ru explained, tracing back his memory of the protest, finding all the relevant facts. The Cutmen tells only the pertinent sections of the truth; some things are best hidden.

"YES, I KNOW THAT, TOO," Ex screamed, pulling back his hands and slamming them into the wooded desk, which yawned under the pressure.

'He is strong but lacks emotional control,' Ru surmised.

"Yes, sir. A man from the crowd intervened, stole my partner's weapon, and helped escort the mark away. My partner fled and did not face the thief. That was the sole reason for the failure."

The man shot back into his chair and launched into a sinister laugh, that rang off the walls. Holding his head in his hands, he rocked forward, still chuckling. "True, true!" he snorted, "If you succeeded, you would be dead. Blood would have painted the city shield, just beyond that window." The crimson color had drained, leaving his grey-blue eyes with the immense focus of a timber wolf. "You keep saying 'my partner,' you keep saying it…right, over and over. Why? Why is your partner not here to tell me?" Irritation filled the void left by the dissipating rage.

Red Sun stepped forward with an outstretched hand. "Final cut," he said, straightening his hand to mimic a blade.

"For fleeing or for failure?" Ex asked, his gaze shifting to Red Sun.

"We do not punish for a simple failure. No, it was for the failure to admit his own fear. Without admitting one's fear, one can never conquer it," Red Sun shared, "His fear led him to sacrifice his mission. Now, that is something that the Cutmen do not forgive." He finished and bowed to Ex.

Ex's large hands clapped. "Sure, sure, whatever," he said briskly, "Why are you here? Really, why?" He seemed like a king on his throne, surveying his subjects.

'My, he does not truly know who rules this planet,' Ru thought, waiting for Red Sun's reply.

"Ex, the issue is between your sons. Like Cain and Abel, one wishes to slay the other."

Angry filled his face again, not as crimson, not brimming, but the same rage was still there. "Tell me, Hong! I need answers! Why did you try to embarrass my firstborn? Of course, you failed, but why?" Ex demanded, his hands trembling, barely holding onto his temper.

His disregard of the Cutmen amazed Ru. 'The audacity! This is really what he had heard about the residents of Skytown. Here respect must be bought, not earned.' He eyed the room, only three were present, but this display only increased his mistrust.

'Wait…his firstborn, the man on the platform was his son?' Ru pondered. 'That was a miscalculation; trouble will come from this. No wonder that Red Sun brought me up here, beyond the clouds. I am really a witness,' Ru thought, measuring the room.

"Sir, you know the policy that has kept us alive for so long. No questions. Understand this, whether you are a prized client or not, that cannot be compromised," Red Sun said with a little heat in his voice. "I only tell this because we have a fortune and destiny to make between us, and we both need each other." Red Sun's head dipped marginally.

Taking the cue, Ex stood and bowed back. "Tell me what you can, then," he marked an order with a question.

"I have dealt with Augustine, private dealing; however, I did intercede on your behalf."

Ex laughed shook the walls again; his fist slamming the desk was the punctuation. Red Sun took another step forward.

"It was to humiliate Richard, make the boy seem weak, or the final cut. That is what we were asked." Red Sun looked Ex in the face, and he finally understood.

Ex sank back into his throne, his face went blank, a questioning king thinking of a disloyal prince. "I see," he said, "thank you for telling me."

'Look into all of August's movements, dealing, schedules, meetings, everything,' he mentally told his AI assistant. 'Brief me in one hour,' he finished.

He turned back to Red Sun, "Anything else?"

"Yes, sir. Please review the memory patch that Ru will send you. The man who stole the flame weapon was seen escorting Richard to his vehicle. I believe that I recognize the man. I will send you the details after you view it. It could be an angle." Ex stood, walked to his real wood liquor cabinet.

"Want something? I have it all," he asked, gesturing to the bottles. The memory patch flashed in his peripheral vision. He queued it up to view after they left.

"No, thank you, sir. We will be leaving. Please contact me regarding the subject in the patch," Red Sun trended to the elaborate double door, followed quickly by Ru.

The click of the door sounded behind him as he stared out to sea. "Play," he ordered.

'Richard was brave with flame inches from his face, sheltering the children, worthless little scumbags that they were,' he thought. He saw it, a mammoth man covered with tattoos running up his body and tracing his pale bald head. The tattoos were new, but he did recognize him, the Druager, the again-walker. The giant played dangerous games and had shaken cities in his time. Now, this killer helped his son, his true successor.

'Plans must be made, just in case,' he began calculating, sipping the drink, the first of many.

In the next volume, The Shadow Steps into the Streetlight, Miguel and Al struggle to cope with Liz's death, and the worst parts of them come to the surface. The veil between reality and illusion becomes thinner for Miguel, who is happily losing touch. The city works to recover from Governor's Mansion fire's smoldering remains as criminal forces set up other traps in the darkness. The fate of the city's soul is on the table.

ABOUT THE AUTHOR

Jt Bailey

JT Bailey attempted a myriad of positions, a repo man, a cook, a security guard, and an international criminal analyst, but daydreams continued to wash over his mind. Begrudgingly, he picked up a pen to scribble out his ideas; though fear stopped him from the rigorous work of completing his stories, and he settled back into banality. Frustrated hands of an aspiring  author continued to wring wages from these jobs, but he knew that his seconds on this spinning rock were counting down. Finally, he decided to compile and distill the tales in his head into…a universe.

The Castle of Electric Bones is his first novel, the beginning of a series.

BOOKS IN THIS SERIES

The Ravin Allegories

In the far future, Miguel Saxon and his sister-in-law, Detective Alicippe Anagnos, hunt down the Draugers gang that opened his wife's throat. Under the direction of a mysterious Darkman, the Draugers rose from Undertown, the wild and beleaguered neighborhoods built into the bedrock under the massive Jersey York city shell. Still mentally and physically recovering from the attack, Miguel stalks his enemies through the mire of corruption in the mountainous city that bulges from where New York once stood. His distraught mind listens to his dead wife's whispers and sees her rotting face in the blackness of the alleys as he is drawn deeper into the city's vicious underbelly. Once roused, his wrath exposes the city's most powerful and forces criminal factions into slaughter. With his sister-in-law and new allies, Miguel mounds a suicidal charge to wipe the city clean by any means necessary.

The Shadow Steps Into The Streetlight Wielding The Digital Moon

Made in the USA
Columbia, SC
16 May 2022

60502546R00191